Trafalgar

By Seth Hunter and available from McBooks Press

The Time of Terror
The Tide of War
The Price of Glory
The Winds of Folly
The Flag of Freedom
The Spoils of Conquest
The Sea of Silence
Trafalgar: The Fog of War

Trafalgar

The Fog of War

Seth Hunter

McBooks
Press

Essex, Connecticut

McBooks Press

An imprint of Globe Pequot, the trade division of
The Rowman & Littlefield Publishing Group, Inc.
4501 Forbes Blvd., Ste. 200
Lanham, MD 20706
www.rowman.com

Distributed by NATIONAL BOOK NETWORK

British Library Cataloguing in Publication Information available

Library of Congress Cataloging-in-Publication Data

Names: Hunter, Seth, author.
Title: Trafalgar : the fog of war / Seth Hunter.
Description: Essex, Connecticut : McBooks Press, [2022] | Series: The Nathan Peake Novels ;
    no. 8 | Identifiers: LCCN 2022017628 (print) | LCCN 2022017629 (ebook) | ISBN
    9781493064670 (hardback : alk. paper) | ISBN 9781493071234 (e-book)
Classification: LCC PR6108.U59 T73 2022 (print) | LCC PR6108.U59 (ebook) |
    DDC 823/.92--dc23
LC record available at https://lccn.loc.gov/2022017628
LC ebook record available at https://lccn.loc.gov/2022017629

♾™ The paper used in this publication meets the minimum requirements of American National
Standard for Information Sciences—Permanence of Paper for Printed Library Materials, ANSI/
NISO Z39.48-1992.

Prologue

Step by Step

It was his recurring nightmare when he was in the prison in Paris. Being on the wrong side in a battle. The wrong flags, the wrong songs, the wrong uniforms.

He saw them through an arc of fire as he sharpened the blades on the spinning stone. The blue-coated soldiers of the French army marching up and down the decks, to the sound of fife and drum. *Rantan-a-tan-rantan. Rantan-a-tan-rantan* . . . The French call to arms—*La Génèrale.*

He could hear it repeated across the water on the other ships, the long, rambling forest of oak and pine stretching over several miles of ocean, and the rumble and squeak of iron on wood as they rolled out the guns. He looked across at Mr Banjo on the next grindstone and shook his head. 'How did we get here?'

> *Allons enfants de la Patrie,*
> *Le jour de gloire est arrivé!*

He remembered the first time he heard it, in Paris during the Terror, just before they had tried to string him up from a lamppost. Death as close then as it was now, perhaps even closer. He'd had his flute with him, and when they took the rope from around his neck, they gave it back to him and he played them a tune—'Yankee Doodle,' because they thought he was an American then, too.

Yankee Doodle keep it up, Yankee Doodle dandy,
Mind the music and the step, and with the girls be handy.

He supposed that was where it had begun. Paris at the time of the Terror. The danger and the deceit, the seductive lure of living with both, and the fear. But it could have been earlier, keeping watch for the smugglers on the hills above the Cuckmere.

'You should be ashamed of yourself, boy, and your father a magistrate.'

Another memory. Of his mother and father having one of their furious rows when he was a child—about him, their lives together, their incompatible politics . . . or all three? His father with his head in his hands plaintively asking: 'How did we get here?' And his mother's grim reply: 'Step by step.'

They say your whole life flashes before you when you are drowning.

'To dangerous liaisons, sir. Where would we be without them?'

That would be Sir Sidney Smith in the Ship Inn at Falmouth. Mephistopheles to his bemused Faust, flushed and jolly over a bowl of punch, with the snow on the hills and the wind from the north-east filled with chips of ice, like the splintered bones of dead armies.

'Oh, we are going to kidnap Bonaparte. Did I not tell you?'

Well, we know how that ended. For some, at least. And now here he was, sharpening blades for the emperor's soldiers so they could conquer Britain.

'Three days of fog, that is all we need, and England will be ours.'

That would be the emperor himself, in the rose garden at Malmaison. Three days of fog. Not a lot to ask for in the English Channel in October.

No fog here, though. Clear blue skies, perfect weather for a battle—if only there was a bit more wind. He looked out across the deck, out to sea through the sparks of the spinning wheel, and saw the English ships in the distance bearing down on them. More creeping than bearing, perhaps, so painfully slow, even under a full press of sail. There would be singing there, too.

Heart of Oak are our ships,
Jolly Tars are our men,
We always are ready:
Steady, boys, Steady!

He should be singing with them. Not here, sharpening swords for the enemy.

'*Merci, monsieur.*'

'*Mon plaisir, monsieur.*'

Now they were lining up to climb into the rigging. The grenadiers and the sharpshooters, the *voltigeurs* and *tirailleurs*. All those weeks of training in Cádiz, throwing their grenadoes and firepots, shooting at the cutouts of the officers at the taffrail.

And there was the sergeant from Naples, waiting his turn. Antonio Scillato. The man they called *Lo Spettro*, the ghost, the revenant. The man who was already dead.

Nathan watched him climbing the ratlines into the fighting tops with his musket slung by a strap at his shoulder. Hand over hand. Step by step.

Chapter 1

Falmouth, Cornwall

Two years earlier . . .

. . . Being New Year's Day, 1803, and a bitter cold day at that, with a brisk
north-easterly whipping across the harbour bringing squalls of rain and
sleet and the threat of snow before nightfall, if the landlady of the Ship
Inn was to be believed. She had consulted her rheumatism on the subject,
and was rarely misinformed.

'Like as not we'll be snowed in for a week,' she declared with grim satisfaction to the two gentlemen who were her only guests at breakfast that
morning. 'But I reckon that won't bother you none, if you's down for the
packet.'

There was a question in her tone, but neither of them being disposed
to utter more than an ambiguous grunt by way of a reply, she left them
with the fresh pot of coffee they had requested and took herself off to the
kitchen to inform her husband that if they were not spies, and very likely
Frogs, then she was the Queen of Sheba.

Mr Penwortham eased the kitchen door a crack to observe the articles
for himself, they having arrived late the previous evening while he was
occupied in the cellar. Britain and France had been at peace for a year now,
but this did not preclude the possibility of another war any time soon, and
the presence of French spies in Falmouth was not implausible. His inspection told him little, however, save that one was a burly ruffian of a fellow—though possibly a gentleman ruffian—with a ruddy countenance,

1

his chin and jowls severely confined by the points of his starched white collar; the other lean and sharp with a longish nose, slightly drooping eyes, and a mouth formed into an expression of mildly amused disdain which the landlord associated with the English upper classes. On arrival he had given his name as Smith and his companion as something so incomprehensible his wife had rendered it as Canoodle, and though they travelled post they had not so much as a valet between them. In mine host's view they were as likely to be bankers as spies, for both species of rogue were drawn to Falmouth by the frequency of the packet boats to those places where their transactions continued profitable, even at a time of peace, but in truth he did not care a fig for who or what they were, so long as they paid the reckoning, so he eased the door shut without further comment and returned to his own breakfast beside the kitchen fire.

In fact, his wife was by no means correct in her assumptions, for although both men had been accused of spying in their time, and with some justification, neither was presently employed in this occupation, and only one might be called French, and even then not without dispute, for he was Breton born and bred, and Bretons were no happier to be called French than the Cornish were to be called English.

'And a Happy New Year,' remarked the man who had given his name as Smith, peering dismally through the hole he had rubbed in the condensation on the window. His tone was sardonic and addressed to no-one in particular, lest it be the recently departed landlady or the world in general, but it brought an instant response from his companion, who had never quite understood this particular form of English humour and was in any case wary of giving offence to those he relied upon for his bread and butter, and a good deal else besides.

'And to you, sir,' he beamed, raising his tankard of small ale. 'And let us hope for a rather better year than the last.'

The previous year being the first for over a decade in which the nations of Europe had not indulged in their normal pastime of inflicting grievous bodily harm upon each other at every opportunity, it might be presumed that the speaker was a military or naval man rendered unemployed by the imposition of peace. This was not strictly true, for although he had experienced more than his fair share of fighting in recent years, he was more in the business of politics than soldiering. His interests being best served by a resumption of hostilities, however, he was desirous of a return to this happy state of affairs as soon as it could decently, or indecently, be contrived.

'Indeed,' drawled Mr Smith, though without removing his gaze from what he could see through the window, which was, in fact, very little. The inn was at the very northern edge of the harbour, conveniently situated for both the London road and the Flushing ferry, and on a better day it would have commanded as fine a view as one might have desired across the mouth of the River Fal to the Carrick Roads, with the great number of vessels that were normally to be found at anchor there. Today, however, all that could be seen through the hole the speaker had rubbed in the misted glass were the bare poles of a few coastal traders moored at the nearest jetty and a huddle of subdued gulls.

'Well, if you do not mind braving the elements and have taken the edge off your appetite'—a hint of irony here, too, for his companion had not stinted in his application to the several courses that had been available to him—'perhaps we might take a turn through the town in search of a somewhat less restricted view. It will blow away some of the cobwebs that have accrued of late.'

Having spent a day and half a night in a hired chaise travelling a hundred miles or so on indifferent roads in the middle of winter, his companion might well have considered that any such cobwebs as had survived the journey were in an even worse state than he. However, some thirty minutes later the two gentlemen, much wrapped against the weather, were to be seen clinging to a flimsy rail below the castle on Pendennis Head, from which exposed prominence they were afforded a panoramic view of one of the deepest natural harbours in the world and the considerable amount of shipping that was assembled there. Falmouth was not a great commercial port in the style of London, Liverpool, or Bristol, but its location made it an attractive proposition for the Royal Mail, which maintained a fleet of some thirty packet ships here, though most of the ships to be seen from Pendennis Point today were birds of passage seeking shelter from the cruel north-easterly that had impeded their further progress up the Channel. Having produced a small Dollond glass from the innards of his cloak, Mr Smith subjected certain of these vessels to as detailed a scrutiny as the weather would permit, frequently removing the instrument from his eye to wipe the rain off the lens with a scrap of linen cloth.

After observing this performance for some little while and finding no enjoyment in it, his companion ventured to enquire if he could be sure the ship was here.

'As sure as I can be,' Mr Smith replied tersely. 'In the circumstances.'

These circumstances had been explained to the enquirer before leaving their base in Weymouth, but he was far from feeling fully informed. This was not unusual, for his hosts told him only what they considered he was required to know, and this was never very much. What was more usual was that he was conveyed from one place to another, often in some discomfort, to meet a number of dubious characters who might, or might not, be of some use to him and his cause, but either way expected to derive some considerable benefit from the encounter. He expected no more of this present expedition to Cornwall.

'Ah, this looks more promising.' The viewer's focus had shifted to one of the vessels moored under what would have been the shadow of the opposite headland, had there been anything remotely resembling a sun. He passed the glass to his companion, guiding the direction with his hand until it was pointing at a three-masted vessel with the distinctive beak of a ship of war, her lean black hull relieved by a single white streak and the chequered pattern of eight gun ports.

'A corvette, you say?'

'The *Mutine*. First of her class, launched in Le Havre three years ago, armed with sixteen eight-pounders. Four hundred tons burthen, ninety-five feet in length, twenty-five in the beam,' Mr Smith rattled on. 'I forget her precise draught, but it will not be much more than twelve feet, I should imagine—you could sail her halfway up the Seine without grounding. Probably designed for coastal protection, or as a cruise raider, but she was taken by a British squadron on her first cruise, just outside Rochefort, without firing a shot. The people who bought her renamed her the *Falaise*. I believe they proposed to employ her as a privateer—that is, a private ship of war,' he added, in deference to his companion's ignorance of things nautical, 'but the war ended before she could see any action. Seen plenty since, though, from what I have heard, peace or no peace. Crew of around one hundred and fifty, fully manned. She would fit our purposes very nicely, do you not think?'

The other man inclined his head consideringly, but actually had no opinion one way or another. A ship was a ship so far as he was concerned, unless it was a boat, apparently. He had frequently been instructed on the distinction between the two, but it was not foremost among his concerns.

'In the service we would class her as a sloop of war,' his informant went on, as if thinking aloud, 'or I suppose, if she could take a few more guns, a sixth-rate.'

'And do we know if her present owner is aboard?'

'That is what I have been informed, though whether he is the *rightful* owner is a matter of some debate.'

'Is that a problem?'

'Not for us,' replied Mr Smith with a smile, 'though it may be for him.'

The gentleman under discussion was at that moment reclining in a well-cushioned armchair in the stern cabin of the vessel that had attracted their attention. It would not have been obvious from his appearance, however, that he had more than a passing acquaintance with seafaring. On his head he wore a silken cap of many colours, such as artists or writers sometimes wore to denote a creative intellect, with a tassel that hung down one side and which he tugged from time to time into his mouth and chewed upon thoughtfully. His body was clothed in a long banyan decorated with exotic birds and luxuriant foliage, such as might be worn by an Asian potentate or a Virginia planter, and around his shoulders, for warmth, he had draped a fur pelisse that had once belonged to an officer of hussars in the army of the Hapsburg emperor, ostensibly to protect against sword thrusts but in essence to impart a degree of swagger. Under this assemblage he wore a reasonably clean linen shirt, buckskin breeches, thick woollen stockings, and a pair of velvet slippers presently attached to a brass warming pan filled with hot coals. Artist or writer, potentate or planter, he was clearly a man of style and possibly substance, though not many would have taken him for a man of action. He was, in fact, a captain in His Britannic Majesty's Navy, and his name was Peake.

'I truly wish it might be contrived,' he was saying. 'For to be perfectly frank with you, I have had enough of the sea and all who sail upon her. Saving your good self, of course. And I would give much for just a few days ashore, but until I can find a way out of our present difficulties, it is out of the question.'

The recipient of this information was of roughly the same age, which was to say somewhat between thirty and forty, but he was as fair as the speaker was dark, and dressed more conventionally for a mariner in a blue reefer jacket over a striped Guernsey sweater, and a pair of loose-fitting seaman's slops. His name was Tully, and he, too, was in the service, with the rank of master and commander, though as his superiors had not seen fit to provide him with a command for some several years now, he was not inclined to give himself airs, thus his somewhat humble attire. Neither gentleman had bothered to shave for at least a week and the stubble on their faces was approaching the status of a beard. Very little natural light penetrated the stern windows of the cabin, and though it was almost mid-day several lamps had been lit to create a rather smoky yellow ambience derived from the oil of whale and seal which might have rendered it cosy, if a little smelly, had it not been so cold. Indeed, the two men had been discussing the possibility of moving ashore and finding more amenable accommodation in one of the inns along the waterfront, but the speaker was reluctant on the grounds of expense, and because, as he was explaining, it might show a shabby disregard for the welfare of the officers and crew who were obliged to remain aboard.

'Your concern does you credit,' the other gentleman replied, 'but do you seriously think they give a tinker's cuss either way? So far as they are concerned, here you are, living in the lap of luxury in a spacious cabin, dining off silver plate, with devoted servants to gratify every whim, while they are crammed into . . .'

But the recipient of this wisdom had begun to express signs of agitation at the word *luxury*, and as the speech continued his outrage could no longer be contained.

'*Spacious?*' He looked about him in affected wonder. In fact, the cabin, while lacking the proportions of a ship of the line or an East Indiaman, was by no means cramped. It occupied the entire breadth of the stern, and though the vessel was officially described as flush-decked, the deck above his head had been raised fourteen inches to permit the occupant to move around without adopting the shambling gait of an ape or cracking his head on the timbers. '*Devoted?* Kidd?' This being the name of his principal—indeed, only—personal servant. 'If you think him devoted, sir, all I can say is, you must have very low expectations of the word. Devoted to who or what, may I ask, besides his own degenerate interests?'

The individual in question not being there to defend himself, Tully uttered a few words, if not to his credit, at least in mitigation of his faults.

'And you knew what you were getting when you agreed to take him on,' he concluded.

'I certainly did not,' his friend responded. 'I had no idea what I was getting. If I had known, I would have left him to the mercy of the hangman. If you recall, he told me he had been apprenticed to a chef in the French royal household. I was the victim of my own unworldly trust. As usual.'

The other man made no comment, though his lips may have twitched a little.

'Any other captain would have had him flogged to within an inch of his life, the way he speaks to me.' This with a raised voice and a sidelong glance towards the cabin door, beyond which the person of whom they were speaking normally lurked in a small storeroom and galley he had appropriated as his quarters. 'And when did you last see me dine off silver plate?'

'I was speaking metaphorically. But you know my meaning. Why should they care if we sleep ashore? You might have urgent business to conduct, such as finding the means to pay what they are owed in the way of wages.'

This caused further agitation.

'They do not get paid off until they finish the voyage, they know that, and it ain't over yet.'

'Well, you cannot blame them for asking when it *will* be over, and why we have lingered a week in Falmouth for no good reason that they are aware of.'

'They are seamen, for pity's sake! When are they ever made aware of anything concerning their welfare?' This was a state of affairs Captain Peake would normally deplore, but his patience had been supremely tested by their most recent voyage. 'By God, I thought the Americans were bad, but this lot . . . I tell you, brother, if I ever have to ship with a crew from Liverpool again, I'll cut my throat and save them the trouble.'

His companion listened to this diatribe with the patience of a man who has heard it all before, or something very like it. 'It would not be so bad if they had money to spend ashore,' he remarked mildly.

'Which I would give them if I had any to give, but until we rid ourselves of this damned cargo . . .'

They were both silent for a moment, as their minds turned to the objects currently residing on the deck below.

'I would have thought we would have heard something by now,' Tully observed.

'It was bound to take a little while to put the word around. A certain amount of discretion is called for, as you know. And it is not as if we can sell to the first scoundrel who comes knocking at the door. We have a duty to ensure they are not used against our own people, or indeed, any whose cause we might be inclined to support.'

Tully regarded him curiously. 'That is very honourable of you,' he declared.

'Well, I am an honourable man,' Peake assured him carelessly. 'Besides, I do not wish to hang for it.'

'But how would we know?'

'That I would hang?'

'Who or what they will be used against once we have parted with them.'

The captain raised his eyes to the deckhead and blew out his cheeks. 'You know what, I have a good mind to throw the whole lot overboard. Should have done as soon as we left the Caribbean. Or before.'

'And how then would we pay the crew?'

'If necessary, I will raise money on the value of the ship.'

They both knew this was easier said than done.

'Well, assuming we do find a buyer, then what?'

'Then we will continue to London, pay off the crew, put the ship in for a refit, and embark on a life of debauchery.' Then, after a moment of reflection: 'Or I might look for a wife.'

'Good God!' This was clearly a shock.

'Is that so astounding? I am of an age when matrimony is by no means to be despised.'

'Really?'

'Well, it can at least be considered without cutting one's throat.'

'Have you anyone in mind?'

'No. My heart is a blank canvas.'

Tully gave some thought to this image, but being unable to respond with anything sufficiently witty or wise, he remained silent.

'However, I do have certain requisites, if that is the right way to put it.'

'Such as?'

'Well, beauty would be welcome, though it need not be disproportion-ate—I do not want someone excessively vain. A measure of intelligence is at least as important—I do not want a lunkhead or a birdbrain. Wit would be appreciated, as we may be compelled to spend a good deal of time together, and it is always gratifying to be amused. A degree of independence—I do not want someone who is overly reliant upon me. And of course, it goes without saying that she must be relatively well-endowed—that is to say, in funds.'

'And you believe you would be regarded as a suitable suitor for such a paragon?'

'My dear friend, I am an officer and a gentleman. I would not be so immodest as to say so myself, but I may even be considered a war hero. I am not ill-favoured, I have no serious vices, and I have the prospect of a considerable inheritance.' But then his face fell. 'If there is any left by the time Molly Egerton has done with it.'

Peake's father, Sir Michael Peake, was a retired admiral and landowner with one thousand acres of prime Sussex downland that would pass to Nathan upon his demise—if he himself lived that long, which must be considered doubtful—but Sir Michael had entered upon a liaison with a younger woman who had already borne him two girls and a boy, and whose expenditure was proving a considerable burden upon the estate. Nathan wished his father a long and pleasant life and was glad on the whole that he had found love so late into it, especially after his marriage to Nathan's mother, but on the other hand, he would have preferred him to have loved someone other than Molly Egerton, a young woman who had aroused Nathan's own passions before her association with his father, the memory of which brought a blush to his cheeks, if not hers, on his infrequent visits to the family home.

'Well, there is always your mother,' Tully remarked provocatively.

Nathan gave him a withering look, for they both knew how little his mother could be relied upon, at least in financial matters. For many years now Lady Catherine Peake had lived an independent, and very expensive, life in London. Initially, she had moved in fashionable society, even numbering the Prince of Wales among her acquaintance, but increasingly she had drifted to what could only be called the fringes, consorting with radicals and freethinkers who challenged almost everything his father had ever believed in. Strangely, this did not seem to have diminished her expenses.

Peake loved both his parents, but he was never more fond of one than when he was with the other.

'That is why my future wife's assets are of concern to me,' he informed his companion tartly. 'Otherwise, I would marry for love and be damned.'

'Except that you do not love anyone,' Tully pointed out. He saw that his friend took this badly. 'I do not say you are incapable of love,' he allowed, 'only that, as you have said, there is no-one at present engaging your affections.'

Further discussion of the subject was interrupted by a brisk, even commanding, knock upon the cabin door, followed by the entrance of an individual whose slight stature and youthful countenance might have identified him as one of the ship's boys, had they had possessed any. In fact, this was the subject of their recent discussion, the much-maligned Kidd, and on closer inspection his features had the peculiarity of being both old and young, and might have been the model for one of those cherubic but menacing gargoyles set above a church porch to frighten away demons.

'Message come for you,' he announced without ceremony, 'from ashore.'

The missive he presented was addressed to 'Captain Nathaniel Peake, Falaise', which caused the recipient some concern, for he had been discreet of late in using his real name, but after breaking the seal and skimming the contents for a moment, his brow cleared.

He saw that his servant was still in attendance.

'Was there something else?' he enquired coldly.

'The boatman was told to bide a reply.'

'Well, tell him to bide a little longer while I discuss it with Mr Tully.'

When the servant had departed, he passed the message to his companion with the remark that 'we may have a bite.'

'S. Smith Esquire,' pronounced Tully dryly when he reached the signature at the end.

'Quite. However, we can expect a certain amount of subterfuge, given the nature of the cargo. What I find more puzzling is that he has come all this way to Falmouth on purpose to pay me a visit, or so he says.'

Tully cocked a head at the stern windows. 'Not the best conditions for a trip ashore,' he remarked.

'Oh, I don't know,' Peake demurred, 'and at least we will get a dinner out of it.'

'What do you mean, "we"?'

'Oh, you are coming too, my lad. We are in this together. Else I will be as a lamb to the slaughter.' Despite his present appearance, Peake's features had less the look of a lamb than a wolf looking forward to its next meal. He eased himself out of the chair and crossed to the small desk where he kept his writing materials.

'The Ship Inn at half past one o'clock,' he said. 'You, me, and the mysterious Mr Smith.'

Chapter 2

The Mysterious Mr Smith

An hour or so later, the two men emerged onto the upper deck of the *Falaise*, dressed rather more appropriately, at least from a nautical point of view, in black oilskins over a reefer jacket with bicorn hats worn fore-and-aft and navy-blue trousers tucked into hessian boots, a style they deemed suitable for half-pay officers in the King's Navy, though *The Gentleman's Magazine* might not have agreed. Neither wore any indication of rank, however, or of which particular species of marine creature they represented: 'for it would be as well,' Peake had cautioned dryly, 'to preserve an element of subterfuge in our dealings ashore.'

'But he knows exactly who you are,' Tully protested reasonably, having experienced his friend's concept of subterfuge on a number of occasions—some called for, some not—but invariably leading to embarrassment, or worse. 'He wrote your name and rank on the letter.'

'I know that,' Peake conceded with a frown, 'but we do not want the whole town knowing.'

They had taken the additional trouble of shaving and of confining their unruly locks in suitable lengths of black ribbon, 'so he will not take us for a pair of ruffians', but after some thought, Peake had decided to leave his pistols behind and content himself with a dirk concealed inside one of his boots.

He had, however, decided to take his bodyguard with him, a tall and striking African by the name of George Banjo whom he had first taken into his service in Louisiana and who had occupied a number of mostly irregular roles off and on since. His particular expertise was gunnery, and there was no-one better in Nathan's opinion concerning the handling of ordnance, of whatever size and description, but there had already been a gunnery officer aboard the *Falaise* when he had assumed command, along with a gunner and a gunner's mate and even an armourer, so an element of diplomacy had been required. He had lately been serving as Nathan's coxswain and the ship's quartermaster, the last man to hold that position having been knocked on the head, literally, by a falling block in an engagement with a French frigate off the island of Hispaniola, but from their earliest acquaintance he had taken responsibility for his captain's personal safety, particularly on trips ashore, where an element of risk was involved. It was unlikely that dinner at the Ship Inn in Falmouth would fall into this category, but Mr Banjo was not prepared to take a chance on it.

His name was derived not from the musical instrument, as most of the crew assumed, but from a shortening of his family name of Adebanjo, whose meaning, as he had wryly informed Peake upon enquiry, was 'he who fits the crown.' Certainly, he was a born leader, and it could only be on account of his colour and circumstance that he had accepted an inferior status in life, though there was a bond between the two men that did to some extent transcend the disparity in rank. Peake tended to avoid giving him direct orders, rather framing them in the nature of a request, which Banjo normally considered favourably, though not always. He was now awaiting instruction on the slightly raised portion of the sloop's stern that passed for a quarterdeck and carrying two bulky objects wrapped in waxed hessian.

'You have brought one of each?' Peake queried. 'And whatever might be needed if a demonstration is required?' A look from Banjo warned him against further enquiry of this nature. 'Very well. But perhaps you had better not bring them to the meeting,' he added. 'We will find somewhere nearby where you may wait in comfort, and call upon you should they wish to inspect them.'

Feeling that he had not come out of this exchange well, Peake moved over to the larboard rail and peered dismally at the mile or so of water that lay between the *Falaise* and the shore. It was one of the ironies of his complicated relationship with the sea that while he was usually stoical in the face of whatever it might throw at him on a long voyage far from land, the prospect of a short trip across an English harbour in an open boat in winter filled him with apprehension. It was for this reason that he had ordered the cutter to be made ready rather than the gig, and it was presently rocking none too gently at the ship's side.

'I think we will achieve a landing without too many casualties,' Tully remarked, being fully aware of his friend's reservations.

'It is not a matter of personal safety,' Peake responded warmly. 'But it is most vexing to sit down to dinner in a pair of wet breeches, or in this case, trousers.'

Tully could not but agree.

'I have no problem with your storms and tempests,' Nathan went on. 'Blow wind and crack your cheeks, so far as I am concerned—is that what your man said?'

'*Your hurricanoes and cataracts spout, till you have drenched our steeples and drowned our cocks,*' quoted Tully, not entirely accurately, from his memory of King Lear on the blasted heath. This usually brought a smile to Peake's lips when he had his own grievance with the weather—(to the despair of his mother and her cultured friends in London, he had always considered *Lear* to be a comedy)—but on this occasion his expression remained severe.

'They may drown as many cocks as they like,' he declared. ' 'Tis this damned rain that puts me out of sorts. It strikes me as a particularly English sort of rain, do you not think? Nothing spectacular about it, and yet it invariably succeeds in making one wet through and thoroughly miserable. What in God's name persuaded us to come back to England in midwinter?'

There were a number of reasons, none of which, so far as Tully knew, would have concerned the Almighty, but he did not bother to list them. When Peake felt aggrieved, he could rarely be diverted from a good moan, and the English weather was a frequent object of complaint.

'We have endured worse,' he remarked shortly.

'Worse in the way of storms, no doubt, but nothing like this. This is the problem with England. It may avoid extremes, in both climate and politics, but it is corrosive of the soul. It rots a body from within.'

Tully made no comment, having heard it all before, or something very like it. He had also heard his friend declare many times that he would give a thousand guineas to be soaked to the skin by a decent English rain, but that would have been when they were sweltering in the heat of the Levant, or the Indian Ocean, or the Caribbean, or wherever in the world there were endless days of unremitting sunshine, for Peake was never more warm for England than when they were in the tropics, or as hot for the tropics as when they were in England.

Happily, the wind seemed to have dropped off a little by the time they climbed down into the cutter, and the rain with it, but the scudding clouds promised more of a brief truce than a peace. This was clearly the opinion of the boat's crew, who had garbed themselves in a variety of oilskin and tarpaulin, and if they did not look especially elegant their expressions suggested this was not the first thing that would concern them. How-ever, they covered the mile or so to the Fal without a resumption of hos-tilities and berthed at a convenient jetty just a few minutes short of the appointed time. After instructing Mr Banjo and the crew to wait for them in one of the nearby hostelries and distributing an amount of coin suffi-cient to cover the cost of a modest meal, he and Tully stepped ashore and hurried into the welcome shelter of the inn.

The atmosphere inside was somewhat morose, even hangdog, possibly due to the revelries of the night before, but Peake was inclined to detect a weary pessimism that may have had something to do with their contem-plations of the year ahead. According to the English journals, and every other authority on the subject, 'war clouds were gathering', and Falmouth from its station near the mouth of the English Channel was bound to be in the way of them. There had been two squadrons of frigates based here during the last war, which had ended little more than a year ago, and although their return would doubtless be welcomed by the town's merchants and tradespeople, the need to keep the King's ships constantly manned and provisioned had far less agreeable consequences for many of their fellow parishioners. A fair number of seamen in Falmouth were employed on the packet ships and thus immune from the depredations of the press gangs, but all that achieved was to make them considerably less particular about those they considered suitable for impressment, and far less likely to observe the exemptions defined by statute.

The two men stood for a moment in the taproom, stamping their feet and dripping water, before making their way to the bar and disclosing the name of their host, whereupon, having been relieved of their oilskins, they were escorted to the rear of the tavern where a private room had been bespoke for them. It was as cheering as Peake might have wished, with a blazing fire and a smell of strongly spiced liquor rising from a large silver bowl on a small table, which was presently being attended by a swarthy-looking individual wearing a white apron over his frock coat and breeches, and a very solemn expression upon his features as if he were mixing a potion to conjure the devil. His expression lightened, however, when he saw who was at the door.

'Captain Nathaniel Peake,' he exclaimed impressively. Excepting the apron, which looked as if it had been borrowed from the cellarman, his dress was of a style and quality that probably put him in the category of dandy, certainly in this part of the world, though he was somewhat past the age when he might be described as a young buck. Despite this, he possessed a profusion of dark curls artfully arranged over a noble brow, a nose that was possibly a little too long to be considered fashionable but gave him a certain hawkish glamour, and an air of consequence that would not have been out of place at Brooks or Whites, though for some reason the image that came to Nathan's mind was of a meeting of the Hellfire Club.

Happily, the room was clearly set for a rather more civilised function. It contained a table and chairs, the former decorated with seasonal boughs of holly, a sideboard containing a number of accoutrements and an even greater number of bottles, several nautical paintings, and two leather arm-chairs, one of which contained—but only just—a very large gentleman with a great slab of a face and several chins who might have been the model for a painting of Bacchus. He beamed at Peake when he caught his eye but did not rise to his feet, and there may, in his eyes, have been a look of apprehension.

'Well, well.' The punch-maker exposed his principal guest to a curious and over-lengthy stare as if he had just encountered a species of animal of whose existence he had not been entirely convinced until this moment, and was still rather suspicious that it might prove an illusion, or fake. 'I am honoured to make your acquaintance, sir. My name is Smith, and this is my associate, Monsieur Cadoudal.'

Not by a twitch of the lips did either of his guests betray any doubt as to the veracity of this information, though it took a remarkable restraint on both their parts—not on account of the names, but because they were somehow expressive of the absurdity of the situation in which they found themselves. The fact that it was not without an element of risk only added to a sense of hilarity to which they were both prone at times, particularly when there were reasons to be nervous, but they made their bows with an exhibition of gravitas that would have fooled all but the most intimate of their acquaintance.

This survived even the intervention of the gentleman introduced by the name of Cadoudal, who rose ponderously from his chair, bowing stiffly in their direction, and then stood there smiling genially and rocking upon his heels but otherwise looking rather like a bull in a china shop who dare not move for fear of drawing upon himself the wrath of the proprietor.

'And this is my friend, Commander Tully,' said Peake.

'Captain Tully, you are most welcome,' declared their host. 'I have read of your own exploits with almost as much interest as those of your esteemed associate. Well, well, well,' he said again, 'Peake and Tully,' with what might have been an air of reverence had it not been for that unfortunate smirk. 'How strange that our paths have not crossed before this moment.'

Nathan tilted his head enquiringly but without eliciting any further explanation of this somewhat alarming statement. He supposed he might have expected a prospective purchaser to make some enquiry as to the identity of the people whose goods were for sale, particularly given their contentious nature, but he had not anticipated so great a degree of interest. He felt a familiar wariness descend.

'But let me offer you both a cup of this excellent punch,' their host gushed as he dipped his ladle into the steaming brew. 'And come warm yourselves at the fire. It looks damned unpleasant out there.'

Nathan accepted both invitations without in the least shedding his growing sense of unease. Why did this Mr Smith consider it strange that their paths had not crossed before, and in what circumstances *might* they have? The possibilities were legion, and most of them involved activities that he would not wish known to someone whose own antecedents were still a mystery to him.

Their host raised his cup. 'To our mutual advantage,' he declared. Then, lifting his free hand in a gesture of restraint or apology, 'No. No, no. That is altogether too uninspiring. To dangerous liaisons. Where would we be without them?'

Almost certainly not here, Nathan thought. It was an odd kind of toast to begin what was, after all, supposed to be a business meeting.

'I am not sure what you have in mind, sir,' he replied, with an attempt at humour, 'but I wish you joy of them.'

He took one cautious sip of the punch and then set his cup firmly upon the mantelpiece. It was imperative to keep a clear head and put their acquaintance upon a more professional footing. Peake and Tully, indeed. As if they were characters in the commedia dell'arte. Any more foolishness, he decided, and they were out the door and be damned to dinner.

'So, you are interested in our manifest,' he began.

'I am interested in your manifest, your ship, your crew, and you, sir,' said Mr Smith with a somewhat broader smile than the smirk that had thus far characterised his features, but was by no means reassuring. He clearly knew a great deal more about them than they did about him. A revenue man, Nathan speculated. He has discovered our secret manifest and demands a cut. But revenue men did not normally invite their quarry to dinner before presenting them with their demands—not unless they were worth a great deal more to His Majesty's Exchequer than Nathan was. He managed to maintain an air of polite interest.

'May I ask, sir, how you came to hear of us?'

'In my line of business, sir, one has to keep one's ear to the ground. I became apprised of certain rumours concerning a vessel in Falmouth Harbour and the goods that it carried. It encouraged me to make further enquiry, and so here we are.'

Nathan's agents in London had clearly done what they were paid to do. There had always been the risk that they would net a shark.

'And what line of business would that be, sir,' he enquired, 'if it is not an indelicate question?'

'It is a good one, nonetheless. I have frequently asked it of myself.' Mr Smith adopted a thoughtful expression. 'It involves long periods of boredom enlivened by brief but frenzied activity, some knowledge of the charts and celestial bodies, combined with a great deal of bluff, bombast, and bluster, an aptitude for browbeating one's inferiors and toadying to those of an elevated rank—and the capacity to consume large quantities of strong liquor without falling into the sea or trying to climb a mast. In short, sir, I am an officer of the Royal Navy, as I believe are you.'

His two guests had listened to this exposition with a measure of stunned disbelief, but as it reached its conclusion a glimmer of enlightenment appeared in Tully's eyes.

'You would not, by any chance, be *Captain* Smith?' he proposed hesitantly. 'Captain Sir Sidney Smith?'

'Ah, you have smoked me, sir,' declared their beaming host. 'The description was perhaps a little too, shall we say, *idiosyncratic*. Ha ha.'

'The Hero of Acre,' announced Tully with a glance towards his companion, to ensure that he appreciated they were in the presence of greatness, and possibly to convey the warning that greatness would not be serving them from a bowl of punch in a waterside tavern in Falmouth in the depths of winter without some considerable advantage to itself, and very likely their own inconvenience.

It was unnecessary. Like most serving officers of his acquaintance, Nathan had heard or read a great deal of Sir Sidney Smith over the years, probably a great deal more than they would have wished to know. He had been reluctantly impressed by stories of his past exploits, however, whether it involved escaping from a French prison, defending the city of Acre from the French army, led by Bonaparte himself, no less, or appearing at London assemblies dressed as a Turkish sultan with a raffish beard and a pair of pistols in his belt, even though the invitations had not proposed fancy dress. It was probably true to say that he was the most famous British naval officer of his day—after Nelson himself, of course—and far more glamourous in his appearance. He had been variously described in the popular journals as Swarthy, Piratical, Mediterranean, or Hebrewical—whatever that meant—one even going so far as to eulogise his 'flashing dark eyes, aquiline nose and jet black curls' as if he were a hero of romantic fiction, but Nathan's own impression was of someone rather on the small side who looked a great deal too pleased with himself to set one entirely at ease. Nor could he overlook certain warnings he had heard about Smith's reputation for double-dealing or for toadying to senior members of the court and ministry to gain advantage over other officers who might be considered rivals by someone less vain of his own accomplishments. Nathan was perfectly aware both of his host's reputation and the dangers it might bring to him personally. Other than making a precipitate dash for the door, however, he was at a loss to know how to proceed other than to raise his cup and murmur, 'Your very good health, sir. I am honoured to make your acquaintance.'

'Nonsense,' declared Sir Sidney briskly. 'You are wondering what I am doing in Falmouth on New Year's Day and why I have invited you to dine with me. This is understandable, and I will do my best to satisfy your curiosity on both counts.'

Nathan responded with a courteous and not entirely mocking bow. He awaited his host's explanation with interest, but before it was forthcoming there was a brisk rat-a-tat-tat upon the door shortly followed by the entrance of the landlord, pushing a large trolley and followed by a number of male and female attendants all bearing loaded trays and festooned with so much holly, ivy, and other greenery associated with the festive season, they looked like they might be officiating at a Saturnalia.

'Excellent, excellent,' declared Smith, tugging off his apron and throwing it over one of the armchairs. 'As you see, we keep shipboard hours here, none of this nonsense of dinner at seven. So let us be seated and become better acquainted over a dish of Stargazy pie.'

He exchanged a knowing smirk with mine host, who was carrying this object to the table. It was a very large pie and endowed with the peculiarity of having a number of fish heads protruding from the crust to gaze with their dead eyes upon the heavens, or those about to feast upon them. Nathan, who had never heard of it and suspected that Smith had only lately been educated in its finer points, was informed that it combined pilchards—a small fish of the herring clan native to Cornwall—potatoes, and hard-boiled eggs. He accepted a large slice but did not consider it a success.

Fortunately, it was not all the first course had to offer. There was also a fish soup, mostly composed of a local species of shark, known as the porbeagle, dressed crab, turbot, and lobster decorated with various whelks, mussels, and other marine creatures that otherwise would have had nothing better to do than cling to a rock. All those that Nathan sampled were excellent, though having subsisted on short commons for most of the long and dreary trip across the Atlantic he would probably have consumed anything laid before him. He had always been a good eater and was rarely distracted by less important concerns than the demands of his appetite, but in this instance he could not help brooding upon his host's motivation in inviting him here, for apart from Tully's unspoken warning, the remark about being interested in 'your manifest, your ship, your crew, and you, sir' had done nothing to diminish his innate wariness. Smith seemed to be in no hurry to enlighten him, but devoted himself to their entertainment with overlong anecdotes, mostly concerning his recent experiences in the Levant, where he had capped an extraordinary career by holding the fortress of Acre against a French siege and, in his own estimate, at least, stopped Bonaparte's march on India.

These stories continued through the fish course and the various species of fowl which followed and were not without interest to his guests, who had both served in the Levant and had been in India while Smith was holding the fort, so to speak, in Palestine. The main question in Nathan's mind, however, was whether Smith had any authority over him. He had been made post during the American war, which made him senior to Nathan by about twelve years, so if Smith was presently under Admiralty orders, he could in theory commandeer the *Falaise*, her captain and her crew—and even her cargo—though it seemed unlikely at a time of peace. In most circumstances Nathan would have welcomed the opportunity for service, but he was not at all sure he wished to serve under a man with the reputation of Sir Sidney Smith. Although he had profited from a degree of favouritism during his career, he had seemed at times to deliberately provoke the animosity of those who could, and would—given the slightest opportunity—contrive his ruin and disgrace, and that of anyone unwise enough to become associated with him. His father had been a captain in the Guards and a gentleman usher at the court of the present king, and it was said by his enemies that this close connection with royalty had caused Smith to be promoted far beyond his abilities throughout his career. He had been knighted by the King of Sweden for his services to that country in their most recent war with Russia, and though he rarely used the title himself, many of his fellow officers referred to him contemptuously as 'the Swedish Knight.' More recently, he was rumoured to be having an affair with Princess Caroline of Brunswick, wife of the Prince of Wales, which might explain the toast to dangerous liaisons that he had proposed at the beginning of the evening.

'Well, having disposed of the last war to our satisfaction, perhaps we should move on to the next,' he declared now. He noted Nathan's faintly arched brow. 'But you must know it is coming, sir. I assumed this is what brought you back to England at such a wretched time of the year.'

In fact, the prospect of another war had played no part in Nathan's decision, but he was aware of the possibility of renewed hostilities. He could hardly fail to be; the newspapers were full of it.

'Depend upon it, we will be at war with Bonaparte before Eastertide,' Smith announced confidently. 'It is but a question of whether we declare war upon *him*, or he upon us. I suppose your success in the Indian Ocean has made you hopeful of a crack frigate, or a '74 at the least.'

'I will be glad to take whatever I can get, given the competition,' Nathan replied cautiously.

'Good God, a realist! How very refreshing. Unusual, too. And of course, with Old Jarvey at the Admiralty . . .'

He did not need to finish the sentence. 'Old Jarvey' was the less than respectful nickname of the Earl Saint Vincent, whose family name of Jervis was similar to the common term for a London cab driver, a species of creature he was said to resemble in both manner and appearance. He had never forgiven Nathan for protesting his decision to bombard the port of Cádiz on the grounds that it would cause heavy civilian casualties, an imprudence that had earned Nathan three months in the Moorish Castle at Gibraltar for insubordination, and he had not held a regular command since.

'We all have our crosses to bear,' sighed Sir Sidney, 'and Old Jarvey is a considerably heavier cross than Our Lord was obliged to endure, if that is not to utter a blasphemy.'

It was, but Nathan let it pass.

'I look no further than the disposal of my present cargo,' he assured him, hoping this might remind him of why they were here.

'Oh, we can always use a few more fireworks,' replied Smith. 'And I propose to make you a decent offer, but I will be frank with you—it is not our most pressing requirement at this moment in time.'

'When you say *we* . . . ?'

A nod towards his companion. 'Monsieur Cadoudal here represents the main opposition party in France—the main opposition, I should say, to Napoleon Bonaparte.'

This was presumably why he was to be found skulking in England, Nathan reflected privately, Bonaparte not being noted for his tolerance of opposition parties. Not if they were in opposition to him. He waited for Cadoudal to say something, but in vain. He had hardly spoken all through the meal, and his only reaction now was to close his eyes and nod his several chins as much as his collar would allow.

'Most of their support comes from the west—Brittany and Normandy, and further south along the Atlantic coast. In the event of a new war, this is where Bonaparte will face the most opposition—at least, from within France. Monsieur Cadoudal and his friends are presently engaged in mobilising that support, and I have the honour of assisting him.'

'As a serving office?' Nathan queried.

A sly smile. 'As a private individual. There can be no official sanction for our activities while our two countries remain at peace. However, between these four walls I can tell you that certain funds have been made available to purchase whatever may be required in the way of material support. Which is where you come in, Captain. The *Falaise* is a French ship, I understand.'

'She was rated a corvette in the French navy,' Nathan replied cautiously. He was wondering how much Smith knew of her recent history and how much he would need to tell him. 'But—'

'My information is that she was taken by a British squadron off Rochefort in the last year of the war and eventually sold to an American gentleman by the name of Gilbert Imlay.'

Nathan kept his features carefully blank, but Smith's expression revealed a degree of pleasure in tormenting him with his knowledge of the circumstances that had led to Nathan's present situation.

'From what my sources tell me, Imlay's intention was to use her, and several other vessels under his command, to run guns to the rebel slaves in Saint-Domingue under General Toussaint L'Ouverture,' Smith went on. 'Or have I been misinformed?'

'As to that, I am not at liberty to say,' Nathan replied, more coolly than he felt.

'Ah. Forgive me. I do not mean to pry into your recent activities in the Caribbean, but I fear I must be blunt, sir, and enquire how it is that the *Falaise* now comes to be under your ownership—rather than Imlay's—and why the guns were not delivered?'

It was a question their lordships of the Admiralty might have asked, particularly Saint Vincent, who had apparently known of Nathan's mission and approved it. At least, according to Nelson.

'The guns *were* delivered,' Nathan insisted. 'The first consignment, at any rate. But by the time we took delivery of the second, Toussaint L'Ouverture was a prisoner of the French and the situation on the island had become—difficult.' If that was an adequate description for the nightmare of atrocity, massacre, and yellow fever that had engulfed the colony. 'Also'—he had to be careful here, but it had to be said, even if it was relayed to Saint Vincent—'I was betrayed by Imlay to the French.'

Smith considered him thoughtfully for a moment. No smile this time. 'Why would he do that?'

'Because he—or his superiors in Washington—wished the French to believe that the rebels were being secretly supported, and supplied with weapons, by the British. American interests in the region, or indeed, anywhere else in the world, being best served by continuing conflict between Britain and France. That is why he had the ship registered in my name.'

Smith shook his head in what might have been silent admiration. He and Imlay probably had a lot in common, Nathan considered. 'And so you decided to keep it?'

'Until Imlay asks for it back, yes.'

'And in the meantime, you feel at liberty to sell the guns to the highest bidder.'

'Within certain constraints.' But he felt compelled to add by way of an explanation: 'Not only did Imlay betray us to the French, he left no provision for paying the officers or crew. It is the only way I can find the means of doing so.'

'Fair enough,' Smith agreed. 'So, what are we talking about?'

At last.

'Eight hundred Brown Bess muskets and two hundred rifles,' replied Nathan diffidently.

Another flicker of a glance towards Cadoudal.

'You do not fear the Americans might feel a little provoked to discover you have kept their ship and sold its cargo to the highest bidder?'

'I imagine this is possible, but I am assuming they would be too embarrassed to do much about it.'

'Well, I doubt they would take you to court, but they would not have to. A word in the right ear . . .'

Nathan inclined his own ear enquiringly.

'Come, sir, I do not suppose you are so naive as not to have considered it. A serving officer running guns to rebel slaves in the Caribbean . . . ? You would be pilloried in the newspapers, those of a certain persuasion, at any rate, and—'

'And acclaimed a hero in others,' Nathan interrupted. 'Slavery is by no means universally supported in England, even in the journals.'

'And how long do you think the present Ministry would last without the support of the slave owners and the dealers and their stooges in the journals and, indeed, Parliament?'

Here it comes, Nathan thought. He avoided looking at Tully, but he knew the same thought would be passing through his mind.

'So, what are you suggesting, sir?'

'I am not suggesting anything. I am merely considering some of the difficulties that might arise should your recent activities in the Caribbean become public knowledge.'

'And do you have a solution?'

'Well, not a solution as such, but'—he frowned as if applying himself to the problem for the first time—'I am thinking that it might be wise to muddy the waters a little. If the *Falaise* were to be hired out to Monsieur Cadoudal, for instance, and you were to undertake certain activities on his behalf . . .' He glanced apologetically at the gentleman in question, as if the notion had just occurred to him. The gentleman's face remained blank, but Nathan imagined they had discussed this down to the finest detail. 'Activities that are very much in the national interest . . . Well, I believe you would find some very powerful voices mobilised on your behalf—in the press and Parliament, and indeed, in the Ministry. Even to the extent of drawing a veil over your recent endeavours on behalf of certain gentlemen in the Caribbean.'

Pure blackmail—you had to allow, so elegantly put—even as you felt yourself sliding from frying pan to fire.

'What activities did you have in mind?' Nathan enquired.

Chapter 3

Snowed In

The snow started on their way back to the *Falaise*. By nightfall it was working up to be the worst blizzard Nathan had encountered outside the South Atlantic, a wild beast, lashed by the north-east wind, howling about the rigging, biting the faces and blinding the eyes of anyone foolish enough or obliged by his duties to venture on deck. He listened to it howling for a while from the comfort of his cot and then fell asleep.

He slept soundly until dawn, by which time the storm had eased a little but showed signs of settling into a prolonged assault, as if determined to erase harbour and haven and indeed most of Cornwall from the map. When he emerged from below, partway into the forenoon watch, he could barely see more than a few yards through the barrage, no ships, no shore, not even the nearest headland of Saint Mawes, just a few shadowy figures garbed as much like an Esquimau as he was, stumbling about the deck or seeking such shelter as was available to them. It felt as if the ship and her crew had been lifted by the wind during the night and transported to an Arctic wasteland, and it would be no surprise to see a polar bear come clambering over the stern, hungry for human flesh. He looked over the rail, just to be sure they were still floating on water, and having confirmed that this was the case, gave orders to the first mate Mr Keppler, who had the misfortune to be officer of the watch, that the decks were to be kept as clear of snow as possible and the yards free of ice, leaving the poor man to work out how best to achieve this remarkable feat, and then retreated to his cabin to consider what difference the weather might make in his present fortunes, knowing full well that it would make no difference at all unless a providential avalanche should sweep the Ship Inn and its occupants into the sea. It might, however, provide him with a day or two's grace to make better preparations for what they had in store for him.

He shook off the mental lethargy that had gripped him since yesterday's dinner and sent for the ship's carpenter, Mr Penn, who presented himself with the wary look of one who has been asked to achieve the impossible many times and expects to be asked many times again. Mr Penn was a Welshman and of dour disposition. Kidd, Nathan's informant on such matters, said that he came from the county of Flint and that his name was Welsh for a tree stump. Nathan seriously doubted if it was true about the tree stump—Kidd had a reputation for calumny—though the carpenter did somewhat resemble that object in stature, being short and stocky with little evidence of a neck and features that appeared curiously crushed, as if it was often sat upon.

'We are expecting passengers, Mr Penn,' Nathan informed him blandly, 'and though I would prefer to accommodate them in the chain locker, or even the bilges, I am persuaded that we must provide somewhere more suitable to their status.'

'Where did you have in mind, sir?' enquired Penn, in a tone that stopped just short of insubordinate, for besides possessing a full complement of 146 officers and men, the *Falaise* was bursting at the seams with her unaccustomed cargo of guns and ammunition. He had long been persuaded by Nathan's previous demands—such as chopping off the ship's figurehead on the grounds that she was bringing them bad luck—that the present owner and captain of the *Falaise* should be consigned to Bedlam as soon as he stepped ashore, and if it were at all possible, confined in a cage in the orlop until his transfer could be arranged. Mr Penn would have had no objections to building the cage.

Nathan had executed a crude drawing on a page of his journal which he now presented for the chippie's inspection. He had divided the fairly generous proportions of the cabin so that it now resembled the quarters available to his junior officers, with an open space down the middle just about wide enough for a table and chairs, which allowed access to the quarter gallery with its seat of ease, and to four small cabins at the side which could serve as sleeping quarters for himself, his two guests, and Mr

Tully, who had previously been obliged to occupy one of the cabins off the gunroom.

'And when would you like to have this done by?' asked Mr Penn, looking about him as if calculating that it might, with some ingenuity, be drawn out to his retirement.

'By tomorrow, Chips, if you please. Or the day after, if the snow persists.'

Mr Penn's jaw dropped, in as much as it was capable of that contortion. He began to explain, as best he could, why this was quite impossible, but Nathan interrupted before he had managed half a sentence.

'Come now, sir, I am not asking for the Taj Mahal.' Mr Penn had not served in India, so the comparison was possibly lost on him. 'A few lengths of fake bulkhead and some canvas will suffice. If you lack for timber, double up on canvas. I will give you a chit for the sailmaker. I have seen you at work—whirligigs ain't in it when you have the wind in your sails.' There were probably better ways of putting this, but he hoped the carpenter would take it as a compliment. 'I am sure you will rig up something acceptable in a few hours, and what else is there to do in this weather? At least you will be working below.'

Mr Penn had no ready response to this, and after muttering some words about seeing what he had in the way of materials, he stumped off to tell his mate the skipper had suffered another rush of blood to the head and they were properly buggered once more. Nathan summoned Kidd to tell him what to expect, though judging from his scowl he had very likely been listening at the door and had already formed a negative opinion of the arrangement.

'And will they be bringing their own servants with them, these passengers?'

It was a reasonable enquiry, but as always there was that in Kidd's manner and tone that verged on the insolent.

'No, they will not, Kidd. You will have them all to yourself, but if you need any assistance, you may ask Mr Keppler to spare you a couple of hands to serve at dinner—only ensure that they will not disgrace us by pouring wine into their laps.' Kidd's expression suggested that they would be lucky to have wine poured anywhere in their vicinity. 'One is a post captain and the other a distinguished foreign gentleman,' Nathan added, 'so I trust they will be treated with all due respect.'

'And will you be staying here yourself,' Kidd enquired, 'while the work is going on?'

'No, I will not. I will move into the gunroom until it is completed,' Nathan replied. 'So, I will have my dinner served there with the other officers. What are we having today?'

He asked this briskly and with a display of optimism, which he did not feel. They had exhausted all that remained of his personal provisions save a few bottles of wine and some spirits, and Kidd derived considerable satisfaction from informing him that they would be having the same as the cook was preparing for the rest of the crew, which was boiled pork with turnip and pickled cabbage, and not even the usual Sunday treat of figgy dowdy, they being out of raisins.

'Good God, is it Sunday?' exclaimed Nathan. 'I had quite forgot.'

He was expected to perform a service on Sundays, with both watches assembled on deck, but it would have been impossible in the snow anyway. More serious was the absence of figgy dowdy.

He considered an alternative, but nothing obvious presented itself. He supposed he could double up on the rum ration, but he would have to check there was enough rum. Not only had the crew not been paid, Kidd included, but they were desperately short on their own provisions, and the salt beef and pork the purser had acquired in Nassau was about as disgusting as anything Nathan had consumed at sea, which was quite an achievement on its part.

One of the few advantages—possibly the only one—arising from Nathan's meeting at the Ship Inn was that he would shortly possess the means to purchase some new supplies, but it was clearly out of the question to send a boat ashore in these conditions, even if the stores were open.

He dismissed Kidd and removed himself and a few personal belongings to the gunroom, where he found Mr Keppler with the purser and the surgeon, swathed in coats, hats, and mufflers, playing cards by lantern light—it was almost as gloomy as it was at night—and begged the honour of sharing their accommodation for a while. To which they readily agreed, of course, though he did not think he had especially brightened their day.

'I will ask my steward to see what wine we still have in store,' he told them, with another appearance of cheerfulness. 'And we will have ourselves a merry dinner.'

This was as likely as a spit roast served by naked dancing girls, he thought, but they forced their frozen features into the semblance of a beaming response. Declining their invitation to join them at cards, he made himself as comfortable as possible and pretended to be engrossed in the study of Hershel's latest offerings on the subject of astronomy while he considered how to deal with the many other inconveniences Sir Sidney Smith was likely to inflict upon him. The main problem was that it meant putting himself at the man's disposal for the foreseeable future, and while he did not have anything against him personally—or at least nothing worth fighting a duel over—he had heard enough unfavourable stories of his duplicity as a commander to make him extremely wary of attaching his lantern to such a wayward star.

And yet their two careers had rather a lot in common. They had both been obliged by choice or circumstance to spend a considerable part of their time ashore, usually on covert missions and occasionally in the service of foreign masters, either with or without the consent of the British Admiralty. They had both been in prison. They had both fallen foul of authority in its various forms. And they had a tendency to engage in dangerous liaisons with women who could cause them a great deal of mischief if so inclined. Or if not the women, then their powerful kin. The main difference between them was that despite his reputation as a blithe spirit, Smith had retained some very important friends in high places, whereas Nathan had never had them in the first place, apart from Nelson, of course, and that had not been entirely to his advantage since the Lady Hamilton affair, which had scandalized the king, the court, and most of high society.

He regretted being unable to walk off his agitation on what passed for a quarterdeck, or to discuss his fears with Tully, but there was nowhere now that was private to them—the noise of hammering and sawing confirmed that Mr Penn and his mates were at work on what had been his cabin—and he could not even distract himself with the thought of a good dinner. However, the liquid situation was not as bad as it was for more solid fare, and he managed to get Kidd to bring up four bottles of claret and one of French cognac from the orlop and hosted as jolly a feast as he could with the miserable sustenance the cook had provided for them. After which, feeling the need to stretch his legs a little, he decided to venture on deck to see how the weather was doing.

He dressed in as many layers as he could without losing the ability to walk and paced the ship from stern to stem, commiserating with those few

hands he had obliged to keep a watch. The wind seemed to have dropped
a little, though the snow was still falling thick and fast, and he could
still see nothing of the anchorage. There had, of course, been no news
from the shore. Even if a boat could be navigated in these conditions, he
imagined that every house and business in Falmouth would be snowed in,
including the Ship Inn, and that it would take a considerable amount of
time and labour to clear them once the snow had stopped falling, which
it showed no intention of doing.

After ten minutes or so of this he was obliged to retreat to the gunroom where he spent the rest of what passed for daylight with Hershel's
astronomy until Mr Penn and his mates had made his new quarters ready
for him and his expected guests. He declared himself well satisfied with
their efforts, though it was a sad reduction of his previous estate. The
cabin they had constructed for him was small but adequate, and if he put
Tully in the one adjoining it, he would have at least the space of a dining table between himself and his two passengers. As it was, for the time
being, he and Tully had the whole area to themselves, and he was able to
unburden himself of at least some of the concerns that had been nagging
at him since their encounter at the Ship Inn.

'At least it solves the problem of selling the guns to the wrong people,'
Tully remarked appeasingly.

'You think they are the *right* people?'

'I take it you do not?'

Nathan let his body do the talking, slumping in his chair as if he had
been struck dead.

'They must have the backing of the British government,' Tully persisted. 'Or at least the Admiralty. Else Smith would not be involved,
surely?'

'I doubt we may be sure of anything where Smith is involved,' Nathan
pointed out. 'When will we learn that the French will never go back to
the old ways,' he went on. 'Most of them would rather die than see the
Bourbons back in power.'

'Then what were we fighting for,' demanded Tully, 'for all those years?'

Nathan wished he knew. Sometimes he did not think Billy Pitt knew.
Perhaps the king did, in his saner moments. But this gave him a clue.

'Madness,' he announced. 'We were fighting madness. Madness and
hysteria and, and—bad theatre.'

He had a sudden sharp memory of a time in Paris, at Sara's place in the Rue Jacob. They had been talking of the *sans-culottes* and the notion that they ran around in striped pants and red shirts with a Phrygian cap on their heads and wooden sabots on their feet, carrying a pike with a head on it. He could recall her words almost exactly, as if she was in the cabin now, except that when she first said them, they were lying naked on her bed.

'*Anyone dressed like that, you may count upon it, will be a student or a man of letters. A journalist or an actor or some such imposter. The workers and the poor wear rags, or the cast-off finery of their betters, picked up for a few sous in the flea markets or taken from a corpse strung from a lamppost. Nobody in Paris is who you think they are. It is all make-believe. Theatre. A masquerade.*'

Sara, who he would very likely never see again.

He felt the sadness settle around him like a sea fret, cold and dank and infinitely depressing, the misery of the past, the lost opportunities, the lost loves . . .

'Bad theatre,' Tully repeated flatly, nodding as if he needed to think about this. Nathan shook off the fret and saved him the trouble.

'What we have been seeing in France for the last ten years. Ever since the storming of the Bastille. Melodrama. The French invented melo-drama—did you not know that?'

Tully shook his head, his expression resigned.

'Rousseau was the first, I believe, but there have been many others since. It has a grip on the entire nation, and we are fighting to stop it from crossing the English Channel.'

Nathan knew this was nonsense—mostly—but while he was generally opposed to nonsense, especially on the tongues of politicians, he was not averse to speaking it himself on occasion when he wished to provoke or entertain, or to counter a propensity towards melancholy.

'It hardly seems worth dying for,' Tully proposed mildly.

'Oh, you would not think that if you had been to Paris as often as I have,' Nathan countered. 'The deputies in the National Assembly baring their chests and inviting someone to stick a bayonet in them if they were false to the Revolution, Robespierre blowing off his own jaw with a pistol . . . And now Bonaparte. Oh dear.' He shook his head. 'Give me a sozzled Billy Pitt and a mad King George any day of the week.'

Although he had not seriously entertained this notion when he started on the subject, he began to warm to it. Bonaparte was certainly inclined to melodrama. Nathan had been at his side when he had saved the Revolution by defending the National Assembly from a royalist mob. With victory in his grasp, however, he had taken it into his head to mount a white horse and wave his sword in the air, upon which the mount had promptly thrown him and bolted towards the enemy, dragging him along with his foot caught in the stirrups, to almost certain destruction had not Nathan stepped forward and grabbed the reins. It had been an instinctive gesture with no consideration of the consequence, but he had felt a degree of responsibility for everything that had happened since.

'I do not think the English are entirely free of melodrama,' Tully remarked with the detached air of the outsider. 'Look at Shakespeare.'

Nathan gave this some thought. He had been obliged to attend several of the Bard's plays with his mother in London, and though he had slept through large parts of them until jolted awake by an irate elbow, he considered himself reasonably well informed on the topic. 'Some of his characters are impassioned at times,' he conceded, 'even a little deluded, but never melodramatic.'

'I would have thought Hamlet verged on melodrama at times,' Tully persisted.

'Really?' *Hamlet* had been one of the plays he had seen, but he had no clear memory of the plot or its characters. There were rather a lot of dead bodies on stage at the end, but he could not rightly recall how they had got there. 'Well, it was not one of his best. How did we get on to *Hamlet?*'

Tully had to think about this. 'Sir Sidney Smith?' he proposed.

'Ah yes. And whoever is behind him. Well, I tell you, whoever it is, they are backing the wrong horse.'

'That being . . . ?'

'Cadoudal,' Nathan declared. 'Doubtless he is brave enough and committed to his cause—but who is he fighting for? The House of Bourbon and the Church of Rome. And who have we been fighting against, as Englishmen, these past two centuries and more? The House of Bourbon and the Church of Rome. Ridiculous.'

This did nothing to clear Tully's puzzled brow.

'Well, I suppose I can always go back to smuggling, or highway robbery,' he sighed. But then he brightened. 'Speaking of which, I picked up a hunk of cheese when we were dining and concealed it about my person.' He felt for it in his pockets. 'Shall we have it toasted with some of that French cognac we have left—if you have not drunk it already?'

'You stole it? From the table?' Nathan was impressed but a little shocked. Tully had been a smuggler before being pressed into the service. Highway robbery was a more recent calling, for which Nathan must take full responsibility, but you had to draw the line somewhere, and stealing food from a gentleman's table was in a different class of felony altogether, like cheating at cards.

'I did,' confessed Tully, unabashed. 'Do you wish to share it or not?'

'I do,' said Nathan hastily. He raised his voice. 'Kidd! Kidd there!'

Chapter 4

. . . And the Cat Jumped
over the Moon

It snowed for the next day and well into the following night, but at the commencement of the forenoon watch Nathan came up on deck to view a relatively clear sky and even a glimpse of wintry sunshine touching the tops of the hills beyond the town. The neighbouring vessels were at last visible, so coated in snow and ice they looked like the sugar-icing ships he had seen on a celebratory cake presented to Old Jarvey on the anniversary of the Battle of Saint Vincent, while the shore had been transformed into a winter wonderland, the hills and vales sculptured into gentle folds and the skeletal trees transformed into a delicate filigree, and even the slate roofs and dung-filled streets of the sleeping town made magical by a white blanket of snow. There was no movement, save for the coils of smoke issuing from the chimneys and the occasional flurries of powdery snow whipped off the surrounding hilltops by gusts of wind, but then as the wintry sun rose still further, stout, stiff-moving figures heavily swaddled in layers of coat and muffler began to emerge from the houses and shops and inns along the waterfront, and after staring about them bemusedly, they began the weary task of clearing the streets and footpaths. By mid-morning, a few boats were moving about the haven, and shortly before the end of the forenoon watch one of them was seen to be heading directly for the *Falaise* with two well-wrapped figures in the stern who were shortly revealed to be Nathan's new employers, Smith and Cadoudal.

He briefly considered piping them aboard, but it was very possible that Smith preferred to remain incognito, so he saved himself the trouble and confined his sense of ceremony to smartening himself up a little and awaiting their arrival at the entry port with Tully and Mr Banjo, who were the only men on the ship apart from himself who knew the purpose of their visit.

The starboard watch was clearing the last of the snow from the decks and the guns and Nathan was conscious of their curious stares in the direction of the two men as they stepped onto the deck. He knew the ship would be rife with rumour, and sooner rather than later he would have to make some formal announcement of their future prospects, but for the time being they would have to remain in ignorance. There was no obvious clue to Smith's status from his dress, but the confidence with which he came aboard would have marked him out as a naval officer to anyone with more than a passing acquaintance with the breed. He looked keenly about him, his eyes sweeping the gundeck and rising briefly to the rigging, and Nathan felt already that he was being given marks out of ten. Smith was famed in the service for having taken and passed his examination for lieutenant, in defiance of the regulations, at the age of sixteen, and he had been made post and given the command of a frigate before he was twenty. Cadoudal, on the other hand, looked as if he would far rather be in his bed, or huddled up close to the fire in the Ship Inn. There was no curiosity in the way he looked about him, only a dull resignation to his fate, like a weary bull being led to slaughter.

Nathan greeted them with a minimum of fuss and hurried them below to what would be their quarters, calling upon Kidd to bring the rum and spices he could smell simmering in the little galley. They had run out of lemons so could not rise to grog, but Kidd was a good improviser, at least when it came to drink. Smith appeared as much at home as he had in the private room of the inn, Cadoudal considerably less so, his bulky presence making the cabin even less roomy than it was. Smith's first words when he was seated at the table were to enquire how soon the *Falaise* would be ready for sea, for he had spent far too long kicking his heels indoors, he said, with this wretched snow.

'As soon as we have taken on provisions,' Nathan replied, pushing his luck, 'for the same snow has prevented us from making proper preparation for your arrival.'

'Be damned to that,' said Smith briskly. 'We will make do with hard tack and weevils, eh, Georges?' He did not wait for a response from Cadoudal. 'Let us make sail while the wind is in our favour. We have brought what we need by way of comfort, and if it is not sufficient, well, it will not be the first time we have been on short commons.'

Nathan frowned, for he had hoped for at least a day to get in a few more provisions, and there was at least one more concern he must address before they set sail. He had mentioned the necessity of an advance on his commission when they first met, and Smith had assured him that it would be arranged, but no funds had yet been made available to him, and from the small amount of baggage Nathan had seen carried aboard he had no great hopes that it was about to be distributed. The crew had been promised their pay at the termination of their present voyage, and while it might be argued that they had not yet reached their final destination, Nathan would certainly have to address the matter before they left their present mooring. He did not suppose for a moment that they would refuse to sail, but they would be surly, slow to obey orders, even to argue the toss, and in his experience one thing could lead to another. He put this to his distinguished patron as tactfully as he could contrive.

'I comprehend the problem,' said he, 'but it is far easier for me to access funds at journey's end than it would be here, and as for the crew, I believe they will find it far more difficult to obtain alternative employment than would be the case in Falmouth. I would advise you to wait until then.'

'Very well, but I will still have to speak to them,' Nathan insisted.

Smith sighed. 'Well, if you must, but tell them as little as possible, and not a hint as to our destination—at least until there is no longer any possibility of contact with the shore.'

Nathan had the crew assembled in the waist. They were not stood in divisions as they would have been in a King's ship, nor attired in anything remotely resembling a uniform, and as he viewed them from the slight vantage of the little quarterdeck, he reflected privately that they came as near as any mariners he had seen to deserving the epithet, 'a motley crew', though he would probably have gone a step further and called them a bunch of pirates. More than half of them had been aboard the *Falaise* when she was fitted out as a privateer towards the end of the last war, so piracy was very much in their veins. Most of them were either Americans, Irish, or from the port of Liverpool, and if they were united in one thing, it was a spirit of rebellion. It seemed to him now as he surveyed the expressions on their faces that it was particularly close to the surface. He had meant to start with some lighthearted remark, even a joke, but decided against.

'Well, men, we have endured many hardships together and have been obliged to remain at our present station far longer than I anticipated'—their stares would have put the Gorgon to shame—'but now we are about to resume our voyage.' The word *resume* was carefully chosen. 'Should the wind remain in our favour, it will be completed in a day or two when we will discharge our cargo and you will be paid what you were promised when you signed on, with a little extra to show my appreciation of your worth.' They continued to gaze fixedly at him without expression. He considered a word of explanation, but anything he might say would risk betraying Smith's confidences. 'Thank you.' He turned to Tully but avoided meeting his eye. 'Mr Tully, prepare the ship for leaving harbour.'

But as he passed Mr Banjo, who had been standing a little behind him in case of accidents, he quoted, or rather misquoted, a line from a nursery rhyme which they had adopted as a kind of private joke, or commentary on their many escapades together.

'And the cat jumped over the moon.'

The cat jumped over the moon was an expression appropriated by Mr Banjo to describe an undertaking of such breath-taking audacity, or folly, it should never have been attempted in the first place, much less rewarded with success. The first time Nathan had heard him use it was after freeing him—at some expense and even greater risk—from a prison van conveying him to a court-martial, and very likely a hanging, on a trumped-up charge of striking an officer. The second was when they had destroyed a French ship-of-the-line with an exploding shell from an *obussier*, a weapon much derided as wildly inaccurate, but which had the good fortune, from their point of view, to start a fire aboard the ship it had been aimed at, igniting the magazine. Nathan had attempted to explain that in the nursery rhyme it was the cow that had jumped over the moon, while the cat played the fiddle, but George persisted with his own version on the grounds that the cat was a far more agile creature than the cow and far more likely to succeed in the enterprise, while the possession of nine lives made it more inclined to accept the risk of failure. There was an unanswerable logic to this.

Mr Banjo, who spoke four languages tolerably well besides his native Yoruba, had a curious fondness for English nursery rhymes—not on account of their childish jingles, but because of the hidden meanings he perceived in them—though he frequently altered the narrative to give whatever meaning he required. The moon-jumping cat was a comment not only on Nathan's agility in the face of danger, but as a reminder that it was becoming something of a habit with him, and he was fast running out of lives.

Nathan was giving some thought to this as he leant on the stern rail of the *Falaise*, watching the coast of Cornwall fade into the distance. While it was satisfying to reflect that he had found a buyer for the embarrassing cargo residing in the orlop, he could not help considering that he had done so by mortgaging his future and putting himself, his ship, and very likely his crew into a situation of considerable jeopardy, or certainly more so than in Falmouth harbour. He was still not sure what Sir Sidney Smith required of them, but he knew it would not be straightforward, and that it would very likely involve a great deal of danger and uncertainty. And although he had often welcomed both as an antidote to boredom and melancholy—a diversion from the relentless march to the grave—he did not feel quite so sanguine about it as he might. Perhaps it was the time of the year. The life force at its lowest ebb. He never felt so attached to England, he mused, as in the leaving of it, or so much regret at the loss of such comfort and joy as it had afforded him over the years. There was regret, too, that he had not had time to visit either of his parents during his brief return. They were of an age now when he knew he should try to see more of them, and he had seriously intended to do so during the present peace. He was particularly concerned for his mother, not on account of her health, which was excellent, so far as he knew, but her propensity for dabbling in politics. She had been an ardent supporter of the independence struggle in America when Nathan was a child and had considerably added to her ill fame by publicly enthusing over the Revolution in France. Age, far from withering her passions, only seemed to intensify them, and every time Nathan received a letter from home, or on the rarer occasions he returned there, he expected to find she had been locked up in prison or confined to an asylum.

A familiar voice at his shoulder distracted him from these gloomy thoughts.

'We could set the stun'sls.'

Nathan raised his head—first to consider the sails, then the sky, and then the expectant face of Mr Tully, who was always desirous of putting on more canvas if it was blowing anything less than a hurricane.

'We are doing well enough without,' he declared at length. At the last casting of the log they had been making between five and six knots, so if the wind held steady from the north-west, they should reach their destination within the next forty-eight hours, and that was quite soon enough for Nathan. But Tully might have a different view, for he had been born and raised on the islands.

The islands. Nathan turned his back on the receding shore and gave some thought to their next port of call. Jersey was the largest of a cluster of small islands off the coast of Normandy. If they had a collective name, Nathan did not know it, and it was not marked on the charts, though they had been in the possession of the English crown since 1066. Tully came from the second largest of the group, Guernsey, but he had not been back there for at least ten years, and appeared to have no great attachment to the place. Shortly after they became friends, he had revealed to Nathan that he was the illegitimate progeny of a Guernsey smuggler and a local squire's daughter who had died bringing him into the world, and that he had been raised as a gentleman by his mother's family. But after meeting his father again at the age of fifteen, he had chosen a life of adventure and lawbreaking over luxury and privilege. By the time he was twenty he was captain of his own lugger—the *Black Pig*—engaged in delivering duty-free liquor to his many customers in the southern English counties, until she was taken by a revenue cutter off Poole and he was given the option of the hangman's noose or a career in His Britannic Majesty's Navy. He had done remarkably well out of it, considering, and rarely spoke of his early life, but Nathan knew that his father had drowned some years back, leaving three young daughters by another Guernsey woman, *not* the daughter of a squire, and Nathan suspected that Tully supported them financially.

He was framing a delicate question about whether he had any plans to visit them when Smith emerged from the aft companionway and spared them both a possible embarrassment.

'What a joy to be at sea again,' said he, beaming about him and sniffing the air with apparent relish, though it was cold enough to take the skin off a man's face. He looked up at the sails. 'Not got the stun'sls out? I would have thought it was worth giving them an airing.'

Tully made some excuse and took himself off.

'I think it may come on to blow during the night,' replied Nathan coolly.

'Oh, well, it is your decision,' conceded Smith.

There was an awkward silence, which Nathan eventually broke with a question of his own.

'So, now we are safely out to sea,' he began, 'and in no danger of having it conveyed to the wrong people, what are your plans for us when we reach Jersey?'

'Oh, did I not say?' Smith responded blandly. 'We are going to kidnap Napoleon Bonaparte.'

He smiled at the expression on Nathan's face. 'I thought you would like that,' said he. 'It will give you an opportunity to renew your acquaintance with him, in rather different circumstances than the last time. Or was that his sister Pauline? I forget your exact dealings with the Bonaparte family. Perhaps in the next few days you will have the opportunity to enlighten me.'

Chapter 5

The Fatal Blow

They convened in what Smith had kindly referred to as the stateroom, though he was probably being sarcastic. In fact, it was more of a passageway between the hastily erected cabins sufficient for a table and chairs and with just enough space left for a body to squeeze through to the quarter gallery if he wished to relieve himself on the seat of ease. Privately, Nathan thought that Mr Penn had done rather well with the limited resources at his disposal, but he was not going to court the mockery of his fellow captain by saying so. There being very little daylight showing through the stern windows, the gloom was alleviated by three storm lanterns hanging from the deckbeams above the table, shedding their jaundiced light upon the three conspirators and a chart of the English Channel.

As they sat themselves down, Kidd appeared with a bottle of Madeira and three glasses and Smith thanked him as if he had brought the Holy Grail, to which Kidd responded with an obsequious smirk of appreciation and a glance at Nathan as if to say, 'Now there is a gentleman', before slinking back to his den.

'So, what do you think of our little plan?' Smith commenced when their glasses were filled. He spoke in French, either for Cadoudal's benefit or because he was aware of Kidd's propensity for eavesdropping.

'Of kidnapping Bonaparte?' Totally insane, Nathan thought, but he kept this to himself for the time being. 'Was it your idea?'

'Ah, as to that, I must refer you to Georges, for I believe it originated in Normandy—but please, your opinion as to its feasibility.'

'Well, it rather depends on where he is,' Nathan countered, 'and how many guards he has about him at the time. But what would it achieve, precisely?'

'What? To deprive the French Republic of its present leader, a man widely regarded as a military genius, even by his enemies? Why, sir, it would be a devastating blow. A fatal blow, even.'

That rather depended on who the enemies were, Nathan thought.

'I think Bonaparte could prove a mixed blessing so far as the French are concerned,' he proposed. 'He will always put his own ambitions before those of the French people, even if he troubles to think about them at all, other than as a means of providing food for his armies.'

He used an expression he had heard on his recent voyage to Saint-Domingue—*la chair à canon*—cannon fodder. Bonaparte was using the French as cannon fodder, but so long as he kept winning victories, they did not seem to mind. Those that were still alive.

'Interesting.' A look of what might almost be respect, though it could just as easily be condescension. 'Yes, that is the opinion I formed of him in the Levant. But of course, you know him as well as any man—any Englishman, at least.'

'Nonsense—with respect,' Nathan protested. And best exposed as such before it got him in any more trouble than it had in the past, he thought. 'We were acquainted for a brief period seven years ago in Paris, when he was a nobody—a *chef de brigade*, without a brigade—and every prospect of being imprisoned for debt—or for backing the wrong horse. I mean in the political sense.'

'But you saved his life, I heard.'

Nathan shook his head, though not in denial. 'I merely restrained his mount when it threw him and dragged him along by the stirrup,' he explained. 'Any man would have done the same.' Smith looked doubtful. 'I did not know then what he was to become.'

'And if you did, would you have let the horse bolt?'

Nathan shrugged. 'Who knows? I do not have the gift of prescience.'

'But you would now agree that he is a significant danger to Britain, as great a danger as we have faced since . . . well, Julius Caesar, when we painted our faces blue and sacrificed people to oak trees.'

'Oh, he is dangerous, yes, but . . .' How could he put it without giving offence to their royalist companion? Nathan knew what Bonaparte was capable of, and not just as a military genius—he could be a cruel oppressor—but there had to be a better alternative than bringing back the Bourbons. The French royal family despised everything Britain stood for—its laws and liberties, its Parliament, its constitution, and particularly the limits placed on the powers of the British monarchy. Moreover, the most recent occupants of the French throne had been weak, indecisive, and inept, and there was no reason to believe their successors would be any different. But perhaps that was the point, at least from the British point of view. Bonaparte was a much more alarming enemy than the Bourbons had ever been, or could be in the future. The real objection to Bonaparte by those who held the reins of power in Britain, and those who supported them in the journals, was that they knew there was not another general to match him—British, Austrian, Prussian, or of any other European power you cared to name. That was why they reviled and caricatured him to the extent that they did, far more than they had any of his predecessors, either in the royalist or republican camp.

'Bonaparte is not the only general in the French army,' he pointed out. 'There are others who are a lot less committed to their own personal aggrandizement and a lot more to be relied upon. His ambition could well be the ruin of him, and France. Look at what happened in Egypt.'

But Smith was shaking his head. 'You underestimate him,' he said. 'If he had taken Acre he would have been in India by now.'

But then he would say that, being the Hero of Acre, Nathan thought. 'And the Prussians and the Austrians might be in Paris,' he said.

Smith frowned. 'What is that supposed to mean?'

'Only that we can never know how things might turn out in the long run.'

'So, we should do nothing but let Fate takes its course.'

'I do not say that. Only that I do not think removing one man necessarily changes the course of history. The reason France is more of a threat to us now than it ever was in the past is because the Revolution released an energy among its people, a fury, one might say, that is capable of destroying everything in its path, regardless of who stands at the head of it.'

Did he really think that? He was sounding disturbingly like his mother, save that she would not have seen it as a threat, of course, she would be all in favour of it. Smith was smiling but in a patronising way.

'I do not think Bonaparte would agree with you about that.'

'This is true,' Nathan conceded.

Bonaparte was always banging the drum of his 'Destiny', even when they had met in Paris. *'My Destiny, my Star.'* He and France were linked by Destiny. More nonsense. At least Nathan hoped it was. But either way, you ended up with a wasteland filled with rotting corpses, a lone cockerel crowing on a dunghill.

'Well, I hope I was never in agreement with Bonaparte,' he confessed. 'But why bother kidnapping him? Why not simply shoot him in the head and be done with it?'

'Well, I suppose that is an option,' Smith considered, 'but I am sure you would not wish us to be thought of as a nation of assassins.'

'Whereas kidnapping . . . ?'

'Oh, is a much lesser offence, surely, much like taking a prisoner of war.'

'Save that we are not presently at war,' Nathan pointed out.

Smith clearly thought he was being overly scrupulous. 'Well, officially of course the British government has no involvement in this. It will be an entirely private venture undertaken by the Chouans, eh, Georges?'

The chins wobbled in apparent agreement.

Nathan felt a stirring of alarm, not far removed from panic. The Chouans were a species of anti-government rebel native to the west of France, fanatically devoted to Crown and Church, and in the right conditions, formidable fighters, but he knew them to be reckless, riddled with informers and hopelessly addicted to glorious defeat.

'But we both hold the king's commission,' Nathan persisted. 'Which would be something of an embarrassment, would it not, if the French discover our involvement?'

'That is why we must ensure they do not,' Smith replied firmly. 'There is clearly a need for discretion, at least while this pretence of a peace endures.

'So, supposing the Chouans succeed in their mission . . .'

'Oh, they will succeed, sir, have no doubt about that. Bonaparte will be in Castle Gorey before he can draw breath.'

'Gorey?' Nathan was startled. 'You intend to bring him to Gorey?'

Gorey was the place they were headed for on Jersey. A small harbour on the east coast of the island, facing Normandy.

Smith frowned, as if he had said too much. 'Strictly between ourselves, and only as a temporary measure—until his future can be determined.'

What future would he have, Nathan wondered, besides a rope or a firing squad? Or more likely, a knife in the back. Whatever you thought about Bonaparte, not only was he a general, he was the French head of state. His murder—as it would be perceived—in an English castle would have consequences, and he said as much to Smith. Whatever the French made of it, it was unlikely to be condoned by King George, who thought of himself, at least in his more rational moments, as the first gentleman of Europe. He would not wish to give his name to an assassination attempt— if anyone had bothered to tell him about it.

'That is why we need to be discreet,' Smith said. 'It must be clear to the world in general that his captors are loyal Frenchmen, motivated by a love of their country and a desire to restore the French monarchy. And of course, it is our duty, as Englishmen, to remind them that they are bound by the rules of civilised conduct.' He gave Cadoudal a sly look that was almost a wink. 'They might put him on trial for treason, perhaps.'

'What—in Jersey? On British territory? Under what law?'

'Or perhaps they will give him a pension and retire him to some distant island to write his memoirs,' Smith breezed on, regardless. 'It is not for us to say. Send him back to Corsica, perhaps, where he came from.' Nathan could tell he had not thought this out—it was only a minor detail. It was the plan that excited him, not its consequences. But who had he found to back him in the Admiralty, or the Ministry, for that matter? Not the Earl Saint Vincent. For all his faults, Old Jarvey was not insane. Nor was Billy Pitt. Often drunk, but not mad. But then, Pitt was no longer in power. While Nathan had been in the Caribbean there had been a change of government. The country was now led by Henry Addington, with Hawkesbury as his foreign secretary. Would they contemplate a stunt like this? Unlikely. They were remarkable only for their lack of imagination, and neither was a risk-taker.

But then, what did Nathan know about it? Politics was an alien world to him. He rarely gave a thought to what went on in the minds of those ruling the country unless it clashed with his own immediate interests. They might well approve something like this—provided they could deny all knowledge of it.

So where did this leave him personally? Apart from on a ship filled with arms and ammunition on its way to Castle Gorey at the behest of a couple of reckless gamblers and adventurers who may or may not have the support of the British government.

Play for time, he thought. It was a mantra that had served him well enough in the past.

'So how exactly are we to carry out this project?' he enquired.

'Well, the precise details are yet to be agreed upon, but the operation will be meticulously planned and executed. Just as it was when I made my escape from Paris.'

So, it was pretty much as Nathan had suspected. Nothing was impossible for the man who had escaped from the Temple prison. His self-belief was impossible to dilute or diminish. And to be fair, it had served him well enough at Acre. In his own opinion he had almost single-handedly stopped Bonaparte from marching on India, and both houses of Parliament had confirmed it by passing a vote of thanks and granting him a pension of a thousand a year. In fact, now Nathan came to think on it, Sir Sidney Smith and Napoleon Bonaparte had quite a lot in common.

'So, what need have you of eight hundred muskets and two hundred rifles?'

Smith gave him what he no doubt considered to be a disarming smile. 'Ah. Yes. Well—they will be used to arm the invasion force.'

'The invasion force,' Nathan repeated flatly. Another detail Smith had neglected to mention until now.

'You are right in saying that after the kidnap there will be a period of great confusion and disorder,' Smith went on. 'There will be some who will be enraged, others relieved—*considerably* relieved at the demise of a man they regard as a threat to everything they believe was achieved by the Revolution—and of course, to themselves. There will doubtless be a move to seize the reins of power. And during this period, we shall land a small but well-armed and well-drilled force of volunteers on the Cotentin peninsula to spark an insurrection across the whole of Normandy, Brittany, and the Charentes. Armed with your weapons.'

Nathan took a moment to absorb this information. It was no crazier than other madcap schemes he had heard, even taken part in, and sometimes they worked. Not often, though.

'And assuming they succeed in their aim, who or what would be installed in Bonaparte's place?'

'Why, the late king's brother, the Count of Provence, but as a constitutional monarch, governing with the consent of the people expressed through their parliament, as it is in England. Eh, Georges?'

Once more he appealed to his associate, who had thus far had so little to contribute to the debate he might as well not have been there. It elicited another vigorous movement of the chins, but his eyes were wary, Nathan thought, as if he was in the company of madmen and brigands and would agree to anything and everything that would stop them from slitting his throat. He probably thought all Englishmen were mad. But perhaps he was just feeling a little queasy. The wind was getting up and the *Falaise* had begun to roll more than was comfortable for someone unaccustomed to life at sea. A glance towards the stern windows revealed that the light was fading faster than it should, even for the time of year. They were in for a rough night.

'So, my role is simply to deliver the guns to Gorey,' Nathan said.

'Good heavens, no! What a waste of talent and experience that would be. No, my friend, you are to play a far more vital role than that. For one thing, our kidnappers will need to be conveyed to Rouen—'

'Rouen?' Nathan was not personally acquainted with the Norman capital, but he knew it was a good way from the sea.

'Because that is where the deed is to be accomplished. We have information that Boney is planning a state visit to assure the Normans he has their interests at heart, ha ha, which would be a considerable achievement, considering they have been in rebellion off and on since the execution of the king.'

'And these kidnappers . . . ?'

'Are presently in Jersey, being trained for their mission.'

So, there was to be training. Nathan did not know if he found this encouraging or not. It would take time, though, and that was definitely a point in its favour.

'And we are to convey them from Jersey to the coast of Normandy?'

'Specifically, to Honfleur, at the mouth of the Seine, and then upriver to Rouen.'

'But Rouen must be at least fifty miles inland.'

'Sixty-one, to be exact. Perhaps a couple of days sailing if one is to lay up at night. A little more if obliged to resort to a tow. The Seine is quite navigable as far as Rouen to shipping of a shallow-enough draught—like the *Falaise*.'

He had it all worked out. But then, this was a curious facility of madmen. Nathan had met men who had worked out exactly how to get to the moon, even down to the exact amount of gunpowder required to fire the rocket.

'Would it not be quicker and easier by road?' he suggested reasonably.

'Possibly, but a large party of cavaliers upon the roads would attract a great deal of attention, do you not think?'

'Whereas a British sloop of war sailing up the Seine will pass unnoticed?'

A tolerant smile. 'Ah, but the *Falaise* bears a proud Norman name and was built in Le Havre'—before Nathan could remind him of her more recent activities in the Caribbean, he went on—'and besides, she will be flying an American flag. Pray, do not look so concerned, Captain. Letters will have been sent to the proper authorities indicating that she is on a visit to the port of Rouen to restore the vessel personally to the First Consul of France as a gesture of goodwill from their friends in the United States, and that the ship will be commanded by his own dear friend, Captain Nathaniel Turner, who saved his life during *Vendémiaire*. I have no doubt he will be more than happy to accept his invitation to the formal handing-over ceremony.'

Nathan was for a moment deprived of the power of speech.

'Turner is the name you used for your espionage activities in Paris, is it not? And the name by which Bonaparte knew you at the time.'

Nathan struggled to take this in. Smith obviously knew far more about him and his past activities than he had ever imagined. But not quite enough. He was looking so very pleased with himself at the audacity of his plan, it seemed almost a pity to highlight its obvious flaws, but it had to be done if Nathan was not to suffer the consequences.

'Unfortunately, it was also the name I used in Saint-Domingue,' he confided. It was the name Bonaparte's sister, Pauline, knew him by, among other rather more personal endearments, and even if she did not suspect him of gunrunning, the French commander, Rochambeau, certainly did, and unless there had been a serious breakdown in communications, he had just as surely conveyed his suspicions to the French authorities in

Paris. 'I am afraid the days of using Captain Nathaniel Turner as a *nom de guerre* are over,' he insisted.

'I am certain that if this was the case it would have reached my informants at the Admiralty,' Smith observed blandly. 'The French are by no means as efficient as you appear to think. Conditions in Saint-Domingue were exceptionally chaotic at the time, as you of course would know better than anyone, and I am informed that they have worsened considerably since you departed the colony.'

'I am afraid I cannot be so confident,' Nathan countered. 'And if your plan hinges on the willingness of Bonaparte to embark on an American ship of war commanded by one Nathaniel Turner, I would respectfully suggest that you consider an alternative arrangement.'

'Naturally we have our contingencies,' Smith assured him, 'but willingly or not, Bonaparte will be brought to the *Falaise* in Rouen harbour and conveyed downriver to the sea. It will be the most audacious coup in history.'

Nathan did not doubt it.

'And when is this coup to occur?'

'Bonaparte's visit is planned for the last week of April.'

'Whether or not Britain and France are at war?'

'Well, that would depend on instructions from our superiors and other circumstances beyond our control, but to ensure the success of our mission we must make all the necessary preparations, do you not agree?'

Nathan inclined his head as if weighing the arguments for and against. In fact, he was utterly appalled by everything Smith had proposed. But April was three months away. A lot could happen in three months. Or nothing at all. The important thing was, it gave him sufficient time to make his own contingency plans. Assuming he would have unloaded the guns by then, received payment for them, and paid off his crew.

Nathan felt some lightening of the gloom that had enveloped him since he had entered the cabin, though not in any physical sense. There was barely any light at all in the stern windows now, and yet they were not much more than halfway through the afternoon watch. He wondered if he should show himself on deck, but if they needed to reduce sail, Tully was more than capable of giving the order without reference to him. Besides, the motion of the ship seemed to have steadied somewhat, and he thought the wind might have dropped significantly.

'As yet we do not know the exact date of the visit,' Smith was saying. 'And if we are at war, it may well be postponed. However, Normandy and the Channel ports are very much in Bonaparte's mind. They are his front line, not only for the defence of France, but for an invasion of Britain, which must be his ultimate ambition. He will want to be at the centre of operations. As to his precise plans, I have no doubt we will be informed nearer the time.'

Which must mean he had informants among Bonaparte's inner circle. Nathan wondered how much they could be relied upon. No more than most royalist spies, he imagined. They had been notorious for passing on wrong information throughout the previous war. They stated as fact what they wished to be the case. But this was only one of his concerns.

'And in the meantime?'

'In the meantime, we will be engaged in making every preparation necessary for the success of our venture. Come, sir. No need for that long face,' Smith chided him. 'Need I remind you of Danton's speech to the French assembly when the Prussian army was advancing on Paris.' He struck a pose that may or may not have been intended as comic. '*L'audace, encore de l'audace, toujours de l'audace!* You were probably there at the time.'

Nathan was not there, as a matter of fact. He had been the youthful commander of a sloop of war ploughing a weary furrow up and down the English Channel in a largely futile attempt to prevent men like Tully from evading the revenue service. But he had been in Paris a year or so later when Danton had lost his head on the guillotine. So much for audacity.

'So let us drink to the success of our mission,' Smith proposed, raising his glass.

It had not quite reached his lips when a violent gust threw the sloop almost on her beam ends.

A confusion of limbs and chair legs and spilled wine, shouted oaths in English and in French, the storm lamps tilted at a crazed angle but still spilling some light on the chaos below. Nathan had been pitched backwards into one of Mr Penn's makeshift bulkheads and only the circumstance of its being constructed of canvas spared him a serious blow to the head. The table, being bolted to the deck, now hung over him like the edge of a cliff with two figures that could only be Smith and Cadoudal clinging to it for dear life. It would have caused him considerably amusement in other circumstances, but his first thought was for the ship, and he had begun to manoeuvre himself along the taut canvas in the direction of the companionway when she as suddenly righted herself and pitched him as violently in the opposite direction. This time he did crack his head and was rendered insensible for a moment. But only a moment. His pressing concern was still for the damage that must have been caused to the sloop, for though she was still afloat, she felt sluggish, as if she had shipped a great deal of water. He immediately thought the worst—that she was wallowing in a trough, very likely dismasted or awash or both, and close to foundering.

There was blood running down from his forehead into his eyes and he staggered almost blindly towards the companionway, calling for Kidd without response. There was no sign of him, upright or prone, in the little galley, but Nathan's view was inevitably restricted by blood and darkness. As he mounted the short flight of steps to the quarterdeck, he heard the fiendish howling of the wind through the rigging and shouted commands that indicated the entire watch had not been swept overboard, and that someone, somewhere, was still exerting a measure of control. Indeed, he thought he detected the voice of Tully ordering men aloft, so the ship could not have been entirely dismasted.

Then he emerged onto the deck. The combination of rain, wind, and spray cleared his brain, and though it would have been an exaggeration to say he took in the situation at a glance, he saw most of what he needed to know. The mainmast and foremast were shorter than they had been when he had gone below, and the foretopsail was billowing out to leeward—still attached to the stump of the foremast, but even in the darkness he could see figures swarming up towards it, either to get it in or cut it away. The courses and topsails had been got in already, almost certainly before the storm was upon them, and the only canvas he could see aloft through the darkness and the rain was the mizzen topsail above his head and perhaps a glimpse of jib and staysail at the bow.

The wind had increased dramatically, and unless he was entirely disorientated, he fancied it had shifted two or three points to the west. Tully was at the con with his hat gone and his hair streaming out to leeward like the torn sail, and two hands were at the helm struggling to bring the ship into the wind, presumably as a means of steadying her, for it was surely in the opposite direction from the course they had set. She was listing heavily to larboard but not too far to cause Nathan any more alarm than he felt already, and though the decks were awash, the seawater appeared to be streaming *out* through the scuppers rather than in.

Then he saw what had made Tully bring her head into the wind, and all other concerns were driven instantly from his head. Rushing down upon them was a truly monstrous sea—surely as mountainous a wave as he had seen anywhere in the world and certainly in the English Channel, black as pitch, but flecked with whitish foam. He took a firm grip on the nearest support and watched helplessly as the bows came slowly, ponderously round, rising sluggishly to meet it, as if they were already lifting a great weight of water. Then it was upon them. But even in his present circumstance, waist-deep in water and blinded by spray, he could tell by the rise of the deck beneath his feet that Tully had done enough to stop it from breaching them.

For a long moment they appeared to be carried sternwards, still listing at a crazy angle, and then they were plunging down the back of it, and Nathan staggered forward to join Tully at the helm. No further commands were necessary. They had taken in all the sail they could, or should—unless they ran before it with bare poles, and in the present sea that could not be advised. They needed the jib and staysails to keep her head into the wind, and keeping her head into the wind was all that mattered for the time being.

But where had such a sea come from? Stupid question. Out of the depths of the Atlantic and into that narrow gap between England and France, that strip of water that looked little more than a river on the charts and could turn into one of the most dangerous seas in the world.

He peered into the binnacle, but the light had gone out and he could see nothing meaningful on the compass. Tully was pushing something into his hands—the end of a lifeline attached to one of the stanchions for the *obussiers* he had consigned long ago to the orlop. Nathan looped it through his belt before the next wave was upon them, but it was nothing like the one they had just survived. He almost felt exhilarated, standing there at the helm, whipped by the rain and the spray, a tide of water rushing across the deck towards him and nothing to do but ride it out, fight every wave as it came. But this was nonsense; there was always something to do on a ship. There was always water to be pumped out, leaks to be plugged, stations to be kept, and everything that was capable of being swept overboard constantly checked and made fast. And so they did, all through that long night with no break in the succession of black clouds and black seas rushing down upon them, with nothing to refresh them but the salt spray and the iron rain.

'I am sorry, it took me by surprise,' Tully admitted when they had time to take stock. 'The wind was holding steady from west-nor'-west and none too violent. We were making steady progress under reefed topsails and jib, and then the wind fell right away. I was thinking what it might mean when we had that sudden gust from the west that lay us on our beam ends. I should have seen it coming. My God, I have known these seas since I was a child, but I have truly seen nothing like it. My fault—my fault entirely.' He almost beat his breast like the penitent Papists, *Mea culpa, mea maxima culpa.* 'I should have known.'

How could he have known, Nathan persisted—it was the sea. But Nathan and Tully held different notions of the sea. Tully *did* know it— or as well as any mariner ever could. He knew it could never be tamed, but he did expect to understand it and predict its moods, anticipate its violence, and harness it for his own purposes. For Nathan the sea was something demonic, a mystery that could never be fathomed or predicted or trusted, and though he might attempt in his supreme folly to ride upon it, he never expected to control it. It was astonishing, in many ways, that he was ever a seafarer.

Later, when it had subsided into, if not passivity, at least a semblance of regularity in its fury, and they had resumed an approximation of their previous course, Tully came to him and apologised—again—for his perceived negligence.

'I was distracted,' he said. 'My mind adrift in the past. I do not mean this as an excuse, of course, but . . .'

Nathan looked at his friend's face, grey and wan as the dawn after a sleepless night on deck.

'No need of one,' he said. Then: 'You mean, going back?'

'Going back.' A pensive nod, his face troubled. 'It is not a journey I thought I would ever make.' Then the ghost of a smile, bleak as the dawn. 'I was not a happy child.'

In the grim light of day they took stock of what they had lost. Two men gone overboard and five in the sick bay with injuries that ranged in gravity from a broken arm to a fractured skull that had rendered the victim unconscious with little hope of recovery, according to the doctor.

'Three dead,' acknowledged Nathan, looking on the dark side. 'Two more than we lost in the Caribbean after nine months of the French and the yellow fever.'

His own gash was not serious, and Tully had helped him bind it with a length of bandage which made him look more heroic than he deserved. Smith had made a brief appearance on deck, looked about him in either perplexity or censure, and after exchanging a few words with Nathan concerning their position and a new estimate of when they might arrive, returned to his cabin. Cadoudal was enduring the miseries of seasickness, he reported, but was otherwise unhurt. Kidd appeared from whatever dark regions had given him shelter with a peace offering of coffee he must have brewed up on his little portable stove. He offered no explanation of where he had been for the past few hours and Nathan did not ask. Back in his natural domain of the Underworld, as like as not.

As for the sloop, she had lost both fore and main topgallant masts and half the maintop yard, but thanks to Tully's precautions, they had saved the ship's boats and all the spars that had been stored on deck. By midmorning, most of the seawater had been pumped out of the hull and Mr Penn reported that there were no serious leaks. The men would endure damp hammocks until they could be brought up on deck to dry, but the stove had been relit in the galley, the chef and his mates were back at work; the crew would have a hot breakfast and a double ration of rum, and apart from those in the sick bay there were no obvious signs of discontent. Indeed, they seemed more cheerful than they had been during all their time in Falmouth Harbour.

'Not a good start, though,' Nathan complained gloomily to Tully before going below to see what breakfast he might cajole from Kidd, 'and I expect it will only get worse.'

Chapter 6

The Castle of Blood

Nathan's first glimpse of Gorey was from out at sea through a dirty squall of rain, looking every bit the archetypal Gothic castle, with a procession of ragged clouds swooping like giant bats above its granite towers. According to Sir Sidney Smith it had been on the front line of England's endless wars with France for nearly five hundred years, but had hardly fired a shot in anger.

It had been built in the thirteenth century for King John, last of the Angevin kings of England, who had lost Normandy and most of his territories on mainland France but kept this little chain of islands off the Cotentin peninsula. Gorey had been intended as their principal defence, but being King John, he had built it in the wrong place, on an exposed headland overlooked by the steep bluffs to the south, where siege engines and later cannon could be mounted to pound it into submission. It had been used as a prison until fairly recently, when it was turned back into a fortress with embrasures for twenty-four-pounder cannon and a barracks for the island militia, though its purpose in the recent war had been to host more clandestine activities. According to Smith, royalist agents, weapons, and counterfeit currency had been shipped across the narrow strait to Normandy in a bid to undermine the French Revolution, a secret war that had succeeded so well, he said, that it had caused more harm to the new Republic than all the armies of monarchist Europe combined.

They approached from the south-west under a reefed main course and staysails, the sea no longer a menace but still restive, agitated, and the torn strips of cloud scudding across the skies with a dirty, bruised look about them, much like the *Falaise* herself. There was a small harbour at the foot of the castle with a stone jetty, and a few fishing boats resting on mud, the only buildings little more than hovels. No taverns, no shops, and very likely no whorehouses—the crew would not be pleased, even if they had the money to spend in them. There was not a single figure in sight, human or animal, either on the ramparts or on the shore, or in the boats in the harbour.

'So shall we give them a salute?' Nathan wanted to know, having no idea who or what he might be saluting. The castle flew the red saltire of Jersey, and the new Union flag with the cross of Saint Patrick recently added to that of Saint Andrew and Saint George, but he had no idea if there was still a garrison based here, or under whose command—admiral, general, or some lesser divinity.

But Smith was shaking his head. 'Let us not make more of a show than we have to,' he said. 'We are not a King's ship—not officially, at least. But you can fly my personal pennant,' he added with a play of nonchalance, 'to let them know I am aboard.'

He had brought this with him from England wrapped in a velvet cloth. Nathan suspected it travelled with him always, or at least since his exploits in the Holy Land. It had been the standard of Richard the Lionheart—John's more successful older brother—who had led the Third Crusade and taken Acre, the city whose defence had laid the foundation of Sir Sidney's own fame. To Nathan's embarrassment they raised it at the mizzen—three golden lions on a field of gules. There was no noticeable reaction from the shore.

'Perhaps you should have fired that salute to wake them up,' Smith remarked with an attempt at humour, but Nathan could tell he was displeased.

But then another flag rose to the top of a third flagstaff—two broad red bands separated by a band of white.

'Ah, the admiral is in residence,' declared Smith with an ironic smile.

'What admiral would that be?' enquired Nathan, for it was unlike any admiral's flag that he had ever seen, certainly in the British navy.

'Admiral Philippe d'Auvergne,' Smith replied with mock ceremony. 'I believe he still calls himself that, though it was a temporary rank conferred upon him during the recent war when he commanded here. With the cessation of hostilities, he has been demoted to captain, and a half-pay captain at that.'

The name struck a chord with Nathan—several chords, in fact, and not all harmonious. He knew the name from the captain's list, of course—he had been made post about ten years before Nathan—but he had not served with any particular distinction, possibly because of his more secretive duties here on the isle of Jersey. There was a more personal connection, though, in that d'Auvergne had been the name of the first great love of his life when he had met her in Paris during the time of the Terror—Sara de la Tour d'Auvergne, Countess of Turenne, was her married name, though she never used it, or at least not when she was with Nathan. Her husband, the Count, had been with the French court-in-exile in Koblenz, but she had never mentioned any kinship to a serving officer in the British navy.

'So, he is our superior officer?' he queried.

'God, no, though he probably thinks he is. He has no authority whatsoever at present, though it were as well to stay on friendly terms with him. He has great influence with the royalist émigrés in Jersey, of whom there are some several thousand.'

'And the flag? What does that signify?'

'Ah, the flag.' A short laugh. 'That is the standard of the Prince of Bouillon,' he declared, 'to which d'Auvergne lays claim.'

'Bouillon,' Nathan repeated. 'Like the soup?'

'Indeed. A tiny principality in the Ardennes on the French border with the Low Countries. It comprises a castle and a few villages, maybe two, three thousand inhabitants, Walloons for the most part. You have not heard the story?' Nathan had not. 'Philippe somehow came to the attention of the present duke, who adopted him as his heir. He decided he was of the same family—the Jersey branch—without a scrap of evidence as far as I can tell. But Philippe is convinced of it. He has been pursuing this claim ever since, thus far without success. The French annexed it during the last war.'

Nathan was struggling with this. As if the Swedish Knight was not enough, with his standard of Richard the Lionheart, now he had another fantasist to deal with. 'So Captain d'Auvergne is French?' he ventured.

'Never say so.' Smith seemed amused. 'He is Jersey born and bred and a loyal subject of King George. He joined the British navy as a midshipman when he was fifteen years old. He is no more French than I am.'

Nathan saw that Tully was regarding him with the look that indicated he needed him to make a decision—and not in a day or two, when he had finished discussing questions of ancestry and inheritance. They had a man taking soundings in the forechains, and his last call had been a quarter less two with the tide still on the retreat. Nathan dismissed d'Auvergne from his mind for the time being and gave his attention to more immediate concerns. Tully was perfectly capable of handling them, but he had to show some interest, or the crew would wonder what he was there for, if they did not already. They came into the wind and the best bower splashed into the choppy waters of the bay about two cables' lengths from the end of the jetty. It was a little before the end of the forenoon watch, almost exactly three days since they had left Falmouth, only a day later than Nathan's original cautious estimate.

'If you will spare me the cutter, I will go ashore and pay my respects,' Smith proposed. 'I will take Monsieur Cadoudal, but it is probably better if you do not accompany us; d'Auvergne will ask all kinds of questions that might be embarrassing for you. If you have no objection, of course.'

Nathan had no objection, though he suspected that Smith had other reasons for leaving him behind. It was perfectly possible that d'Auvergne had a much more important role than Smith was prepared to concede. There was also the matter of their remuneration, which Nathan had been assured would be paid on their arrival in Jersey, and which the crew would certainly be expecting.

In the meantime, they had salt beef for dinner with pease pudding and hard tack and spent the afternoon repairing some of the damage inflicted by the storm. Two of the spare yards served to jury-rig their crippled topmasts, and the sailmaker had fashioned new royals and topgallants from the canvas he had in store, though darkness was upon them before they were able to fit them to Nathan's satisfaction. However, in the meantime Kidd had succeeded in purchasing a large turbot and a half-dozen crab from the local fishermen, and Nathan and his officers had a rather more substantial supper than usual to make up for their miserable dinner. They could not feed the entire crew on fish, however, even in the abundant waters off Jersey, and the purser had brought grim reports of their diminishing supplies. There was still plenty of hard tack, salt beef, and pork, but no more cheese or dried fruit, very little flour to make bread, and they were perilously low on rum, beer, and tobacco. The men might tolerate food rationing for a few days or so, but not of rum or tobacco, and it was imperative that their new patron returned from his trip ashore with sufficient funds to avoid a mutiny. There was no obvious source of supplies in Gorey, but the island's chief port of Saint Helier was only a few miles along the coast, and Tully was confident that it could supply most of their needs, if only they had sufficient funds.

Later that night the two of them settled down in the stern cabin with a half-bottle of brandy and some stale cobnuts Kidd had dug out for them, speculating on their immediate future. Aware of the presence of Kidd on the far side of the bulkhead, they spoke in the Guernésiais dialect Tully had taught Nathan over the years for whenever they wished to keep their conversation private.

For the first time Nathan spoke of Smith's plans for them to sail up the Seine to Rouen and assist in the kidnap of the French First Consul. Tully's reaction was similar to his own but expressed rather more colourfully, even in the local dialect.

'It will never come to anything,' Nathan declared, more confidently than he felt. 'It is one of Smith's madcap schemes for ending the next war before it has started. The wonder is that it has even got this far.'

'How far is that?' Tully wanted to know.

'Nowhere at all, so far as I can tell. However, I imagine that someone in government must have approved it, else he would not have any funds at his disposal.'

'We have no evidence that he does.'

This was depressingly true. 'At the very least they must have authorised him to liaise with the French royalists,' Nathan insisted. 'Or Cadoudal would not be here. And he appears to have the use of the castle—for what that is worth. Do you know anything about it, and what goes on there?'

Tully shook his head. 'Not lately, though I knew enough ten years ago not to want to come anywhere near the place. It has an evil reputation on the islands. For over a hundred years it was used as a prison for English dissidents, political and religious. Many were kept in chains and left to rot.

Quite a few of the locals, too. Behave yourself or you'll end up in Gorey, my nan used to say.'

'That did a lot of good.'

Tully gave him a look. 'I had kept clear of it thus far,' he said, 'until you brought us back here.'

In the morning, when Nathan went up on deck, the sea was less agitated, the sky lighter, and the castle somewhat less foreboding. At some point the walls had been rendered with limewash and they were still streaked here and there with white, as though buckets of paint had been poured down from the battlements. Though if Tully was to be believed, it should have been blood.

The tide was in, and the harbour looked more picturesque with the fishing boats bobbing at their moorings and the nets hung out to dry on the jetty and the gulls swooping about in a generally satisfactory manner, without being too raucous. And here was a pinnace with a blue ensign heading out towards them under a lateen sail. Nathan recognised the slender figure of Sir Sidney Smith in the stern, and rather more interest-ingly, a large sea chest in the centre of the boat with two redcoats seated beside it, their muskets held upright between their knees. He considered whether to have him piped aboard but decided that his earlier insistence on discretion could save him the bother, but he was at the entry port to greet him as he climbed the steps. He looked somewhat the worse for wear—Nathan suspected drink rather than the rack—but he had brought good news.

'I have arranged for our cargo to be stored in the castle,' he said. 'And I have brought something in return that I trust will be to your satisfaction.'

Under his careful supervision, the chest was hoisted aboard and carried by the soldiers to the improvised stateroom, where it was deposited on the table. Nathan had summoned Tully and Banjo to follow them below and all three watched with interest as Smith, with the air of a magician about to perform an especially clever trick, produced a large key from his coat pocket, turned it in the padlock, and raised the lid.

The chest was filled with a number of black leather bags each closed with a wax seal and containing a quantity of coin to the value of one hundred pounds, Smith declared with the air of one who kept his promises. There were at least fifty of them, possibly more. Nathan sent for Mr Babb and Mr Bent, ship's purser and paymaster, with their muster books and accounts.

At their meeting in the Ship Inn, a price of £5,500 had been agreed upon for the guns, with a sufficiency of powder and shot for 30,000 rounds. Mr Bent calculated that the officers and crew were owed a little over £2,000 for their last voyage from Boston to Jersey via Saint-Domingue, which, minus a generous bonus, left Nathan with a handsome profit. On top of which, Smith had agreed to £1,145 a month for the hire of the *Falaise* with a full complement of 150 officers and men.

All of which was most satisfactory. But then came the first note of discord.

Smith proposed that the cargo should be unloaded and conveyed to the castle before the crew were paid, and that before receiving his share each man should be required to sign on for a minimum of six months' service.

'Else I might find myself with a ship but no crew,' he reasoned.

'The law is quite straightforward on the issue,' Nathan retorted, 'and they all know it as well as any lawyer. "Freight is the mother of wages". Once the freight is discharged, they must be paid. And in a place like this, I fear they may be inclined to take the law into their own hands. They are not blue jackets, and I do not have a squad of marines at my disposal to restrain their wilder emotions.'

'We have soldiers enough at the castle,' Smith affirmed, 'should we have need of them.'

They locked eyes across the open chest.

'They have been fighting the French navy for the last year in the waters off Saint-Domingue,' Nathan persisted. This was something of an exaggeration, but Smith was not to know that. 'I do not think they will be overawed by the Jersey militia.'

Smith brooded for a moment. He glanced at Tully, who smiled at him. Tully had the kind of smile that was either wholly engaging or convinced you of his absolute willingness to have you strung up from the yardarm in the blink of an eye. The two redcoats at the door stared fixedly ahead as if they had not heard a word.

'Very well,' Smith conceded. 'But I hold you entirely responsible for ensuring that you are fully crewed and ready to sail at a moment's notice.'

This was, in fact, of some concern to Nathan, though he did his best to disguise it. However, he had little choice in the matter. He could not keep the crew locked belowdecks. The boatswain and his mates piped all hands and Nathan gave them another little speech from the slight elevation of the quarterdeck. Once again, he thanked them for their services over the past year and declared he would pay a large bonus to anyone signing on for the next cruise, which would be much less perilous and even more lucrative. He had no idea if this was true. There was a great deal of cheering, but no-one rushed to enter their names in the muster roll. Then they lined up to receive their pay.

Nathan had indicated he was ready to sail the sloop round to Saint Helier once the wind permitted, but they were not prepared to wait. By the time the last man had been paid there was a long line of boisterous mariners lurching along the road to the capital. A few had managed to acquire the use of a farm cart, and went bowling past, whooping and hollering and blowing horns. One man was riding a donkey; another was trying to ride a pig. Nathan was left with barely enough of a crew to moor the *Falaise* in deep water before the tide was out. Tully had stayed with the ship, of course, along with the two officers, Keppler and Cole, and a few of the petty officers, mostly the older, more respectable men like Mr Babb and Mr Bent. Dr Drew had stayed to tend to his patients in the sick bay, though two of them had left their beds and gone hobbling off to Saint Helier on sticks. Kidd had gone, too, and even George Banjo—to keep them out of trouble, he told Nathan with a grin.

Nathan watched them out of sight as the sun went down, a substantial part of him wishing he could have gone with them without major loss to his dignity. He felt a growing sense of melancholy. It was like the last act of a drama which, for all its horrors, had left not a few fond memories. The island of Tortuga, *Le Belvédère* and the Garden of Eden, the lovely Adedike and Citizen Dubois, and of course, Pauline Bonaparte. And now it was finally over.

The sky grew dark. There were a few lights on in the castle, but they did little to alleviate its overwhelming air of oppression. Smith had gone back earlier. Unfinished business, he said. Nathan wondered if he had a woman there. Lucky man.

'They will be back when their money runs out.' He heard the voice of Tully behind him. More fool them, he thought. He was in that kind of a mood.

'Well, we will still be here,' Nathan replied gloomily. 'We have nowhere else to go.'

But Tully apparently did. He announced his intention over a poor supper of stale bread and cheese, washed down with cold tea and rum. With Nathan's permission he wished to travel to Guernsey to find his sisters— or rather, his half-sisters, the daughters of his father's second marriage.

'I would just like to make sure they are safe and sound and in no financial need,' he said, with a measure of embarrassment. 'I will not stay long.'

Nathan felt his heart sink to a new low, but he insisted that Tully take the cutter and three of his depleted crew. Then he unlocked the strongbox in his cabin and tossed two bags of coin onto the table.

'Take them,' he said. 'They are as much yours as mine.'

Tully protested that he had already had more than his fair share of the profits from their last voyage, but Nathan would not take no for an answer. It was difficult for him to look anything but downcast, however, as Tully prepared to leave at first light the following morning.

'For God's sake, why this long face?' Tully chided him gently. 'I will be back before most of the crew.'

'You do not wish to see the other half of your family?' he queried, meaning the rich half.

'No,' replied Tully firmly. 'I will not be seeing them.'

Nathan's depleted crew spent the rest of the day finishing off the repairs to the masts, Nathan working with them in canvas ducks and a fisherman's Jersey sweater with a Monmouth hat on his head. In the evening he dined alone in his cabin off cold salt beef and mustard, bulked up with hard tack and washed down with small beer. He had instructed Kidd to pick up fresh supplies from Saint Helier but he did not expect him back in a hurry, if ever, so after spending an hour or so fishing off the stern without catching anything but a small crab, he resolved to go ashore and see what he might bag in the way of game. He had no notion of what wildlife existed on the island, which was a mere nine miles long and five miles across at its widest point, but he imagined there must at the very least be rabbits and possibly geese, duck, and woodpigeon, any of which would make a welcome change from salt beef, or even fish. Besides, it would give him some welcome exercise and stop him from brooding.

There were several fowling pieces in the armoury and plenty of shot, so appropriately armed and suitably attired, he had himself rowed ashore in the gig and set off into the interior with his gun and his leather pouch. He was aware, of course, that you could not just shoot anything, anywhere, and that the necessary permissions must be sought to avoid being taken for a poacher, and though this had not troubled him as a boy, it would be more of an embarrassment to him in his current situation. However, he considered that a gracious manner, possibly backed by an offer of remuneration, should be sufficient to persuade one of the local farmers or landowners to allow him the freedom of their estate.

The skies were clear and the wind not especially troublesome, and after about an hour of tramping down country lanes without encountering either man or beast, he observed a fairly substantial manor in the style of a French chateau across the fields to starboard. He walked a little further and came upon two large stone gateposts, but no gate, with a drive apparently leading to the house. There were no obvious signs of human habitation, but as he approached, he heard a sound that could have been hammering, or more like a light tapping upon metal or stone. It appeared to be coming from an outbuilding, about the size of a barn but with arched windows and a cross on the roof indicating that it might be some form of chapel. The door being open, he advanced to a point where he could see inside.

It was quite dark but there was a little natural light penetrating from the open door, and at the far end, beside the altar, a number of candles on tall iron stands had been placed to provide a circle of light, in the centre of which a young woman was chipping away with hammer and chisel at a sculpture which appeared, by virtue of its wings, to be an angel. He could see from the chips that flew from under the chisel that it was made of wood, but it was the sculptor who occupied Nathan's immediate attention. She had only to turn her head to see him standing in the open doorway, but she was so engrossed in her task she had no sense of being observed, and Nathan for his part did not wish to disturb her. Initially he thought she might be a nun because her hair was hidden by a sort of coif, and she wore a plain blue robe with a white apron. But whatever species of creature she was, she was extraordinarily beautiful. In fact, she could almost have been an angel herself. A strand of dark hair had escaped from under the coif and was hanging across her cheek. Probably not a nun then.

She stepped slightly to one side to reveal more of her face. It might have been the combination of the candles and the light from the stained-glass windows, but she looked like someone from another world. A pagan goddess, perhaps. Angel, nun, pagan goddess—whatever she was, he thought her the most enchanting creature he had ever seen. Or at least, for some considerable time. There was a purity in her features that was yes, angelic. But she had such lips; they held a promise of delights that were surely forbidden to angels and nuns. And perhaps most alluring to Nathan personally was the rapt concentration on her face. She was entirely, utterly focused on what she was doing. She bit upon her bottom lip, the eyes raised to the face above her, measuring, calculating where to place the next blow, deliver the next cut. He loved observing a woman when she was concentrating on something, unaware of being observed. Music, a painting, a sculpture, even a meal. He had never encountered a woman sculptor before, or even heard of one. He might have stood there forever, but the sound of horses' hoofs recalled him to his situation, and he turned to observe a party of riders approaching across the forecourt. They consisted of a lady and two gentlemen. They reined up before him and gazed down with the hauteur of the upper classes at an importunate peasant. Nathan informed them that he was looking for the owner of the house.

'Well, you have found her,' said the woman. 'How can I assist you?'

She spoke good English but with a perceptible French accent. She wore riding clothes, including a top hat and a half veil, and he would almost certainly have found her attractive if he had not been blinded by the vision in the chapel.

'My name is Peake,' he said, 'Captain Peake of His Britannic Majesty's Navy.' He could give hauteur for hauteur if required. The woman continued to stare at him without comment. 'I have lately berthed at Gorey,' he went on, 'and thought to take a turn ashore. I had a notion to shoot a few rabbits, but I thought to seek permission of the landowner first.'

The woman glanced sideways at one of her companions, who was looking down at Nathan with an expression that indicated, to Nathan at least, a wish to strike him with his whip. Go ahead and try, thought Nathan.

'Rabbits,' repeated the woman, as if the word was unfamiliar to her.

'Les lapins,' said Nathan, in case this helped. 'Or pigeons. Anything you would consider a pest. We have been at sea a long time and not had much in the way of fresh meat.'

'Please.' The woman inclined a languid wrist to indicate her surroundings, first one way, then the other. 'Be my guest, *monsieur le capitaine*. Good hunting, as they say.'

Nathan made her an elaborate bow that fell just short of sardonic. 'Your servant, *madame*.'

As he straightened up, he glanced towards the open door of the church. They could clearly hear the tapping. He wondered if he could venture an enquiry. But no. Now was not the time.

He put on his hat and walked away.

He returned to the *Falaise* with four rabbits and two pigeons. It had occurred to him to deliver two of the rabbits to the house by way of a thank-you, and in the hope of seeing his divine sculptress again, but they may have been taken from him by a servant at the door, and besides, it would have left him a little short of the means to feed himself and a hungry wardroom. He could always go back tomorrow, he thought.

But the following day, the Swedish Knight was back and in a foul humour.

'See here, Peake,' he began. 'We have been inspecting your guns, and these rifles will not do, you know—they will not do at all. How the hell do you fire them? The breech screw keeps jamming, and one of our sergeants has blown his thumb off.'

Nathan shook his head wearily. He had explained all this, but he knew at the time that Smith had not been listening. He thought it was like any other breech-loading rifle. It was not. The Ferguson rifle was in a class of its own. Use it the right way, and it had an amazing rate of fire. Six, even ten rounds a minute. Use it the wrong way and it would blow off your thumb. If you were lucky. Nathan tried to explain this again, but it would not do. Smith insisted he must find someone to demonstrate. In the absence of George Banjo—or the gunner, Mr Caine, or the armourer, Mr Newton, who distrusted the gun anyway—it would have to be him.

So he spent the next two days ashore drilling some several hundred French exiles in the use of the Ferguson rifle. They were young countrymen for the most part from Normandy, fiercely independent, driven to rebellion by the attacks on their traditions and religion, but more particularly by the imposition of the draft to find men for the revolutionary armies. They had fought in the wars of the *Chouannerie* and been forced into exile by the savage retribution dealt out by the victorious republicans. Their commanders were from the old Norman country gentry, bitterly opposed to the 'new men' of the Revolution, the bourgeois lawyers and teachers and educated elite of the French cities, especially Paris. All of them appeared to be experienced soldiers, if not in the handling of the Ferguson rifle, and they wore the red coats and white breeches of the Jersey militia.

Nathan quickly adapted to his new role as drilling instructor. The breech was closed with a screw, he demonstrated, the trigger guard serving as a crank to turn it. One turn dropped the screw low enough to drop the ball into the breech. Then you poured in the powder and screwed it up again, blowing off any residue from the breech. This was most important, or an accident could happen.

The drill went well for the most part. They only lost one more thumb, and they were delighted with the rate of fire when things were going well. The Fergusons were an experimental weapon, he explained, but they had been used with great effect at the Battle of Brandywine during the American rebellion. Unfortunately, the British high command did not like them. They were too sophisticated for them, too expensive to manufacture, and to be fair the breech screw did keep jamming if you did not keep it constantly greased with tallow or bees' wax. Privately, Nathan suspected the real reason for their dislike was that they allowed a certain independence of action, and they preferred their soldiers to stand in a line firing disciplined volleys, even if they could not fire more than three shots a minute, and rarely hit anything more than a hundred yards away.

They were just finishing for the day when they were joined by an officer in the uniform of a British naval captain who turned out to be the putative Prince of Bouillon, Captain Philippe d'Auvergne.

He was a big, bluff man with none of the airs and graces Nathan had been led to expect from Sir Sidney Smith's description. Had it not been for the uniform, he would have taken him for an English country squire, though he had led a particularly adventurous life even for a British naval officer. He had begun his service career in the Arctic where, as a young midshipman, he had been involved with the equally youthful Nelson in a futile search for the North-West Passage. He had subsequently served in the American War, then in the Caribbean, the Cape, and the Indian

Ocean. He had been a prisoner of war, a castaway on a desert island, and an explorer before returning to his native Jersey, officially as the administrator of relief grants to émigrés, but effectively as a spymaster, sending them back to France as agents of the British government and keeping them supplied with arms, money, and supplies from his base at Gorey. Most of this Nathan knew from Smith, but d'Auvergne was not at all reticent about filling in the gaps, and after the drill he invited Nathan back to his quarters in the castle where over a bottle of cognac he entertained him with the story of how he had become the Prince of Bouillon. This also had its share of adventure.

It had started with an engagement with a French frigate off Ushant when his own ship was badly damaged and later driven on the rocks and wrecked, but while he was being held as a prisoner of war his name had been drawn to the attention of the aged Duke of Bouillon who was head of the d'Auvergne family, and one of the wealthiest men in France. After meeting the young Philippe, the duke had formed a close attachment to the young officer and arranged for his parole, later adopting him as his son and heir. Unfortunately, with Bouillon in French hands it was a title in name alone, though d'Auvergne was hopeful that a return of the French monarchy might see the principality restored to him one day. Common courtesy prevented Nathan from mentioning it, but it was clear that he had personal reasons for supporting the royalist cause.

He was an agreeable-enough host, however, with a warmth of manner that took the edge off his obvious vanity, and they parted on good terms, with an invitation for Captain Peake to return the following evening for a reception he was holding for some of the local émigrés.

'You will find it entertaining,' he said, 'if only as a study in anthropology, for they are something of a lost tribe, forever bemoaning the theft of their birth right, though I believe they did nothing but complain when they were at Versailles in the days of the king.'

Their new Versailles was Castle Gorey, he said, where he was obliged to play the Sun King, or at least entertain them from time to time. It turned out he had an ulterior motive, however. Bonaparte had offered an amnesty to all returning émigrés who were prepared to honour the new constitution, and he knew some of them were considering it.

'They think they will get their old lives back as they were before the Revolution,' he said, 'and when they are disappointed, as they surely will be, they may be open to other offers. Most of them make hopeless spies, but they do occasionally pass on a useful piece of information, and at the very least they can provide a safe house for our more useful agents.'

It was dark when Nathan returned to the castle, now wearing his dress uniform and with Mr Penn's nephew, a young man by the name of Bentham, to act as a linkboy. As they walked up the hill from the jetty, they were obliged to step aside on several occasions for the carriages bringing d'Auvergne's guests in from the country, who, he said, made a great effort to impress, even if they were living in straitened circumstances.

'The majority of them manage to maintain a carriage and a few ancient retainers,' he said, 'though carriage horses are in short supply.'

Nathan presented his pass to the sentries at the gate and was directed up several climbing pathways and flights of stairs to the reception room. Clearly, d'Auvergne was not entirely careless of appearances himself, and the way was illuminated by a great many coloured lanterns and flares, with soldiers stationed at regular intervals to act as guides. It still looked like an ogre's castle out of a fairy tale, but an ogre who had put himself out to charm his victims before putting them on the menu.

The reception was being held in the medieval hall of the main keep, decorated with tapestries and lit by hundreds of candles, with more soldiers on hand to put out the fires that might occur as a result, and as many servants to dispense drinks. A quartet in a minstrel's gallery provided chamber music, and d'Auvergne, in his regalia as Prince of Bouillon, circulated among the guests, many of whom bowed and curtseyed as if he truly were the Sun King. They were dressed in all the finery a French émigré could contrive, though plastered with far more makeup than the current fashion in Paris, the men as well as the women. Nathan's first impression, in fact, was of a charade, or the carnival at Venice, with everyone wearing a mask, even if it was their own painted face.

One of the first faces he saw, however, was that of Sir Sidney Smith, which was as unpainted as his, and his dark hair was unpowdered. Disappointingly for Nathan, he wore the full dress uniform of a post captain in His Britannic Majesty's Navy, rather than the court dress of a Turkish pasha, as he had in London on his return from the Levant. He had come up with a cover for their presence on the island—they had been sent by the Admiralty to inspect the island's defences—and he greeted Nathan like a long-lost friend.

'Rum old do,' he said. 'Bit like the House of Wax in Paris. You ever been there?'

Nathan had, as a matter of fact. He had even met Marie Grosholtz, the daughter of the proprietor, who had been making a mould from a human head, fresh from the guillotine on the Place de la Revolution. It did not seem worth mentioning.

'I think if I had been a Frenchman by birth and seen this lot ambling about the Tuileries, I might have been compelled to start a revolution myself,' Smith remarked.

Nathan had entertained the same thought himself. He had been observing the faces in the room with a distinct lack of enthusiasm when there was a movement towards the buffet and he saw his divine sculptress. She was no longer wearing a blue smock and a white coif, nor was she carrying a hammer and chisel, but he was in no doubt it was the same woman. Their eyes met, and he thought he detected a hint of recognition. Then she looked away.

He turned towards his companion and saw that he was observing him with his knowing smile.

'Who . . . ?' he began.

'Ah, that is our beautiful assassin,' said Smith. 'Let me introduce you.'

Chapter 7

The Avenging Angel

'Assassin?' Nathan gazed across the sea of bobbing heads. She was talking, or rather listening, to an old gentleman in a wig and frock coat decorated with the ribbon of some ancient order of chivalry. His expression verged on the besotted; hers was politely attentive. She was one of the few guests dressed in the current Paris fashion, though her muslin gown was by no means as transparent as some he had seen in the French capital, and as a concession to modesty, or the season, she wore a red drape that covered most of her upper works. Her chestnut hair was piled high on her head and threaded with pearls, a single strand artfully escaping, as it had from under the coif she had been wearing in the chapel. She was certainly the loveliest assassin Nathan had ever seen. Not that he took Smith's contention at all seriously. An assassin of the male ego, perhaps. A breaker of hearts, or balls, or both. Had she broken the Swedish Knight's?

'Keep your voice down,' his informant cautioned him. 'We do not want the whole room knowing. I have a list of her previous victims somewhere, but I would have thought you would be more interested in the next one.'

'And who would that be?'

'Can you not guess?'

Does he mean himself, or me, Nathan wondered. Am I to be stretched on the rack of her charms and then led to the block? It might be worth it.

'It could save you a trip to Rouen.'

He had that irritating smile playing about his lips, but something in his eyes and manner suggested that he might be at least half serious.

Nathan was suddenly wary. 'I thought the intention was to kidnap him,' he said.

'Oh, it is. Louise is our contingency plan. Do you wish to meet her or not?'

Nathan invited him to lead the way.

Her gentleman admirer had been replaced by the woman whose arrival had interrupted his worship in the chapel. Even without the advantage of a horse, she still contrived to stare down her nose at him.

'Ah, *monsieur le capitaine*. Did you shoot many rabbits?'

Smith shot him a look of enquiry.

'We had a brief encounter on *madame*'s estate,' Nathan informed him, 'but were not formally introduced.'

'I see.' He clearly did not. 'Well, if you will permit me—Captain Peake, Madame le Comtesse de Rochefort, and this'—with a small bow to her companion—'is Mademoiselle Louise de Kirouac.'

A Breton name, though this was not as interesting to Nathan as the indication of her marital status. She was taller than the impression he had formed of her in the chapel, and a little older, though probably not much above twenty.

'But what is this about rabbits?' Smith persisted.

'The countess was kind enough to permit me to do some shooting on her estate,' Nathan explained. 'As we were in want of supplies.'

'It is not my estate,' the countess corrected him firmly. 'I am in temporary residence only, until my country is cleared of thieves and murderers.'

That might take some little while, Nathan thought, even if Bonaparte and his crew were shown the door.

'The countess has extensive estates in Brittany, where you would probably find the shooting rather more to your liking than on the islands,' Smith put in smoothly.

'If I am ever able to return there,' the countess responded. 'At present the only shooting in Brittany is of those who do not bow the knee to Bonaparte and his cutthroats.'

'So, you will not be taking up his offer of an amnesty?' Smith quizzed her mildly. 'You can return any time you like, you know, provided you swear an oath of loyalty and promise not to mix with rogues like me. Surely that is not too much to ask, and we will have one less mouth to feed.'

His tone was provoking, and the countess was duly provoked. She offered a few words in French which Nathan translated roughly as fuck their constitution, fuck their amnesty, and fuck you. Fair enough, he thought. They clearly knew each other rather well.

'And how is your angel coming along?' he addressed her companion, thinking to sail the conversation into less troubled waters. He slipped as easily into French as Smith had.

She did not seem surprised by his remark. Either she had noted his presence in the doorway of the little chapel, or her hostess had apprised her of it later.

'I am having some trouble with the face,' she said.

This was not a subject Nathan could converse upon with any authority or wit, but he did his best. 'Does he have a name, your angel?' he enquired.

'Not really. He is meant to be the Avenging Angel. Some say he is called Azrael, but that is the Angel of Death. Perhaps they are one and the same. But the way he is coming along, I may have to call him Lucifer. The mouth, for all my efforts, has formed itself into a knowing sneer. The Devil is in my hands, I hope, not my mind.'

Her voice was deep, almost husky, though there was no discernible trace of a Breton accent.

'So, you have hidden talents, my dear,' Smith teased, in a tone that suggested they, too, had more than a passing acquaintance.

'I would not call it a talent,' she murmured. 'I am a mere amateur. A carver of wood. It is just a way of passing the time, which goes very slowly here on Jersey.'

'She is her father's daughter,' the countess remarked. 'He taught her a great deal. Before they nailed him to a cross.'

Her friend glared at her, but the countess had locked eyes with the Swedish Knight. There was some chemistry between the three of them that was beyond Nathan's comprehension. He would have liked to know more, but there was no coming back from that remark so far as the conversation was concerned.

Happily, the entertainers came to their rescue. Clowns, jongleurs, and a fire-eater. Home-grown or imported for the occasion, they succeeded in distracting the company from other concerns, or at least from talking about them.

'I trust you found that entertaining?' Smith queried, as they walked back through the castle grounds.

'It had its moments,' Nathan acknowledged. 'But what was that about the man nailed to the cross?'

'Ah, yes. The countess. Do not let her disconcert you. She likes to shock.'

'It certainly seemed to shock her companion. Why would she say such a thing?'

'Perhaps because she wished to remind us of the nature of the beast, so to speak—not that we need any reminding.'

'And was her father truly nailed to a cross?'

'It was not unusual as a means of execution by the Blues during the *Chouannerie*.'

The Blues were what the Chouans called the republican army, Nathan recalled. Both sides had been guilty of the most appalling atrocities during the long war in the west.

'I believe it is in mockery of their affinity to the Church of Rome.'

'So Mademoiselle de Kirouac's father was involved with the Chouans?'

'Actually, I am not sure that he was. I do not think he was very political at all. Just in the wrong place at the wrong time. He was a quite famous sculptor apparently. Perhaps they did not like his sculptures. He had a lot of commissions from the Church.'

'So, she has personal reasons to . . . ?' He did not complete the sentence. Hate? Kill? Sculpt an avenging angel? But he did not need to.

'You might say that. Especially as the revolutionists killed her mother, too, though in her case they employed the guillotine.'

'Was her mother also with the Chouans?'

'I believe this was earlier—during the Terror. For presuming to advise Robespierre on the best way to govern France.'

He would not have liked that. Nathan had met Robespierre on a number of occasions during the time of the Terror, and although he was by no means as tyrannical as his accusers maintained, he was not an easy man to advise. He had more than a touch of misogyny in him, too, he recalled, though he tried to pretend otherwise.

'She was a very outspoken woman by all accounts,' Smith went on. 'Though mostly it was expressed through her writing. She was a great writer of pamphlets during the Revolution.'

'And her name was de Kirouac?' Nathan was trying to recall if he had come across a woman by that name while he was in Paris.

'No. She and the father were not married. Her name was Olympe de Gouges.'

'The playwright?'

'Another of your acquaintances in Paris?' Smith observed him slyly. He had given Nathan several indications that he knew rather more of his activities in the French capital than Nathan would have wished.

'No, but I heard talk of her.' She had been an associate of both Mary Wollstonecraft and Thomas Paine when they were in Paris. 'And how old was her daughter at the time?'

'If she *was* her daughter. It has not been conclusively established, though there was certainly some kind of a relationship. She was thirteen or fourteen, I believe. Old enough for them to throw her in prison in case she was afflicted with the same disease. I am not sure it cured her entirely.'

'She was in prison—during the Terror?'

'She was indeed, and rather more interestingly, became closely acquainted with a fellow prisoner we now know as Josephine Bonaparte, though she called herself Rose then, and was married to an aristocrat by the name of Beauharnais. But of course, you know that. I believe you knew her quite well yourself at the time.'

They were in and out of the light from the torches on the castle walls, so it was difficult to read his expression. Mocking, no doubt. In fact, Nathan had formed no close attachment to Rose Beauharnais when he was in Paris. Apart from anything else, it would have been too dangerous. She had been the mistress of Paul Barras, the top man in the Republic at the time, and Bonaparte was besotted with her. But it was not Rose Beauharnais that he wanted to talk about.

'So what of Mademoiselle de Kirouac? She never married?'

'No. Strange that, with such looks. But she has had a great deal to distract her. After her release from prison, she went to live with her father in

Brittany. I believe she kept house for him. Then came the *Chouannerie*. I do not suppose marriage was the first thing on her mind.'

'So, she lost both parents to the Revolution?' Good enough reason to want to assassinate someone.

'Well, that is what the countess told me, though she is not always to be relied upon.'

'I take it you are well acquainted?'

'With the countess? I would not say that, but I have dined once or twice at her current residence, which is called Rohan Manor, should you ever seek directions.'

'And Mademoiselle de Kirouac?'

'Oh, she and I know each other tolerably well.'

Unfortunately, the conversation had to end there. They had reached the outer gate and here was poor Bentham waiting for him, huddled in a boat cloak.

'What are you doing out here?' Nathan was shocked to see him out in the cold, but he muttered something about the company not being to his liking. Nathan did not push him. He was a good-looking lad, often importuned. He relit his flare from one of the sconces in the wall and off they went down the hill to the harbour and the lights of the waiting ship.

Next morning Nathan took an inventory with Mr Babb. With most of the crew gone ashore the supply problem was no longer urgent. On the other hand, the provisions they had left were not of a nature to tempt the appetite. Besides, as Nathan pointed out, 'If they do come back, we must ensure we do not lose them again for want of food and drink.'

Clearly, Mr Babb thought this was dangerously close to mollycoddling, but he raised no objections in principle, only as to the best means of securing the necessary provisions. The wind remaining stubbornly in the south-west, Nathan proposed that the purser travel to Saint Helier by road and arrange for their purchases to be brought back the same way, and Mr Babb being amenable to this, he and his assistant set off almost immediately by donkey cart. Nathan, in the meantime, decided to avail himself of Captain d'Auvergne's invitation to dine at the castle, where he possessed the luxury of a French émigré cook.

Despite these practical diversions, his mind was still occupied with thoughts of Louise de Kirouac, the nature of her relationship with the Swedish Knight, and, this notwithstanding, how he might contrive to meet up with her again. The most direct means was to pay another visit to the chateau on the pretext of shooting rabbits, and he was about to set off in the gig with this in mind when he was informed that a boat had arrived from the shore with a letter for him.

It was from the Countess de Rochefort; inviting him to dinner.

'Well, *monsieur le capitaine*, I hope you were not looking forward to rabbit. It appears that you have shot them all, or rendered them so terrified they will not come out of their bunkers, or wherever it is they reside when they are not in a pot.'

The countess was considerably more welcoming than on Nathan's last visit to the manor, and Nathan replied that her company was more than sufficient, whatever was on the menu. In fact, he was not as anxious to satisfy the needs of his stomach as he would normally have been. His chief concern was that Louise de Kirouac would be present on the occasion, coupled with a faint disquiet that the countess might have designs on him herself. She had sent her carriage for him but advised him to be prepared to spend the night, as they dined so late, and the roads were not safe after dark, though from what cause he could not imagine. It could hardly be brigands on an island the size of Jersey.

He need not have worried. Mademoiselle de Kirouac was awaiting him in the withdrawing room, dressed for the occasion in a manner that caused his temperature to rise considerably, if not hers. There was another gentleman present—one of those he had encountered on his last visit—who was introduced as Monsieur le Comte de Vervais, but his attentions to the countess suggested that he was her chosen partner for the evening, if not on a permanent basis. His manner, too, was somewhat more agreeable than on the previous occasion, and they made a convivial foursome for an impressive dinner whose main components were a very appetising fish soup and a *gigot d'agneau* in an anchovy sauce with enough side dishes to considerably improve upon Nathan's diet aboard the *Falaise*.

As for the conversation, it was dominated by the current situation in France and the much-anticipated renewal of hostilities between the new republic and the crowned heads of Europe, Britain in particular. Bonaparte came in for a predictable amount of vitriol in a household of émigrés, but there was nothing in the conversation that suggested one of them had been designated as his assassin, though it was probably not something they would discuss in front of a stranger. Naturally Nathan said nothing of his own association with Bonaparte—or any other of his family. Of more significance to him than the topic of conversation, however, was the occasional glance he encountered from Mademoiselle de Kirouac, which indicated to him that his hopes of a greater intimacy were not entirely fanciful, and there was a flippant exchange between her and the countess about the chateau being haunted, which gave him the precise location of her bedchamber, which was just across the passage from his own.

Even so, when the time came for him to retire, he was by no means resolved to act upon these indications—not from any lack of desire, but rather for fear of being mistaken in hers. Besides, despite the conversation about the ghost, could he be sure of finding the right room? There were few things more ridiculous than creeping around a strange house in a nightshirt with a candle like the character in *Goosey Gander* and hoping to find the room of a woman who may or may not welcome one's attentions. He lay undecided for an appreciable length of time before resolving to take a chance on it. Even then, he garbed himself in the Indian banyan he had brought with him, considering it to be a more romantic alternative to a nightshirt. He agonised for a moment or two over the Moorish curled-toe slippers which normally accompanied this garment, but decided it was more masculine to go barefoot, though by this time he was so cold there was no feeling in his feet at all.

Thus garbed, he moved quietly into the corridor and tried the door immediately opposite his own. It opened easily enough, and he found her standing in the middle of the room. In a nightdress with a candle.

'I thought you had got lost,' she said. 'I was just coming to find you.'

She was shivering, from cold or nerves, or both. He wrapped his arms around her and kissed her on the lips. Then she led him to her bed.

✸

In the morning when he awoke, she was still sleeping soundly beside him. He watched her for a moment in the light that filtered through a gap in the curtains and thought her even more beautiful than when he had first seen her in the chapel, though perhaps not as pure. Her long hair was spread on the pillow, more tawny than chestnut, and her mouth was slightly parted in what was almost a smile. He wondered briefly if he should rouse her or quietly return to his room before they were discovered by a maid. But the countess was surely in on the plot, and no-one else mattered. There were certain houses where the correct form had to be maintained, but Rohan Manor was probably not one of them.

He found his banyan robe among the tumbled bedclothes and slipped it on as he padded across to the window and drew back the curtains. The sky was a startling shade of blue and there was no hint of movement in the trees, which relieved him of any lingering guilt he might have felt for being away from his ship.

'What on earth are you wearing?'

He turned to see her face in a vignette of bed-curtains. His heart skipped a beat, and it was not for the slur on his treasured robe. He looked down at the exotic birds, the tropical foliage. He supposed it was a little exotic for Jersey.

'It was given me by a maharajah,' he lied, 'for saving his life.'

In fact, it had been a parting gift from Sister Caterina for services of a different nature when they were in India.

'Well, keep it on if you like,' she said, 'but come back to bed.'

There were times over the coming weeks when he wondered what he thought he was doing, but they were few and far between. For the most part he sailed under clear blue skies with the merest breath of a wind to remind him of his duties. Which were not, in any case, especially arduous. Sometimes he was called upon to drill French exiles in the use of the Ferguson rifle, but not often. He saw very little of Sir Sidney Smith, and when he did there was no more talk of kidnapping Bonaparte or of invading mainland France. He seemed to have other things on his mind. For several weeks he was away from the island—on urgent business in London, according to d'Auvergne. Presumably he took the packet boat from Saint Helier, for he made no demands upon the *Falaise*.

Tully returned after a few days and took over any responsibilities that might have distracted Nathan from his other pursuits. He had seen his sisters and they were well enough, he said, and in good spirits, but he had no desire to spend a great deal of time with them. True to his prediction, the crew also came drifting back, all but a dozen or so of the Americans, who had found berths on a barque bound for Southampton from where they would make their way homeward. Tully had the rest of them making a thorough overhaul of the ship and painting everything that did or did not need painting. They even practised with the guns, the gunner having secured a sufficiency of powder along with the stocks of food and liquor the purser had obtained in Saint Helier. This was the only reminder of what the *Falaise* had been designed for. Otherwise, she remained idle in Grouville Bay, with the occasional cruise along the coast to keep the ship and crew in trim. There was some grumbling, according to Tully, but then there always was. It was nothing to worry about.

As for Nathan, he spent every day he could with Louise. It was an early spring on Jersey, and when they were not at the chateau they explored the island together, riding through the woodlands or walking the empty beaches and netting for shrimps in the rock pools when the tide was out, as he had in Sussex as a child. But they did not need much in the way of diversion. They were completely engrossed in each other.

The Avenging Angel was mostly neglected, though from time to time, Louise would attack it with a chisel. Nathan examined it more closely and found it vaguely disturbing, though he could not say why. Perhaps it was the mouth. Despite what she said about being an amateur, he thought she was immensely talented, but then he would. He was as much in love as he had been with Sara when he had first met her in Paris during the Terror. More, perhaps. He told himself it was more. He tried not to think of how that had ended.

They talked sometimes of the past. He told her of his war, or at least some of it. He did not speak of his undercover work in France. He thought it would be better for her not to know. She told him about the woman who had raised her in Paris, Olympe de Gouges, though she had never owned to being her mother. Publicly she had always referred to Louise as her ward, the daughter of her best friend who had died in childbirth—and it was not something her father had ever wished to talk about. Madame de Gouges had been kind to her, sometimes loving, but she was too occupied with her writing initially, and then with the Revolution, to have a great deal of time for mothering. But then she was not very different from most women of her class and pursuits. Nathan's mother had been the same.

Louise told him about the bad time that had followed her guardian's arrest and execution and her own imprisonment in the former convent of the Carmelites, where she had met Rose Beauharnais, who had been like a big sister to her. It was the time of the Terror, and they were all living in the shadow of the guillotine.

Within a week of her release her father had come for her and taken her back to his home in Nantes. He was older than Madame de Gouges, by a decade or so, the son of a wealthy merchant and shipowner who had left him sufficient money to pursue his love of art. An accomplished scholar as well as a painter and sculptor, he had no wife, or any other children besides Louise, and he took pleasure in tutoring her in many subjects, not just art.

She did not know how he had become involved with the Chouans, or even if he was, but he was a Breton patriot and a devout Catholic—probably that was enough. The fighting in lower Brittany had been spasmodic, a war of skirmishes, night attacks, and savage government reprisals. Her father was a victim of one of these. He had been working on a sculpture of the crucifixion in a church in Vertou, not far from Nantes, when the village was attacked by the Blues. That was probably what gave them the idea of nailing him to a cross, Louise said. When the soldiers left, she had gone there with some of his friends to take him down and bury him. After that, she had joined the Chouans herself, but she had nothing much to say about that, other than they had been on the run for most of the time, pursued by dragoons, hitting back with the occasional ambush or night attack. She was reticent about what part she had played in these skirmishes. He did not know if she had been a fighter or a cook or supplied some other form of support. Perhaps he should have asked, but he was not sure he wanted to know.

By 1800 the Chouans had been reduced to a few starving bands, and Louise had fled with some others to Jersey. The countess, who had been a patron of her father's, had invited her to stay at Rohan Manor, and she had been there ever since. She had some money from her father's estate, but she lived from day to day; she tried not to think about the future. She said nothing of her relations with Sir Sidney Smith, and again, Nathan did not like to ask her for fear of what it might reveal.

But then one day he told her what Smith had said about her at the reception at Castle Gorey.

It did not come entirely out of the blue.

Smith had returned from his visit to London with a promise of more ships, very soon, but he provided no details. The international situation was extremely grave, he said. Bonaparte had been throwing his weight around even more than usual, treating the smaller states of Germany as if they were French provinces, and when the British government had protested, he had told them to mind their own business—they had no say in the affairs of Europe. The king, who was also the Elector of Hanover, felt deeply insulted. They must be prepared for war at any moment, Smith said.

Then he sent Nathan off to cruise the Normandy coast, taking soundings and noting the best beaches for making a night landing. As d'Auvergne had been landing agents there for several years, Nathan suspected this was just to keep him out of the way. But why? However, he dutifully took the *Falaise* on what he was convinced was a fool's errand, spending three days cruising the sixty or seventy miles of coast between Cap de la Hague and Granville, doing as instructed and drilling his crew to a point of readiness for whatever might be required of them. Whatever the reason for his mission, he could at least remind them that they were on a fighting ship and not a private yacht. Then, when he returned to Gorey, he discovered from d'Auvergne that Smith had spent the previous night away at Rohan Manor.

When he next went there, he found Louise working on the angel again. She seemed pleased to see him, but he thought she was distracted. Perhaps it was the angel. Looking at it now, Nathan thought he saw in it something of Smith's sneering smile. He kept this to himself, but later in her bedchamber, he found her cleaning a pair of duelling pistols which she said had been her father's. He watched her for a moment, thinking how well she handled them, but then she had been a fighter with the Chouans. Even so, with his mind on by what d'Auvergne had told him, he blurted out what Smith had said about her being an assassin—and that her next target was Napoleon Bonaparte.

He made his tone light, as if it had been intended as a joke, but she was clearly shocked. Shocked and angry.

'Why would he tell you that?' she demanded.

He shrugged. 'I have no idea. Perhaps just to see how I would react. He plays games with people.'

His eyes dropped to the pistols on the table before her.

'But it is so ridiculous—and dangerous.'

'Why dangerous?'

'What? To say I plan to assassinate Bonaparte? How can you ask? When the place is crawling with spies.'

She was looking at him as if he was an idiot. He had not seen her like this before.

He shrugged. 'I am sorry. I did not take it seriously.'

'Well, believe me, plenty of other people would.'

'Why?' Provoked himself now. 'Do they know something about you that I do not?'

She shook her head, but in exasperation rather than denial. Then she laughed, not quite convincingly.

'But this is absurd. You think that is why I am cleaning my father's pistols?'

'Of course not, I told you . . .'

'You did not take it seriously. No. Well, perhaps you should have.'

They had been speaking French as they usually did when alone and she used the formal—*vous auriez peut-être dû*—and he was more concerned with that than with what she had actually said.

'I am sorry to have made you cross,' he told her, taking her hand.

'I am not cross—not with you. Only with him, for saying something so stupid.'

They left it at that, but he felt a constraint between them, and he still did not know if Sir Sidney Smith had visited the chateau while he was away, or why.

He had to go back to the *Falaise* that night for a dinner with d'Auvergne and some other guests, and it was two days before he was free to return to Rohan Manor. The servant who let him in said that the countess wished to speak with him in the library.

'Louise is not here,' she said as soon he appeared at the door. 'She has gone back to France.'

He stared at her in disbelief.

'Please,' she said. 'Sit down.' She waved him to a chair, but he did not move. 'She left you this note.'

He took it and broke the seal. It was in French, but it did not say much.

'*Cherie*, I have had to go back to France on business concerning my father. I do not know when I will be free to return. I am so sorry. It was arranged in a great hurry, and I was not able to come out to your ship to tell you in person. I am not sure that I would have been able to. I am so sorry, *Cherie*. I love you. Louise.'

He could get nothing more out of the countess, though he did not try very hard. He could not find the words.

He rode back to Gorey and sought out Sir Sidney Smith, finding him in his office high in one of the towers.

'You have sent Mademoiselle de Kirouac back to France,' he began without preamble.

Smith eyed him warily with no hint of that supercilious sneer, which was just as well, given the mood Nathan was in.

'It had nothing to do with me, sir. So far as I am aware, it is a family matter. She has taken advantage of the amnesty to reclaim her father's estate. I expect she needs the money. I do not suppose it was easy being a guest of the countess.'

Nathan was certain he was lying but unsure what to do about it. He was furious with Louise, furious with Smith, and most of all, furious with himself for appearing at such a disadvantage.

'So, she has returned to her home in Nantes?'

'As to that I have no information, but I expect that will be the case, yes.'

Smith was sitting at his desk with a view of the bay through the casement window behind him, the *Falaise* riding at her mooring off the harbour wall. She was ready to sail at a moment's notice and the wind had shifted to the north-west. If Louise had taken ship from Saint Helier, it might not be too late to stop her.

'Then I must request a leave of absence,' he said. 'For personal reasons.'

Smith shook his head. 'For heaven's sake, Peake, sit down and think on it. You cannot go to France, with or without the *Falaise*.' He sounded more resigned than angry.

'Why not? We are not at war.'

'No, but we soon will be. By the end of the week, if my information is correct. So, if you ever wish to see Louise de Kirouac again, you had better have regard to the means of winning it as soon as possible.'

Chapter 8

War

The news reached Jersey two days later by the Weymouth packet. It was not unexpected, though no-one seemed to know the precise reasons, and accounts in the English journals varied. Bonaparte's interference in the affairs of Switzerland was given as the main cause of hostilities but was not generally taken as anything more than a pretext.

'But a pretext for what?' enquired d'Auvergne when they met at Castle Gorey for a council of war with several of the royalist exiles. 'I mean, if it is not Switzerland, what is the real reason?'

He seemed to think that Smith would know, but Smith smiled his superior smile and said that it did not really matter what the reason was; it was better to confront Bonaparte now than when he had conquered the rest of Europe.

'For that we need troops,' said d'Auvergne gloomily, 'and depend upon it, they will not come from Britain. We need alliances—with Austria, Prussia, Russia, wherever else we may find allies. And without Billy Pitt at the helm . . .' It had been Pitt who had put together the coalitions that had fought the last war, paying vast subsidies from the English treasury for the European powers to maintain their troops in the field, but the present government had not secured a single ally on the continent of Europe, d'Auvergne pointed out.

'We can do our best,' said one of the Frenchmen, 'by getting rid of Bonaparte.'

He had been introduced to Nathan as General Jean-Charles Pichegru, a recent arrival in Jersey with the reputation of a competent, even brilliant, military commander. He had been on the side of the Revolution at first and had led the French armies into early victories on the Rhine and in the Low Countries, but had since become a royalist. Nathan was not at all sure why, save for a deep personal dislike of Bonaparte.

Plans for the kidnap were well advanced, he intimated, but if something went wrong at the last minute they were prepared to 'manier le poignard'— which Nathan translated as wield the dagger, presumably a reference to the assassination of Julius Caesar. It was clear that Pichegru and Cadoudal saw themselves in the roles of Brutus and Cassius, though their names would not ring as resoundingly throughout history, Nathan suspected. An agent Cadoudal referred to by the nom de guerre of Chandell had been planted at Malmaison, the home of Madame Bonaparte on the western outskirts of Paris, which was occasionally used by her husband as the government headquarters, and the tyrant's movements were under constant surveillance, he said. But it was vital to have more agents in position to ensure a simultaneous uprising of royalist forces. Otherwise, some other member of the Bonaparte family, or one of his generals, would simply step up to take his place.

'Once we remove Bonaparte, the whole pack of cards will collapse,' Pichegru predicted confidently, and he added that arrangements for landing agents and arms on the French mainland were well in hand.

Nathan glanced at Smith, but he did not react. He was staring straight before him, his chin resting on his hands, his face impassive.

'Does the British government know of this plan?' Nathan demanded a little later, when he had joined him in his turret.

'Broadly speaking,' Smith replied, in what might almost have been a yawn. 'I doubt they have read the small print.'

'Such as the plan to kill him if all else fails.'

'Did they say that?' he frowned.

'They did.' And so did you a few months ago, he felt like reminding him.

'Well, the devil is in the details, as they say.'

'And what is that supposed to mean?' Nathan was not in the mood for Smith's games.

He shrugged. 'The details of the operation are down to the royalists. We are merely giving a certain level of support.'

'You mean, by landing men and arms on the French coast.'

'You always knew that to be the case. You supplied most of the arms. You knew how they were going to be used.'

Nathan sighed. In truth he had never taken the plan to assassinate Bonaparte seriously. Perhaps he should have.

'For the purposes of rebellion,' he said. 'Not murder.'

'I think that is a fine distinction. Would you call the execution of King Louis murder, or rebellion? Or our own King Charles, for that matter.'

This was typical of Smith. You tried to pin him down on something specific and you found yourself debating the English Civil War, or Caesar's conquest of Gaul.

'I never signed up for an assassination,' Nathan persisted.

'No-one is saying you did. I understand it is a contingency only, and as I say, nothing to do with us. But given that we are talking about the assassination of a tyrant, a man who has seized power by military coup, what are your principal objections, as a matter of interest?'

'I would prefer to wage war openly, not in this weaselly cloak-and-dagger fashion.'

'Good God, Peake.' He affected profound shock. 'When did this come upon you?'

'I think you have a mistaken impression of my past activities,' replied Nathan coldly. 'I have never done anything that has not been approved by my superiors in the Admiralty.'

He was sounding unusually stiff and pompous, but Smith had this effect on him lately.

'Have you not?' Smith raised a quizzical brow. 'Well, we will not discuss that for the moment. But what makes you think they do not approve of this?'

'You said the British government did not know of it.'

'Ah. Well, perhaps I should have said the British government does not officially know of it. Nor do they want to.'

'So, who are we answerable to?'

Smith observed him thoughtfully for a moment and seemed to come to a decision. 'If I told you the warden of the Cinque Ports, would that satisfy you?'

Nathan was not amused. The Cinque Ports were the five fishing ports of Dover, Hythe, Hastings, Sandwich, and Romney, which had traditionally raised ships and men for the defence of the realm, but they had not done so since the Middle Ages, and the warden had long been a purely ceremonial role. But then it came to him. The present warden of the Cinque Ports was Billy Pitt. He had been given the title as a consolation prize when he had resigned as the king's chief minister, and with it, the residency of Walmer Castle on the Kent coast.

'Billy Pitt is still answerable to Parliament and to the British public,' Nathan insisted. He was not at all sure he believed this, but Smith's smug air of certainty annoyed him.

If anything, the smile widened. He appeared genuinely amused. 'I think you have the wrong impression of Parliament,' he said, 'and I speak as a member. As to the British public, when did they ever know anything, and what would they do about it if they did?'

Nathan shook his head determinedly. 'I cannot accept that.'

'And yet you have been involved in activities on behalf of the British government of which my fellow Members of Parliament knew nothing, and would certainly not have approved if they did.' Smith's tone remained light but there was an edge to his words. He did not mention Nathan's recent activities in the Caribbean, but he did not have to.

'I do not mean to be critical,' Smith soothed him. 'You acted in the belief that it was in the national interests, to prevent Bonaparte from building a new French empire in North America. It might interest you to know, by the by, that the recent sale of those territories to the United States was facilitated by an old acquaintance of yours, one Gabriel Ouvrard of the Bank of France.'

Nathan frowned. It was nine years since he had been acquainted with Ouvrard, who had been his chief contact in Paris at the time of the Directory. Not for the first time, he wondered how Smith came to know of these clandestine activities. It put him at a considerable disadvantage.

'Ouvrard helped arrange the deal,' Smith went on. 'But the amount agreed upon for the purchase—fifteen million US dollars—was made available by Barings Bank, of the city of London, with the tacit approval of the British government. That money is now available to Napoleon Bonaparte to wage war upon Great Britain, and I have it on good authority that it will be used to raise and equip an army of two hundred thousand men for the invasion of England.'

'What is your point?'

It seemed to Nathan that these were Smith's usual tactics of diversion and distraction, aided by a great quantity of smoke and mirrors.

'Only that there are a number of confidential dealings that the British government would not wish Parliament or the British public to know about.'

'And the assassination of Napoleon Bonaparte is one of them?'

'You should not give too much credence to Pichegru. He is a bitter man who feels ill used by the Republic. I can assure you that the present arrangement is to kidnap him and house him in Castle Gorey pending peace negotiations with either him or his successors. How could you object to that?'

Nathan shrugged. 'And would it matter in the slightest if I did?'

'Excellent. I am glad to have you aboard,' beamed Smith. 'Not least as you will have the job of landing our royalist friends on the shores of France.'

Which was why, some several months later, His Britannic Majesty's hired vessel *Falaise*, as she now was, slipped out of the Bay of Grouville on a mission that would, in the opinion of at least one man aboard, change the course of history.

That man was not the ship's captain.

Even in the most buoyant of moods, Nathan had never seen himself as a man of destiny, much less a shaper of world events. He left that to such forces of nature as Napoleon Bonaparte, or indeed, Monsieur Georges Cadoudal, who, on coming aboard earlier that evening, had made this extraordinary declaration and congratulated Nathan on the privilege of carrying him on the first part of his journey. Cadoudal's own mood was buoyant, and a strong whiff of spirits suggested that he had prepared himself for their present voyage by resorting to the brandy bottle, it being recommended by some, if not Nathan, as an antidote to seasickness. He was rather more reticent about revealing the precise nature of their historic mission, and Nathan was not inclined to waste time on conjecture. All he had been told by d'Auvergne was that he was to land the Breton and his associates with a quantity of arms on the north-east tip of the Cotentin peninsula. As to their subsequent plans, these were none of his concern,

Nathan told himself, whatever contribution they may or may not make to the British war effort.

They had been waiting on the weather for several nights now, but at last conditions were as right for them as they would ever be, with a fresh south-westerly wind and a new moon flitting in and out of cloud, providing just enough light to see what they were about without making it too obvious to hostile eyes ashore. Or so Nathan hoped. The more likely danger he anticipated was from meeting up with a French cruiser that had managed to evade the British blockade, for which reason he had taken the precaution of part-clearing the ship for action, with the guns loaded and prepared for firing, if not yet run out, and the ship's boats towed astern. But d'Auvergne's orders had been explicit: They were to avoid conflict if at all possible. If forced to defend themselves, they were to aim at disabling their opponent and making a swift escape. Nathan had his own feelings about this, but he had complied to the extent of ordering the guns to be double-shotted with chain. Ruinous to an enemy's rigging at short range, quite useless at anything greater. But then, as Mr Banjo had remarked in his hearing, at night they were unlikely to hit anything much further than he could spit.

Once they had rounded St Catherine's Point, he set a course for the nor'-nor'-east on a broad reach that would keep them well out from the Normandy coast until they reached their designated landing point. The wind had freshened a little since they had left Gorey, and there was enough of a swell running to warn of worse to come, though the depression that had settled over him for several months now had left Nathan as indifferent to the weather as he was to most other aspects of life.

Even the renewal of hostilities with France had done little to distract him from the personal torment that had followed the abrupt departure of Louise de Kirouac—a deep sense of loss, combined not only with the hurt and humiliation of what he could only take as a rejection, but also a bitter self-reproach for leaving himself vulnerable to such emotions. He still did not know the reason for her leaving. It might have been to take advantage of Bonaparte's amnesty and recover her lost inheritance, as Smith and the countess had informed him, or it might have been simply because she was so bored with her life on the island—and with him—she could not bear to remain a moment longer. There was also the suspicion that she had been sent on some secret mission on behalf of the royalists, a possibility which

Nathan would have dismissed as unlikely had her departure not followed so soon after he had teased her with Smith's remark about her being an assassin.

Whatever her motives, to Nathan's mind it showed how little he had mattered to her, despite the words and deeds of love. Nor could he shake himself of the notion that she and Smith enjoyed a much closer relationship than she had been prepared to admit, and whether or not this was sexual in nature, he could not look upon it as anything other than a betrayal.

As if this was not demoralising enough, Nathan's own career was as much in the doldrums as it had ever been. In fact, he could not remember a time when his prospects had appeared as bleak, saving the time he had been incarcerated in the Moorish Castle of Gibraltar. At the beginning of the last war, he had been the master and commander of a sixteen-gun brig in the English Channel. Now, after ten years of almost continuous conflict, being made up to post captain and successively commanding a crack frigate and a flotilla in the Indian Ocean, he was back where he had started. In fact, it might be argued that he was worse off now than he had been then, for although he was a rank higher in the chain of command, the *Falaise* was a mere hired vessel in the service of King George, and he was arguably in more of a backwater now than he had been when he was supporting the revenue service in the port of Rye.

Smith, of course, continued to assure him that they were playing a vital role in the war effort. While Bonaparte was moving two hundred thousand troops to the Channel coast with a view to invading England— with the funds made available to him by Barings Bank, if Smith could be believed—he and d'Auvergne and their royalist friends continued with their preparations for invading France and marching on Paris, though the combined strength available to them amounted to no more than a few hundred French exiles in borrowed British uniforms and one sixteen-gun corvette, formerly of the French marine. He was, he informed Nathan, anticipating the arrival of several regiments of regular British infantry, and a sizeable force of fighting ships which he had been promised by his friends in the Ministry, and to which Nathan would be appointed as his second in command. In the meantime, he continued with his plans to take the war to the enemy, as he put it, by landing a number of agents and guns on the French coast to promote the counter-revolution. The one thing Nathan could be grateful for, he supposed, was that there was no further mention of either killing or kidnapping the First Consul, though it would be foolish to think the idea had been abandoned. In fact, given that the French had over a million men under arms compared to the fifty thousand regular soldiers stationed in England, it appeared to be one of the few ideas in circulation that would do anything to redress the balance.

He was distracted from these gloomy thoughts by the reappearance of Monsieur Cadoudal, who had spent most of the time since leaving Gorey in the stern cabin with his fellow conspirators, playing cards and fortifying themselves with more cognac than Nathan would have considered advisable in the circumstances, even if its properties were as curative as they imagined. He half-ran, half-staggered down the slope of the deck, for they were canted sharply to starboard, reaching out to grab the rail with both hands, and for a moment Nathan thought he was going to be sick over it, but he just stood there, arms and legs braced, gazing out towards the darker mass of night sky that was Normandy some four or five miles to the east. Nathan considered sending a polite but firm request to return to his temporary quarters below deck, but he was safe enough where he was provided he did not move, and the sea air would be a lot better for him than the alcohol-infused fug down below.

Cadoudal presented in many ways an oddly incongruous, even ludicrous figure, his massive bulk further enlarged by a military cape with several overlapping collars and a bicorn hat worn athwart, the way Bonaparte wore his, and pulled down low over his ears. Whatever he had been doing with himself on Jersey for the past few months, it had clearly not involved losing any weight. And yet both Louise and the countess had spoken of him with respect—he had been a charismatic leader of the Chouans, they said, inspiring a fierce loyalty among his followers, though Louise claimed never to have met him. Nathan had believed her at the time; now he was by no means sure. She had also told him that the name Cadoudal, in the Breton language, meant 'warrior returning from the fight'. Nathan suspected he was far more of a politician than a soldier, a conspirator rather than an active participant in the kind of combat at which the Chouans excelled—a war of night attacks and hit-and-run raids announced by the fiendish shrieking of an owl. He could not see Cadoudal creeping through the darkness making bird noises before rushing upon a lonely republican outpost or crouching in a ditch for several hours, in hopes of ambushing a troop of dragoons. Nathan trusted that whoever had been sent to meet him would bring a mount for him, or preferably a coach and four, and that he would swiftly be conducted to a nearby hostelry, rather than spend the night in the open. Even if his mission was not as historic as he appeared to believe, it had to be important enough for d'Auvergne to put the *Falaise* at his disposal, instead of entrusting him to one of the local smugglers. But then, why bother, when he had Nathan at his beck and call?

Nathan was diverted from his deliberations by a subtle alteration in the movement of the ship. Tully's appearance at his side indicated that he had noted it, too, and they both raised their eyes aloft to study the appearance of the sails. They were not feathering exactly, but there was a slackness about the edges that advised them of a minor shift in the direction of the wind.

'Maybe a point to the west,' remarked Nathan, hopefully. 'No more.'

Tully did not contradict him, and it required only a slight trim to maintain their present course and keep them well clear of Cap de Flamanville, which was looming darkly off the starboard bow, but Nathan's mind was now focused on the coast beyond. He had the natural sailor's fear of a lee shore, and even a slight shift to westward would compound their problems considerably. Although Tully had not spoken, Nathan could sense his unease.

'What do you think?' he enquired, without taking his eyes from the sails.

'It will help on the way back,' said Tully, who had a tendency, which Nathan did not share, to communicate the good news first. 'But it will not make the landing any easier.'

Nathan knew this already.

'So, what do you suggest?' he demanded.

But for once Tully appeared reluctant to commit himself. Nathan watched his face in the dull glow of the binnacle light, which was the only light he had permitted to be shown on their approach to the shore.

'I would advise standing well out to sea—but in the present circumstances . . .'

He did not have to say more. They had been instructed by d'Auvergne to wait offshore until they saw the agreed signal—three exposures of a lantern light, repeated at intervals of one minute. Then they were to land their passengers in the cutter. But with the wind shifting to the west, even by as little as a point, and the swell that was running, there was a real danger of the *Falaise* being driven upon the shore. Normally—if there was ever a normal in this situation—it would have made sense to stand well out to sea, but this would have given the cutter that much further to travel to the landing point, and then it would have to find the darkened *Falaise* on its return. The sloop might have to wait, hove-to or cruising up and down the exposed coast for up to two hours or more, which was difficult enough at the best of times, and without the added complication of the Alderney Race.

Tully had briefed Nathan on this phenomenon before setting out from Gorey. It was the name given to a strong sea current that flowed between the Cap de la Hague, on the extreme tip of the Cotentin peninsula, and the isle of Alderney, ten miles to the west, where the full force of the Atlantic Ocean, already compressed into the English Channel, was diverted into this narrow strait. When the wind and the Race were going in opposite directions, the sea became extremely turbulent, Tully had explained, with waves reaching a height of twelve feet or more, and less than fifty yards between them. Their landing point was a good ten miles to the south-east of the most dangerous point, but it could still be a problem for them, and more particularly, for the cutter. Apart from the violence of the waves, the opposition of wind and sea could create a great deal of wind-blown foam, which made visibility very poor, he said, especially in the darkness.

Nathan had, of course, passed on Tully's reservations to d'Auvergne, who had argued that the very notoriety of the Race made it much less likely that they would encounter a French patrol in the vicinity, either on land or at sea. Besides which, as an islander himself, he prided himself on knowing the nearby waters as well as any man alive, even Tully, and he insisted that if they made their approach with the tide on the ebb, the Race was nothing to be concerned about, even with the wind from the south-west. Tully clearly had his doubts about this, but they had set out from Gorey to be as sure as they ever could be that they would arrive at a favourable time. However, by Nathan's estimation, they had less than three hours to complete the operation before the tide changed from ebb to flow, and then they were in trouble.

'I think we must hold to our present course,' he said, 'and try to maintain our position until the cutter returns.'

'Very well.' Tully's formal assent did not disguise his considerable misgivings. 'I will take the cutter in if you like,' he added after a moment. 'And if we cannot find you in the dark, I can always sail her back to Jersey.'

This was true, but Nathan was by no means persuaded. Tully's knowledge of the local tides and currents was a lot more valuable to him aboard the *Falaise*, especially in the troubled waters of the landing point.

'Cole can manage the cutter,' he said, with a confidence he was far from feeling. 'We have three hours before the turn of the tide. That should be plenty enough.' Even for Cole, he added silently.

They both knew this was uncharacteristically optimistic.

Neither of them spoke again for the next hour or so as they cruised the dark waters of the bay, their eyes smarting from the effort of peering towards the even deeper darkness of the shore, for there was not a light to be seen. Nathan had a dozen lookouts aloft, half of them keeping a watch for any dangers from out to sea, the rest scanning the long expanse of shore for the signal. Nathan was forced to wear ship twice to avoid running into the Nez de Jobourg, and was on his third run back towards the opposite headland when at last he heard a cry from the watcher in the foretop—'A light, four points off the larboard bow'.

Nathan saw it almost at once, there being little else to distract him— the three swift flashes that came from the repeated twitching of a cloth from a lantern. He gave the correct response and they clewed the mainsail and braced the main yards back until the ship was hove-to a mile or so from the shore. The cutter was hauled up alongside and Cole climbed down into it with three of the hands. Two cases of muskets were passed down to them with kegs of powder and shot. Then Cadoudal and his three associates.

Nathan and Tully stood together at the rail and strained their eyes to follow the cutter's movement towards the thin line of breakers that marked the line of the shore. It seemed noticeably closer than when Nathan had last looked, but they had a hand in the mainchains taking soundings, and there were six fathoms of water under the keel; they could afford a little leeway. Even so, he felt a distinct sense of unease, and he knew Tully felt it too. The swell seemed much heavier, probably because they were hove-to, but even with the tide on the ebb there was a noticeable surf. Cole must have lowered the mainsail as they neared the beach, and for a long anxious moment Nathan lost them. Then Tully let out a cry and he saw the crimson sail against the lighter shade of the sand. This close to low tide there was an appreciable stretch of open shore before they would reach the cover of the dunes, and if this was a trap, now was the moment to spring it. The moment lengthened into minutes. Longer. There was no discernible movement on the shore, but it was impossible to make out much in the way of detail. Tully thought he saw ponies on the strand, but they could have been rocks or moon-wraiths to Nathan, and even if he was right there was no knowing whether they were the reception party or a troop of dragoons. He braced himself for gunfire. Nothing. Another longer wait, and then with immeasurable relief they saw the sails of the cutter again, coming back towards them.

Slowly the distance between them narrowed, but the *Falaise* was rolling badly now. It would be no easy business getting the crew aboard. In his mind's eye, Nathan saw the white surge of the Race rushing towards them out of the darkness. He had no idea what it was like in reality; no desire to find out. Mr Banjo had the line ready, weighted with a belaying pin, judging the distance. The cutter was almost under their bow. Now! Nathan urged him silently. He waited another second and then threw. Straight and true, the line hurtling into the space between jib and mainsail and dropping into the sea beyond. Cole made it fast, and then lowered the sail. There were a dozen men hauling on the line, drawing in the cutter like a gaffed whale. When they were close amidships and just clear of the roll, Banjo threw them another line and they made it fast to the stern. One by one the four men leapt for the mainchains on the downward roll and were hauled aboard, laughing like kids at the funfair—all except Lieutenant Cole, who was of a more sober disposition and whose breeches were soaked through from the waves.

Their exuberance was short-lived. They were scarcely aboard and the cutter still alongside when there was a cry from one of the lookouts.

'Sail! Three points off the weather bow!'

Every face turned into the wind, every eye searching the sea to the north-west. And there she was, emerging from beyond the Nez, three-masted with the long, lean lines of a ship of war, and although it was too dark to reveal a single detail that would reveal her nationality, much less her identity, every nerve, every expectation of catastrophe, told Nathan that she was French.

Chapter 9

The Dark Shadow

Even by the uncertain light of the moon, in the midst of more pressing concerns, Nathan felt a strange sense of recognition, almost of what the French called *déjà vu*, as he observed the vessel that had emerged from beyond the Nez de Jobourg. She was running close hauled to the south on a course that would take her across the mouth of the bay, and from what he could see of her rig against the lighter sky to the west, she was almost certainly a French corvette, built along very similar lines to the *Falaise*. In fact, it almost seemed as if a trick of the moonlight had produced a mirror image emerging from the other side of the headland.

His immediate concern was whether she was in British hands, or still part of the French navy. There were other possibilities, of course, but although the gentlemen at Lloyd's, who had an interest in such affairs, maintained that the English Channel accounted for about a fifth of the world's shipping, not many of those ships would risk the Alderney Race, certainly not at night and in the teeth of a brisk south-westerly, unless they were up to no good. The British navy maintained a presence off Cherbourg, but as far as Nathan was aware it consisted of two or three brigs on a watching brief, and they had no reason to venture further south unless they were in pursuit of an enemy. The chances were that she was French. The question was, what to do about it?

There were not a great many alternatives. They could wear ship and run in the opposite direction and hope to weather the opposite headland—or they could make for the narrow gap between the Nez de Jobourg and the approaching ship, with the risk of coming under fire, losing a spar or even their helm, and being driven upon the rocks. There was no disgrace in running. Not public disgrace, at least. D'Auvergne had been quite clear that they were not on a cruise to destroy the enemy or take prizes.

'We have to wear ship,' Nathan concluded without enthusiasm.

'All hands to the braces,' bellowed Tully, who had probably come to the same conclusion some moments earlier and had been waiting with admirable self-control for Nathan to make his mind up.

There was a rush of feet across the upper deck.

Then Nathan changed his mind.

'Belay that!' he roared. Then turning towards the astonished Tully, for he rarely countered an order: 'We will go straight at her,' he said, quoting Nelson, though for more practical reasons than mock heroics. He raised his voice again: 'Roll out the larboard guns!'

Several moments of what appeared to be utter chaos, of shouted orders and curses and colliding bodies and men hurrying here and there with no apparent purpose than to give their officers and petty officers apoplexy, though in fact every man knew exactly where he had to go and what he had to do, if only every other man would keep out of his way. This was what they had been doing all those months since early spring in the seas off Jersey, with their wages spent in the stews of Saint Helier, such as they were, and nothing much better to do. Loading up the guns and rolling them out and firing them at a succession of makeshift targets until they had achieved a creditable three broadsides in just under five minutes—at a cost of three hernias, a broken leg, and two crushed fingers. Now they had a bigger and better target, if only they could avoid running up on the Nez.

But first he had to establish that the approaching vessel was French— or at least a legitimate target.

'We need absolute silence,' he informed Tully in as low a voice as would carry for the wind. 'Not a word.'

Even in the darkness he could see that Tully was giving some thought as to how he might convey this to the officers and crew.

'Naturally, you may give the order first,' Nathan instructed him, with a hint of prickliness. 'But then—absolute silence. Until I give the word to fire.'

As these instructions were passed along the gundeck, Nathan made his way forward and stood at the rail by the larboard cathead, straining his ears as much as his eyes as he peered into the darkness. The other vessel was still coming on with no apparent change of course, though she had little room for manoeuvrability, with the Nez so close to leeward and the wind on her bow. But there was no indication that she had seen them against the darker background of the shore. The distance between the two vessels was narrowing rapidly and Nathan was still weighing the odds. Could she be British? There were still a few former French corvettes in British hands—captured during the last war, like the *Falaise* herself—but why would a British ship risk a passage through the Alderney Race in the teeth of a brisk sou'-westerly unless she was trying to escape something worse? If she was French, as seemed likely, had she been sent on purpose to intercept them at the landing point—in which case their mission had been betrayed long before they had set out from Jersey—or was her appearance purely fortuitous, a routine patrol or an unforeseen dash for some port of refuge on the Cotentin? Much depended on the answer, for if the former, her guns would be run out and ready to fire, and in her current situation, with her back against the wall of the Nez, the *Falaise* would be fighting for her life.

They were perilously close to the headland now, the tall granite cliff rising high above them, but it was not her height Nathan feared; it was the rocks at her feet. He could see them extending for about a hundred yards into the sea, a line of black molars with the white rollers breaking over them. He could hear the noise they made as they broke, and feel the spray thrown back on his face.

But now he heard another sound, and it was the sound he had been listening for, raised in indignant alarm, if not panic. He could even hear some of the words.

Putain, qu'est-ce que c'est? Nom de Dieu!

It was not conclusive. He had tried the same trick himself, and there were plenty of other British officers who spoke fluent French, but they had rarely been trained as actors. He almost laughed with the absurdity of it all. The long lance of the bowsprit appeared to be coming straight at him, but he saw that the two ships would pass each other at a distance of a few yards.

He waited another second and then as he felt the swell lifting the bows, he turned his back and raised his voice in a bellow that would carry above the sound of the wind and the breakers on their lee.

'Fire as you bear!'

The urgent echo from Cole in the waist and then the night ablaze with light, the rippling roar of the cannon thrown back from the cliffs, the air filled with smoke and the acrid smell of gunpowder.

And they were past. Not a shot fired in return unless he had missed it. It had certainly missed him. And ahead of them, the open sea. The cat had jumped over the moon again. But not yet landed on its feet.

He looked back towards the cliffs, fading now into the darkness, if not as rapidly as he would have wished, and then grabbed for the nearest support as the ship began to pitch and roll as violently as if it were an unbroken steed attempting to unseat its rider.. He made his way back across the heaving deck as fast as his dignity would allow and joined Tully at the con.

'Is this the Race?' he asked more cheerfully than he felt.

'It surely is.' Tully made no such pretence. His tone was grim.

Nathan looked to see what their opponent was doing. The moon was behind cloud, and it was difficult to see anything very much, but then he saw the light of her stern lantern a little way into the bay, though not as far as he would have thought she should have been by now.

Then the moon came out and he saw why. One of her masts appeared to be down—or at least, the top part of it. If any quantity of sail was attached, it must have been dragging in the water like a giant sea anchor.

He felt a brief exultation. Be damned to d'Auvergne. If he could wear ship, he could be up with her in a matter of minutes.

He looked back at the cliffs, judging the distance. Half a mile, perhaps, lengthening by the minute—and the Race was not all bad; it would help bring their bows around. But if there were more rocks, just under the surface of the water . . . There were none marked on the charts, but charts were not that reliable, particularly when it came to underwater rocks.

He told Tully what he was thinking and heard the exhalation of breath.

'Are there more rocks,' Nathan pressed him, 'apart from those we can see?'

'It is too long since I was last here,' Tully said. 'I do not think so, but I cannot be sure.'

He could lose the ship. For the sake of—what? Glory? Precious little glory in the taking of a French corvette, and yet . . . What was he here for, if not to fight?

She still seemed to be lying dead in the water, but they would be hacking away at that mass of canvas and cordage dragging her over to leeward, and unless they were total incompetents they would have her moving and back on course in a matter of minutes—or coming back at the *Falaise* to give blow for blow.

He looked at the sea in his wake. Black as night—blacker, with no white breakers that would reveal the presence of rocks.

'We must give it a try,' he said.

Tully did not point out that there would only be one try, but then he did not have to. Besides, no matter how close they were as friends, when they were at sea Nathan had never known him to question an order. He had often thought it might help sometimes, provided he was discreet about it.

Tully raised his voice. 'Hands to the braces! Prepare to wear ship!'

They fell off the wind and at once Nathan felt the fury of the Race. It hurled them about like a plaything, but the men were heaving on the braces, the bows coming round, the sails filling on the opposite tack. . . . And they were racing, almost flying, back towards the Nez. However, they had a little more sea room now, and though they were leaning far over to leeward, their motion was far easier with the Race behind them, the bows plunging deep into the swell and throwing the spray back along the length of the deck. Nathan's face was wet with it, his hat in his hand, his hair like strands of seaweed blowing to leeward . . . Not happy, exactly, but with a wild exhilaration that was almost akin to happiness. Later he knew he would regret this, if he lived that long.

He summoned the two lieutenants, Keppler and Cole, to the quarter-deck to tell them what he had in mind. Both were former naval officers, dismissed from the service for what might have been considered minor offences if they had not been serving under Old Jarvey at the time, and though he had not taken to them especially—they were both on the dull side and somewhat lacking in imagination—he had no option but to give them command of the guns, even though Mr Banjo and the master gunner, Mr Caine, were both far better gunners.

He looked at them now standing expectantly before him and wished it were not the case, but they were competent enough if you told them exactly what to do.

'I intend to come close across her stern and rake her with the starboard guns,' he told them. 'And then come up to leeward.' It would mean losing the weather gauge, but it was worth it for that one raking broadside if they could make every shot count. 'Reload double-shotted with round shot and grape—and this time, fire low.'

Even in the dim glow of the binnacle light he could see them frowning with the effort of taking this in.

'And Mr Cole, I would be obliged if you would have your men assist with the starboard guns.' They had rehearsed this many times in the waters off Jersey, working the guns both sides and singly. 'And prepare the men for boarding,' he added, before dismissing them. If that did not stimulate the imagination, nothing would.

And now here was Mr Banjo, respectfully awaiting his attention, though inwardly Nathan knew he would be seething with impatience.

'Request permission to fire the bowchasers, sir.'

The bowchasers were Banjo's special concern. Unlike the rest of the guns, they were loaded with round shot and they would at least add to the confusion as the French crew sought to get back on course.

'Very well,' he said.

They were past the Nez now and closing rapidly, but the other ship was moving too, if not so fast. He watched carefully to see if she would wear and come back at them, in which case he would be forced to change his tactics, but no, her bows were still turned towards the distant hulk of the Cap de Flamanville. Did she even know the *Falaise* was coming up on them? She might think they were halfway to Alderney by now. He was about to send to Banjo to hold his fire when both guns went off almost simultaneously. So be it. If they did not know already, they did now. But he felt rushed into making a decision he might regret. He crossed to the weather rail, searching for the other ship. And there she was, falling off the wind, and unless she planned to run onshore that could only mean she was turning to meet them.

'Starboard your helm!' he roared, and then as the bows swung further to leeward: 'Fire as they bear, Mr Keppler.'

They were crossing the enemy stern at an acute angle and at a distance of about two cables' lengths, perhaps less. His guns would be able to fire a rippling broadside while she was still wearing, but then they would have to reload. He had the usual qualms about making the wrong decision, but too late now.

The first gun fired, and then the others as they came to bear. The smoke blew back on them, darkening the night and masking whatever damage they might have caused, but at that range, with the other ship heeled right over towards them, the chain shot would sweep her deck like grape. But she was still coming round, and now they were taking fire themselves, the fierce stabs of flame through the smoke, the ships so close now Nathan could see the white faces of the officers at the stern. Their gundeck was steeply canted and their guns would have to be at maximum elevation.

Nathan looked down the length of his own gundeck and could see no sign of the mayhem he could have expected from flying splinters, which meant most of their shot had either ploughed into the lower part of the hull or gone straight into the sea. But his own gun crews were still struggling to reload. It seemed to be taking them a lot longer than it had in all those months of practice in the waters off Jersey, but then no-one had been firing back at them.

He returned his gaze to the other ship. She was still coming round and there was a single burst of flame from one of her bowchasers. A few moments more and her starboard broadside would bear. His mind was filled with options, all poor. Continue on his present course, wear with her, and run back for the Nez?

But then he knew exactly what he had to do.

'Port your helm!' he roared, and then: 'Prepare to board!'

The bows swung to starboard, and they were heading straight at her. He could hear the shouts of alarm as they realised what he was about, but there was nothing they could do, the two ships barely yards from each other now.

'Brace yourselves, lads!' he heard Tully shout, and then the shock through the whole length of the hull as they ploughed into her just abaft her starboard bow, their own bowsprit tearing through her fore course, and the two ships like two giant stags with their horns locked, struggling for advantage. But both ships still had way on them, and they were grinding along each other's side, snapping spars like branches in a storm, a mass of canvas and cordage hurtling down to the decks.

Nathan saw his boarders leaping from rail to rail; more men running along the bowsprit and dropping down onto the enemy deck, others swinging down from the yards. He had thirty soldiers aboard, men of the Jersey militia, given him by d'Auvergne in lieu of marines, and they fired a disciplined volley and then clambered over the rail with their bayonets, but most of his men were like savages, armed with pistols and cutlasses, tomahawks, pikes, and whatever else came to hand—belaying pins, lengths of chain—and nothing disciplined about them at all, just a wild rush up the cant of the enemy deck, stumbling over dead and wounded.

They had practised boarding over the last few months, using an old hulk from the Saint Helier shipyards as the enemy, and he was sure it had been more organised than this, but again, no-one had been fighting back. They were firing at him now. He felt the wind of it at his ear and raised his eyes to the enemy tops. He could see nothing but sails and night sky, but they could probably see less. Then the flash of musket fire. Only then did he realise he had neglected to arm himself. He had taken one of the Ferguson rifles for his personal use and it would have come in handy now. He cursed Kidd, who should at least have brought him his sword and his pistols. He tried not to think about it—if he was hit, he was hit—but he looked to his own tops to see if they were firing back. He should have marines up there, but he had no marines, only the Jersey militia, and climbing the rigging was not in their contract. A handful of topmen were lashing the yards together so the ships would not drift apart, though the rigging was already so closely intertwined, this was the least of their troubles, and the wind was pushing both ships towards the shore.

Tully was shouting in his ear. 'We must take in the courses!'

'Yes, yes, carry on.'

Always a useful standby at times like this. Carry on.

A grenade fell at his feet with a hissing fuse and he stooped to pick it up and threw it over the larboard side. Perhaps he should have thrown it back. Another ball whipped past his head close enough to make his ear sing. Be damned to this, he thought.

'The ship is yours, Mr Tully,' he said. 'I am joining the boarders.'

'Take my sword,' said Tully. 'If you must.'

Nathan could not see his expression in the dark, but he knew it would be between resigned and disapproving. He took the proffered sword with an embarrassed thank-you and used the mizzen shrouds to hoist himself onto the rail. It was a mere step onto the other ship and he jumped down onto the deck, but had barely taken a step when he slid on a patch of blood. He was climbing up and wiping his palm on his jacket when a French marine came at him with a levelled bayonet before falling to the deck, though it was for another reason than someone else's blood.

Nathan turned to see George Banjo at his side with a levelled pistol and smelt the burnt powder. He wondered, not for the first time, where he had come from. When last seen he had been with the bowchasers.

But now there was another man coming at him—with a sword this time. He parried the blow and by way of a riposte punched him in the face with his left fist. He staggered back against the binnacle and by its light Nathan saw that he wore an officer's uniform. He knocked aside his sword and pulled him to his feet.

'This is madness,' he told him, repeating it in French for his better instruction. 'C'est de la folie.'

The Frenchman seemed to agree, but Mr Banjo was pressing the point of a cutlass into his neck.

'You are the captain?' Nathan enquired, though he seemed a bit on the young side, even for a captain of corvettes.

'Lieutenant, second class,' the man said. 'The captain is dead.'

Nathan looked about him. There seemed to be no-one else alive on the quarterdeck besides the two of them and Mr Banjo. A lot of bodies, though. He looked down the French gundeck. Chaos still, but as far as he could make out, more of his lot than theirs, and they had their backs to the sea, crowded against the weather rail.

'Call on them to throw down their arms,' he instructed the French offi-cer. 'There is no point in losing any more lives.' Though how the fellow would make himself heard above the racket they were making was quite another matter.

The man nodded, and Mr Banjo took the cutlass from his throat. It had drawn blood, and Nathan saw the dark stain on his white stock.

And then it was over, as suddenly as it had begun. The men on the rail were dropping their weapons and raising their arms in surrender, and the Jersey militia, discernible by their red jackets, were singing something ribald that Nathan did not know. Possibly the Jersey national anthem.

Both ships were in more danger from the sea than from each other. But now they had the sea to worry about, for they were dangerously close to the breakers.

'Work with us and we will put you and your men ashore,' he told the lieutenant who looked once towards the shore and then nodded in urgent agreement.

Nathan took him kindly by the elbow and led him forward. Then he barked a series of orders, first in English, then in French, and invited the French lieutenant to repeat them. He did not need much urging, for now it was a different kind of battle: French and English united in a desperate fight for survival, seizing spars to pole the ships apart and then heaving on the braces to claw away from that hungry shore. More men in the tops try-ing to restore order to the chaos aloft. The *Falaise* seemed in better shape, and even with her smaller crew she was already pulling away, her bows pointed towards the open sea. They made it past the Cap de Flamanville with a cable's length to spare.

Nathan looked at the French lieutenant. He was sitting down on one of the quarterdeck cannon with his head slumped between his shoulders and one leg stretched out straight before him. He had a splinter wound in his thigh that had lost him a lot of blood and he seemed exhausted. In fact, all of the Frenchmen seemed exhausted, more so than Nathan might have expected after a short battle. Many of them were sitting or lying on the deck, all the fight knocked out of them. Their captain and first lieutenant had been killed in that first broadside off the Nez de Jobourg, it appeared, and the crew seemed to have little appetite for renewing the conflict. The deck had been strewn with bodies when his men had boarded, the timbers greasy with blood. It still was, despite the sand that had been liberally sprinkled over them, and Dr Drew and his loblolly boys were working with their French counterparts on treating the wounded below, though the dead still lay more or less where they had fallen.

Looking down at the bodies from his vantage on the quarterdeck, Nathan felt a familiar sense of remorse. But it was an indulgence to dwell upon it, the suspect guilt of the recurrent killer.

He asked his clerk the time. A quarter past three. Barely fifty minutes since they had fired the first broadside. So impossibly short a time for so much violence and death and destruction. He would have said three or four hours at least, and yet it had gone in a flash. How long was a flash? Fifty minutes apparently. The time it took to brew a cup of coffee on Kidd's little stove. Time was not to be trusted. It was not consistent.

'I think it is time we broke out the rum,' he said.

They did not make the same fetish of rum in the French navy, but they had plenty of wine and brandy, and the captain's steward brought a bottle of cognac up for them to share.

They both needed it, the lieutenant probably more than Nathan. His name was Letellier, he revealed, and he was from Le Havre, where the ship had been built. He was as astonished as Nathan by the similarity between the two ships—in fact, his captain had thought at first she must be French—and now they discovered they were sister ships—the *Aurore* she was called, meaning 'dawn,' in the sense of the Revolution being a new dawn for mankind, he explained to Nathan, in case he did not know. The *Falaise* had originally been called the *Mutine*, which translated as 'rebellion against authority.' They were even more astonished by the coincidence of meeting up at dead of night off the coast of Cotentin.

'And what were you doing there?' Nathan got in first, 'if it is not to betray a confidence.'

The lieutenant seemed glad of the opportunity to unburden himself. They had, he said, been fighting under a serious handicap after an encounter with an English frigate off the west coast of Ireland, which had left twelve of their crew dead or wounded and the rest driven to the point of exhaustion after a long chase across the Celtic Sea and up the Channel. And then, within a few miles of safety under the guns of Cherbourg, they had run into a British squadron. The captain had decided to brave the Alderney Race only to encounter their dark shadow waiting for them at the far end, though the French lieutenant did not quite put it like that. He probably thought it was impolite. He did not care to ask Nathan what he was doing there, but he did nervously remind him of his promise to put them ashore.

'I *will* put you ashore,' Nathan agreed, 'but not here.'

He needed to give Cadoudal and his men time to find a place of safety, if there was such a thing, before the lieutenant reported to the French authorities and they came to their own conclusions as to what the *Falaise* was doing off the tip of the Cotentin peninsula at dead of night.

The two ships continued to follow the line of the coast until shortly before dawn, when Nathan decided it was safe to land them on a deserted stretch of sandy beach to the south of Carteret. Firstly, however, they buried the French dead in a short ceremony using the tricolour from the stern of the *Aurore*—thirty-three of them, including those killed in the earlier encounter, not counting the captain and the first lieutenant, who Letellier decided to take with them for burial ashore. There were almost twice as many wounded, the least serious of whom were lowered into the boats with the rest of the crew. Nathan had lost just five men killed and nine wounded, all in those frenzied few minutes of hand-to-hand fighting.

It took three trips to ferry them all ashore, Letellier being among the last to leave. He looked like a corpse himself in the pale dawn light. They shook hands and Nathan gave him back his sword. He was nineteen years old.

They reached Gorey halfway through the afternoon watch after making a long detour to the south to come back on the opposite tack, the wind still in the west-south-west and freshening. Two battered ships for the price of one. The rigging of the *Aurore* was a shambles and the bows of both vessels would need some work, but it could have been a lot worse, Nathan thought, when he had a proper chance to take stock.

They moored some way out in the bay, it being low tide, but he knew d'Auvergne would be watching through his glass and wondering how the *Falaise* had succeeded in duplicating herself in the short time since she had left Gorey. Indeed, they had scarcely moored when they saw the pinnace coming out from the shore with the blue ensign d'Auvergne still used, though he was no longer a rear-admiral. It did not bring d'Auvergne, however, but the Swedish Knight, back from his trip to England.

Nathan told him the story over coffee laced with rum in the stern cabin, more or less as it had happened, only skipping a few details that he thought might not resound to his credit. Smith seemed pleased enough— he would probably be angling for a share of the prize money, though he was not officially in a position to do so—but in any case, he had doubled the size of his fleet, if only they could find enough men to crew her. However, he seemed oddly distracted, as if forcing himself to be more interested than he was, and finally Nathan asked him how his recent trip to England had gone, thinking it must have gone badly.

'Very well,' he nodded, as if to reassure himself. 'Very well, indeed.' Then, after a short pause, 'I have seen a vision of the future, and it is under the sea.'

Nathan inclined his head politely. Smith was given to making oblique remarks of this nature and he tended not to take them too seriously, but then perhaps he should, given what he had said about Louise de Kirouac.

Smith leaned forward and gazed at Nathan with the intensity of a prophet seeking a disciple. 'I am speaking of submarines, sir, if you know my meaning?'

Nathan nodded warily. He had heard of submarines. They had been around for a long time as an idea—rather like flying machines—and some of them had actually been built, though he was not sure how well they worked. They seemed to go up and down all right, if only for a few feet, but not to move in any other direction, which rather limited their usefulness, Nathan would have thought, as a weapon of war, if not as a toy for sportsmen to play with, or children in a lake.

'I have had the privilege of meeting the man who is making them,' Smith went on. 'He is an American by the name of Fulton, and I believe I have persuaded him to come to Jersey to further his experiments.'

'You met him in London?' enquired Nathan, while he struggled to take this in, and assess what it might mean to him personally.

'No. I did not go to London,' said Smith. 'I was in Paris.' As if this was the most natural thing in the world, in the middle of a war with France, and he had just popped over there for a day or two to take in the sights. 'Incognito, of course,' he added with a smile. 'Mr Fulton has been working for the French government, but there has been a cooling in their relations of late. He does not feel properly appreciated, so I have put to him the advantages of working for us. Interesting man, full of ideas, lots of energy. And yet he has had no formal training as an engineer. He was an art student when he went to France. Wanted to paint landscapes. Ended up building a submarine. Is that not extraordinary?'

Nathan agreed that it was.

'Well, I have invited him to Jersey to build one for us,' Smith went on, as if this too was entirely routine. 'My colleagues in the Admiralty are sceptical, but believe me, it is an invention that could play a vital role in the defeat of Bonaparte—and you and I, sir, are going to be at the beating heart of it.'

At the time Nathan was not at all sure what he meant, but later, when he did, he would be glad he had used the word 'at' and not 'in'.

Chapter 10

The Assassins

'You know what he calls us?' demanded the man Nathan had been told to call Mr Francis. 'Assassins. Submarine assassins.'

Mr Francis was not his real name. His real name was Fulton—Robert Fulton—and he and Nathan had come to know each other tolerably well over the past few months, but Nathan had been instructed to call him Mr Francis for reasons of security, and he was perfectly happy to do so until he was instructed to call him something else. That was the way things were under the present chain of command. Anyone of any importance had a *nom de guerre*, as did quite a few people of no importance at all. He probably had one himself, though no-one had told him what it was yet.

'That is the way he is, Old Jarvey,' said Nathan, for they were talking of the First Lord of the Admiralty. 'He is rude to everyone under the rank of sovereign, and that is only because the king keeps well out of his way. I shouldn't worry about it.'

'Oh, I am not the least bit worried,' declared the American. 'In fact, I think it is quite apposite. I had thought of calling my *Nautilus* a *killer* submarine—as opposed to one that simply explores the depths of the ocean—but it did not translate so well into the French.'

Again, Nathan made no comment. As far as he was aware, the object in question had not managed to kill anyone during its short life in the French navy, and as it had only managed a descent of twenty-five feet, the depths of the ocean remained as untroubled by its activities as the enemies of the French nation. It had been dismantled by its designer and sold for scrap metal shortly before he left France, though his detractors said it had foundered on its last dive in the River Seine, never to rise again.

He peered over the rail of the *Falaise* to where the inventor's latest creation lay almost submerged in the choppy waters off the Kent coast, attached to the corvette by a long length of cable, though not long enough in Nathan's view. It was known as a torpedo, named after a species of stingray, though it was also known by its creator, for rather more obscure reasons, as a 'coffer'. In appearance, when you could see it clearly enough, it was not unlike a large coffin, some twenty feet long and weighing about two tons, with a hull of caulked timber and a wedge-shaped bow and stern. The hull was lined with lead and covered with tarred canvas that rendered it more or less waterproof, though this was about to be put to the test. At present it was ballasted with leather bags filled with water so that most of the hull lay under the surface, and Nathan's present concern was that if the waves became much choppier, it might sink entirely.

This was nothing, however, to his concern that the ten kegs of gunpowder that had been packed into its hull might explode prematurely, destroying not only the torpedo but also the *Falaise* and a not insignificant section of the Kent coast, taking with it the former First Lord of the Treasury, Mr William Pitt, his niece, Lady Hester Stanhope, Sir Sidney Smith and his brother Spencer, and a number of senior Admiralty officials, who were watching the exercise from Walmer Castle, perched on a small eminence just above the shore.

'What do you think they are they waiting for?' Fulton-Francis demanded, gazing in that direction.

'I expect they are waiting for Billy Pitt,' said Nathan. 'As is usually the case.'

Walmer Castle had been built during the reign of Henry VIII to repel a French invasion, but like Gorey, in Jersey, its only experience of action had been during the English Civil War when it had surrendered twice in a matter of weeks—once to the forces of the king, and once to the forces of Parliament. Now it served as the official residence of the warden of the Cinque Ports, though its current occupant still spent much of his time in London angling to get his old job back as the king's first minister. Lately, it had become the centre of clandestine operations against the French Republic, nominally under Pitt's leadership, but effectively controlled by

Sir Sidney Smith, who now appeared to find Gorey 'too remote' for his needs, by which he presumably meant too far from London, where all the decisions were made.

Nathan had no objection to the change of location, Jersey having lost much of its appeal since Louise had quit the isle. His new role was to assist Fulton-Francis in testing what Smith called his 'infernal machines' in the waters off the Kent coast, though this was the first practical demonstration before spectators. Anchored about a mile offshore, just off the western end of the Goodwin Sands, was an old, unmanned brig called the *Flying Fish*, which Nathan had rescued from the breaker's yard and was now destined to be the target ship, in honour of which his crew, with the gallows humour that passed for wit in the maritime world, had rechristened the *Frying Fish*. To replicate the conditions of a real attack, she should have been moored closer to the shore, with the *Falaise* further out to sea, but if the torpedo missed there was a danger it would run up onto the beach and explode at the foot of the castle walls, so the positions had been reversed. The large amount of shipping moored in the Downs between the Goodwin Sands and Deal was effectively prevented from approaching the danger area by a fresh westerly breeze, and the *Aurore*, now under Tully's command, was stationed off South Foreland to prevent the incursion of any ships from the other direction. Even so, the delay was making the inventor nervous, and this had transmitted itself to Nathan and various other members of the crew. A lot depended on calm—calm operators, calm sea—and as far as Nathan was concerned, the sooner the demonstration was over the better. There would be a massive bang, the *Frying Fish* would be well and truly fried, and they could all go home for dinner.

Unfortunately, they were still waiting for the signal from the shore, and they were now more than halfway through the forenoon watch. He supposed ten in the morning was a little early for Mr Pitt, especially after a night on the bottle. When Nathan had met him up at the castle, shortly after the summons from Smith, he had been shocked by his appearance. The former minister had always had a weakness for drink, but it had finally taken its toll, no doubt aggravated by his resignation from high office. The official duties of the warden were negligible; his niece Lady Hester saw to all the domestic arrangements, including the entertaining; his clandestine operations against the French were mostly handled by the

Smith Brothers; and Fulton and Nathan ran the practical side of things with the infernal machines. There was nothing for Pitt to do but drink, so he drank.

Nathan watched the submarinist covertly as he waited for the signal from the shore. Despite his misgivings about the purpose and efficacy of his inventions, he found Fulton engaging enough as a person, though of course you had to accept that he was barking mad. This was probably true of all inventors. They had to believe in the impossible or they would not be inventors. They also had an exceptional degree of self-belief, which was all very well, but in Nathan's view it was always useful to retain a level of self-doubt, or at least the self-knowledge to know when you were talking cobblers. This facility seemed to be completely lacking in Mr Fulton-Francis.

Nathan himself was something of an inventor. He had invented a machine for exploring the universe which he called a spaceship, and which was propelled by magnets, rather like sails, moved by the invisible magnetic currents, just as more conventional ships were propelled by the trade winds. In his imagination, Nathan navigated this craft through the universe, descending upon such of its planets, moons, and other astral bodies as appealed to him and having intercourse with their inhabitants. This helped pass the time when nothing much else was happening—a frequent condition when you were at sea. One day, he hoped to write a novel about it. But he would never have attempted to explain the workings of this machine to another human being, outside the realms of fiction, much less expect them to cough up the money to build it. Apart from anything else, he would have been worried that they might have ostracised him from society, or even had him confined to an asylum. Fulton-Francis seemed to have no such reservations. Nathan supposed you had to admire him for this.

He was somewhat less admiring of Fulton's willingness to sell himself and his inventions to the highest bidder. He had told Nathan that he was the son of poor Irish immigrants who lost their farm in Pennsylvania when they could no longer pay the mortgage, so Nathan supposed he had as good a reason as any to better himself at the expense of others, especially those who had more money than sense. Or the vision to recognise genius, as Fulton might prefer to put it. He had come to England as a young man back in the 1780s, ostensibly to study painting, but he was caught up in the canal mania of the time and began to design earth-digging machines and tugboats powered by steam, attracting wealthy patrons, such as the manufacturer Robert Owen and the Duke of Bridgewater.

For one reason or another, nothing seemed to have worked out for him, so in 1797, in the middle of the last war between Britain and France, he had taken himself off to Paris and offered his services to the French Minister of Marine who had provided the funds to build his first submarine—the *Nautilus*—with a view to using it against the British fleet. Fulton claimed that the initial trials were promising, but then a new Marine Minister had been appointed who was far more sceptical of the notion. At any rate, the funding had dried up and Fulton came back to Britain and offered his services to the British navy. He said nothing of his recruitment by Sir Sidney Smith in Paris, but Smith was certainly his mentor now. Others, notably the Earl Saint Vincent and Admiral Lord Keith, thought him something of a charlatan, Nathan had heard, but Fulton did not seem overly perturbed by this. He had been educated by Quakers and claimed to be a pacifist, arguing that his submarines would prove so destructive that if every nation had them, it would make war unthinkable. Nathan perceived certain flaws in this logic, but he did not pursue the matter. On the whole he rubbed along with him pretty well, provided he did not have to take him too seriously.

'There is the signal!' Fulton exclaimed, looking towards the shore where a flag had been run up on one of the turrets.

'Pass the word for Mr Banjo,' Nathan instructed Mr Keppler.

But Mr Banjo was already standing by, waiting for orders.

He had been the first member of the crew to volunteer to help the inventor with his experiments—and his interest in ordnance and explosives had swiftly advanced him to the role of chief assistant. Unfortunately, from his point of view, Fulton's new submarine was still confined to the drawing board. Either Pitt had his doubts about its effectiveness, or lacked the funds to build the vessel, which was a good deal bigger and more complicated than the one he had built for the French.

Instead, Fulton was obliged to use a ship's boat as the delivery vehicle, ballasted so that the gunwales were barely above the surface of the water. At night, in a real attack, the crew would wear dark clothes and have their faces blackened, none of which was deemed necessary for the purposes of today's demonstration. All that was required was to tow the torpedo into position behind the ship's gig, release it at the appropriate point, and row back as fast as possible to the *Falaise* while it drifted down onto the target and blew it to pieces.

'Which should not be beyond our limited resources,' Fulton had professed confidently to Nathan when they had emerged from the planning meeting at Walmer Castle.

He looked a mite less confident now, Nathan thought, as he watched him climb down to join Mr Banjo and his four crewmen in the gig. He had expressed some concern about the state of the weather, which was a little overcast, but no more than was normal for an English summer's day. The sea was a little on the choppy side, but nothing like as bad as it could be in the vicinity of the Goodwin Sands, and the tide was doing more or less what you expected it to do at any day of the year, ebbing and flowing without reference to the needs of the human race, much less inventors. At present it was flowing, which was what they wanted it to do. This did not diminish Nathan's own anxieties, but he had been reluctant to put them into words for fear of being thought a Jeremiah. He was glad to see the back of the torpedo, however, as it was towed steadily towards the target.

The explosive was to be detonated by a clockwork device which fired a small charge of powder, in much the same way as a flintlock. Fulton would set this in motion at a distance of about four hundred yards, before releasing the weapon and making his escape. Time and tide would do the rest. In theory. Fulton had estimated that with the tide at its present rate of flow, the torpedo would reach the target in approximately seven minutes and attach itself to the ship's cable by means of a grappling hook, which projected out from its blunt bow.

Nathan entertained serious doubts about all of this, but Fulton had explained that even if the torpedo did not run directly into the brig, the force of the explosion would sink it at a distance of at least two hundred yards. If the charge inexplicably failed to detonate, the torpedo would drift harmlessly onto the Goodwin Sands, where it could be recovered later. Some of his present anxiety could be put down to the fact that with the delay in starting the exercise, the Sands were now almost underwater, but Nathan estimated that he still had about half an hour before they were completely covered by the tide.

The gig had now reached its station—a distance of about two cables' lengths from the brig. Nathan watched through his glass as the torpedo was hauled up alongside the gig for Fulton to scramble aboard and start the clockwork, which was in a waterproof container sealed with a cork. He experienced a tense few moments before Fulton climbed back into the gig, which cast off and began to row furiously back towards the *Falaise*.

The torpedo began to drift slowly down towards the target. Nathan could barely see it above the surface of the water, and soon he lost it altogether. Seven minutes went by. Eight, nine . . . The brig was still bobbing composedly at its mooring. Nathan could see no sign of the torpedo. At ten minutes the gig was back, and Fulton joined him at the rail.

'Can you see it?' he enquired anxiously.

Nathan could not see it.

Fulton scanned the area with his glass.

'I cannot understand it,' he murmured.

Nathan made no comment.

'Either the clockwork has stopped,' said Fulton, 'or the priming powder has got wet. Conditions are not ideal.'

They rarely were, Nathan reflected. That was the problem with the sea.

'So what now?' he ventured.

'I suppose we must try to recover it,' said Fulton doubtfully.

'They are signalling from the tower,' said Mr Cole, who had been appointed signals officer.

Among the distinguished guests watching the demonstration was Captain Home Riggs Popham, commander of the squadron blockading the Channel ports. He was another inventor. He had recently invented a new signalling system to replace the old one, which had fallen into French hands. Like Fulton's infernal machines, it was still in the experimental stage.

'What does it say?' asked Nathan, after a long silence.

Mr Cole was leafing through a book of instructions.

'I do not know, sir,' he confessed miserably. 'I cannot find it in the book.'

'If there is no flag for a particular instruction, you are supposed to spell it out,' said Mr Keppler, who interested himself in such matters and rather resented Mr Cole's new status as signals officer.

'Well, I am damned if I can spell it,' said Mr Cole irritably. 'Begging your pardon, sir,' he added for Nathan's benefit.

'I imagine it says, What the fuck is going on,' offered Nathan. He turned to Mr Fulton: 'What do you suggest we tell them?'

While Fulton pondered this, Nathan asked if there was a flag for 'Stand by'. Mr Cole consulted the book.

'Can we go any closer?' asked Mr Fulton.

Nathan sighed. 'How close can we go without it blowing us up?' he wanted to know.

'Oh, there is no danger of that,' Mr Fulton contended. 'If it has not gone off already, I do not see how it can.'

'Even so,' Nathan persisted.

'Well, I would say about—half a mile?'

'We are about that already,' said Nathan. But he ordered the yards hauled around and they moved a little closer. They still could not see the torpedo.

'If we had been on schedule, it would have drifted onto the Goodwin Sands,' Fulton complained.

The Sands were now completely submerged by the tide.

'So where else could it be?' Nathan feared he already knew the answer.

'Well, it will most likely drift through the Downs,' Fulton advised. 'Or out to sea.'

'There are at least three hundred ships moored in the Downs,' Nathan pointed out. He was trying to keep his temper. It never helped to lose your temper, even with a man who had invented a machine that could cause more damage to British commerce and to the British navy, and to himself, personally, than the entire French navy and army combined, even under Napoleon Bonaparte.

'Well, obviously, if we can find it, I will defuse it,' said Fulton.

'Bring the cutter alongside,' Nathan ordered.

'They are signalling again,' Cole said.

'Is there a signal for affirmative,' Nathan asked.

'Yes. A white cross on a red background,' said Cole happily.

'Well, signal that, then.'

'But—what are we affirming?' Mr Cole enquired miserably.

'Their last signal,' said Nathan.

'But I could not understand their last signal,' the officer pointed out.

'It does not matter,' Nathan said. 'Affirmative always does the trick. If they signal again while I am away, find a signal that says Advise.'

'While you are away?' Mr Keppler repeated. He looked alarmed. 'Sir? Where are you . . . ?'

'To find the torpedo, in the cutter,' said Nathan.

The Downs was the most crowded anchorage on the south coast. If the torpedo blew up in the middle of it, there would be a massive inquiry, and he would be held responsible. They would not blame Pitt or Smith because it would be harmful to national morale. As for Fulton, he was an American who had recently been in the service of the French, and no-one would dare admit that he had been put in charge of a deadly weapon off the south coast of England. Besides, he did not exist officially. Nathan was the obvious scapegoat. He suspected this was why he had been chosen in the first place.

They found the torpedo in less than an hour. The grappling hook had caught up on the cable of an East Indiaman on the outer edge of the anchorage. None of the crew had noticed yet. The coffer was barely breaking the surface of the water, but they put a line around Fulton and sent him aboard to defuse it. An officer aboard the East Indiaman shouted down to know what the blazes was going on. Nathan considered telling him that a highly explosive secret weapon belonging to the navy had gone astray, just to teach him some manners, but in the end he said he was recovering one of his ship's boats. Fulton took out the cork and delicately removed the clockwork. Then they towed the torpedo back to the *Falaise*.

Nathan put on his dress uniform and took Fulton with him to report to the castle.

'Well, that was all a bit of a shambles,' Smith greeted him cheerfully. 'What went wrong?'

Fulton embarked on a lengthy explanation, but Smith cut him short. 'These things happen,' he said. 'I expect it will be all right on the night.'

His lack of concern puzzled Nathan a little. He was noted for his indifference in the face of disaster, but he had invested quite a lot of personal prestige in this venture. He had anticipated a storm, or at least a serious sulk.

'What did Mr Pitt think about it?' asked Fulton anxiously.

'Nothing,' said Smith. 'Lady Hester was a bit scathing, but she always is. Pitt wasn't here. He has been unavoidably detained in London. Come with me,' he said to Nathan. 'I want to talk to you in private.'

Nathan followed him wearily up the stairs to his apartment in one of the turrets, expecting a delayed explosion. But Smith's manner did not change.

'There has been a much worse balls-up in France,' he said when they were alone, 'but it might work to our advantage.'

He poured them each a bumper of Madeira and told him the story. The agents they had been landing in Normandy had all been arrested by the French police.

'What—all of them?' Nathan was astonished. He had not expected it to end well, but not this badly. 'Even Cadoudal?'

'Cadoudal, Pichegru, Moreau—all of them. All the big fish, all the little sprats. Cadoudal was the last. He went on the run, but they cornered him in Paris. He shot two gendarmes, but they got him in the end. He's being held in the Temple with the others. I don't give much for their chances.'

'But . . .' Nathan was lost for words. 'How?'

Smith shrugged. 'I do not know all the details. We have only just heard. From what we know, they picked up one of the agents in one of the safe houses and he cracked under pressure. Gave the rest of them away. But there is more.' He filled his glass from the bottle.

Nathan was shaking his head, but not at the indulgence. He was wondering how Smith had persuaded himself that this could work to their advantage.

'When Bonaparte heard what they were plotting, he took it personally,' Smith went on.

'Well, he would, would he not?' Nathan put in. 'They were planning to kill him.'

'Only as a last resort,' Smith objected. For the first time he looked rattled. 'The idea was to kidnap him and bring him back to Gorey. You know that. For God's sake, man, if anyone asks you about this, do not say there was any talk of assassination.'

Nathan forbore to remind him that it was he who had first mentioned it.

'We do not wish to be known as a bunch of assassins.' Smith lowered his voice as if there was the slightest danger of being overheard on top of a turret overlooking the English Channel. 'Especially not now.'

'Why not now, rather than at any other time?'

'Because Boney has dicked his nob and is set to be cast as the villain of this little drama, not us.'

'Dicked his nob?' Smith was fond of using thieves' cant and even if Nathan did not know the precise meaning, he could usually make a stab at it, but not on this occasion.

'Lost his head, thrown a fit, gone to Barking. He sent a troop of dragoons across the border into Germany to kidnap the Duc d'Enghien.'

He looked as if he expected Nathan to be more shocked by this than he was.

'Who is the Duc d'Enghien?' Nathan enquired.

'Louis Antoine de Bourbon,' Smith frowned at his ignorance. 'A prince of the royal blood. He would have been the Prince of Condé, had he lived.'

Nathan was puzzled. 'I thought you said they kidnapped him.'

'Yes, and then they killed him,' Smith announced with satisfaction. 'On Bonaparte's orders. He was taken to a chateau on the outskirts of Paris. Tried for treason by a bunch of colonels and shot by firing squad. In the castle moat.'

'*In the moat?* What, with a firing squad?' He wondered if one of Fulton's inventions had been involved. It seemed unlikely.

'Oh, for heaven's sake, Peake, it was a *dry* moat. But whether the moat was dry or not, you do not seem to grasp the significance of this. To send troops into a foreign country with whom you are not at war, kidnap a guest of the ruler, and murder him. In cold blood. Or even hot blood. Good God, man, it is beyond barbaric, do you not think?'

'Well, I suppose, but . . .' Privately, Nathan was thinking that sending secret agents into France to kidnap the head of state might be considered in a similar light, but it was probably better to leave this unsaid.

'It has yet to make the London journals, but the courts of Europe are in uproar,' Smith exulted. 'The King of Prussia, the Emperor of Austria, the Russian Tsar . . . The Holy Roman Empire is under his personal protection.'

Nathan must have looked as if he was wondering how the Holy Roman Empire came into it.

'Baden is part of the Holy Roman Empire,' Smith informed him helpfully. 'Baden is where the prince was living at the time—as a guest of the duke. And you know who the Duke of Baden is?'

Nathan confessed he did not. 'He is the son-in-law of the Tsar Alexander.'

'We have always agreed that Bonaparte is a creature of impulse,' Smith went on. 'And here is the proof of it.'

'When you say "we" . . . ?' Nathan submitted cautiously.

'You and I, sir. We may not have discussed it, but we are in perfect accord on the subject. You do not think so?' For Nathan was frowning sceptically. Smith dug into his desk and produced a plain sheaf of writing paper on which some words had been written.

'This is from your report, written at the request of Billy Pitt when you came back from Paris in ninety-five.'

Nathan looked at it. 'This is not my hand,' he said.

'No, it is a copy I had made, but they are your words, I believe, and remarkably prescient, I should say.'

'As to Bonaparte,' Nathan read, 'he is essentially an adventurer, driven almost entirely by personal ambition, though he does have a strong attachment to family and friends and a determined animosity towards those he perceives as his enemies, a permanent sense of blood feud. He never forgets a favour or forgives what he considers to be a slight.'

He remembered now. This was after the attempted coup of *Vendémiaire* in the autumn of 1795, when he had first encountered the young Bonaparte in Paris. He read on:

'He is a meticulous, even obsessive planner, but he requires his subordinates to follow his plans to the letter. The slightest divergence from them enrages him beyond reason. Associated with this is an ambiguous attitude towards convention. Like many who consistently break the rules, he requires others to follow them absolutely, in warfare and in society. The two things he most abhors, and fears, are subordinates who do not follow his exact orders and enemies who employ unconventional methods against him. He depends upon those who oppose him to follow the rules of warfare, of society, of God; in short, to do what they have always done, to fight as they have been trained to fight, to obey the conventional doctrines. Any deviation from this approach drives him to extremes of rage and frustration. It disturbs the balance of his mind. He loses his judgement and is driven to make rash decisions.'

'There you have it!' exclaimed Smith. 'That is our man.'

Nathan was astonished that he had ever written such a report. He must have been more affected by his experiences in Paris than he had thought at the time, or since. It was, he thought now, by no means accurate. Bonaparte was a much more complicated individual than was suggested here. He might fly off the handle at times, but he rarely allowed it to affect his judgement. He was much more composed than the report suggested, and much more dangerous.

'Where did you get this?' he demanded.

'From Billy Pitt,' said Smith. 'He had it among his private papers. I would say it informs many of his actions, especially now. It was to some extent behind his support of the kidnap plot. Even if it failed in its stated aims, it could not fail to provoke the target. To bring out the Corsican in him. *He loses his judgement and is driven to make rash decisions.* And so he has. It could give us the coalition we need. Prussia, Austria, and Russia in a Grand Alliance with Great Britain.'

'You think?' Nathan was doubtful.

'I do. And what is more, so does Billy Pitt. That is why he has stayed in London. Addington is useless as a war leader. The country needs Pitt—and Parliament will demand it gets him. I am going up to London tomorrow to cast my vote.'

Smith was still an MP. He was also Pitt's cousin, Nathan had discovered. He would probably be minister for war when he came back.

'So—no more submarines,' said Nathan with relief. He assumed Pitt would now have other priorities. Smith, too.

'On the contrary. They are the very thing. The unconventional methods that Bonaparte fears. They will enrage him beyond reason, especially as he considered them himself and then rejected them. I have proposed an all-out attack on the invasion fleet with all the infernal machines at our disposal.' His eyes gleamed as he thought of a more heroic way of putting it. 'We will light such a fire as will be seen across the whole of Europe.'

Chapter 11

The Infernal Machines

Through his Dollond glass in the foretop of the *Falaise*, Nathan watched the late-afternoon sunshine glinting on the helmets of the French cuirassiers drilling on the parade ground of what had become known as the Great Camp at Boulogne. Above them on the heights above the port and stretching inland as far as the eye could see were tents for up to sixty thousand soldiers of the French army. Similar, if smaller, camps were to be seen all along the coast, providing accommodation for an army of two hundred thousand men, including cavalry and artillery, with a fleet of over two thousand flatboats and barges to ferry them across the English Channel. According to the British journals, Bonaparte was to take personal command of the operation, which would secure the subjugation of Great Britain and its transformation into a republic on the French model—or a province of republican France, depending on which journal you read. His battle headquarters were said to be in the chateau of Pont-de-Briques, on the outskirts of Boulogne, though to date he had confined himself to a few short visits to make speeches and hand out medals for heroism during earlier campaigns. He had assured his troops that once they had landed, they would make short work of an army that could call upon fewer than the fifty thousand regulars based in the British Isles. Only the Royal Navy prevented a victory march on London. But they had been here for two years now, and the only marching they had done had been on the parade ground.

Thus far, Britain's response had been limited to a series of defiant editorials and mocking cartoons depicting Bonaparte's preparations, which were said to include barges powered by windmills, hot-air balloons, and even a tunnel under the English Channel. But all that was about to change. The British navy was about to go on the offensive, and with its own wondrous devices.

Since the failed demonstration off the Kent coast, Fulton had made a number of improvements to his infernal machines. Instead of the crude coffer aimed at the *Flying Fish*, he had developed a craft he called a 'torpedo-catamaran', based on the outrigger canoes of the South Sea islanders, ballasted with lead to make it ride low in the water, and with the explosive balanced on the platform between the two wooden hulls. Eighteen of these vessels were now available for an attack on the invasion fleet at Boulogne, each steered to its target by a lone helmsman equipped with a paddle and dressed in dark clothing to make him all but invisible to the enemy lookouts at night. After hooking the torpedo to the ship's cable, he would activate the firing mechanism before paddling away on the catamaran. Additionally, Fulton had invented a smaller device called a 'carcass', which was a copper-lined cask filled with gunpowder and combustible 'fireballs' and detonated by clockwork. These would be floated down to the target on the tide, like his earlier inventions, but they would be sent in pairs, linked together by a line that would snag on the bows or stern of the target vessel and bring them up on each side of the hull before they exploded. Rather more conventionally, Fulton's infernal machines were to be reinforced by three fireships, loaded with the usual combustible materials and explosives. Each would be guided towards the target by a skeleton crew who would set the clockwork timers before taking to the boats.

This deadly flotilla had been conveyed across the Channel by a squadron of frigates and was now standing by off the French coast, some two miles back from Nathan's advance guard, ready to move into position under cover of darkness. The overall command had been given to Admiral Lord Keith aboard the seventy-four-gun *Monarch*, with Sir Sidney Smith as his principal adviser on all matters infernal.

The setbacks that had befallen Smith's previous operations across the Channel had not diminished his enthusiasm for taking the war to the enemy. Indeed, he continued to argue that the Cadoudal conspiracy, despite failing in its immediate objectives, had caused Bonaparte to make a serious blunder and exposed him in his true colours as a murderous tyrant. However, there was no tangible sign of the grand coalition that had been anticipated as a result, and Bonaparte's power in France appeared to be greater than ever. After the exposure of the plot against his life, he was enjoying a surge in popular support. Even his more moderate critics had been rounded up by the police, and the alleged assassins had been put on trial and condemned to death. Louise was not among them, Smith told Nathan, though he claimed not to have heard from her since she had left Jersey. Georges Cadoudal, however, had been guillotined in Paris in July, going to his death with courage and dignity, according to Smith, and assuring the hostile crowd that they would now see how a Christian, a royalist, and a Breton could die.

Despite the arrest of so many of his agents, Smith still seemed remarkably well-informed about events in France. He had told Nathan that Josephine had been horrified by the decision to kidnap and execute the Duc d'Enghien and had pleaded with Bonaparte to change his mind, but had been told to mind her own business. He had known several days before the official announcement that Bonaparte had decided to change the constitution, turning France from a republic to an empire, and himself from First Consul to the Emperor Napoleon—the first emperor of the French since Charlemagne, over a thousand years since. His coronation was to be held before Christmas in the cathedral of Notre Dame. The pope was said to be lined up to place the imperial crown on his head, as his predecessor had crowned Charlemagne, and Josephine would be crowned empress. France would have a new royal family to replace the Bourbons.

Whatever Smith's opinion now, this was not the result he had hoped for when he had sent Cadoudal and his men into France, but he did not seem to have suffered any loss of prestige with his friends in government. Lord Melville, who had been brought in to replace Saint Vincent at the Admiralty, had made more funds available for the secret weapons that Smith confidently predicted would destroy Bonaparte's invasion fleets before they had even left their moorings.

Nathan continued to have his doubts about that, and even if they worked as well as Fulton predicted, he did not think that Boulogne was the right place to use them. There were some serious obstacles before the torpedoes could even reach their targets. Besides the forts and batteries on the cliffs, a double line of gunboats and brigs had been moored directly in front of the harbour entrance, with a great many guard boats and pinnaces rowing up and down at night, filled with armed men. Nathan's task was to prevent them from intervening while the fireships and the torpedoes were being manoeuvred into position. He had the *Falaise* and the *Aurore* at his disposal, and two gun-sloops, the *Roebuck* and the *Raven*, with a total of seven hundred sailors and marines, but he was under strict instructions to do nothing that would alert the French to the danger they faced. This effectively meant that his hands were tied until the first torpedoes exploded.

Nathan had expressed these concerns to Smith and Fulton. Neither seemed much bothered. Whatever the results of the raid, Smith said it would demonstrate to all of Europe that the British were not simply waiting for the French to invade—they were 'taking the war to the enemy'. This confirmed Nathan in his view that they were simply putting on a show to provoke Bonaparte into making another rash decision, and to aid Pitt in his mission to win an alliance with the Russians or the Prussians or the Austrians, or all three. At the same time, he had a suspicion that if the raid was a total fiasco and his superiors at the Admiralty needed someone to blame for it, he had once more been pushed to the front of the firing line.

The light was rapidly fading from the sky. Out to sea he could make out the sails of the blockading squadron against a bank of orange and purple cloud. Red sky at night was supposed to be the sailor's delight, but the barometer was falling and there was a slight swell running—there could be a storm on the way, but not soon enough to halt the attack. The ship's boats were drawn up on the weather side, so they would not be observed from the shore, and small arms and cutlasses were being handed out to the men selected to crew them.

Nathan had decided to command the boats himself. He had told his officers it was because he was the one whose head would be on the block if it all went wrong, particularly if a gun went off prematurely and alerted the French to an attack. But he knew it was more than that. He had an overwhelming sense of disaster, and he did not want to be standing helplessly on the quarterdeck of the *Falaise* when it happened. Better to be in the thick of it. Nelson had always felt the same, apparently, though his record of leading small boats in an attack on the enemy was not encouraging.

There was a cry from the lookout on the topmast. They were on their way.

Nathan climbed into the mizzen shrouds with his glass. Keith seemed to be bringing the whole squadron in. If the French were not already alerted to the possibility of an attack, they would be now. Perhaps he planned to use the conventional ships as a diversion while the infernals made their approach, but it was just as likely that his adviser had told him they were too far out to see the show.

Nathan could not entirely explain his antipathy towards Sir Sidney Smith. He had never tried to top it over him, or suggest they were anything but equal partners in a daring if somewhat irregular adventure. Smith even seemed to be quite attached to Nathan in his way. He claimed to respect him for his apparent indifference to promotion, or public acclaim.

'You are as susceptible to flattery and the allure of celebrity as an American backwoodsman,' he had declared.

Nathan might have wished for a different analogy, but the admiration seemed sincere enough. Nathan had protested that he was not in the least bit indifferent, but that he knew a lost cause when he saw one, and that if he did not bugger things up for himself, his mother could always be relied upon to do it for him. Smith had laughed and clapped him on the back and told him this was exactly what he meant. But Nathan knew they would never be friends. And if tonight's work turned out badly, he would have no hesitation in throwing Nathan to the wolves.

The fleet began to turn into the wind about a mile from the inshore squadron, but as they counter-braced the yards, three smaller ships continued towards them. These must have been the fireships, though unless you knew they were packed with explosives you would have taken them for ordinary gun-sloops or brigs. As they drew nearer, Nathan saw that each of them was towing six catamarans in a long line astern, but again, an uninformed viewer would have taken them for ship's boats, especially in the poor light. At least Nathan hoped so.

It was almost dark when the first ship reached the *Falaise* and came up alongside. He heard Fulton's voice hailing him from the stern. He sounded cheerful enough. But then he had reason to be. According to Smith, he had negotiated a bonus on his salary for every vessel he managed to destroy. Perhaps this was no different from the prize money awarded to the crew of a King's ship for every enemy vessel they captured, but it felt different to Nathan, and he was not alone in that. Lord Keith had been heard to remark that he did not see how it was any different from an intruder sneaking into your home, slitting your throat while you were asleep, and taking all your money before he set fire to the house. But the operation had been sanctioned by Lord Melville and Mr Pitt, so he did what he was told, like Nathan.

One by one the catamarans were drawn up to the side of the brig for their pilots to climb down and take up their positions. Nathan did not envy them. The sea had grown noticeably choppier and the waves were practically breaking over their heads. The same thing was presumably happening on the weather side of the *Aurore* and the *Raven*, though it was too dark now for Nathan to see that far. It was a new moon and shed very little light on the proceedings. Plenty of lights towards the shore, though, from the line of guardships and in the port beyond.

Now Fulton was lowering the carcasses into the water from the deck of the brig—presumably having set the clockwork timers. Nathan called out to ask when he would be ready to go.

'Any minute now,' came the distracted reply.

Any minute was not quite good enough, not with those timers ticking away.

Nathan ordered the ship's boats up from the stern and the crew began to descend hastily into them. He called out to Fulton again to say: 'Ready when you are.' Silence for a long moment. Several tons of explosive bobbing in the waves at the side of the ship. Then, finally: 'We are ready now.'

The first catamaran came drifting round the stern of the *Falaise*, just about visible in the light of the stern lantern. It barely broke the surface of the water, but Nathan could see the dark figure of the helmsman, attempting to steer it with his paddle. It caught the tide and began to move rapidly towards the shore. A second followed, but it was barely a few yards from the *Falaise* when it turned beam on to the waves. The pilot seemed to be struggling to bring the head round, and then a large wave swamped it.

Nathan called down to the gig to find out what was happening. No-one could tell him, but a minute or so later the dripping figure of the pilot was brought aboard.

'Bastard slid into the sea,' he said, presumably referring to the torpedo. 'Begging your pardon, sir.'

He heard Fulton call across from the brig.

'The waves are too high. I have lost two more of them over here.'

Nathan swore. 'How long before they explode?'

'Oh, the torpedoes will not explode,' Fulton replied a little tetchily. 'The operator sets the clockwork when he attaches it to the target. It is only the carcasses that are charged.'

'And where are the carcasses?' Nathan demanded.

'They are on their way,' said Fulton.

This was something, if he could be believed. 'Well, you had better send the fireships in,' he advised.

There was another long moment and then the first fireship began to move away from the *Falaise* and head towards the shore. Nathan watched it go with relief. He looked out towards the *Aurore* and the *Raven* and saw the same thing was happening there. It was time to join Mr Banjo in the cutter and set off with his flotilla of small boats. Their purpose was to stop the French from boarding the fireships before the crew set the clockwork timers and made their escape. They had scarce moved a hundred yards from the *Falaise*, however, when there was a large explosion from inshore. Then another. Nathan saw the line of French ships briefly highlighted, as if in a flash of lightning, but the explosion seemed to have occurred between them and the port. There were several more. He could see one of the fireships just ahead of them. The crew should have taken to the boats by now, but he could see no sign of them. Then the moon came out of cloud, and he saw a single boat, but it was not one of theirs. It was heading straight towards the fireship from the direction of the shore.

'Row for that boat,' he shouted. No point in keeping quiet now. It was like every bonfire night he'd ever been to rolled into one. In fact, the more noise they made, the better. It might divert the French from boarding. He could see now that it was a large pinnace, loaded with men. He pulled one of his pistols out of his belt, cocked the hammer, and took aim.

The instant he pulled the trigger the fireship exploded.

Chapter 12

The Arsonist

It was pitch black, blacker than night, and he concluded that he was deep underwater and probably drowning, if not drowned already. He struggled to move, to propel himself towards the surface, but his limbs would not respond. It felt as if something thick and heavy was wrapped around them, like seaweed or the tentacles of some monstrous beast, and it was keeping him trapped down there in the depths of darkness. Then he saw a light, a flicker of light, no more, like the pale glow of a lighthouse from far out to sea, or a wrecker's treacherous lantern, and he renewed his struggles to break out from whatever it was that had a hold upon him.

'*Allez-y, doucement. Ne vous dérangez pas.*' A distant voice from somewhere beyond the light. Then it grew in size and intensity until it filled his vision and within it there was a face, indistinct at first but then taking shape and substance as the face of a man, or a demon, depending on one's expectations of life, or indeed, death. The nose was bulbous and red, the lips thin and pale, the eyes somewhat bloodshot, and they looked down upon him with an expression of what might have been concern or malicious satisfaction. Again, it depended upon one's expectations of people. In Nathan's present state of being, a demon seemed more probable, but a demon of some maturity, not your youthful sprite, wearing an unfashionable grey wig and a blue uniform jacket. Naturally, it spoke French.

'*Calmez-vous, monsieur, vous avez eu un coup sur la tête.*'

A knock on the head. Yes. That would explain a great deal. Even as this information transmitted itself to the part of his brain that was still functioning, other more visual clues were being noted and subjected to analysis. The timber beams and lanterns, swaying somewhat dizzily above the demon's head, the canvas hangings, and above all, the foul stench alerted him to the probability that he was in the surgeon's cockpit on the orlop deck of a ship of war, or in one of the lower reaches of Hell, which some would find preferable.

'Where am I—who are you?' he enquired, considering it advisable to speak in English until he was better informed regarding his situation.

'You are in the *frégate Revanche, monsieur*, and I am a surgeon in the French marine.'

Startled, Nathan looked to see how many limbs he had left, if any. He lifted his arms. Both there; also hands. He attempted to raise his head to look down the length of his body to check the legs and feet but the dull pain that was behind his eyes increased to such an intensity that he thought better of it. He raised his hand to his head and felt the texture of a bandage.

'*N'ai pas peur, monsieur, vous êtes intact.*' The demon/surgeon attempted English again. 'Only it is the knock on the head. *Débris* from the ships of fire you send against us.' Sternly, and with a frown. Fireships were generally frowned upon by all navies. Within the rules of war perhaps, but only just.

It was coming back to him now. The fireships, the infernal machines, Fulton, Sir Sidney Smith . . . more visions of Hell. He had been in the cutter, pulling towards one of the fireships. Then the explosion. But he could remember nothing after that.

'How did I get here?'

'You were saved from the sea—by your servant, Monsieur Banjo.' The name, or some other memory, brought a smile to the doctor's lips.

'Banjo?' Nathan repeated, to give himself time to think about this. He knew who Monsieur Banjo was, but he had no memory of being in the sea, or saved from it.

'*Le nègre.* He is your servant, yes?'

No point in contradicting him—yet.

'Where is he?'

'I send for him in a moment. But please to be *tranquille, monsieur*. With the wound to the head, is important to be calm, you understand?'

Nathan promised to stay calm.

The surgeon was observing him carefully but not unkindly. 'So, who do I have the honour of addressing, *monsieur*?'

Nathan thought about it. To lie or not to lie? Safer to lie, usually, but he did not know what George Banjo had said. He told the truth for once. 'And you, *monsieur*?'

'Blanchett, *monsieur*, *à votre service*.' He briefly ducked his head. 'I will send for your servant.'

Nathan closed his eyes. He thought about where he was and how he had got here and where he might be going next. In normal circumstances, as a prisoner of war and a post captain, he might expect to be treated with respect and exchanged for a French officer of equal rank at the first opportunity, but the circumstances were not normal. It rather depended on how the French felt about Mr Fulton's infernal machines and how much damage they had done and how much blame might be attached to him for this. In the absence of Fulton and Smith, quite a lot, he suspected.

He heard a voice he recognised and opened his eyes.

'Hello, George,' he said. 'I hear you saved my life, again. How many times is that?'

'I am not counting,' said Mr Banjo. 'How do you feel?'

'Could be worse.'

Banjo himself looked his usual unruffled self. He was wearing a clean white shirt and white cotton ducks and his hair was tied back with a ribbon. He might never have been in a battle, or the water. Nathan marvelled, not for the first time, at how he managed it.

'How long have I been here?' he asked.

'Twenty-four hours, almost. It is now eight o'clock on Wednesday evening.'

Nathan put his hand to the bandage again and probed tentatively with his fingers, wincing as he felt a sharp jab of pain just above his left eye. A different pain from before.

'You were cut,' said George. 'Bad enough for stitches.'

'How many stitches?'

George regretted he could not say, but Nathan could feel them now through the bandage; not more than five or six, he calculated.

'And how are they treating you?' he asked, as if it was not apparent from his appearance.

'Well enough. I sleep in the sick bay and am permitted up on deck from time to time to take the air.' He considered Nathan thoughtfully. 'Is there anything I can do to make you more comfortable?'

Nathan thought about it. He would like something less hard to lie upon—he seemed to be on a plank, or an arrangement of chests. But his immediate priority was drink, and then food. He mentioned this. It seemed to be cause for amusement.

'I will see what I can find for you. But I will have to ask the doctor. I told them I was your servant. I thought it might help.'

'So I hear.'

'Also, I gave them your name. I was not sure if it was advisable—but they knew your rank, and if I said I did not know it would make them suspicious.'

'No reason why you should not.' Nathan hoped this was the case. He and Banjo were so used to lying, in the course of their professional activities, it felt uncomfortable to be telling the truth. But he had been right to give his real name to the doctor. 'Any more of us here?'

'No. I do not know what happened to the others—in the cutter—but unless they were picked up by our own people . . .'

'And the attack?'

'One French pinnace destroyed—in the same explosion that wrecked the cutter.'

'And that is all?' Nathan was astonished. This far exceeded even his most pessimistic expectations.

'That is what I have heard. One of the fireships exploded in the gap between two of the frigates—it might have caused some damage, but nothing serious. The third sailed right through the line and blew up just off the shore. I do not know what happened with the torpedoes. But they did not sink anything. I think most of them exploded in the sea, just off the shore, or on the shore itself.'

'None in the harbour?'

'No. Not that I have heard. The conditions were not ideal,' he added, with a strange formality, as if it was for him to offer an explanation of their failure. He was alone among the crew of the *Falaise* in being an advocate of Fulton and his machines. If there had been a submarine available, he would have been down in it. 'It blew up a gale in the early hours of the morning.'

Nathan had seen that coming; it was a pity it had not come earlier.

'And the French, what do they make of it all?'

A Gallic shrug. 'Here, on the *Révanche*, they seem to be more amused than anything. They say the British hold Guy Fawkes early this year.'

Amusement he could deal with, even mockery. Better than anger, certainly.

'They know about the torpedoes?'

'They know we were using something new. I think they found some of the carcasses that did not explode. I said all we were told was there was to be an attack with fireships and that we were to pick up any men we found in the water—French and English. But they will want to question you, I think. There is talk of taking you ashore. They do not know I speak French.'

Banjo had spent over a year in France as a prisoner of war and had taken the opportunity to add French to the several languages he spoke already. It would be an advantage if they remained in ignorance of this.

'Did they say where they are taking us?'

'I heard them speak of a castle—something like Pont-de-Briques?'

That would be Bonaparte's headquarters, just outside Boulogne.

'And are there any other prisoners that you are aware of?'

But before he could answer, the surgeon reappeared. George stepped back.

'Is it permitted for the captain to have something to drink?' he requested. 'And some food?'

It was permitted for the captain to have water and a little gruel. Nathan groaned but turned it into a groan of pain. It might be wise to appear weaker than he felt, but he saw the look Blanchett gave him and did not think he was fooled. Sure enough, in the wake of the gruel came the ship's captain to see how he was and to inform him that on the morrow he was to be sent ashore.

The captain's name was Brionne, and his manner was reserved but not openly hostile. Nathan asked if his servant might accompany him and was told he could, but Brionne would answer no other questions.

Nathan was assisted by Banjo and one of the surgeon's mates into the adjoining sick bay, where a cot was available for him, and he passed a reasonable night, considering. In the morning Blanchett came back to check on his condition and to tell him they were ready to take him ashore.

Banjo had dried his uniform and sponged down most of the stains, and he was able to dress without assistance, settling his hat somewhat gingerly on his bandaged head. He shook Dr Blanchett by the hand and thanked him for his ministrations. Then with a junior officer and two marine sentries in attendance, he made his way to the upper deck. The gale had just about blown itself out, but the sea was still restless, the sky mostly blue with a few high white clouds, the wind westerly.

A glance out to sea showed him the sails of three ships at not too far a distance. His inshore squadron, most probably. No sign of Keith's larger flotilla. He wondered if Tully was watching through his glass.

The captain had provided his own barge as transport and Nathan was handed down with a care he would have taken amiss if he had not been exaggerating his own feebleness.

As they approached the shore Nathan had the opportunity to view the invasion fleet which completely filled the harbour and lined both banks of the river for as far as he could see. It did not tell him much more than he had learned from the topmast of the *Falaise*, except that they were the real thing, not some Potemkin imitation, and they looked pretty much ready for sea. There were soldiers everywhere, but that was only to be expected. So far as he knew it was the largest concentration of troops in Europe.

A closed carriage was awaiting them on the quayside with a dragoon captain and four mounted troopers to escort them to wherever they were going. Nathan did ask, but the captain regretted he was not at liberty to say. It was a short journey, however, and when they were permitted to descend from the carriage, they found themselves in the forecourt of a modern-looking chateau, which, judging from the number of military officers striding about in elaborate uniforms, was almost certainly the Pont-de-Briques—Bonaparte's headquarters for the Army of England.

If the new emperor was in residence, he clearly did not intend to welcome them personally. Instead, they were left to kick their heels in a starkly furnished guardroom with no fire and high windows they could not see out of until their escort returned to conduct Nathan, alone this time, up two flights of stairs and along several corridors to another room, considerably better furnished but on first impressions not likely to be any more relaxing. At a long table in the window sat three officers, sitting very straight and flanked by two grenadiers standing at rigid attention. Two of the officers wore military uniform; the third was a naval captain.

At the far end of the table sat another military gentleman of more junior rank, and at a separate, smaller table, a non-commissioned officer, armed with paper, pen, and ink. On the near side of the long table and at some little distance from it was an empty chair, possibly for Nathan. And on the opposite side of the room, untouched by the light from the window, sat a gentleman in a dark suit decorated only by the tricolour cockade. Despite the uniforms and the formal air of ceremony, as if they were conducting a court-martial—perhaps they were—it was the civilian who troubled Nathan the most. On his previous visits to France in the guise of Captain Turner of Nantucket, it was the civilian officials who then had the most authority and were certainly the most dangerous to him. But Bonaparte might have changed all that.

He was led to the empty seat and the proceedings began. They were to be conducted in French, the senior officer informed him, but a translator was present if he required assistance, he said, gesturing to the gentleman at the far end of the table.

Nathan indicated, in halting French, that this would be helpful, as he regretted his grasp of the language was very poor. He thought he saw the twitch of a brow, but the request was granted. He was then informed, first in French and then in English, that this was an informal court of inquiry into the recent attack on Boulogne.

Nathan replied, through the interpreter, that as a prisoner of war he was not obliged to assist the enemy in any way whatsoever, and that he would only answer such questions as were permitted under the laws of war. This provoked a lengthy exchange among the several officers, during which Nathan, who adopted an expression of bewildered incomprehension throughout, gathered that his status as a prisoner of war was in dispute, and that there was a strong case to be made that he was an arsonist who had been engaged in an incendiary attack on French shipping, involving the deaths of twenty Frenchmen. After some minutes of this, the interpreter informed him that he should answer the questions accordingly and his replies would be noted. He was then asked to confirm his name and rank, which he did.

'And your status at the time of the attack?'

'I had the honour to command His Britannic Majesty's sloop *Falaise*.'

'So why were you found in the water?'

'I do not know.'

A muttered oath from the senior officer. 'How is it that you cannot know?'

'I was unconscious,' replied Nathan, when the interpreter had put this to him. He put his hand to the bandage on his head.

'Let me put to you that you were thrown from a small boat by the force of an explosion which you yourself contrived.'

Nathan pretended to consider this with an expression of baffled ignorance, which he had learned from his father's servants as a child. This was accompanied by a shake of the head, but no reply.

The senior officer leaned forward and fixed him with a stern eye. 'Come, sir, you are a post captain of—what is it?—near ten years standing and some considerable achievement.' In other circumstances this information would have been welcome. He would have been glad if it had been made known to the Earl Saint Vincent when he was in office. 'Do you expect us to believe you were in command of a mere sloop of war and that you were unfortunate or foolish enough to fall into the sea?'

Nathan waited for the interpreter to translate.

'You may believe what you wish, sir,' he said, 'but that is the case.'

The officer was losing his temper—or pretending to. Nathan had the impression that this whole performance was just that: a performance. But why?

'What I believe, sir, is that you were the commander of a murderous attack upon the port and population of Boulogne with a number of incendiary devices that were it not for the courage and vigilance of the French navy would have caused a great many civilian casualties. What have you to say to that, sir?'

Again, Nathan waited for an approximate translation before stonewalling a reply. The only incendiaries he knew of were the fireships, he insisted, his only orders to rescue men from the water—French as well as English.

'Very well, *monsieur*, if that is all you have to say for yourself, I am under instruction to transfer you to the custody of the Ministry of Justice.' He turned to the gentleman in the shadows and said in French and, Nathan thought, with a certain amount of relief, 'Citizen Arnoult, *il est tout à vous*.'

He is all yours.

Nathan was led outside where Mr Banjo was waiting for him under guard. There was also a carriage, with four horses, and a mounted escort.

'Please to enter the diligence,' said Citizen Arnoult.

Nathan entered the diligence. Mr Banjo followed. And then Citizen Arnoult. Nathan and George sat on the side facing the rear of the coach, Arnoult on the other.

Nathan smiled at him.

'Where are you taking us?' he enquired.

'You can speak French now, *monsieur*,' said Citizen Arnoult, in French. 'The pretence is no longer necessary, and it would be a lot easier for us both.'

Nathan considered. He might have a point.

He repeated the question in French.

'To Paris, *monsieur*, so make yourself comfortable. It is a long journey.'

Chapter 13

The Prisoner of the Temple

Nathan felt a familiar mixture of anticipation and apprehension as they approached the outskirts of the French capital. A half-remembered line from Shakespeare groped through the fog at the back of his mind. Something about old age and infinite variety. He did not think it referred to Paris, but it could have. And yet it was a city of as many horrors as delights: enchanting, malign, and murderous. He had experienced moments of great happiness here, and even greater sorrow, and there was no other place on earth where he had come so close or so often to violent death.

They had been four days on the road and it was a relief to be nearing journey's end, whatever it might bring for him personally. They had stopped at a number of inns on the way, and though he had no complaints about either the food or the accommodation, he could not speak so highly of their transport. It was an ancient vehicle, long preceding the Revolution, and neither its springs nor its upholstery provided much cushioning against the rigours of the French roads. The worst of it, though, was the boredom. They had spent at least eight hours every day almost literally thrown together in that confined space, and the company of the taciturn Arnoult did nothing to relieve the tedium of the journey. He had refused to answer all but the most mundane of questions regarding their eventual destination or the fate that awaited them there, but it was unlikely to include a tub of heated water and the services of a masseur.

This was his fourth or fifth visit to the city, and it brought back poignant memories. He had been here at the time of the Terror when the streets were filled with violent mobs and the tumbrels rolled daily to what the authorities called the Humane and Scientific Execution Machine, and everyone else, the guillotine. It had seen off a number of his acquaintances and even some of his enemies. He had himself been imprisoned and tortured here, strung up from a streetlamp, lost in the sewers, and buried alive in the catacombs. He had fallen in love. And on his last visit he had saved the life of the man soon to be crowned the Emperor Napoleon. It was not the kind of place you came to relax, or for the good of your health, but you could never call it boring.

For most of the journey from the coast they had followed the *Grande Rue*, the old Roman road between Calais and Paris, but there had been so many diversions along the route, either due to flooding or some other obstacle, Nathan could not be sure from which direction they were entering the city, or make an informed guess as to where they might be heading. They passed through one of the great *barrières* erected by the tax farmers in the days of the old regime, but there were no aggressive demands for their papers as in the early days of the Revolution. Perhaps security was a little less tight than it had been then, though this seemed unlikely in the wake of the Cadoudal conspiracy and with Fouché back as minister of police.

As they passed into the inner city, he pressed his face to the window but could see no landmark that was familiar to him. The streets seemed cleaner than he remembered them, the people better dressed, and none of them appeared to be carrying a head on the end of a pike as in former days. It was said that Paris had recovered her reputation as the style capital of Europe, and during the brief year of peace a great many English tourists had flocked here for the food and the fashion—and the frisson of horror from visiting scenes of slaughter that had taken place during the time of the Terror. It would be a while, Nathan thought, before they came again.

The carriage slowed to a crawl and then turned off the road, jolted along a particularly fierce stretch of cobbles, and came to a halt at a stone archway with two massive doors which had to be laboriously opened for them. This time their custodian was obliged to show his papers before they were allowed to proceed, but they advanced only a short distance before stopping again. For once Arnoult met Nathan's eye. He even spoke, though the information he imparted was superfluous.

'*Nous sommes arrivés.*'

The carriage door was opened by one of their escort and they stepped down into a closed courtyard. Although it was barely halfway through the afternoon, they were in deep shadow. Nathan looked up at the stone walls and Gothic turrets of what might have been a castle from a fairy tale if you did not know its history, for though he had not been here before, he knew at once where they were.

Everyone in Paris, possibly all of Europe, knew the Paris Temple, if only by its notoriety. It had been built in the twelfth century by the Knights Templar as a fortified monastery to guard their wealth, and, as was widely believed, to practise their occult rituals, and when the order was suppressed, the knight commander and his close associates had been tortured to death here in the hope of making them reveal the whereabouts of their hidden treasures. However, it had earned more recent infamy as the prison where the French king and his queen had been incarcerated before they were led to the guillotine, and where their only surviving son had died of some wasting disease at the age of ten.

But it was an even more recent death that occupied Nathan's mind as they entered the building itself, for the Temple was where several members of the Cadoudal conspiracy had been imprisoned, and where General Pichegru, whom he had met in Jersey, had been found hanged with his own scarf in his cell. Suicide, said the authorities. Murder, said the royalists.

Either way, it was not the most reassuring of thoughts for a new arrival.

They were conducted into a large chamber with stained-glass windows and a selection of ancient weaponry on the walls where they were formally handed over to the prison authorities. They were not consulted in this process. Indeed, they might as well have been cattle or a delivery of merchandise for all the notice that was taken of them. Arnoult produced a paper for one of the officials to sign, presumably by way of a receipt. Then, with no more than a brief glance and a curt nod, he left them with their new custodians.

For the first time they were subjected to a grim appraisal.

'I am the chief warder, Citizen Fleury,' announced the man who had signed for them. He wore civilian dress with a tricolour ribbon to denote his status as a superior being. 'You will please to turn out your pockets.'

He indicated a long table at which two other officials were seated. They did as instructed. A handkerchief, a Monmouth cap, a flint, a few crumbled leaves that might pass for kindling, a small compass, and a few English coins.

'This is the only money you have?'

'All that is in our possession,' Nathan agreed. 'If that is a problem, we can always look for somewhere else to stay.'

It was a poor joke, made with some vague notion of lifting the atmosphere. It did not work. No-one so much as cracked a smile, not even Mr Banjo. They both had sufficient experience of prison life to know that without money or any other means of survival, things could go very badly for them indeed, and not just in the way of sustenance.

Citizen Fleury shook his head sadly and announced that Citizen Bazille would conduct them to their quarters. The flint and the kindling were retained but everything else given back to them, for what it was worth. It was all very civilised—no armed guards, no shackles or leg irons—but it did not make Nathan any more optimistic. The warder indicated they should walk ahead of him, but besides this, he took no other precaution. He did not appear to be armed, but there seemed little point in attempting escape until they had a clearer idea of the layout of the place and where to go next.

They preceded him down a long passageway and up a spiral staircase that ascended one of the turrets. On the first two landings a narrow window let in some light from the sky and permitted the glimpse of a garden and the high wall enclosing it. On the third, Nathan could see over the wall to the city beyond, though it was obscured by mist or smoke, or both. Their escort stopped them here and selected a key from the large ring at his belt. This opened a small door leading to what were apparently to be their quarters.

Bazille gave them a tour of inspection. It did not take long. There were two small bedchambers, each the size of a monk's cell with a single narrow bed. A high barred window showed a glimpse of sky. Another slightly larger room contained table and chairs, and a fireplace with a cooking range. The window here was also barred, but not so high, and with a view over the city. The only other room was the privy, or shithole, as the warder more accurately described it, for it was the size of a cupboard with a stone ledge with a hole in the centre, presumably opening onto the castle walls. Even so, Nathan had seen a lot worse in terms of both privy and the quarters themselves. They would be permitted access to the exercise yard for one hour every day, Citizen Bazille informed them, and to the library every three days, but these privileges were dependent upon their good behaviour.

This was all reasonably encouraging. On the other hand, the beds had a single blanket but no linen, there was no fuel for the fire, and no means of lighting the single stub of a candle on the table.

Did they have any questions, their host wished to know.

Nathan had a lot of questions, but he limited himself to one for the time being.

'When is dinner?'

'You have missed dinner,' came the dispiriting reply. 'The next meal is breakfast.'

'We have not eaten since breakfast this morning,' Nathan informed him, with more hope than expectation.

'Prisoners can send out for food,' the warder pointed out, 'have they the means to pay for it.'

Not for the first time Nathan cursed his lack of provision when he had left the *Falaise*, but there had been other things on his mind at the time. He did not even have anything he could use in lieu of coin, his sword, pistols, and chronometer having been lost in the sea, or in the first few hours of captivity while he was still unconscious.

Was there no-one in Paris to whom they might apply for funds, the warder wanted to know. It would, of course, be almost as much in his interests as theirs if they had the means to alleviate their condition, for he would take a healthy commission on every transaction.

Nathan considered. There was always Bonaparte. Nathan wondered how he would respond to a request for a loan—especially from someone rotting in one of his own prisons. He might think it would go some way towards repaying Nathan for saving his life. There were also several members of the Bonaparte family who might retain favourable memories of their association, though he could not rely upon it. But even if he could summon up the nerve to write to them, and risk the consequences, they had all known him in his guise as the American shipowner, Captain Turner, and the last thing he wanted was to alert the authorities to the fact that Turner and Peake were one and the same.

Otherwise, there was his bank. He had only lately deposited his prize money for the *Aurore* with them, so he was unusually flush in funds. So far as he was aware they did not have a branch in Paris, but bankers always had a way of moving money around, even in the midst of a war. However, it would take some considerable time to arrange, and he could be dead by then. He searched his mind for someone else he knew in Paris, someone with a few francs to spare, and out of the fog came a name. Gabriel Ouvrard. The man who, according to Smith, had set up the deal with the Baring Brothers that was now paying for Bonaparte's invasion army.

He had been Nathan's chief contact on his last fraught visit to Paris in the year '95. At that time he had been financial adviser to Thérèse Tallien, wife of one of the leaders of the new Republic. He had also been close to Rose Beauharnais, now referred to in polite circles as the Empress Josephine. If he remembered Nathan, and still had a good opinion of him, he might be willing to arrange a transfer of funds with his bank in London and advance him a sum of money in the meantime. The trouble was, he, too, had known Nathan as Captain Turner.

'Well, if you can think of someone, let me know,' said their jailer as he prepared to leave.

Nathan sighed. 'I would need pen, ink, and paper,' he said.

He thought about the wording very carefully, and as he did so the germ of an idea came to him. There were others who knew of his double identity and some of them might well be in Paris. There was a strong possibility that his activities in the waters off Saint-Domingue had been the subject of a report to the French Ministry of Marine. In which case he might face other charges besides attempted arson. But there might well be some confusion, not only about his role in the French colony, but also about the name that he had used while he was operating there. To some, like Pauline Bonaparte and her husband Leclerc, he had been known as Turner, an American seafarer in the service of the US ambassador; to others, like Leclerc's successor, Rochambeau, he was Captain Peake, a British naval officer running guns to the rebels. It occurred to him now that he could capitalise on this. It might muddy the waters for a while.

He took up the quill, dipped it in the inkwell Bazille had provided, and began the letter.

He had no seal, but he folded it and wrote Ouvrard's name on the out-side, giving his address as the Bank of France, which should find him—if he was in Paris. But it was the thinnest of lifelines. It might also provide a rope to hang him—not that they hanged people anymore, in France. Not officially. More likely it would be the guillotine, or the garrotte.

He handed the letter to Bazille, who lit the candle for them before he left.

Night fell. It was cold. They did not have a coat between them. They had to make do with the blankets off the beds, and they huddled on either side of the table with their hands stretched out to the tiny blaze of the candle until it went out. The prison was strangely silent. No sounds of other prisoners, or any other sounds you might expect in a prison—the slamming doors, the turning keys, the footsteps of a warder doing his rounds. Perhaps there were no other prisoners. Just them.

Nathan stood at the window for a while, staring out over the city. A city of lights. Somewhere in that city, if he was lucky, the banker Ouvrard would soon be opening his letter. But what next? Would he screw it into a ball and toss it onto the fire before heading out for the evening? He was an important man; why would he concern himself with a nobody who had been of some small use to him nine years ago? Smith had said that Thérèse Tallien was now his mistress and that they remained close to the Bonaparte family. It might help; it might not. Napoleon's younger brother Jérome had reason to remember him with gratitude, for Nathan had saved him from the sea, but then he had put him there in the first place. Pau-line might have even fonder memories, but they would be mixed with the guilt she had felt when her husband died of the yellow fever. Rose, or Josephine, as she was now, would probably not even remember him. And then there was Napoleon himself.

He closed his eyes and pressed his head against the bars. Prison was becoming like another home to him. It had been predicted by his father's servants. 'That thar varmin' will likely end up in prison', they would say after some childhood prank, or piece of mischief, 'or dangling at the end of a rope'. But even they would have been surprised at how many prisons he had frequented in his short life. Four in Paris, one in London—if only for a night, for duelling. Three months in the Moorish Castle on Gibraltar on the order of Earl Saint Vincent, for insubordination. The Doge's prison in Venice . . . What had that been for? He had forgotten. He had been cold, hungry, miserable—close to despair on a number of occasions. The trick was to keep yourself occupied, in your thoughts if not by more physical means. Cleaning the cell worked, but you needed something to clean it with. Drawing pictures on the walls or on the floor. Keeping a journal. But again, you needed something to write or draw with. He had used soot from the fireplace before now, and blood from his finger, but you could not even use soot or blood without light. Failing all else, you could fall back on your memories. To remind yourself of who you once were, and who you could be again, if you were ever let out.

Looking out on Paris in the dark he remembered his nights in the Rue de Conte with Sara. They were good memories, even if they had been under the constant threat of discovery, imprisonment, and death. But Sara had been a long time ago. There had been other women since, though not that many, he told himself, for he did not care to be thought a philanderer. He liked being in love, even though it so often involved sadness.

Inevitably, of course, this brought back memories of Louise. He could not recall those months in Jersey without bringing to mind the pain of her leaving, and the months that had followed. He still felt betrayed. He could not believe anyone could treat him so shabbily. After the words of love she had spoken, all those months they were together, her apparent delight in his company, her sadness when he was obliged to leave her, even for a short while—and then to leave him without a word, just a scrap of a letter, saying nothing.

He knew this probably said more about him than her. He had too high an opinion of himself, that was the trouble. Odd, that, for he did not value himself that highly as a naval officer, and as for his aspirations as Renaissance man—an astronomer, an artist, a musician, a writer and a poet—he did not deceive himself that they were anything other than that—aspirations. Conceits, singularly unblessed by talent.

And yet he expected a woman like Louise to love him. To adore him so much it was impossible to think of loving anyone or anything else, much less to leave him with no expectation of ever seeing him again. Why was that? The adored, adorable child of loving parents? Hardly. He knew his mother and father loved him, in their way, but they had not spent a great deal of time with him when he was a child, and he had not spent much time with them since. He had been spoiled by their servants, of course, for all the abuse they heaped upon him. Perhaps that was it.

But he was inclined to think it was something else—something that made betrayal the worst of all crimes for him. He remembered what he had written about Bonaparte, a man whose self-esteem was so important to him, and yet so fragile, that he considered any form of personal betrayal a crime that could never be forgiven, but cried out for the most cruel revenge.

Best not to dwell on such things. But what else was there to dwell upon? How hungry he was, how miserably cold? The guilt he felt when he looked at George Banjo, huddled in his horsehair blanket, with his head on his arms. What was the point of rescuing him from slavery, or a prison van, only to lead him to a place like this?

A sound at last. A door opening and closing. Heavy footsteps.

Bazille was back. He carried a lantern which he set down on the table before reaching into the folds of his greatcoat to produce a letter—and a leather purse, which fell with a satisfying thud upon the table—and a faint clink of coin?

Nathan read the letter first.

My *dear Nathaniel,*

I was very glad to hear from you, though sorry it brought news of your present plight. I hope it will be of short duration and that we can do something to alleviate the conditions. Despite the restrictions imposed by the current state of hostilities between our two nations, I will endeavour to make funds available to you from your bankers in London. In the meantime, I am advancing a sum that I hope will answer to your immediate needs. Should you require any further assistance, please do not hesitate to call upon

Your devoted servant

Gabriel Ouvrard

Nathan broke the seal on the purse and carefully tipped its contents onto the table. A low whistle from the warder. Twenty gold coins. Nathan picked one of them up. A cockerel on one side, the head of Bonaparte on the other. *Germinals,* the gold francs that had replaced the *louis d'or.* People were already calling them Napoleons. Each worth about three English pounds. A generous man, Ouvrard, if he was so disposed.

'Would it be too late to send out for some supper?' he enquired of the warder.

It was not too late, not in Paris. Paris, like London, never slept where there was money involved. In the streets about the prison there were any number of shops whose owners could oblige them with most of their needs, Bazille informed them.

They dined that night on roasted fowl and sausages, with a salad of leaves and green beans, and an apple tart for dessert, washed down with two bottles of red wine. The warder threw in a few candles from the prison stores and wood for the fire, along with tinder and flint for lighting them. Later several packages were delivered with sheets, pillows, and more blankets. Less urgent supplies could be ordered in the morning, Bazille told them. By then they had made a long list.

Over the next few days they purchased most of what they needed to make life bearable. Fresh rolls and coffee were delivered every morning at eight o'clock. Dinner at the shipboard hour of one, and a light supper at seven in the evening. They purchased writing materials and warm clothing, sending what they had worn on arrival to be laundered. They obtained brooms and mops and other cleaning materials and religiously swept and washed the floors every day before breakfast. They blocked the draught from the windows with bolster cases and bought two colourful rugs for the floor. They did not neglect their personal hygiene, sending out for soap and toothbrushes, towels and combs for their hair.

'I know we will not be receiving guests,' Nathan acknowledged, 'but it is important not to let our standards slip.'

Bazille regretted they could not purchase mirrors in case they broke them to cut their throats.

'Do you get that a lot in here?' Nathan asked him.

'It has been known,' Bazille confessed.

Razors were banned for the same reason, so they let their beards grow until eventually Bazille secured the services of a barber who came in fortnightly. The days grew into weeks, the weeks into months. They were on the whole pretty comfortable, but for the first time in his life, Nathan had nightmares. They were always variations on the same theme. He was on the wrong side of a battle at sea. He did not know how he had got there, but he did not seem to be a prisoner. There was a fog, or something like it, possibly smoke, and ships would emerge from it, with monstrous figureheads of mythical beasts, or birds with cruel beaks, or spiteful women with hair like snakes. He suspected this was from his memories of Saint-Domingue and of the old figurehead on the *Falaise*, of a vengeful goddess, but he did not want to think about it too much. He did not know the meaning of these nightmares, if they had any. He supposed it was because he was in a French prison and feared he might die here.

In his waking hours he continued to make the best of things. At Christmas they had a goose. Nathan wrote letters to his parents and to Sir Sidney Smith but received nothing in reply, and had no means of knowing if they had received them. There were no other communications, either from friends in England or from Gabriel Ouvrard. And no word from the authorities. Nathan had been prepared for another interrogation, but it did not happen. They appeared to have forgotten him. This was worrying in itself, but Nathan's requests for an interview with the prison governor went unheeded.

Winter passed into spring. Every day they exercised in the prison yard or strolled in the gardens. They saw the chestnut trees come into leaf and then burst into pink and white blossom. Their only news was from the French journals that Bazille brought them every morning with their breakfast. They read of Bonaparte's coronation at Notre-Dame in a ceremony conducted by Pope Pius VII, who had travelled from Rome for the occasion only to have Napoleon take the imperial crown from his hands and place it upon his own head. Then he had gone on to crown Josephine as his empress. The only news of the war was of ongoing French preparations for the invasion of England. More ships had been launched, more troops were arriving daily at the Channel ports. There was nothing about all of this being funded with money provided by Barings Bank of London, but if there had it would doubtless have been taken as another example of the emperor's genius.

Then one morning, Bazille arrived with their croissants and their coffee to inform Nathan that he was summoned to the Ministry of Justice for questioning. His escort would be arriving at eleven o'clock.

After waiting so long it was a shock. For the first time in months he dressed in his naval uniform. He lacked a sword and a hat but he would probably pass muster at a court-martial. He smelled of the rosemary and lavender the laundry had used as a deterrent to moths.

They had sent a fiacre for him with an escort of three gendarmes. None of them spoke on the short journey to the Ministry. On arrival he was marched straight up to a room on the first floor which was set up pretty much like the court at Boulogne, with three men seated at a table, flanked by guards, and a clerk at a separate desk to take notes. But this time there was no interpreter, and only one of the men wore military uniform.

Nathan sat down in the chair facing them.

'My name is Colonel Laurent,' the man in uniform informed him, 'and these are my colleagues, Citizen Popelin and Citizen Thibaud.' They had been convened as a court of inquiry by the Ministry of Justice, he said, to determine the nature of the charges against Captain Peake under the Act of Accusation and to determine if he would face trial.

The official shuffled the papers before him and cleared his throat before fixing him with the eye of a man going through a weary charade.

'Your name is Captain Nathan Peake, of the British Royal Navy.'

'It is.'

'You are accused in the first case that on the night of Tuesday, October the second, in the Year Twelve, you did attempt to set fire to the town and docks of Boulogne in the Pas-de-Calais regardless of the danger to civilian property and life . . .'

This time Nathan got as far as opening his mouth before the colonel raised a hand to quell his protest.

'You do not have to register a plea at this time. This is not a court of law, it is a court of inquiry, and you are here to answer the questions we will put to you before proceeding to a formal charge—or not.'

Nathan spoke anyway. 'I would remind you, sir, that I am a prisoner of war and not obliged to answer any questions other than those concerning my rank, the ship I had the honour to command, and the number of crew.'

'As will be noted.' Laurent gave a nod to the clerk. 'However, it is for the court to determine whether the actions of which you have been accused merit the status of a prisoner of war or that of a common criminal. I would remind you that your cooperation with the court, or the lack of it, will be taken into consideration. In the meantime, you would be advised to reflect on the fact that the charges, if they are sustained, are punishable by death.'

He consulted his papers.

'Your participation in the attack has been well documented, and your replies to the court of inquiry in Boulogne is a matter of record. Do you wish to add anything to what you stated on that occasion?'

Nathan did not.

'Then in the light of the evidence before us and the written statements of the witnesses, I believe there is no need for further questioning on that issue.' He looked to each of his companions, who nodded. 'So, I will proceed to the events of the night of August thirty-first off the Nez de Jobourg, on the coast of Cotentin, where it is alleged that you did land a number of agents, including one Georges Cadoudal, with the intent, of which you were fully aware, to abduct or murder the then First Consul of the Republic, Citizen-General Napoleon Bonaparte.'

This was a shock. Nathan had been prepared for the first charge, but not the second.

'I know nothing of that,' he protested.

'You do not deny that on the night in question, you were in command of the sloop *Falaise*, an armed vessel in the hire of the British Royal Navy?'

'I do not deny that, but as to her mission—'

'The mission has been attested to by a number of those since apprehended and convicted before the courts. As to whether you knew of it . . .'

Nathan decided to make a speech, not so much for the benefit of his present interlocutors as for the unknown audience beyond their facade.

'May I state—for the record—that I do not believe the British government or Admiralty would have countenanced such a mission had they known of—of what you declare to be the object. And even if they had, I would have declined to play any part in it.'

This caused a raised brow from Laurent and another exchange of glances with his companions.

'Even if that meant disobeying the orders of your superior officers?'

'It would, I regret, not be the first time.'

If they knew his service record, and they probably did, they would be aware of this.

The chairman consulted his papers once more.

'Moving on, do you deny that along with the agents in question, you also landed a quantity of arms intended for the use of insurgents against the Republic?'

'I have no comment to make on that, or on the nature of the authority you uphold.'

This was provocative, but so be it.

The chairman eyed him sternly. Another glance towards the scribe to make sure it had been noted.

'And that these arms were part of a consignment formerly intended to be delivered to insurgents in the French colony of Saint-Domingue.'

'Again, I have no comment,' said Nathan, though he was alarmed at the course the inquiry was taking.

'You do not deny that you were the commander of the *Falaise* when it was operating in the waters off Saint-Domingue between the months of Floréal and Thermidor in the Year Ten?'

'That is not something for me to confirm or deny. As a serving officer in the British navy, I am not obliged to offer any explanation of my conduct in the pursuit of hostilities.'

'But Britain and France were not then at war,' declared Laurent in a tone that verged on the triumphant, as if he had caught the prisoner out, and perhaps he had. 'So, the activities of the *Falaise* would be categorised under international law as piracy.'

'Without evidence of those activities I can make no comment.'

Laurent bestowed a glance on each of his fellow judges. 'The court will have noted the report of Citizen-General Rochambeau, deputy commander of French forces on the island at that time, and of Citizen-Admiral Villaret de Joyeuse, who commanded the navy.'

The two heads bent over the documents. Nathan dearly wished he could see them for himself. He had met the admiral only once, on the flagship *L'Océan*—at a ball to commemorate Bonaparte's victories in Italy. His only meeting with Rochambeau had been as his prisoner when he had threatened to have him torn apart by killer dogs.

Laurent held Nathan's eyes for a long moment. Nathan gazed blandly back. He felt much as he had during his childhood in Sussex, when he had been interrogated by one of the several authority figures in his life—his teacher, the village curate, his father's servants, sometimes even his father himself—to find the truth behind some imaginative falsehood of his. You would think there would be other, much more fraught memories of being caught in a lie, but it was always that early experience that came back to him. Probably because it was where it had all started.

'Have you ever met a man called Turner? Captain Nathaniel Turner, an American sea captain?'

Nathan had been braced for this. It did not make it any easier. He hoped this did not show in his face or his voice.

'I do not believe so, but I have met a lot of sea captains in the cause of my duties, and a good few of them have been American. I cannot always recall their names.'

'This Captain Turner was in Cap-Français and later at Tortuga at the same time as we know you were commanding the *Falaise* in the waters off Saint-Domingue.'

Nathan took the liberty of giving a small shrug. 'If you say so.'

The shrug was probably a mistake. Laurent coloured slightly, his stare grew harder, if that were possible. 'Very well, Captain Peake, or Turner, or whatever you care to call yourself, your lack of cooperation has been noted, and you will now be escorted back to your quarters. The next time you are called upon to answer these questions will be in very different circumstances. In the meantime, you would be advised to reflect upon the perils of your situation. I would remind you, yet again, that the penalty for conviction on just one of these charges is death.'

'How did it go?'

Nathan tilted his head as if considering. 'I've done better,' he concluded.

George stated the obvious. 'But you're back. And in one piece.'

'For the time being.'

Nathan sat down at the table. George poured him a glass of wine. From one of the good bottles.

'I have ordered dinner,' he said. 'A hearty beef stew. Unless you have lost your appetite.'

'I have not lost my appetite,' Nathan assured him.

'So, what happens next?'

'I really have no idea.' He drained the glass and poured again. 'I do not suppose they are any keener on a public trial than I am, but of course, it may not be public.'

Their daily routine continued much as before. The journals carried news of Bonaparte's new designs for Italy and the Holy Roman Empire. A number of principalities and minor states were abolished. There were protests from Prussia, Austria, and Russia. Particularly Russia, which was said to be preparing for war. It was reported that Britain was offering to pay the tsar for every soldier he put in the field. Bonaparte had repeated his remark that Britain was a nation of shopkeepers, but added that they should stick to keeping shops. An editorial in the Moniteur, which could only have been written with his consent, advised that another general European war was 'inevitable'.

Closer to home, Bazille informed them that a new prisoner governor had been appointed. Citizen Gaudet. Pompous ass, he said. They did not meet.

Then, on the first day of June, Bazille entered their quarters to tell them to pack their bags—they were being transferred to the Conciergerie.

It was not good news. The Conciergerie was a name that, even more than the Temple, conjured up all the horrors of the recent past. A former royal palace in the heart of the old city, it had been turned into a court-house and a prison shortly after the Revolution. At the time of the Terror, when France was ruled by the Committee of Public Safety, many of its victims had been transferred from other prisons for their trial here before being sent on their final journey to the guillotine. Marie Antoinette had been among them. For her and thousands of others, transfer to the Con-ciergerie was a sentence of death.

'Why are we being moved?' was Nathan's first question.

'You are asking the wrong person,' Bazille said flatly. His manner was unusually terse. 'Probably on account of being too important a prisoner to be entrusted to the likes of me. All I know is that your escort is waiting in the governor's office, and the order was signed by Fouché himself. So you better get your arses moving.'

Despite their many purchases they had not thought to provide them-selves with luggage. Nathan put on his uniform and wrapped some spare clothing and a few other possessions in one of his sheets. George took whatever of their recent purchases he thought might be useful, including what remained of their wine. Nathan still had Ouvrard's purse, but it was down to the last two coins.

This time there were two other warders waiting to escort them to the guardroom. They were instructed to sit on a bench and wait. They waited. No-one spoke.

After a few minutes the door opened and five men entered. One wore civilian dress and had about him a look that fitted Bazille's brief description. The others wore the uniform of the Corps of Gendarmerie, and one of them was a colonel. The warders snapped to attention.

'Stand up,' said the civilian.

They stood up.

'I am the prison governor, Citizen Gaudet,' he said.

Nathan gave him a courteous bow, though he did not feel at all courteous. He felt disrespected and ill-used. Most of all, despite his uniform, he felt like a tramp. It did not help that his belongings were wrapped in a sheet on the floor.

'You are now in the custody of these gentlemen,' said the governor. 'Good day.'

He might as well have said good riddance.

Nathan looked at the colonel. A youngish, hard bastard of a face with bad skin, a thin moustache, and an inflated opinion of itself. He did not bother to give his name.

'You will follow me' was all he said.

They were marched out into the courtyard where a fiacre awaited with draped windows—and a mounted escort.

The colonel mounted one of the spare horses and they were left standing outside the closed door of the carriage. The curtain was twitched back a little from the inside and Nathan felt himself under inspection. He frowned. The sunshine was very bright and the interior correspondingly dark, too dark for him to see a face, but the hand that drew back the curtain was the hand of a woman, wearing a black lace glove. The door was opened from within.

The woman was the only occupant. Nathan felt as if he had been punched in the stomach.

'Get in,' she said.

Chapter 14

The Bad House

Nathan's mind was in another place, but his limbs moved as directed. He climbed into the coach and sat there, clutching his bundle.

'You, too,' the woman instructed Mr Banjo. Nathan moved up on the seat to make room for him. 'You can put that down now,' she said.

Nathan put the bundle on the floor.

'Are you not well?' She was peering carefully into his face. Her own face was exactly as he remembered it, but she seemed less real to him now than she had been in his thoughts for all those months in prison.

'Is he all right?' she said to Mr Banjo. 'I mean, still in his right mind?' He looked to Nathan for guidance.

'This is Madame Louise de Kirouac,' Nathan informed him. 'You met her in Jersey.'

He did not know how much the crew had talked of his affair with Louise, and the effect of her sudden disappearance from his life, but he imagined it had occupied at least some of their time.

'I remember,' said George.

'Well, then,' said Louise. 'If we are all set.'

She lifted the white parasol that was resting against the seat at her knee and banged it on the roof of the carriage. The driver cracked his whip and the carriage clattered across the cobbled courtyard towards the prison gate.

'How?' Nathan demanded, spreading his arms to indicate the interior of the carriage, though in fact he meant much more than that.

'Later,' she said. 'Let us get out of here first.'

They were delayed only briefly at the gate, and then they were moving through the streets of Paris. Louise pursed her lips and blew out a long sigh, putting her head back against the seat.

'Where are you taking us?' Nathan asked her.

'Somewhere you can lie low until we can get you back to England,' she said. 'It is not far.'

For a moment he thought she meant England, but no, she meant the place where they could lie low. It was good to know, however, that England was where she eventually had in mind.

'Who is "we"?'

She shook her head. 'Better not to know. We may yet be stopped—and there are other people whose lives are at risk besides your own.'

He raised a corner of the curtain. They were travelling through the streets of Paris and at a steady lick, the way being cleared for them, he imagined, by their mounted escort. From what he could see he reckoned they were heading west down the Rue Saint-Honoré—the route the tumbrels had taken to the guillotine on the Place de la Revolution in the time of the Terror.

He was aware that Louise was studying him carefully.

'How have you been?' she said.

'Well enough,' he answered coldly. 'Been better. And worse.'

This was probably very annoying, but he could not help himself.

The carriage came to a halt. He reached for the curtain again but this time she stopped him with her hand.

'We are at the *barrière*,' she said. 'The colonel will deal with it.'

The carriage door remained closed. Whatever the commander of their escort was telling them, it was working. Perhaps he was a real colonel. They moved on again and Nathan closed his eyes, letting himself sink into the jolting of the carriage. He felt like a blind man playing chess. Worse, for a blind man can always feel the pieces.

They were, by his reckoning, about half an hour on the road before they stopped again. A longer delay this time. Then they moved on, but not for long. Louise banged on the roof again and raised her voice so that it carried to the coachman. 'Not the house. The stables.'

Nathan caught George's eye. She leant forward, touching his arm.

'There is a need of discretion. Do you have a change of clothing in there?' She nodded towards the bundle at his feet. 'Something less obviously—British.'

'Now?'

'In a moment.' The carriage stopped and she opened the door and jumped lightly down. 'I will leave you to your . . . Be quick.' And then she closed the door.

He changed into the white ducks and shirt that had been his everyday wear in prison, folded his uniform as best he could, and stuffed it into the bundle. Then Louise was back.

'You can get out now.' He descended into a stable yard. Grooms in livery were walking horses that were not designed for pulling carts, or even carriages. No-one paid him any attention. 'If you would not mind waiting here for us,' she said to George. 'We will not be long.'

Nathan looked at the back of the house. A chateau—a palace? Whatever it was, it did not look like a prison.

'Yours?'

'Not mine, no. But come, I will introduce you to the lady of the house. If you do not mind using the rear entrance.'

He followed her across the yard and into the servants' quarters. A few people about, a few curious looks this time, but they seemed to know Louise. The men bowed, the women curtsied. She bestowed a gracious smile.

Up a flight of stone stairs and then into the main part of the house. Long corridors universally tiled in black and white, potted palms, a great many paintings depicting scenes of battle and a brace of footmen at every door, until at length they entered a large conservatory filled with exotic plants and mature trees, even live birds, darting plumage among the foliage—and in their midst a woman in a straw hat and an apron, seated at a rough wooden table, potting seedlings. She looked up at their approach and laughed, covering her mouth with her hand in a gesture he still remembered as though it were yesterday.

'Eh bien, monsieur le capitaine, quelle surprise.'

It was a surprise for him, too. The last time he had seen her was in a little house off the Champs-Élysées trying to cover her nudity with a tablecloth when her lover Paul Barras had unexpectedly joined them to declare that the counter-revolution had started.

'Oh, for God's sake, man, you look like you've seen a ghost,' said the Empress of France. 'I have not aged so much, I trust.'

He pulled himself together, at least so far as his manners were concerned.

'On the contrary, *madame*, you do not look a day older than'—but he must avoid specifics—'than when I was last in Paris.'

This was not quite true, and in those days she would not have been seen dead in what she was wearing now. A tablecloth, yes; an apron, never. But then, he had never seen her gardening before.

'I am delighted to see you looking so well, *madame*, and in such . . .' But once more words failed him, or perhaps there were just too many. He spread his arms, gazing about him as if in helpless admiration, though it was more apprehension he felt, for this must be the house she had bought while Bonaparte was fighting in Egypt, as their family home. He had read about it in the English journals. A palace fit for a king, and that was before he made himself emperor. For all Nathan knew, he was here now, lurking behind one of the exotic plants, ready to jump out like a pantomime villain.

She was laughing at his expression, the hand once more raised to her mouth. Her teeth were her least attractive feature, and she invariably shielded them with a hand or a fan, even when she spoke. 'It is a little different, I grant you, from my little house in the Rue Chantereine, though I was very fond of it at the time, as you know.'

He wondered if she remembered that last evening when he had been there with Ouvrard and Murat, and she and her friend Thérèse had performed their masquerade, as they called it. Something in her eyes suggested she did.

'But let me offer you some refreshment.' She clapped her hands and a figure appeared from nowhere: not the emperor, but a young woman, dressed in the height of fashion—one of the servants, it must be presumed, though she would have ladies-in-waiting now. 'Tea or coffee? Oh, get them to bring both, Célestine, and a bottle of Jamaica rum; I am sure he will drink that.'

This was the old Josephine, brimming with mischief and damn-your-eyes, the woman he had known as Rose Beauharnais. Her full name was longer and more imposing, and Josephine was in it somewhere, or Marie-Josèphe, to be precise, but no-one had ever called her that—not then. It was Bonaparte who had insisted on Josephine. She was *his* Josephine.

Rose was the name she had when she belonged to Paul Barras, the man who had ruled France before he did. She must be in her early forties now, and there was something of the matron about her. But she carried it well, even in gardening clothes. She had always carried herself well, always made the best of herself, and look where it had got her. Bonaparte had been besotted with her in those days, when she was a leader of French society, an icon for the Paris of fun and games that had succeeded the Terror, and he a penniless officer of artillery desperate for preference. She had treated him like a doting spaniel, though more of a nuisance than a pet, to be kicked from time to time to remind him of his place.

He tried to wipe the past from his mind; he had enough problems with the present.

'It is a—a Paradise,' he struggled. 'I take it these are all from the South Seas.' Knowing as much about plants as she did about ships.

'Many are from the Americas and the Caribbean,' she said, looking about her, 'including my native Martinique, of course, but I have a fine collection from New Holland—all via England, of course, these days.'

He wondered how to phrase the obvious question—via England, with a war on?—but then a procession of servants arrived with their refreshments. A silver coffee service, a ceramic teapot with dragons, delicate China cups, a tiered cake stand—and incongruously, a bottle of Jamaica rum with one glass. Josephine kept up the flow of small talk while the servants distributed coffee and cakes, but not rum. Perhaps he was supposed to help himself. She talked about the house, which was a far safer subject than the war, or the past, probably for both of them.

'It was in a ruinous state when I bought it,' she said, 'and now it is accounted one of the most beautiful houses in France, and I have almost a thousand hectares of land to go with it.'

She rattled on—about the river that ran through it and the wonderful meadows, the woodland and the farm, the meandering pathways—while Nathan's mind rambled off on a course of its own. According to the English journals, she had bought it with borrowed money while Bonaparte was in Egypt, raised in the expectation of the loot he would bring back with him to France. But there had been no loot, not after Nelson had disposed of his fleet in the Bay of Aboukir. He was reported to have been furious with her when he found out what she had done, leaving him with a home he did not want, and a pile of debt he wanted even less, but he had only been a general then. Perhaps it was more to his taste now that he was an emperor. *Malmaison* it was called, a strange name for paradise. The English papers had made a lot of that—the Bad House, the House of Evil, a house fit for a Corsican ogre. But from what Nathan had heard in prison, Bonaparte spent most of his time in the old palace of the French kings, at the Tuileries. Nathan dearly hoped he was there now, or in Boulogne. Anywhere but here.

He sat there, straight-backed in his chair, holding his cup and saucer delicately at his chest and listening politely, his head still warped by the unreality of his situation, still trying to take it in. It felt like a spider was crawling across the back of his neck. A tarantula, perhaps, from Martinique, to remind her of home. He reached up a tentative hand to brush it off, bracing himself for the paralysing bite, but it was the frond of a plant. He wondered if she was playing a game with him. At any moment he expected her guards to come bursting in and march him back to the Temple, or somewhere worse. But they would probably wait until he returned to the carriage. She must have asked to see him, he thought, to remind her of old times before he was sent back to prison, for trial and execution.

The lady-in-waiting was here again, murmuring in the empress's ear.

'I am afraid I have to leave you,' she said. 'Duty calls.' A tinkling laugh, the hand to the mouth. 'But Louise will look after you, and I hope we will meet again before you leave us.' Nathan stood up and bowed low. Then she was gone.

'You have not touched your rum,' Louise pointed out, 'but you can take it with you, if you like.'

She was being sardonic, but he picked up the bottle, and she led him back through the house. Out to the carriage with the waiting coachman and horses. A footman stepped up to open the door. George appeared to be asleep, but he opened his eyes when the door opened.

Nathan made to step into the carriage, but Louise put her hand on his arm.

'We walk from here,' she said. 'Leave your belongings. I will have them sent on.'

She led them across the stable yard, down a short drive and into a walled garden where at least a dozen gardeners were at work. Along a maze of pathways until they reached a quaint little cottage with a thatched roof, the walls covered in roses. Louise produced a key from her reticule and opened the door onto a small but cosy drawing room, comfortably furnished with floral-patterned armchairs, small tables, and a pine dresser.

'I hope this will be satisfactory for you,' she said, like a landlady showing them their lodgings. 'There are two bedrooms upstairs, a bathroom, and a kitchen. I have had the larder stocked up with food and drink, but I will have meals sent from the house. There is a little private garden at the back, but please do not venture into the main gardens in case it causes talk among the gardeners. I will come by from time to time to make sure you have everything you need.' A glance at Nathan that might have been ironic, and then she was heading for the door.

Nathan was still standing there, overlarge and awkward in the small room, still clutching his bottle of rum, but before she could reach the door he managed to beat her to it and pushed it gently shut.

'Just a minute, if you will.'

'I will take these upstairs,' said George, picking up their bundles and beating a hasty retreat.

'Please sit down,' Nathan invited her.

She looked for a moment as if she might refuse, but then with a small shrug she sat in one of the armchairs, looking up at him with polite expectation. He sat down opposite, putting the bottle down on the floor.

'What is going on?'

'I told you—'

' "It is better I do not know". Quite. But there are some things I need to know if I am to sit here quietly potting plants, waiting for you to decide my future.'

'No-one is asking you to pot plants, and it is not for me—'

'How long are we staying here?'

She sighed. 'Until your ship comes in.'

'What ship?'

'I cannot tell you that. You have to trust me.'

'Why . . .' He was about to say, Why should he trust her, after what had happened on Jersey, but he thought better of it—for the time being. 'What are you doing here?'

'I am staying here. For a while. We are old friends, Rose'—she corrected herself—'the empress and I. I told you that. We met in prison, during the Terror.'

'That was a long time ago.'

'Yes, but we have kept in touch.'

'Even when you were in Jersey?'

'Even then.' Her look was defiant.

'You did not think to mention that—at the time?'

She answered with a shrug.

He wondered if Sir Sidney Smith had known. Almost certainly. It had probably played a vital part in the conspiracy. They had always meant to kidnap Bonaparte on the road to Malmaison, or assassinate him, depending on whose version you believed.

'So, you were a plant?'

He saw her lips twitch, but he had not meant it as a joke. His own face remained rigid, though he could feel it redden. He might have been sitting on a court-martial.

'She invited me to come and visit her and—yes, it was encouraged by certain people in Jersey.'

'So that you could kill him?'

That wiped the smile off her face. She made to rise. 'If you are going to be insulting . . .'

'Why is that insulting? No matter. It is none of my business. What I need to know is how you came to hear I was in the Temple—and why you got us out—and what is going to happen next. If you are not prepared to say, we will walk out of here right now, and take our chances with the police.'

A reluctant sigh as she sank back into the chair. 'Very well, if you cannot bring yourself to trust me. You wrote to Gabriel Ouvrard.'

It was a statement, not a question, and he made no reply.

'Well, he told Thérèse, and she told Ro—the empress. And I think—though I am only guessing—that she told the emperor and he—arranged matters.'

'Bonaparte?' He was astonished.

'He may not have been involved personally. I believe Fouché signed the order, either at Napoleon's request, or because he knew that is what he wanted.'

'But—why?'

'I imagine that if it came to a trial, it might have been embarrassing for him—and all the others you managed to deceive.'

She sounded critical, and he wondered if she included herself in this. If so, she had a hell of a nerve. But then, she had never lacked nerve.

'But I think the main reason was to clear a debt.' The ironic smile. 'You are his lucky star.'

His sister Pauline used to tell him that, and he had told her what he told Louise. 'Nonsense. I do not believe he thinks anything of the sort.'

'But you do not know him.'

'And you do?'

'Rose does, and she says he believes in his star just as other people believe in God.'

'That is not to say he thinks I am it. Descended to Earth to aid him in his endeavours.'

'Well, he has a few of them, I believe. Like guardian angels. And if you must keep saving his life—'

'Once. Accidentally.'

'And his friend Junot in Italy, I hear. And his favourite brother in Saint-Domingue, and'—she obviously could not think of any others, but it was not the full extent of her knowledge—'not to speak of pleasuring his sister.'

'What?'

'Do you deny it?'

'I . . .'

'And probably Rose, too, though if he knew that, it would be a different matter.'

'I never pleasured Rose.'

This was true. He had been quite fond of Rose Beauharnais, but not in that way, and if he had felt any more lustful feelings, he would have had the sense not to indulge them.

'I am not interrogating you. You are asking the questions. What else do you want to know?'

'Does she know who I really am?'

'Ah. Well, as to that—who are you? Or am I not among those you feel obliged to confide in?'

'You know who I am.'

'Do I? I am not sure about that.'

This was playing games.

'So, who are you working for—Bonaparte, Josephine—or Sir Sidney Smith?'

He was never going to get a straight answer, but she still managed to surprise him.

'I am working for the empress at present, making a statue of her, for her garden. Gardening.'

He shook his head in disbelief, or astonishment. But why not? It made as much sense as anything else he had heard recently.

'And what about him?'

'Who?'

'Bonaparte. Still planning to kill him?'

'I was never . . . Look'—she glared at him, and he had a sudden sharp memory of the time in Jersey, the last time before she left, and perhaps the reason for her leaving, but then she seemed to consider, and when she spoke it was more reasonably—'at one stage I might have thought about it, even said things that were . . . inadvisable. My father had been murdered. I was out of my mind with grief—and rage. People probably thought they could use that to their advantage.'

'So what changed?'

'Nothing changed. I am not a killer, whatever you seem to think, or have been told, and besides, Rose loves him.' She shrugged dismissively. 'And I love her. We were in prison together. I was fourteen years old, and my mother had just been sent to the guillotine. Rose was as—not a second mother, but a big sister, certainly. I could never betray her.'

'So you betrayed them?'

She looked confused.

'Cadoudal and the others.'

'What?' Then she realised what he meant. 'How could you think that?'

'I am sorry. I do not think that. So, you did nothing?'

'If you like.'

They sat there, at opposite sides of the little room, with the whole world between them.

'Is that all?' she said. 'Can I go now?'

'What happens next? How long are we meant to stay here?'

'Sometime in the next few days a ship will leave London for Calais—a cartel, I think it is called.'

A cartel was an arrangement—a means of communicating at time of war—but the name was used for the ships, too. They carried messages between the two governments, or prisoners, even scientists from time to time.

'For an exchange of prisoners?' This would be the usual cartel. But it was not for prisoners.

'No. Much more important than that. For plants. There is a nursery in the village of Hammersmith, near London—the Vineyard. Famous, not only in England. Josephine has always bought her plants from there. And sometimes a botanist comes with them—to advise on planting and care.'

Of all the things she had said, this was possibly the most astonishing. He was shaking his head in disbelief.

'It is quite true. It is arranged by the British Admiralty, I believe. The blockade is lifted temporarily so it can enter Calais.'

He did not know why this should surprise him. While he and others like him were killing each other, Fellows of the Royal Society came to lecture in Paris; why not botanists to plant bulbs in the empress's garden and tell her how often to water them?

'So, how does this help us?'

'The botanist will bring two assistants with him—Frenchmen, who will stay here at Malmaison, and you and Mr Banjo will go back with him, with passports that have been prepared for you. Anything else?'

This, surely, was enough to think about. But he did not want her to go.

'Have you finished the statue?'

He meant the statue for Josephine, but he could not help thinking of the other statue on Jersey, when he had first seen her, and possibly she was thinking of it, too.

'Almost.' She held his gaze. 'I just have to get the mouth right.'

Perhaps it was the look she was giving him, and the memories it stirred. It was only later that he regretted not being gentler with her, or the noise they made, for it was a small room with far too much furniture to be making love in, and with Mr Banjo upstairs, but Nathan had been in prison for a long time, and not just physically.

The next two weeks were like Eden before the Fall, despite the danger they were in, and they were not much in the garden. She would only allow them out at night, or late in the evening, when no members of staff were there. George went further afield than he should have one night and came back looking a little shaken.

'Something jumped at me,' he said. 'Big brute like a moose, but on two legs. Leaping.'

'That will be the kangaroo,' said Louise, laughing. 'It is from Australasie. I do not think they are dangerous.'

There were a great many exotic animals, and birds. Ostriches and emus, gazelles and zebra from Africa, llamas from South America, peacocks . . . They heard them at night. Sometimes for Nathan, it felt like he was back in Tortuga, in the gardens Pauline Bonaparte had created to rival her hated sister-in-law. But he did not talk of that.

There had once been a castle here for Norman raiders, Louise told them, where they would bring back their loot and their captives; hence, the name—the Bad House—though another word for it was the Hideout.

'So, you see, it is appropriate,' she said.

Mostly when Louise was there, they stayed in the bedroom, or they would dine, all three of them at the small table in the kitchen, off the best foods the grander kitchens of Malmaison could provide. Often there were visiting emissaries at the house, entertained by Josephine, and once a state banquet with Bonaparte himself as host. The grounds were patrolled by armed guards, but they stayed indoors while the emperor was there, until Louise came back the next day with some delicacies from the feast and announced that he had returned to the Tuileries.

Then the botanist arrived from Calais.

He was to stay for just two days, Louise said, and then return to England with his new assistants. She stayed at the cottage for all the time he was there, but it was not long enough. Nathan felt the minutes go by like they were torn from him, as from a raw wound. He felt like one must feel on that final walk to the scaffold, with every step forced against your will, but you make it all the same. Step by step.

On their last night, he asked her to come with him.

But she shook her head. 'I have no passport. It would be to risk all our lives.'

'Can you not get one, from Rose?'

'Rose cannot do that. It would have to be Fouché. There is no time, even if he agreed. It would be to risk everything.'

She was close to tears, but she would not be moved.

'I cannot leave,' she said. 'Not while Rose is here—and Bonaparte is still in power.'

'So, you cannot leave because you love the empress and hate the emperor?'

'Yes, if you want to put it like that. I can still be of use. I get to hear things. I can . . . I can even influence them. Josephine has power, more than you think. She pretends to be stupid, but only because she knows men prefer that—men like Bonaparte, certainly—but she is far from stupid.'

'What use can you be?' he demanded brutally. 'The agents are all dead. And so will you be, if you stay.'

But he was wasting his breath, and the little time that was left for them.

'Well, then, I will stay with you,' he said. 'I can pass for French. I can help you.'

'You know you will not do that,' she said. And he knew she was right.

'And what would I do in England,' she said, 'while you spend your life at sea? Stay with your mother?'

She was right about that, too. He had tried that with Sara. You cannot love a woman and leave her with your mother. It is unfortunate, but there it is.

They stayed awake most of the night, with their arms wrapped around each other, listening to the cries of the peacocks in the garden, and he did not think he had ever heard so sad a sound.

'Listen, there is something I have to tell you,' she said, as the first streaks of dawn appeared, like a thief in the window. For a moment he thought she would say she had a lover, and was to be married next week, with Josephine as her maid of honour, and Bonaparte giving away the bride. He would not have been entirely surprised. But it was not that.

'It is something I overheard from Bonaparte himself when he was here. I do not understand it properly—but you might. It concerns the British fleet.'

Chapter 15

The Master Plan

'Ah, Peake, welcome back to London. You have had a hard time of it, I hear, in recent months, but it don't seem to have knocked the varnish off you. Wish I could say the same for meself.'

There was a new First Lord at the Admiralty, Lord Melville having resigned over a small matter of having public funds paid into his private account, and his place had been taken by my Lord Barham, who was possibly the most ancient mariner to hold this office, being but four months short of his seventy-ninth birthday. He carried his years well, however, from the physical point of view, and apart from a certain tetchiness, appeared to be at least as much in command of his faculties as any of his predecessors. 'He moves ships about the globe with the skill of a chess master,' Nathan had been informed by an associate he had met on the way into Admiralty House, adding less impressively, 'though I doubt he has been to sea for thirty years or more.'

'So what is this great plan of Boney's that you wish to tell me about?' he demanded of Nathan. 'A matter of the utmost urgency, I am advised.'

'They were not my words, my lord,' Nathan corrected him. 'But I did think it was important enough to bring to your attention personally.'

'Quite. Everyone does. Well, carry on, sir, carry on. The floor is yours.'

The floor in question was that of the Admiralty boardroom, which possessed not only the distinction of a Grinling Gibbons fireplace and a wind dial connected to the weathervane on the roof, but a quantity of large maps which could be rolled up and down from the ceiling in the manner of blinds whenever their lordships wished to remind themselves of the seas at their command. The current map on display showed most of Europe, including the Mediterranean and the Atlantic Ocean, to the shores of North America.

The First Lord made himself comfortable in one of the chairs and folded his arms in anticipation. He was Nathan's only audience.

'Well, my lord, it is much the same strategy as Bonaparte has deployed in the movement of his armies,' Nathan began. 'Divide your enemy and concentrate your own forces to attack the weakest point.'

'I see. Well, I suppose there is no reason why it should not work at sea, as it does on land,' conceded his lordship, though in a tone that suggested a degree of doubt, 'give or take a few imponderables, such as the winds, the tides, and a few others I have not yet thought of. But pray continue.'

Nathan took up the long pointer that lay upon the table for the purposes of demonstration. 'It involves three French squadrons and one Spanish, my lord, a total of around fifty ships of the line, presently located here at Brest, Rochefort, Ferrol, and Toulon.' The pointer moved from the tip of Brittany, down the Atlantic coast of France to Spain, and on to the Mediterranean, a distance of above a thousand miles. 'The plan is for each squadron to break out at roughly the same time and head across the Atlantic to rendezvous in the West Indies—off Martinique.'

The pointer made a leap of four thousand miles to the west.

'When all are assembled, they will return across the Atlantic in such force as to outnumber our naval defences by more than two to one and escort the invasion barges across the Channel.'

'Landing two hundred thousand French troops on the south coast of England,' Barham finished for him laconically. 'Well, it is certainly ambitious. But tell me, even if it were possible to evade all four of our blockading fleets, why choose a rendezvous four thousand miles to the west? Why not to the south of Ireland, or indeed, anywhere off the coast of Europe?'

'I have been thinking about that, my lord. I think the idea was to choose somewhere sufficiently remote that there would be no danger of the individual fleets being attacked at the rendezvous before all were assembled. And in the meantime, they could do appreciable damage to our commerce in the West Indies.'

A flicker of the hooded eyes from the map to Nathan. 'And how reliable is this information?'

'I believe Sir Sidney Smith considers the informant to be one of his most reliable agents,' Nathan advised him. In fact, he had no idea of Smith's opinion of Louise, so far as her talents as an agent were concerned. Nor, for that matter, of Barham's opinion of Sir Sidney Smith.

'Well, it is not impossible to evade our blockades, as you know.' Barham's eyes had returned to the map. 'It happens a good deal more often than one might prefer.'

They both knew that the winds frequently blew the squadrons off station, though for all four to be dispersed at the same time would be unfortunate.

'However—assuming they do break out, what does Boney think our admirals might do next, when this great escape is discovered?'

'Well, that is not for me to say, my lord.'

'Make an informed guess. From your knowledge of the subject, as it were.'

First Lords came and went, but they all appeared to cling to the same myth that Nathan and Napoleon were the best of friends.

'I should think he would assume they would go looking for them, my lord. But perhaps individually, in their own sphere of operations, and according to the information at their disposal.'

They both knew the difficulty of finding an enemy fleet in the Atlantic, or even the Mediterranean. Nelson had lost the French for over a month when they last broke out of Toulon on his watch, and by the time he found them Bonaparte and his army were in Cairo.

'Divide and conquer.'

'Precisely, my lord.'

'Well, if you had told me this a month or two ago, I would have damned you for a gullible fool, or worse,' Barham declared. 'But as it is, we now know that Villeneuve did exactly as you have indicated—and Nelson has followed in pursuit, after spending several weeks going the wrong way. Our information is that both he and Villeneuve are now in the West Indies, though whether or not they have been privileged to meet is anyone's guess.'

'And the other French squadrons?'

'Ah, that is a better prospect, from our point of view. None of them succeeded in slipping the leash, as it were. However—our recent information is that Villeneuve has up to twenty ships of the line and seven frigates at his disposal. Now we know what the master plan is—provided, of course, that your informant is as reliable as you or Sir Sidney Smith suggest—we must presume that when he has had enough of waiting for the others to join him, he will hasten back to Europe. He may already be on his way, leaving Nelson hunting about the islands in search of him. In which case we have to give some thought as to where he will turn up. He might try to break the blockade at Brest—or further south. If he can unite with any one of those squadrons, we will have a formidable force to contend with.' He regarded Nathan with a thoughtful eye. 'So, what are *your* present plans?'

'Mine, my lord?' As if this was the last thing on his mind, which it pretty much was. After the cartel had landed him at Dover, he had come straight up to London to report to the Admiralty. He had no idea if what Louise had told him was true or not. He did not suspect her of lying, but it was entirely possible that her cover had been blown and she had been fed misleading information. It was even possible that his escape had been contrived so that he could take it back to Britain to mislead his superiors. But he had felt duty-bound to pass it on. Beyond that, as he expounded to his lordship, he had no plans other than to take a short leave and return to his ship.

'Ah yes, the *Falaise*.' Barham either had a mind for detail or he had been recently briefed on the subject. 'And remind me why a post captain of ten years' seniority and some considerable achievement finds himself in charge of a sixteen-gun French corvette?'

'It occurred when we were at peace,' Nathan told him, 'when I was a half-pay officer.' It was probably better not to mention the enmity of the Earl Saint Vincent and what had occasioned it. 'And to be fair, my lord, there are two such vessels under my command.'

'Oh yes, I was forgetting you took the sister ship as prize. Permit me to congratulate you. I have read the report of your action off the Nez de Jobourg. And how do you get on with Sir Sidney Smith?'

'Tolerably well, my lord.'

'Tolerance is another of your virtues?'

'I would not have put it among the foremost, my lord.'

'Quite.' A dry old smile. 'Well, Peake, I have it in mind to give you a choice. You can re-join Captain Smith off Deal with his submarines—I understand that he is planning a new attack on the invasion fleet. Or there is a frigate at Portsmouth in need of a captain—the *Panther*, of thirty-six guns; I am inclined to send her off at once to join Lord Cornwallis with the Channel fleet—but what would be your preference?'

Chapter 16

The *Panther*

She was moored on the outer edge of Spithead, just off the Isle of Wight, looking very fine in the early-evening sunshine with her sails hung out to dry in the warm summer breeze. The *Panther* of thirty-six guns, a fifth-rate of the *Perseverance* class. Nathan had ample time to look her over on the tender that brought him out from Portsmouth, for the anchorage was sparsely employed at present, with most of the navy's ships on blockade duty or hunting down what remained of the enemy's commerce. She was not so much bigger than the *Falaise* in terms of her hull dimensions, and she probably would not match her for speed, but that long line of chequered gunports gave a strong hint of her firepower. She probably had three times the weight of the corvette's broadside with her long guns alone, and from what he had gathered from the sketchy research he had been able to do at the Admiralty, she carried a number of carronades as well. Not a new ship, by any means—in fact, she had been built in 1783, the same year he had joined the navy—but she had fought and won so many engagements since, in the East Indies, the Med, and the North Sea, that she was accounted a crack frigate, capable of holding her own against the new generation of heavy frigates that were emerging in France and America.

He wondered how her officers would receive his appointment. Lord Barham had said he would send word by the shutter telegraph, but Nathan was not counting on it, and in his present mood he did not much care; he had his commission in his uniform coat pocket, and that was all that mat-tered. He was not in the most conciliatory of moods. He had not thought he could feel any worse than when Louise had left him in Jersey, but he found that he could, and did. Finding her when he had least expected it, only to lose her again so soon after, probably forever, was a shattering blow. The dark cloud had descended from the moment he had left Mal-maison and stayed with him on the journey to Calais and beyond, not especially lifted by Mr Kennedy's lengthy lectures on the genealogy and maintenance of plants. It was still here now, for all the pristine glory of the summer sky. Even so, he did not wish to be seen as one of those surly, morose buggers who make life a misery for all who serve under him. He would sooner get on with people than not. God help them, though, if they tried to slight him.

He knew little of the ship's previous commander, Robert Taylor, except that he was a few years senior to him on the Navy List and had not been with the *Panther* long. This was something in Nathan's favour, as the men would not have had time to form an attachment, though most sailors sub-scribed to the philosophy 'Better the Devil You Know'. There was always a worse devil in the offing. The other thing in his favour was that Taylor was only on sick leave, having succumbed to some mysterious affliction of the bowels, though the First Lord had said he did not expect him back in a hurry, if ever. 'Not that we need tell his officers that, for it will doubtless ease the transition if they think you are only a temporary inconvenience.'

Nathan had assumed this was Lord Barham's notion of wit, but you could never be sure with a man of his age and temperament. However, it meant that the invalid's servants were still available to Nathan, an important consideration when his own entourage was now reduced to Mr Banjo, who had no more aptitude for the role of valet than he did. He was wondering, in fact, if he could come to a financial arrangement concern-ing Captain Taylor's private stores, rather than let them go to waste, for he had not had time to provide himself with more than a few delicacies from his mother's larder and a couple of bottles of wine before travelling post from London. It was odd how a broken heart never seemed to affect one's appetite. The two organs did not appear to have any practical means of communication.

He was distracted from these obtuse reflections by a challenge from the frigate and Mr Banjo shot him an enquiring look before cupping his hands to his mouth and bellowing back: '*Falaise*' to let them know her new captain was aboard—or the old one miraculously recovered.

'But let us take a turn around her first,' Nathan instructed the helmsman, as much to give them time to prepare for his reception than to prolong his own observations. For all he knew, most of her officers had gone ashore and the lower decks were filled with women from shore. Whoever had been left in charge might appreciate an extra few minutes' before he came aboard.

There was nothing in her outward appearance to cause concern. Her canvas was weathered but otherwise unworn, her rigging impeccable and her paintwork spotless—and as an added bonus there was the snarling head of a black panther at her prow instead of the ghastly harridan that had greeted him on the *Falaise*. They travelled down the long line of gunports and then round by her stern, the dark row of windows that graced his cabin, the gilded lettering of the ship's name, and the white ensign lifting in a languid salute to the pale summer sky. If it had not been for the sorrow of his lost love he would have been as happy as at any time in his life.

But now they were docking at the entry port, and he put all other thoughts out of his mind as he reached out for the side ropes—elegantly sheathed in white canvas—and climbed nimbly aboard to the familiar wail of the boatswain's pipe and a reception party of officers, the blue-and-white uniforms, a phalanx of red-coated marines, and the crew lined up in the waist. One of the officers stepped forward, his own hat in his hand.

'Welcome aboard, sir. Simpson, first lieutenant . . .'

And so it proceeded: the introductions, the uniforms, the names, the faces . . . more youthful these days with his own advancing years. And such a quantity of gold lace, so many more officers than aboard the *Falaise*. A first, a second, a third lieutenant, a lieutenant of marines . . . a half-dozen midshipmen ranging in age from twelve, at a guess, to a pair of ancients of eighteen or more. Then the warrant officers: the sailing master and his mates, the surgeon, the purser, the carpenter and the bosun, the chaplain—by God, they had a chaplain, this was a first for him—the gunner, Mr Jenks . . .

'Ah, Mr Jenks, tell me about the guns—the eighteen-pounders I can see'—they were the ship's main armament, twenty-six of them lined up on the gundeck, dull black iron and scrubbed timber, every accoutrement in place, anything that was capable of a shine, shining—'but what of the rest?'

'Eight nine-pounders, sir, on the quarterdeck'—with a glance to the first lieutenant to make sure he was not talking out of turn—'and two more on the fo'c'sle. Then there are the smashers, sir, two for'ard, two aft, thirty-two-pounders.'

A swift exchange of glances with Mr Banjo, who was lurking in the background, though he was a bit on the large side for lurking. He would be wondering what Nathan was making of all this, after six months in the Temple prison. Confused, overwhelmed, apprehensive? But no, he did not feel any of these things. He felt like an imposter. But then, he always did. He *was* an imposter. It was all right.

'*Does she know who I really am?*'

'*Ah. Well, as to that—who are you?*'

They proceeded to the quarterdeck—a proper quarterdeck, not the fourteen-inch step that passed for one on the *Falaise*—and he took out his commission. A terrible moment when he thought he did not have it, then the cry of 'Off hats!' as he found it in his coat pocket. The stamp of several hundred feet and then the dead silence, with just the flap of that giant ensign in the wind.

'By order of the right honourable Lord Barham . . .'

The solemn assumption of powers that might enrage a jealous god.

'. . . hereof nor you nor any of you may fail as you will answer the contrary at your peril, and for so doing this shall be your warrant. Given under our hands and the seal of the office . . .'

At last he put it away and the order was given to dismiss. Back to work.

'Is it your wish to inspect the ship, sir, or would you prefer to go straight to your cabin?'

'The cabin, if you please, Mr Simpson. We can leave the ship for later— but what I have seen thus far does you credit. Great credit.'

Picking his words with care, but meaning them. Nathan's eyes had hardly been still since he came aboard, save when he was reading his commission, and he had not observed the slightest cause for complaint— rigging not so much taut as quivering with tension lest it be flogged for slacking, the decks holystoned to a sheen that would have done credit to a ballroom, and even the cook's slush that greased the wheels of the gun trucks looking like it might have been filtered through muslin before it was permitted to be applied. He was a small, dark man, Simpson, a slightly shrewish face that might be given to petulance if everything was not just so. But petulance Nathan could live with; he would have to consult the ship's log to know where he stood on flogging and other means of imposing order. He caught George's eye again, a subtle inclination of the head to follow them, for his position would have to be settled in the next hour or so, or he would be sleeping in the manger on the orlop deck.

But between them and the companionway there was another phalanx, not so orderly as the marines, and more anxious. These were the captain's servants, and there were a great many of them. More introductions. The steward, Mr Fox, his valet, his cook—he had a valet, his own private cook! Several others whose precise function was not immediately clear to him. Captain Taylor had clearly not stinted himself where his personal well-being was concerned. Nathan had met fewer servants in the average country house. But finally, down the steps and along the passageway, to the cabin itself. A bit bigger than on the *Falaise*, but not much, and he had to share it with a pair of thirty-two-pounder carronades, but he could live with that. The evening light was pouring in through the stern windows, the reflections of the seas dancing on the deckhead . . . Polished oak panels and gleaming brass, a chequered canvas stretched across the floor, and a cherry-wood dining table that would seat over a dozen, according to Mr Simpson, who must have dined here often, of course, and would again—Nathan was already planning the menu, his own cook, forsooth! Two cabinets, a writing desk, and his cot, discreetly curtained. And two quarter galleries, one of which provided him with a balcony over the sea, the other presumably containing his own private throne room, though he gave that a miss for the time being. All things considered, the cat was over the moon again, and down to another soft landing.

He saw Simpson shoot a glance at Mr Banjo, not for the first time, and decided it was time for his own introductions.

'This is Mr Banjo, who saved me from a watery grave off Boulogne'—just the once would do; he did not want to give the impression he made a habit of it—'and then had the misfortune to share my captivity in the Temple.'

Mr Simpson nodded curtly and received a perfectly respectable knuckle to the forehead in return—not a hint of irony that Nathan could detect.

He was about a foot taller than the first lieutenant, even with his head at a subservient angle, if only to avoid banging it on the deck beams.

'Mr Banjo is an experienced master gunner. I do not expect him to replace Mr Jenks, but if a position could be found for him as a gunner's mate, I can promise, he will not disappoint you.'

He avoided Mr Banjo's eye.

'Of course, sir. Yes. I will see to it. Banjo, you say?'

'Short for . . . ,' Nathan began, but thought better of it. 'Yes, Banjo.'

And so it went on. It had been easier to settle into the Temple. He sent for the purser with his muster roll and his other lists. They were 25 short of their full complement of 270 officers and men, but had recently provisioned for a three-month cruise. There was nothing to stop them sailing at once if he was so minded. He confirmed this with Mr Simpson, whose face was an unasked question.

'We are to join the Channel squadron off Ushant. If you have no objection, we will sail at first light.'

Mr Simpson had no objection, but at first light there was a tender from the shore with new orders. Nathan read the terse missive from Lord Barham. The French fleet had been sighted in the mid-Atlantic on a course that would take them to the north-west coast of Spain, and Admiral Calder had been ordered to lift his blockade of Rochefort and Ferrol and hasten to intercept them with his fifteen ships of the line. Captain Peake was hereby requested and required to join them without delay—off Cape Finisterre.

Chapter 17

The Fog of War

Finis Terrae, the Romans named it—World's End, at the western extremity of the Empire, where the sun slid into darkness at the end of the day and there was nothing beyond save the realm of monsters. They would have known better now, but the odd monster might have been a welcome relief from the total absence of shape or form that confounded Nathan's vision as he paced the quarterdeck of the *Panther* out in the Atlantic off the north-west coast of Spain.

They were six days out of Portsmouth. Six days of mostly favourable winds and clear skies, until now. And now—fog.

A patchy, summer fog. A blurring of the distinction between sea and sky, all the more impenetrable in that there was no point of reference, not a sail, not a rock, not a single image, even indistinct, on which to focus the eye, so that it felt to Nathan as if a milky cataract had formed across his vision, rendering him even more helpless than usual in this world of illusion—a blind pawn pushed across a vast, featureless board by the Grand Chessmaster of Whitehall.

But not so blind he could not see gunfire. For as the marine sentry waited on the forecastle to strike three bells into the evening watch, the opaque sky to the west was shot through with a rapid flashing of orange light, and a sound as of distant thunder came rolling back across the tranquil sea. It *could* have been thunder. Or even monsters. If you knew no better.

Nathan knew better. Or thought he did. If he was not greatly mistaken there was a great sea battle raging out in the Atlantic thirty leagues to the west of Finisterre—almost exactly where Lord Barham, in his omniscience, had placed Admiral Sir Robert Calder and his fifteen ships of the line, and while Nathan was not so vain or deluded as to imagine that he or his forty guns could make much difference to the outcome, he was loath to record his contribution with a graphic description in the ship's log of the abstract effects of gunfire in fog.

'Well done, Mr Shaw,' Nathan remarked to the sailing master, 'but now you have brought us to the right place, perhaps you would be good enough to whistle up a wind.'

For a moment he thought the sailing master might take him literally, for whilst you could not fault his navigation, thus far, he was a few degrees adrift in his grasp of irony. Then the pursed lips formed the ghost of a smile, and he nodded his belated appreciation of the jest. The exchange was typical of the awkwardness, not only between Nathan and the sailing master, but between him and all of his officers. It was not the first weak joke he had made in the last few days, nor the first time he swore it would be the last.

'Perhaps we might come a point to leeward and see if we can join in before it is too late,' Nathan advised. 'And it would be as well to clear the ship for action, Mr Simpson,' he instructed the first lieutenant, who was like a little ferret at his side, sniffing for the least scent of weakness or fear. 'And beat to quarters.'

There may have been no noticeable effect on the ship's progress, but her inner world was transformed upon the instant. Simpson barked a series of commands, a little marine drummer popped up on deck like the pantomime demon from a hidden trap—all it lacked was a puff of red smoke—the off-duty watch tumbled up from below to the beating of his drum, the armourer and his mates staggered about under armloads of muskets, pistols, and other instruments of death, and most impressively of all, the guns were run out with a long, satisfactory rumble of iron on timber that an imaginative soul might compare to the growl of lions, or perhaps panthers released from their cages—give or take the odd squeak.

It might be thought premature when they were moving at such a snail's pace, but it was impossible to judge distance in the present conditions.

The sound of gunfire was strangely muffled by the fog, the flickering lights playing tricks upon the eye. The battle could be ten miles away, or two. Besides which, Nathan told himself, there was a strong possibility of a frigate or two lurking on the fringes of the battle, as frigates did. According to the report he had read, Villeneuve had seven frigates to accompany his twenty ships of the line, Calder just two. And now the *Panther*, if she could only get there in time.

It was possible, of course, that Lord Barham had sent greater reinforcements. Nelson might have returned from the West Indies. Cornwallis might have spared a few ships from his blockade of Brest. But if not, Calder was going to face a devil of a fight, and nothing Nathan knew of him suggested he could pull off a brilliant victory against heavy odds. From what he had gleaned from his fellow officers, he had been promoted to rear-admiral as a matter of seniority, rather than for any great achievement on his part, though according to Mr Simpson, who kept abreast of such things, he was one of the navy's greatest experts on manoeuvring a fleet by signal flag. Ironic, then, that he faced his first critical test as a fleet commander in a fog.

Nathan's immediate concern had been for Calder's outnumbered fleet, but now as the *Panther* crept through the featureless sea, he began to give some thought to his own problems. A frigate had no business joining the line of battle, but when he could not see the disposition of either friend or foe he had to make up his own rules. If he had any kind of plan, it was to discover how the two fleets were placed and engage with one or more of the enemy frigates, but if the visibility did not improve, he was as like to catch a tiger by the tail.

The thunder and lightning were now pretty much incessant, and though he could still see no movement in the mist, he was persuaded that the battle was much closer than on his first impression, and distributed across a broader expanse of ocean. And yet it was almost as if there were two parallel worlds that normally led a separate existence but had been drawn eerily close, with only a thin membrane separating them— the tranquil world of the *Panther*, apparently alone in its isolation, and the world of chaos and confusion just beyond the veil. And then, as if an especially violent exchange of gunfire had blown it away, they saw a cluster of ships no more than a half-mile or so off their starboard bow, slugging it out, broadside to broadside.

Nathan crossed to the leeward rail in hopes of disentangling the various individual elements of the action, but if the guns had dispersed the natural miasma, in so doing they had created their own artificial fug of smoke. After a moment or two of silent contemplation through his Dollond glass he was joined at the rail by Simpson and several other of his officers, all training their own glasses upon aspects of the conflict and offering their own interpretations of what it involved. Nathan did not find this especially helpful to begin with but was reticent to enjoin silence, and eventually was able to form a picture, of sorts.

There were four, no five, or even six ships engaged. They were French, no Spanish. There is the San Rafael, *do you see her, sir? Spanish third-rate, eighty guns, I saw her in La Habana in '98. And that is the* Espanol, *sir, you can tell by the flag. What—are they firing upon each other? No—see the ensign! It is the* Malta, *she was at the Nile, only then she was the* William Tell. *French eighty-gun two-decker, do you remember, sir? You were there, were you not? I brought you a message from the admiral when you were in the maintop of the* Vanguard *after the battle, only you were dressed as an Arab and I was a mere midshipman in those days. The* Guillaume Tell, *he means, sir. Fled the battle, but then she was trapped in Valetta by the blockade, that is why we renamed her the* Malta. *Captain Buller, eighty guns. But I say, she is alone against five of the enemy!*

Finally he snapped and told them all to stow their banter, they were like a gaggle of squabbling seagulls. Instant silence. But now they were waiting to see what he was going to do about it, and he was damned if he knew. One British ship of the line engaged with five of the enemy. Where were the rest of Calder's fleet? Were they fled, defeated? He could see more clearly now. The five Spanish ships were more or less in a circle, covering perhaps half a mile of sea, and the *Malta* was at the centre, like a bear surrounded by slavering hounds, and yet some of the hounds were bigger than the bear. But she was firing both broadsides and the Spaniards seemed to be keeping their distance, for the present at least.

What was he to do?

To throw the *Panther* into such a shambles would amount to the useless sacrifice of ship and crew, for what could a frigate achieve against five ships of the line? And yet he must do something, and soon, for already they were drifting past. But then while he was still thinking about it the fog came down again. One moment the ships were there, pounding away at each other in their fury, the next they were gone, rubbed out as if by a giant eraser and just that strange, flickering light in the mist to show that the battle continued in the parallel world.

'Look, sir! To larboard!'

Nathan looked. They all looked. Over to the east, the curtain had rolled back to reveal a different tableau. A long line of ships stretching into the middle distance, suddenly clear of fog but each shrouded in a dense cloud of smoke pierced with the flame of forty, fifty guns. And above, stirring feebly in the still air, the blue ensign of Admiral Calder's command. They had found the British fleet, gloriously intact and undefeated—but what were they firing at?

Their heads turned as one, back to starboard, and there they were, like ducks in a fairground stall, but ducks that fired back. The enemy fleet. Not so clear, but clear enough at a distance of about two cables' lengths from the British line, and both fleets blasting away with their broadsides. A thousand guns at least, not that anyone was counting, for it was immediately, painfully obvious that if the *Panther* continued on her present course and at her present rate of knots, she would cruise sublimely between the two fleets. Save that there would be nothing sublime about it. She would be torn apart by the first decent broadside, whether it was British, French, or Spanish.

'I think, gentlemen, it might be advisable to wear ship.'

Nathan heard his voice and was surprised at its calm, but an instant later he realised it was the wrong order. To wear ship would mean falling off the wind and moving directly towards the enemy fleet. If they were spotted by the last ship in the enemy line, a slight adjustment would bring her broadside to bear, and they would be pounded by at least forty heavy guns for as long as it took them to come upon the opposite tack. Fortunately, the instruction had been confined to the small group of officers at the rail, which included the first lieutenant and the sailing master, and it had not yet been relayed to the crew.

'Belay that,' he uttered in the same calm tone, and then, as he often did when caught amiss, he raised his voice to issue a stream of orders himself.

'Larboard watch to the braces. Starboard to the counter braces. Stand by at the helm. Helm a lee, Mr Garrett. No higher. Bear up, bear up.'

He was keeping an eye on the trim of the sails, looking for the slightest sign of feathering, for they were sailing very close to the wind now, such wind as there was, and it would not do to be taken aback before the eyes of the whole fleet, though it was to be hoped they had more serious matters to occupy their attention.

'Steady, steady. Keep her so. Captains at the braces—now! Brace up! Steady, steady. Haul on the weather brace. Brace up, brace up . . .'

Slowly, laboriously, the frigate came up into the wind and began to cross the stern of the lattermost ship in the British line. Nathan could see her name now—*Thunderer*—a two-decker of seventy-four guns. He remembered her when he was with Nelson at the Glorious First of June, Albemarle Bertie had been her captain then—you did not easily forget a name like that—but he was an admiral now, sent God only knew where, save that Lord Barham would know better. Nathan could not recall who commanded her in his stead, if he had ever known. Whoever it was, Nathan hoped he could make out their flag, for the *Panther* would be a stranger to him, and if he took her for French or Spanish, he would not hesitate to fire upon her.

But they were crossing her stern now and she was holding to her course. He came up on her weather side with some notion of hailing her, to report the plight of the *Malta*, but he could never have made himself heard in such a barrage, and he doubted there was a signal for it. He crossed to the weather rail to see if there was anything further out to sea. There was. A flotilla of smaller ships flanking the British line, two frigates, a lugger, and a cutter, all flying Calder's blue ensign, and presumably hoping to pick off some straggler or engage with the enemy frigates, of which, thus far, he had seen no sign.

And then suddenly they were gone. Either they had sailed into a patch of fog, or he had, but they were no longer there, and looking back he saw that the *Thunderer* had vanished, too, and the entire British fleet with her, though he could still hear the thunder of the guns. And so it went on, in and out of the fog, worsened now by the fading light, the two fleets targeting each other only by the flash of their broadsides.

And then a series of rockets burst in the darkening sky and he knew from the slackening of fire that it was the order to break off the action. There were spasmodic outbreaks of gunfire for the next hour or so, but gradually it stopped altogether, and Nathan took in the courses and countered the fore- and maintops, waiting in the suddenly silent sea for further instruction.

He was waiting all night. Shortly before the end of the first watch the fog cleared and he could see a few ships to the south under a great display of stars, but if it was the British fleet, it was scattered over at least a mile of sea and pretty much becalmed. Of the enemy fleet there was no sign. Then, a few minutes into the middle watch, the little cutter *Frisk* came alongside, working under sweeps, and Nathan exchanged a few words with her commander, Lieutenant Nicholson. He had been sent by the admiral to report on the condition of the fleet and advise his captains to hold their station, not that there was any question of doing otherwise in such conditions. They had taken two enemy ships, Nicholson reported, both Spaniards, and lost none, which must count as a victory, though everyone expected the battle to resume at first light. What of the *Malta*, Nathan wanted to know, describing that he had seen her surrounded by five enemy ships and sorely pressed. But it turned out that it was the *Malta* that had taken the two Spaniards. Nicholson had the story at first hand from her commander, Captain Buller. She had been in the rear of the British line when the two fleets met, but in the confusion of the fog had found herself cut off and surrounded. Even so, she had fought back to such effect that at about eight o'clock she had forced the eighty-gun *San Rafael* to strike and then sent the *Malta*'s boats to take possession of the seventy-four-gun *Firme*. Both ships were now in British hands, and *Malta*, though much shot about, was still able to take her place in the line.

He would take news of the *Panther*'s arrival to the admiral, Nicholson said, which he was sure would be very welcome to him. Both men knew that five ships of the line would have been a great deal more welcome, if the battle was to be resumed in the morning.

The night continued clear but with very little wind. At dawn Nathan could see most of the British fleet, still scattered over a mile or two of sea, and far to the south the sails of Villeneuve's combined fleet. The wind such as it was had shifted slightly to the west during the night and now favoured the enemy, but they showed no sign of taking advantage of it. Calder, for his part, concentrated on forming his ships into line of battle and making such repairs as they could. Presumably Villeneuve was doing the same. By nightfall there had scarcely been a change in the disposition of the two fleets.

By morning the wind had backed to the north and freshened. The advantage was now back with Calder, and when the flagship signalled for all captains to come aboard, Nathan was sure it could mean only one thing.

They assembled in Calder's stateroom. There was a great air of expectancy. The loss of the two Spaniards had brought the two fleets closer in number, and according to Nicholson, who had been sent off on a scouting mission, three more were so badly knocked about as to be useless in a fight and barely able to keep at sea. Everyone anticipated the order to resume the engagement.

It was not forthcoming. Calder was a man of about sixty years old and had first fought in the Seven Years' War. He was old-fashioned in his appearance and, it became clear, in his approach. There was no straight at 'em so far as he was concerned. He believed in the time-honoured tactic of sailing parallel to the enemy and pounding away at each other until one was forced to withdraw, trusting that with their slower rate of fire it would be the French. But this meant coming up at the rear of the enemy line and gradually gaining on them until the two lines were directly opposed, a hard-enough manoeuvre in the best of conditions.

Besides, the admiral had something else on his mind. He was wary of the ships he had been blockading in Ferrol before he had been ordered south in search of Villeneuve. At the last count there had been eight Spaniards there under Admiral Grandallana, and four French under Gourdon. If they came out—and there was nothing to stop them—the British fleet would be caught between two major enemy fleets totalling thirty ships of the line.

There were murmurings of dissent. With the wind in the west, it was simply not possible for the enemy to emerge from Ferrol, declared Buller. There were nods of agreement. But winds could shift, C—alder insisted, as they had done in the last two days. Besides, there were other factors to consider. Two of their ships, the *Malta* and the *Windsor Castle*, were badly damaged, and there was a need to protect their two Spanish prizes— evidence of their triumph in the last battle. This was something they could be proud of, he said. They had fought against heavy odds and pulled off a famous victory. They must now resume the blockade of Ferrol and wait for reinforcements from either Nelson or Cornwallis before taking any foolish risks.

There were some angry mutterings from the captains as they waited to return to their ships.

'Foolish risks!' Nathan heard one of them growl—Griffith, he thought, of the *Dragon*. 'You might say that of any battle, and to save the country from invasion . . .'

'It is certainly no way to win a war,' agreed Buller, who was put out at being told the *Malta* was not fit for combat.

'No, but I tell you what,' said Griffith, 'it is a damn sure way of losing one.'

Chapter 18

At Pistol Shot

'So, what is the plan?' demanded Nathan, eyeing his companion warily across the several bottles of wine that were lined up on his table, some opened, some not.

'My personal plan?' considered the American, measuring the level of liquid in his glass. 'I'll tell you what my plan is, sir—to get drunk as an English lord and be damned to it.'

The frigate *Panther* was on a close reach, some thirty leagues west of Vigo, in the company of an American wine merchant, and Nathan was already three sheets to the wind.

'I was thinking more of your government's plan, sir—in so far as the present war is concerned,' he clarified, though he had been losing track of their debate for the last half-hour or so. As he recalled, they had covered the natural disposition of mankind towards wine, women, and song set against its propensity for unleashing horrendous violence at the drop of a hat, the virtues of philosophy set against the dangers of taking ideas too literally—liberty, equality, and fraternity being quoted as famous examples of this—and the current parlous state of Anglo-American relations, which had been the most recent topic, if Nathan had not missed something along the way. His visitor was clearly not constrained by the convention of avoiding the subject of politics, women, or religion at the table, though his discourse was alleviated by frequent references to the quality of the wine they were sampling, with some amusing asides on its producers, who were all, obviously, French. It was the kind of occasion, and conversation, Nathan enjoyed, and which had been missing for most of his time aboard the *Panther*.

'Ah, the government,' returned the American. 'Ha. Well, I cannot speak for the president, sir, who, if you want my opinion, don't know his arse from his elbow as far as the world outside Virginie is concerned, but anyone with the slightest bit of nous would be keeping the pair of youse kicking the shite out of each other while we get on with enjoying the good things of life. What is it your man said? The pursuit of happiness? Well, hear him—for all his blether.'

He drained his glass and selected another bottle.

'Well, that's as may be,' muttered Nathan. *The pair of youse* he interpreted as the French and the British, and had he been wholly American himself, and not just on his mother's side, he would probably have concurred with the sentiment. As it was, and having been the victim of this stratagem on more than one occasion in recent years, he felt mildly vexed at the level of manipulation involved—not that it was ever hard to manipulate John Bull and Johnny Crapaud into kicking the shite out of each other. 'But if it were not for His Britannic Majesty's Navy, they would be laying into the Americans, sir,' he pointed out, 'just as they were before the rebellion.'

'Which we call the Independence War,' said the American, politely setting him straight. 'But we'll not be falling out over it.' His name was Campbell, a short, stocky gentleman of forty years or more with a ginger beard, turning grey at the edges, and a fair bit of the Highlands about him still, though his family had been driven from Scotland by the Clearances, he had told Nathan, before making their way to America by way of Ulster shortly before the altercation between Britain and her former colonies. They had clearly prospered in their adopted country, for Mr Campbell was now skipper and part-owner of the brig *Grampus* of Philadelphia, heading back to her home port with a cargo of Bordeaux wine. They had run into each other in the Atlantic some few leagues off the west coast of Galicia, Nathan having been sent to shadow the French fleet with the other frigates while Calder resumed the blockade of Ferrol.

Unfortunately, a gale had driven them far out to sea, and by the time it blew itself out and the *Panther* had clawed her way back towards her station, there was no sign either of friend or foe—only the neutral American. Any hopes he had of enlightenment from Mr Campbell had been swiftly dashed—at least so far as the opposing fleets were concerned—for he had been battling the same gale, he said, since leaving Bordeaux, and had scarce seen a single sail except at a distance until he had run into the *Panther*. He could, however, offer Captain Peake the consolation of some of his finest vintage for a very reasonable price.

'I'll not have another,' said Nathan, covering his glass, having sampled the best part of three bottles already. 'But I'll take two crates of each if we can agree on a fair recompense.'

Mr Campbell dug in his pocket for a pencil and made some rapid calculations on a scrap of paper. Nathan had no idea what was fair or not, not being an expert on Bordeaux wines and his head befuddled by drink, but they came to an amicable agreement and Nathan called for his steward to pay the man.

Mr Campbell transferred the coins into his purse and sat back with a satisfied beam, but there was a quizzical look in his eye.

'I have tae admit that when I saw you coming up on us, I had a notion my trading days were over,' he confided.

'Oh, and why is that, sir?' enquired Nathan, disingenuously. When he had first assumed command of the *Falaise* half her crew had been Americans illegally pressed into the service of King George.

'Oh, let us say that my compatriots have not always profited from an encounter with an English cruiser,' Mr Campbell disclosed, 'the world being the way it is.'

'To be fair, I do not believe the French are any better,' Nathan answered reasonably.

'True, sir, very true. In fact, you're all bastards, the lot of youse,' declared Mr Campbell, laughing heartily. 'And now let us seal our understanding with another glass,' he insisted, reaching for the last unopened bottle. 'This is the Chateau Margaux which Jefferson himself praised most highly when he was in France, for he was a fine one for the wines, did you know, and compiled a list of the best of the Burgundies while he was ambassador there? 'Tis a rare vintage, and I'll throw in a couple of bottles gratis in the interests of harmony between our two great nations.'

'Go on,' said Nathan, pushing his glass across the table with feigned reluctance. He strongly suspected that Mr Campbell favoured the French over the English, like most of his compatriots, but he was not prepared to be ungracious about it. His mother was of the same inclination.

Over a final bumper he disclosed that he was himself an American on the female line, his maternal relatives being very big in the shipping interest, and that he had been born in New York before the Great Falling-Out, as he wisely opted to call it. He greatly admired the Americans for their absence of convention, he said, and their lack of deference. He did not say how he would feel about seeing these qualities transferred to a ship of war, nor that his father had spent seven years fighting for King George while his mother cheered on the rebels, and that this had been the cause of their own spectacular falling-out.

He and his guest parted on excellent terms, however, and Nathan accompanied him up on deck to make arrangements for sending the launch over with him to pick up the wine. The light was fast fading. It would be dark soon. Not impossible for the brig to slip away with Mr Campbell and his money, and their cargo no lighter. He put such churlish thoughts out of his mind.

'A very fine ship,' Mr Campbell declared, gazing blearily about the gun-deck, which was obscured by lines of washing, it being a day for drying out after the recent gale. 'Very fine indeed. How many guns did you say she has?'

'Twenty,' said Nathan, who had said nothing on the subject of guns at all, but was naturally inclined to lie about it for reasons he was not always clear about, save a habit of deception, at least when it came to warfare. He did not quite trust Mr Campbell, for all his amiability, and like as not the next ship he would run into would be a Frenchman.

He stood at the rail watching the man making his way back to the *Grampus* and reflecting that another officer would have taken his ship prize, pressed her crew to make up his numbers, kept half the wine for himself, and sold the rest. Truth be known he half-regretted not doing it himself, certainly for not having pressed a half-dozen prime topmen. They were probably British deserters anyhow.

In fact, there was no legal case for taking her prize—not in the present state of play between the two countries—but by the time it was thrown out of court the poor man might well have been ruined. Which was what Mr Campbell had doubtless been thinking while they were sat in his cabin drinking his wine and setting the world to rights. It reminded Nathan of the fable of the fox and the wolf, or any other story of predator and prey when cunning is the only recourse of the underdog against the over-mighty. But here was the launch coming back with his purchases, plus, it later transpired, the free bottles of Chateau Margaux Mr Campbell had promised—a sure sign that Nathan had paid over the odds, though he was well past caring.

When it was unloaded, Nathan had a dozen bottles sent round to the gunroom with his compliments and staggered back to his cabin to pass out.

He emerged the following day with a sour mouth and a sore head to find the American ship still with them at a distance of about a mile. This was surprising, for the wind was north-west by north and the weather fair—not quite fair for Philly, but not far from it—and he could conceive of no good reason why Mr Campbell was proceeding with them towards the coast of Galicia, unless he had been considerably more drunk than Nathan, which did not seem likely. It was possible, he supposed, that he had further business this side of the Atlantic that he had not wished to disclose, but it stirred his suspicions, even though he could think of no special reason for them.

They had just changed the watch and he was finishing his second cup of coffee when he heard a call from one of the lookouts. A sail—three to four points on the starboard bow.

He hurried up on deck and after a brief exchange with the officer of the watch climbed into the foretop to take a look. She was still hull down, at a distance of about three or four miles to the south-east, but they were on a converging course and closing fast. He noted with concern that the *Grampus* had parted company with them and was already halfway towards her. Mr Campbell might be anxious to conclude another deal, of course, but Nathan did not think so. On the other hand, what other reason might he have—except to give them information? He struggled to hold his glass steady—the gale might have blown itself out, but there was still a swell running.

Mr Simpson came up to join him and they observed the approaching ship in silence for a few moments. She was hull up now and they could see the gunports, but no guns yet. Even so, gunports, topgallants, and royals—odds on she was a ship of war, but of what nation? There was no indication of that yet—she could be one of their missing frigates—but she appeared to be coming straight out from the Spanish coast, probably from Vigo, on a course that would take her to the Azores or beyond, so the far greater likelihood was that she was French or Spanish. A moment later, and he was sure of it.

He snapped the glass shut and gave the order to clear for action.

They had practised every day at the guns since leaving Portsmouth, and Nathan had found there was very little room for improvement. His predecessor had drilled them to as near perfection as they would ever be and had clearly not stinted on powder and shot. They could invariably fire three rounds in five minutes, and their accuracy, at least in firing at a target that did not fire back, was as good as he had seen since his days on the *Unicorn*. The only improvement he had made was in having two extra gunports cut in the stern gallery on each side of his cabin, for he had noted there was a blind spot that could not be reached by the quarterdeck guns, a common failing in English frigates. The new ports had not been equipped with guns, but rings had been sunk into the deck for the tackle, and it was a simple matter to transfer an eighteen-pounder or a carronade from one of the other ports if the need arose. His only other concern was the shortfall in his crew. It had not been noticeable on the voyage out, but it might well become so during an engagement. He could have used those topmen from the *Grampus*.

He climbed up the mizzen shrouds a little way to see what she was up to. Both ships had shed their wind and were riding alongside each other like a pair of old friends. He did not see anything pass from ship to ship, though they were close enough, certainly for an exchange of information. But now the frigate was moving away and heading towards them. And finally she showed her colours and he heard the drumbeat, beating to quarters. *Branle-bas de combat!*

She was clearly up for a fight, and he was surprised—not because he thought she was shy, but for a lone French frigate to be out here in the Atlantic far from any port, it must mean she was on a mission, either to deliver dispatches, to cruise for prizes, or to find the enemy fleet and report back. In each of these cases she would be under orders to avoid conflict with an enemy she could not be confident of defeating.

He swept his glass slowly along her gundeck. They were about evenly matched, he thought, for size and speed, and she probably carried more or less the same number of guns, maybe a few more. Not enough to be sure of victory. He wondered if Campbell had passed on the erroneous information that the *Panther* had just twenty guns. It was quite possible, and he knew that from a distance she seemed no bigger than a corvette. He had thought so himself when he had first set eyes on her off Portsmouth.

They would discover the mistake soon enough, though. Then, if her captain thought better of it, she would fall off the wind and run south. Nathan did not want that to happen. He could not afford to go off on a long chase and leave his station unguarded. It occurred to him that she might be enticing him to do just that.

'Port your helm, Mr Bateman,' he ordered.

He was conscious of the surprise among the officers on the quarterdeck, for this would mean losing the weather gauge. One of the midshipmen came running up, touching his hat—Clinton, the youngest of them, his voice not yet broken and even more high-pitched with excitement; it was an embarrassment, as if they were playing at war in the schoolyard.

'Mr Bounton's compliments, sir, and permission to fire the bowchasers as they bear.'

It was a long shot, but Nathan gave his assent and the midshipman was almost back at the guns when the Frenchmen fell off the wind, just as he had anticipated, and fired a rippling broadside. She was heeling hard over and most of the shot went high and wide, but two holes appeared in the flying jib and another round struck the best bower with a clang that could be heard the length of the ship, the shattered pieces taking out two of the gun crew at the starboard bowchaser—and poor Clinton, who had just come running up to them with Nathan's orders. He saw the boy thrown to the deck and Mr Banjo scoop him up in his arms and hurry him below, but he looked lifeless to Nathan, and he could see the smear of blood he had left on the deck.

She was running to the south-west now with the wind on her starboard quarter, too far off for them to intercept her, but they would cross her stern at a distance of about six hundred yards, and he gave orders to double-shot the guns with chain and langrel, and to aim high. Some surprised looks there, too, for langrel was a villainous kind of shot comprised of various fragments of iron bound together, seldom used by anyone but privateers and aimed high into the rigging—but his chief concern now was to stop her running back to Vigo, and the only way they would catch her would be to bring her sails down. He could see her name now—*Perle*—one of the new *Pallas* class of forty-gun frigates, he thought—so new it was possible she had yet to see action. The guns would be a little heavier than their own eighteen-pounders, and he had an idea she carried the French equivalent of carronades, too, though not how many.

They fired a rippling raking broadside as they crossed her stern, but either the range was too long or their aim too poor, for he saw no visible effect. A poor start.

'Port your helm, Mr Bateman,' he called out again.

They came up on her lee but at a distance of three or four cables' lengths. They were set for a long chase, he thought, unless the long guns in his bow could bring down a spar, but to his surprise he saw that the *Perle* did not seem to be increasing her lead. In fact, if he was not much mistaken, she was dawdling, with both courses reefed, as if content to let him come up with her. She was either leading them on or she wanted to make a proper fight of it, broadside to broadside as they ran along together, with the minimum of manoeuvre, which must mean her captain was pretty confident of having by far the greater firepower.

He looked for the *Grampus* and saw her sailing serenely along a mile or so off their larboard quarter and on the same course. Damned hyena, he thought, running at the heels of the tiger, ready to strip the carcass when the fighting was done. He thought of giving her a shot to warn her off, but it would only have been a distraction.

They were coming up fast now, and he called out to Mr Phillips to stand by with the starboard broadside. From what he had seen, the *Perle* handled well, and she was heavily enough armed to give them a fight, but he very much doubted if she could match their rate of fire. It was the received wisdom, though he was not sure if it was based on experience or pure prejudice. Closer, closer, he could see her officers gazing back over the taffrail, seeing that snarling beast bearing down on them. He was close enough to see their faces, and he thought they did not seem overly concerned. His bowsprit was level with the tricolour, and at the last moment he wondered if they were coming up too fast, but it was too late now.

'Fire as you bear!' he called out.

They exchanged broadsides at little more than the range of a pistol shot, racing neck and neck like a pair of thoroughbreds, but he had been right—the *Panther* had a tad too much way on her and she was pulling ahead before his crews could fire a second round. He was framing an order to brace back when the *Perle* luffed up and crossed his stern. He almost ducked as her bowsprit swung towards him, just clearing his taffrail, and then she fired a raking broadside. He felt the wind of the shot on his cheek and a piece of flying metal took off his hat.

Others were not so lucky. The helmsman was cut in half, the bottom half still standing horribly at his station before toppling to the deck, the crew at the carronade thrown about like ninepins. Simpson was down in the scuppers clutching what was left of his arm, and a shower of cordage and tackle came crashing down onto the netting above their heads. Even before he could give the order, Nathan saw men rushing to the unmanned helm, others throwing the bodies that were obviously dead over the side and bearing the rest below.

He crossed deliberately to the taffrail, grasping it with both hands, staring out through the smoke. For a moment he thought she was going to carry on running to the south, but then she came swinging back, crossing his stern again to windward. He had just enough time to call out for the crew to throw themselves flat but forgot to do it himself, and was lucky when the hail of grape and roundshot had passed to find himself still in one piece. One of the French officers, possibly the captain, took off his hat and waved cheerfully to him as they passed, but then the twenty-six-pounder carronade Nathan had mounted in the quarter gallery fired at point-blank range and wiped more than the smile off his face. He wondered if there was anything in the rules of war to stop you mounting a gun in what normally served as the officers' latrine, but it was the last frivolous thought he had for some time.

The Frenchman was now coming up on their weather side, and for the next fifteen minutes or so they ran together on the starboard tack, exchanging broadside for broadside. Nathan had ordered his eighteen-pounders reloaded with round shot, firing straight into her hull—he was no longer afraid of her running for Vigo—but he kept the carronades firing high with chain and langrel, for he had seen that it was having a decisive effect, not only on the ship's handling, but as a distraction to the gun crews. There was so much debris and even bodies falling from above, the protective netting had collapsed onto the gundeck in parts. Then the main topmast came down, bringing the mainyard with it, and a tangle of rigging. There was a noticeable slackening in her rate of fire—Nathan calculated that his crew were firing at least three shots to every two of theirs—but the *Panther* had sustained plenty of damage herself, especially aloft, and there was no fear of pulling ahead of her again. Again, the Frenchman tried to cross his stern, but the crew were ready for it now and smartly backed the mainsail, losing so much way the two ships lurched together like a pair of drunks in Wapping.

'Stand by to repel boarders!' Nathan called out, for he had seen a horde of sailors and marines massing on the enemy forecastle. There was little chance that anyone had heard him, but others had seen the danger and the cry was taken up by the marine sharpshooters in the rigging.

The marine lieutenant, Mr Denton, was leading a squad of his men aft, though most of them had shed their red coats and black shakoes to work at the guns, and were in checked shirts and colourful Barcelona scarves. They met the first wave of boarders with a disciplined volley and then charged with their bayonets. A less-disciplined mob followed with whatever weapon they favoured, swords, pistols, pikes, tomahawks, lengths of chain, but the Frenchmen were now pouring over the rail.

Nathan fired both his pistols and exchanged sword strokes with one of the officers, possibly the same one who had waved to him earlier. Then they were separated by a mass of struggling men. To his surprise, Nathan saw his right arm was soaked in blood and there was a slash in his sleeve from wrist to elbow. Then Mr Banjo was at his side, laying about him with a cutlass in one hand and a tomahawk in the other. Nathan took a moment to see what the ships were doing, in as much as he could see for smoke from the guns that were still able to bear. Their bowsprit was caught up against the enemy mizzen, but there was no other entanglement that he could see. He looked to his helm and saw it was still manned with the new helmsman guarded by marines.

'Starboard your helm!' he called out to him, and with a sound very like a bough splintering from an oak the *Panther* pulled away, leaving about a score of boarders stranded up against the starboard rail. One of them tried to jump back to his own ship but fell into the widening gap, and the others, seeing they were well outnumbered, threw down their arms. Nathan was surprised that they had not lashed the yards together, but looking up he saw the reason why—there were few yards left to lash, and no-one aloft to lash them.

The two ships drifted further apart and the firing ceased. The *Perle* looked a perfect wreck with her mainmast a mere stump and at least half her yards down on the gundeck with a shambles of canvas and cordage.

Nathan looked to his own ship. Two of the guns were dismounted, and almost all the masts and yards seemed to have suffered some damage or other. He sent as many men aloft as he could spare while the rest saw to the guns and brought up more powder and shot from below. Meanwhile, he dragged off his coat and examined his own wound—a long slash from wrist to elbow, probably a sword, fortunately not deep. The surgeon and his mates were all busy down below, so he submitted to the attention of one of the midshipmen, who fumbled with nervous fingers until Mr Banjo intervened and finished it off for him.

By then they had made enough running repairs to be on the move again, and as they closed on the crippled Frenchman the foretop came crashing down across her bows, bringing down what was left of her jibs and staysails. She was wallowing in the swell, unable to bring her guns to bear, and as the *Panther* came up on her weather side she bowed to the inevitable and struck her colours. It was a quarter to eleven, three hours after the first gun had fired.

Nathan sent the marines over to take possession and a prize crew under the sailing master, Mr Caine.

'Send me a damage report as soon as you can,' he told him. 'And your assessment of whether you can sail her to Gibraltar.' He saw the man's eyes light up, for it would almost certainly mean a promotion for him. 'And send back her captain if he is still alive,' he instructed the marine lieutenant, 'and any of his officers still standing. I don't want them trying to take their ship back.'

While they were away, he made his own assessment of how much the *Panther* had suffered, but it was not enough to stop them from keeping their station off Finisterre. He was more concerned about the butcher's bill, but it would be some time before he had the exact number—roughly a dozen dead and twice as many wounded was the early estimate. Yet it could have been much, much worse. He was all too aware of the mistakes he had made in the early part of the battle—the most basic error being to think she was planning to run downwind after the first broadside.

He was distracted from his own inadequacies by the sight of the French captain coming aboard with two of his officers under a midshipman and a marine escort.

The midshipman stepped up for a private word.

'Mr Caine presents his compliments, sir, and begs to report that the prize is a forty-four-gun frigate with a crew of three hundred and thirty men'— he recited the figures in the manner of a schoolboy who has learned his lesson by rote—'some two dozen of whom are reported killed in action, above twice as many wounded, and as many again taken prisoner—which he will have the exact figure for you shortly, sir. And that in his opinion she is not capable of making her own way to Gibraltar or anywhere else, sir, in her present condition, and will have to be taken under tow.'

Another problem, but somewhat preferable to the situation the French captain found himself in.

'*Capitaine de frégate* Pierre Milius,' he introduced himself, presenting his sword to Nathan with a stiff little bow. He was a youngish man, probably in his early twenties, putting on a brave face but close to tears. Nathan did not blame him. He had felt the same when he had lost the *Unicorn*, and he was not even aboard her at the time.

'Keep your sword, sir, and your honour,' he said to him in French. 'You fought a good fight and have no reason to feel ashamed.'

He was about to send him below with instructions to his steward to make him and his officers as comfortable as their circumstances would allow when he saw the *Grampus* coming up on their starboard bow, close enough to indicate that Mr Campbell intended an exchange of views.

'Tell me, sir,' he addressed the Frenchman, 'how is it you were so keen to offer battle with no certainty of victory.'

'I deeply regret it,' said the captain, 'for it has cost me dear, but I had word that you were a twenty-gun sloop. Had I known you were so heavily armed I would never have taken the risk of jeopardising my mission.'

And what mission would that be, Nathan wondered? But the captain was unlikely to tell him, and he had another question for him: 'And am I right in saying that would have come from the American gentleman?'

Milius regretted he was not at liberty to say.

Fair enough, thought Nathan grimly. I will ask him directly.

When the French officers had been escorted below, Nathan called the boatswain over to issue a double ration of rum to the men still standing at the guns. Then he composed himself at the weather rail with his arms clasped firmly behind his back and his most severe, no-nonsense expression as the *Grampus* came alongside. Mr Campbell was waving his hat and beaming broadly.

'I give you joy of your victory, Captain,' he shouted. 'I would join you in a dram to celebrate, but I fear we must be on our way. We have delayed long enough to watch the fireworks.'

'And I fear I must insist,' Nathan called back, po-faced. 'Heave to and come aboard with your papers, sir, if you please.'

He was disposed to argue, but Nathan was having none of it.

'Quick as you like, sir, or I shall be obliged to hasten you with a quantity of grape,' he told him, 'and I do not mean the kind you are used to.'

By the time he came aboard, Nathan had been given the full butcher's bill. Twelve dead, twenty-eight wounded—three dangerously. The dead included the young midshipman, Clinton, the second lieutenant, Mr Bounton, who had been killed at his guns, the master's mate, Mr Telford, and the quartermaster, Mr Young. Nathan had scarcely known them—they had not served more than six weeks together—but they had been shipmates and now they were dead, and he blamed himself for it, at least in part. If he had not been so intent on stopping the *Perle* from escaping he would have fought a different kind of battle and they might have been alive now.

But if he needed someone to share the blame, there was always Mr Campbell.

'Never trust a Campbell', someone had said to him once. Another Scotsman, inevitably, but it did not mean it was not true.

This Campbell came stumbling up to the quarterdeck, clutching his ship's papers and looking something between fearful and indignant.

'Now then, Mr Campbell, I have evidence that you gave information to the enemy,' Nathan rebuked him sternly. 'Information that may well have cost the lives of a dozen of my men, and I would be entirely within my rights to hold you to account for it, sir, and render your ship and her cargo forfeit.'

This was for the court to decide, but it would do to be going on with.

Mr Campbell appeared bereft of the power of speech, but after several false starts he managed an impassioned rebuttal.

'Never in life, sir, never in life, upon my word as a gentleman, and my word is my bond, sir, in my occupation.'

'Do you deny that you informed the French captain that we were a twenty-gun sloop and ripe for the taking?' Nathan demanded.

'As God is my judge,' protested Mr Campbell. 'Never in life, sir.' He appeared to consider. 'But now, hold on a minute. Yes, yes. I was not going to claim the credit for this, but as you mention it—I did indeed tell him you were a twenty-gun sloop, and why? Because I knew it would seduce him into combat and he would be the loser by it. And see! See what is the result of it!' He threw a dramatic arm in the direction of the wreck that was the *Perle*. 'Tell me who is the winner and who is the loser?'

'That is no thanks to you, sir,' Nathan retorted, shocked by the brass neck of the man. 'I dare say you will be telling us you next that you—'

'And not only that, but see what I have here, sir, that was entrusted to my care, and without asking for it, mind, or giving any indication of whether I am for Boney or the Emperor of China.'

Campbell thrust one of the rolled-up documents at his accuser with an expression of outraged innocence, but before Nathan could take it from him or make any other response worthy of the name, they were interrupted by a cry of 'Sail, ho!' from the maintop lookout.

'Ten points on the starboard bow,' the man called out, and Nathan could tell by the urgency in his voice that she was a lot closer than she should have been if he had been keeping even half an eye open, and indeed, he had only to scramble a short way into the mizzen shrouds to see the worst.

'Belay on the rum,' he shouted to the bemused boatswain, who was in the process of dishing it out to a line of eager hands and had very possibly never heard such an order in his twenty years of service, 'and beat to quarters.'

Chapter 19

Ruse de Guerre

'Sorry to put the wind up you, Peake, but a level of deception seemed advisable in the circumstances, d'you see?'

Captain the Honourable Edward Colpoys Griffith possessed the affectedly languid air of a certain type of English gentleman who has been raised in the belief that his natural superiority can only be conveyed by the appearance of extreme boredom at all times. In fact, Nathan did not at all see, but Captain Griffith maintained a lofty indifference to the opinion of others less gifted than himself, in which category he clearly placed his junior colleague, along with most of the human race. They were seated at the table of his stateroom on the *Dragon*, which for reasons Nathan was far from understanding had been flying the French flag on her approach—thus prompting his hasty call to arms—but he accepted the apology, if that is what it was, with as good a grace as he could muster.

The *Dragon* had been one of the seventy-fours with Calder's fleet when it was scattered far out into the Atlantic by the recent gale. She had been heading back to the rendezvous off Ferrol when she had felt bound to investigate what her captain described as the 'rather odd ménage' of *Panther*, *Perle*, and *Grampus*. Perhaps the different flags had confused him, but Nathan harboured the suspicion that he had been hoping to get close enough to demand a share of the prize money before Nathan could justifiably claim to have the situation under control.

Griffith was no more than a year or so ahead of him in the Navy List but had done rather better for himself in terms of command, a circumstance which Nathan attributed to his being the nephew of a prominent admiral and having served as the flag lieutenant of Sir John Jervis in his youth. He accepted that this opinion was not unprejudiced. Griffith's career had survived an infamous confrontation with the mutineers at Spithead in '97, which had left a number of men dead and resulted in the seizure of his ship and his imprisonment by members of his own crew. Clearly his air of detached ennui had its limits, but he seemed affable enough now, if you overlooked the somewhat calculating look in his eyes which suggested, at least to Nathan, that he was overly conscious of his status and the ever-present menace of those who might challenge it. However, he toasted Nathan's victory over the *Perle* with a bumper of champagne which his steward brought up chilled from the orlop and demanded a detailed account of the engagement, which, with his constant interruptions and demands for clarification, Nathan found more exhausting than when he had been fighting it. He concluded his account by describing the part Mr Campbell claimed to have played in deceiving the French captain and producing the document the American had thrust into his hands.

'He maintains that it was given to him for safekeeping,' he said, 'with instructions to ensure that it was delivered if the action did not go quite the way Captain Milius intended.'

Griffith peered at it down the length of his nose. 'It is in French,' he complained.

'That is because it was written by Admiral Villeneuve,' Nathan pointed out, but he obliged with a translation. 'It is addressed to Admiral Allemand, whom he expected to find in the Azores with five ships of the line, requesting and requiring him to proceed to Ferrol to unite with the ships under Villeneuve's command, before sailing north to join with Admiral Ganteaume at Brest.'

Griffith peered down his long nose at the offending document.

'And do you think it is genuine?'

'It has every appearance of it.'

'But why would your Frenchie entrust such a missive to a complete stranger, and an American at that?'

'It is surprising, I agree, but the French are often sentimental in their attachment to Americans, equating them with Rousseau's noble savage.'

Griffith looked further perplexed. 'However, it was, as I have said, a pre-cautionary measure in the event of his being unable to continue with his mission to the Azores.'

'Indeed.' Griffith was still staring at the despatch as if the longer he looked the more sense it might make to him. 'Ferrol, you say?'

'That is what it says here.' He indicated the name of the port for Griffith's inspection.

'Well, it does make some degree of sense,' Griffith conceded reluctantly. 'The fact is, Peake, we have had information that while we were driven into the Atlantic, Villeneuve took the opportunity to slip into Ferrol.' His languid air had dissipated somewhat, and a frown of what could almost be concern had appeared on his brow.

'So he has joined forces with the Spanish,' Nathan reflected. This would give him thirty ships of the line, and with the French fleet at Brest—he did a swift calculation—even without Allemand's squadron, the allies would have a fleet of over fifty ships of the line at their disposal. Cornwallis and Calder had no more than thirty between them.

Bonaparte's grand plan was beginning to look considerably less fantas-tical than when he had first heard it.

'And where is Admiral Calder at present?' Nathan enquired.

'I presume he is heading back to Ferrol—as I was—but the expectation of his blockading such a large fleet must be considered, well, shall we say optimistic?'

Nathan considered that Captain Griffith did not have a lot of time for Admiral Calder, not that it surprised him.

'And there is no news of Nelson?'

'None that I have heard.'

'So, what do you advise?' Nathan enquired tactfully.

'Well, I am not a fleet commander.' For once, this might have been a relief to him. 'I suppose we can only stand off Ferrol and wait until the rest of the fleet comes up with us—but what of the *Perle*? Can she be saved, do you think?'

Nathan thought not, unless she be taken under tow to Gibraltar.

'I am afraid I cannot advise that, in the circumstances.' Griffith frowned. 'We will need every ship at our command.'

'Then we must burn her,' conceded Nathan regretfully, for she would almost certainly have been bought into the service and he would have been some several thousand pounds the richer for it.

'And what of the American—is she a legitimate prize?'

'That is a matter for the courts,' Nathan conceded.

'I was thinking of commandeering her to send a despatch back to England,' Griffith revealed. 'I think you will agree that it is vital for Lord Barham to be advised of our latest intelligence as soon as possible.'

'There is something else we might do,' Nathan offered diffidently. 'Something in the nature of a *ruse de guerre*. It is not without risk, but I believe it is the best chance we have of keeping Villeneuve shut up in Ferrol.'

The port of Ferrol had been chosen by the Bourbon kings of Spain as their principal naval base on the Atlantic and the capital of the maritime department of the North, but it had never quite attained that exalted status, more from inertia on their part than from any practical difficulties, for it was one of the finest natural harbours in Europe, with a basin that could provide safe anchorage for some several hundred ships, and an especially narrow entrance which, with its several forts, had proved a successful deterrent to enemy incursion and could even be shut with a boom. It also had the advantage of being virtually impossible to blockade, the strong Atlantic winds driving the blockading force far out to sea or along the treacherous Costa da Morte to the north, named for its preponderance of shipwrecks.

It was with only mild concern, then, that on an evening in late August 1805, the watchers on the battlements of Fort San Felipe observed a brigantine flying the American flag heading towards them under a full press of sail, pursued by an English frigate. The general alarm being sounded, it took no more than a few rounds from the twenty-four-pounders on the ramparts to persuade the frigate of the folly of this enterprise, and she turned away with a parting shot from one of her bowchasers, which missed.

Nathan had observed the fall of this shot with professional interest from the deck of the *Grampus*. It was a near-enough miss to appear convincing, he thought, without being so close as to cause discomfort to his new shipmates, who might have resented even superficial damage in the interests of his present subterfuge. He was even more relieved that the shots from the fort came nowhere near the *Panther*, which was now falling off the wind and moving swiftly out of range. He exchanged a glance with George Banjo, the only member of his crew he had permitted to accompany him. So far, so good, but there was a long way to go.

Captain Griffith had been reluctant to authorise his mission, if not so much out of concern for Nathan's safety as the possibility of being held responsible if it resulted in his capture, or indeed, the loss of a perfectly good frigate.

'Why can we not send Mr Campbell?' he had demanded when the venture was put to him.

'To put it bluntly, because we cannot trust him to give the right information,' Nathan had replied.

And so Mr Campbell was being held hostage aboard the *Panther* while Nathan took his place, relying on the crew's concern for their employer's welfare to dissuade them from betraying him to the French navy. He had convinced Griffith that he was the right person—if not the only person—to play the part, having played a similar role many times in the past, and assured him there was very little risk. The wind had shifted to the northeast, which would permit him to sail into Ferrol on a bowline, deliver his message, and come out with the wind on his quarter. He would be back by nightfall.

Privately, however, he was not so confident. He knew that it was the kind of reckless and vainglorious action he would have deprecated in Sir Sidney Smith.

But then, as Smith frequently reminded him, they had much in common. Nathan could hear his voice now. 'Come, sir, admit it—there is far more of a thrill in being a spy than in being the captain of a ship.'

Smith was far the better actor, though. He lived whatever part he took upon himself, for as long as it suited him to do so, whether it was a Turkish pasha or a Westminster politician. It was all part of the game. Not that this was to diminish its importance in his eyes; life itself was a game. Nathan had more of his father's moral rectitude, or so he liked to think. Others would not have agreed.

But it was too late for regrets, for there was a two-decker of the French navy bearing down on them out of the morning haze, and an officer with a loud hailer instructing them in French and in English to heave to and present their papers for inspection.

Nathan greeted the officer who led the boarding party with every appearance of affability. He was a fresh-faced youth of about twenty years with the rank of ensign, which did not exist in the British navy but was somewhat above that of midshipman, without conferring the status of a lieutenant. This in no way diminished the young man's sense of importance. Nathan longed to kick his backside, but entering into the character of Mr Campbell, he led him down to his cabin and offered him a glass of wine instead. It was coldly refused.

'Your papers, if you please, *monsieur*.'

Nathan had them to hand. They showed the *Grampus* to have been built and registered in Boston in 1793 and acquired eight years later by the Messrs Duncan and Alexander Campbell, master mariners and wine merchants of Philadelphia.

'And who would you be?' demanded the officer.

'I would be Alexander,' replied Nathan, 'at your service, sir.'

'And your manifest?'

Nathan showed him the cargo list.

'Bordeaux wine? That is all you are carrying?'

'That is all, sir. You are sure I cannot offer you a sample?' His hand hovered above the bottle of Château Lafite which he had appropriated from Campbell's private stock.

It stayed hovering.

'Then why were you running from the English frigate?'

A resigned shrug. He must be careful not to overact. 'For the reason that any American must who does not wish to lose his prime hands to the British navy.'

The officer picked up the ship's log. 'You have come directly from Bordeaux?'

'I have, sir. Though we were considerably delayed by the recent gale.'

Nathan had ensured there was no reference in the log to the encounter with the *Panther* and the frigate's subsequent engagement with the *Perle*.

'And did you observe any other English vessels in the course of your journey south?'

'I did indeed, sir. A fleet of above thirty sail, no more than a few hours north of here off the Costa da Morte.'

The ensign lost his air of cool detachment.

'You are sure of that?'

'I was close enough to read some of the names. I have listed them in the log.'

He showed the officer the page. He had scribbled down the names of fourteen ships, thinking that to write them all down might arouse suspicion, but several of them would have meant a great deal to anyone who had served with Villeneuve in the Mediterranean.

'Thirty, you say?'

'That is the number I counted. There may have been more.'

'You had no closer contact?'

'I did not. I clapped on as much sail as we could carry and made directly for Ferrol. Unfortunately, one of the outlying frigates gave chase, as you will have observed.'

'Why Ferrol?'

Nathan permitted himself another shrug. 'It was the nearest refuge. Even then, it was a close call.'

The officer studied him carefully for a moment. Then abruptly he climbed to his feet.

'I must require you to come with me, sir, and report to my captain. And bring your papers with you.'

Nathan made a show of protest.

'And who is your captain, sir?' he enquired.

'Captain Lucas, sir, of the *Redoutable*.'

Chapter 20

The *Redoutable*

Nathan took off his hat and held it in both hands in front of him, as he imagined Mr Campbell would have done in similar circumstances. He composed his features into an expression of respectful supplication. The wind was picking up a little. He could feel it in his hair and it lifted the tricolour at the stern of the French ship. She was a third-rate of seventy-four guns, the ships that formed the backbone of the French battle fleet, as they did of the British. Beyond her stern, he could see down the length of the Ferrol anchorage. It was filled with a great many ships of war, and to his concern, though he hoped it did not show on his face, they appeared to be coming out.

Captain Lucas was in any case intent on a study of the ship's log the ensign had just delivered to him. He looked sharply up at Nathan.

'You are sure you did not imagine this?'

'I am not blessed with so powerful an imagination, sir,' Nathan confessed.

Lucas looked down again and read from the log. '*Temeraire, Neptune, Belleisle, Victory* . . .'

At the last name he looked up again, his eyes searching Nathan's. He was a man of about forty years, so small and slight he appeared quite doll-like, not much more than five feet high, Nathan thought, his face pitted with the marks of smallpox and with pointed, slightly prim features and a small tight mouth that suggested he might be something of a martinet.

Everything Nathan had seen since coming aboard the *Redoutable* suggested that he ran a tight ship.

'Do these names mean anything to you?' he demanded.

'Other than being British ships of the line . . . ?'

'Nothing more?'

'I regret—'

'And yet you considered them important enough to enter in your log.'

Nathan said nothing.

'You are aware that *Victory* is the flagship of Admiral Lord Nelson?'

'I was not aware of that, no.'

'But you do know who he is?'

'I do.'

Lucas again consulted the log.

'*Ajax, Warrior, Dragon, Defiance* . . .' He looked up again. 'These are the ships of Admiral Calder.'

Nathan looked politely interested.

'So, this would suggest the two fleets—of Nelson and Calder—are combined.'

Nathan spread his arms in hapless ignorance. 'All I know is that it appeared to be a very large fleet.'

Lucas exchanged a glance with the lieutenant who stood at his side. Then he turned to observe the ships in the anchorage at their stern. It was obvious now that they were coming out.

'I must speak with the admiral,' he said to the lieutenant. 'If it is not already too late.' He addressed Nathan again. 'I fear I must oblige you, sir, to await my return.'

'But, sir, I must return to my ship . . .' Nathan made a gesture towards the *Grampus*, still hove-to in their lee.

'I will not be long. You may wait in my cabin.'

Lucas was gone for above an hour. Nathan remained under guard in his cabin. It was apparent, however, that they were under way. For the sake of form, he asked the ensign if they were heading into Ferrol and received, as expected, no reply.

At length, however, another officer appeared to present the captain's compliments and request his presence back on deck. As he emerged from the companionway he saw that they were at sea, a mile or so out from Cape Priorino Grande, to the north of the Ferrol estuary. They were bearing north-west, with the wind on their beam, and the *Grampus* a little way off their starboard quarter on the same course. But then he looked astern and saw the other ships. An entire fleet, standing out to sea in line ahead.

Lucas was at the weather rail with his glass, looking further out to sea. He called Nathan over and passed the instrument over.

'Recognise them?'

Even at a distance of well over a mile Nathan had no difficulty in knowing the *Panther*. Behind her was another ship that he guessed must be the *Dragon*, with the *Perle* in tow. He was glad to see that they were keeping their distance.

'I regret not,' he said. Lucas took the glass back.

'One of them is the frigate that pursued you into Ferrol,' he pointed out.

'I fear one frigate looks to me very much alike to another,' Nathan told him with a genial grin. 'Is there to be a battle?'

'I regret that is beyond my control,' replied the captain.

An officer approached to inform him that there was a signal from the flagship. Lucas trained his glass for a moment and then shut it with a snap.

'I fear you must remain with us a little while longer, Captain, but you may rest assured there will be no battle. Not in the immediate future, at least. We are heading south.'

Chapter 21

The Revenant

For the next four days and five nights the combined French and Spanish fleet made its stately and sometimes ponderous progress down the Atlantic coast of Spain and Portugal—rather like the Spanish Armada, Nathan thought, in reverse. There was no further sign of the *Panther* or the *Dragon* or any of the British fleet. Nor, after the first night, of the *Grampus*.

'I fear that in the confusion of our retreat, if I am permitted to call it that, she slipped into the night,' Lucas informed him the following morning. 'It appears that you have been abandoned, *monsieur*.'

Nathan wondered what would happen to Mr Campbell as a result. He would probably not be thrown to the sharks, or whatever other species of fish dwelt in the Bay of Biscay, but it would be a long time before he got back to America. For the time being, however, he was more concerned with his own fate.

'I am afraid you must accept our poor hospitality for a while longer,' Lucas informed him. 'I will ask the purser to find you a berth and a place to mess until we can put you ashore.'

This translated into a share of the same rations provided for the crew, which at least included wine, and a stall among the animals on the orlop deck, which Nathan was to share with his 'manservant'. Fortunately, after his recent experience of French hospitality he had thought to bring his purse with him, and a few coins distributed in the right place provided them with a few extra comforts in the way of food and bedding—and there was no restriction on their freedom of movement. They were even permitted to climb the rigging and perch in the tops, from where they had a view of the entire fleet—thirty-three ships of the line and seven smaller vessels, covering almost three miles of ocean. They included four ships of over a hundred guns, including the giant *Nuestra Señora de la Santísima Trinidad* of four gundecks and one hundred and thirty-six guns, which Nathan had heard was the most heavily armed ship in the world. It also seemed to be one of the least manoeuvrable, but even so, it seemed extraordinary to Nathan that with such a fleet at his disposal, Villeneuve had not proceeded northward in accordance with Bonaparte's instructions for the conquest of Britain.

Mr Banjo had the answer.

'*Erujeje*,' he said simply. A Yoruba word which loosely translated as 'terror', he explained, 'only something greater than that.'

Admiral Villeneuve was terrified, he said, of Admiral Lord Nelson. The very name reduced him to a state of unspeakable dread, not unlike that inspired by the *houngans*—the priests of voodoo they had encountered on the island of Saint-Domingue.

'And how have you come to this conclusion?' Nathan wanted to know.

Mr Banjo had come to this conclusion because, unlike Nathan, he mingled freely with the crew, and possessed a charm and ease of manner that invited confidences, even from people he had only just met. It had been one of his chief advantages in his former life as a secret agent. It probably helped in this case that he spoke fluent French and was always willing to help out if there was a heavy weight to be shifted or a rope to be hauled upon. He was also an expert armourer, adept in the repairing and firing of guns. By the evening of the second day he had been invited to share meals with the gunner and his mates, who provided him with some of his most useful nuggets of information. The French admiral, he told Nathan, was by nature weak and indecisive. He had no confidence in himself, his men, or his ships, and was paralysed by dreadful forebodings, invariably involving Admiral Nelson.

Villeneuve, he reminded Nathan, had been one of the French commanders at the Battle of the Nile. He had seen Nelson and his fleet sweep down upon them when they believed themselves to be in an unassailable position and simply blown them away. Villeneuve had only survived by cutting his cable and running, and he had been running ever since.

Whether this was true or not, it did not bode well for either the admiral or his fleet that this was what his own men were saying. And according to George, it was a view shared by the Spanish admiral, Gravina, who had transmitted it via diplomatic channels to Napoleon. George had this from the *Redoutable*'s gunner, who had it from the gunner on Gravina's flagship, the *Principe de Asturias*, who heard it from Gravina himself while listening at the skylight of his stateroom.

The one thing that George could not discover was where they were going. No-one seemed to know. He did not know if Villeneuve did.

When the fleet turned south out of Ferrol, it had been expected that they would double back during the night and attempt to evade the blockading British fleet and proceed on their journey northward. But they kept going south—as if the French admiral was anxious to put as much distance as possible between himself and his nemesis—or at least where, thanks to Nathan, he believed his nemesis to be.

But finally, on the morning of the fifth day out of Ferrol, they arrived at Cádiz.

It was as far south as Villeneuve could have gone without leaving Europe altogether, and probably the safest refuge he could have found anywhere on the Atlantic seaboard. This was where Francis Drake had singed the King of Spain's beard at the time of Elizabeth, but since then it had been considerably fortified, and the English had failed in every attack since. It was also the scene of Nathan's great falling-out with Admiral Jervis, which had cast such a blight on his subsequent career. It was not, for him, the most auspicious of destinations.

After consulting the ship's purser, he was informed that he would be handed over to the American consul at the earliest opportunity. Nathan hoped he might then find a berth on a ship to neutral Lisbon, and thence, England. But for two days he was left kicking his heels on the *Redoutable*, at its mooring in the outer harbour.

Then came a summons from Captain Lucas.

Nathan knew the moment he entered the cabin that it was not to wish him bon voyage. Lucas was seated at his table in the stern windows, flanked by two of his officers. Their faces were stern, and there were two armed guards in attendance, along with several other individuals seated in the background.

Nathan was kept standing.

'I regret to inform you, sir, that a charge has been laid against you,' Captain Lucas began. He raised his voice in the direction of the men seated along the side of the cabin. 'Sergeant Scillato.'

A man in the blue-and-white uniform of the French army stepped forward and saluted smartly. He was a man of about thirty years of age, with a dark complexion and the kind of moustaches that looked designed to be twirled, though he did not look like the twirling sort. His features were gaunt, his expression grim. Nathan could not recall ever having met him, but this was not conclusive.

'State your name for the record,' Lucas instructed him.

'Sergeant Antonio Scillato.'

'You are a Neapolitan in the service of the French army."

'I am.'

'And is this the man you claim to be Captain Nathaniel Peake, an officer of the British navy?'

It was a question Nathan had been braced for on many occasions over the past few years. This in no way lessened the shock.

'It is,' said Sergeant Scillato.

'And what grounds do you have for this accusation?'

'In the Year Five I was serving as a lieutenant of marines aboard the *Minerva*, flagship of Admiral Prince Francesco Caracciolo of the Royal Neapolitan Navy.'

He stared straight ahead of him, speaking French with a heavy Italian accent. Nathan's apprehension, already acute, increased.

'In the spring of that year an English frigate, the *Unicorn*, entered the Bay of Naples and the commanding officer came aboard the flagship to pay his respects.'

Nathan remembered the occasion as if it were yesterday—not so much because of that particular event as for what had happened afterwards. He also remembered Prince Caracciolo, for much the same reason. He was a man of great charm and charisma who had joined the British navy as a young man and served with distinction during the American Independence War and later, against the French at Genoa. They had conversed very agreeably, in English, over a bottle of Campania wine.

'Later, I was ordered to escort the officer ashore with a squad of marines and conduct him to the residence of the English envoy, Sir William Hamilton,' Scillato went on.

Nathan remembered that, too. It was the first time he had met Lady Emma Hamilton. He had no memory of the officer of Neapolitan marines.

'And you are in no doubt that this is the same man?' Lucas ascertained.

'No doubt at all, sir. I stood as close to him as I am now, and later I escorted him back to his ship.'

'You have not met him since?'

'I have not.'

'And you have no prejudice against him?'

'Other than believing him to be a British naval officer?' put in one of the other officers with a grim smile.

'No, I do not.'

'Do you have any questions for this witness?' Lucas asked Nathan.

'I . . .' Nathan shook his head bemusedly. 'I am completely at a loss. I have never been to Naples. So far as I am aware, I have never met this gentleman.'

'He is lying,' said Scillato calmly.

'Thank you, Sergeant. You are dismissed,' said Lucas.

Scillato saluted, turned smartly on his heel, and marched from the cabin.

'Believe me, sir,' began Nathan, spreading his arms in what he hoped appeared to be helpless bewilderment.

Lucas raised a hand. 'There is one other witness.' He glanced towards the men seated in the shadows. 'Lieutenant Morel.'

Another man stepped forward. This one wore the uniform of a French naval officer. Nathan vaguely recollected seeing him on the quarterdeck of the *Redoutable* during the voyage south. He tried to think where he might have seen him before but had no recollection of it.

'State your name for the record.'

'Lieutenant Jean-Baptiste Morel of the French Imperial Navy.'

'And do you recognise this man?'

'I do.'

'Identify him, if you please.'

'Under his present guise?'

'As you knew him previously.'

'Previously I knew him as Captain Nathaniel Turner, an American sea captain.'

'And in what circumstances?'

'In the Year Ten I was serving aboard the flagship *L'Océan* in Saint Domingue when we had a visit from the envoy of the United States government, whose name I recall as Imlay, and with him was another American who was introduced as Captain Turner, who later accompanied the emperor's sister to the island of . . . '

'Thank you, Lieutenant,' said Lucas sharply, 'And this was definitely the man you now see standing before you?'

'It was.' He hesitated a moment before adding: 'And I later heard that he was accused of running guns to the insurgents.'

Lucas addressed Nathan. 'Do you have a question for this witness?'

Nathan shook his head. He maintained his expression of bemused innocence.

'Thank you, Lieutenant, you may stand down.' He looked at Nathan again. 'Do you have anything to say to these accusations, sir?'

'What can I say, save that I was never in my life in Saint-Domingue and never in Naples,' Nathan declared. 'And how can I be two different people—a British naval captain called Peake and an American called Turner?'

Lucas conferred for a moment with his two associates. Then he addressed Nathan again. 'There is clearly a case to be answered,' he said. 'Further investigation must be made, and I am afraid that in the meantime, sir, you must consider yourself under close arrest. Master-at-arms.'

Another man stepped forward and took Nathan by the arm. But one of the other officers was murmuring in Lucas's ear.

'One moment,' Lucas said. 'It has been brought to my attention that you have a servant with you.'

'That is right. My manservant, Mr Banjo.'

'How long has he been with you?'

'Oh, almost ten years now.'

'And is he slave or freeman?'

'He was a slave when I acquired him—in New Orleans. But slavery was abolished in Pennsylvania some years since, so I gave him his freedom. He has been with me ever since.'

'Aboard your ship?'

'Mostly, but also at my home in Philadelphia.'

Lucas instructed the master-at-arms to have Banjo brought before them.

A few minutes later he was led into the cabin. He wore the same bemused expression as Nathan. He confirmed that Captain Campbell had bought him as a slave in New Orleans and later given him his freedom. He had worked for Mr Campbell and his family at their home in Philadelphia and had shipped with him to a great many parts of the world, but never to Naples or to Saint-Domingue. This was as they had rehearsed before leaving the *Panther*, and despite a tendency to overact the role of a frightened servant, Nathan thought he did very well.

Lucas had words with his two confreres and announced it was clear that additional enquiries would have to be made. There were a number of men among the fleet who had served in Saint-Domingue at the time in question who might, he said, be able to shed more light on the matter. It might also be necessary to send to Paris for instruction. In the meantime, he was prepared to accept the gentleman's parole.

As soon as they were released, they headed for their usual spot in the maintop where Nathan filled Banjo in on the details of the charges that had been made against him.

'This man Scillato,' he said. 'Do you know him?'

Banjo shook his head.

It was not altogether surprising. The ship's complement numbered more than six hundred and forty men and boys, including almost two hundred soldiers, a far larger contingent than there would have been on a British ship of the same size.

'See what you can find out about him,' Nathan said.

They met in the same place two hours later.

'They call him *le revenant*,' Banjo said.

'Why?'

'Because he came back from the dead. He is a phantom—a ghost.'

'Did they say any more than that?'

'Oh yes, plenty. He was a supporter of the Revolution in Naples in '99, and when the royalists got back in, they strung him up from a lamp-post. Somehow he managed to survive, but when he returned to his home he found his wife and children had been butchered.' He took Nathan's expression for incredulity. 'They killed the families of anyone who had anything to do with the Revolution,' he went on, 'thousands of them—men, women, children . . . It was much reported at the time, and Admiral Nelson was widely held responsible, but you would have been in India . . .'

Nathan had heard the reports, even in India. It was after the Nile when Nelson took the fleet into Naples and met Lady Hamilton. But shortly after his arrival, there had been a revolution—inspired and aided by the French, it was said—and Nelson had transported the royal court to Sicily for their safety. The Hamiltons went with them, Emma being a close personal friend of Queen Carolina. While they were away Naples was retaken by the royalists, but a deal was struck to give the rebels safe conduct to French territory, signed by representatives of the British, the Russians, and the Turks—united then in an alliance against the French. When the royal family returned, however, they reneged on the deal, and convinced Nelson to support them. There were hundreds of executions. Admiral Caracciolo, who had agreed to serve the revolutionary government, was hanged from the yardarm of his own flagship, and then the mob went berserk, butchering the families of everyone suspected of supporting the rebels.

Nelson had been made Duke of Bronte by the king in gratitude for his assistance, but the atrocities had cast a dark shadow on his reputation, even in England. Among republicans in Italy, he was known as the Butcher of Naples. This had provoked one of Nathan's rare fallings-out with Tully, who had been loud in his condemnation. Although he was not strictly speaking British—the Bailiwick of Guernsey having its own laws and constitution—he had a highly developed sense of British 'honour', and he felt this had been severely compromised by what had happened at Naples on Nelson's watch.

Nathan thought he was probably right, but he would not say a word against Nelson. Nor would he blame the malign influence of Emma, as many of Nelson's friends did. If anything, he blamed the wound suffered by Nelson at Aboukir, his sense of order and his justifiable fear of revolution. He even blamed Vesuvius, the volcano that loomed over the Bay of Naples and was said to infect the atmosphere with its chthonic vapours. Since then, he had largely succeeded in putting the events of Naples out of his mind. Much worse had happened in Paris, at the height of the Revolution, he told himself, or more recently under the French in Saint-Domingue.

But now the ghost of Naples had come back to haunt him.

'His shipmates say he lives only for revenge,' George said.

Over the next few days Nathan observed Sergeant Scillato on a number of occasions, usually up in the rigging, at firing practice with the other soldiers. Scillato's usual station was the mizzentop, and his targets were the officers on the enemy quarterdeck. Life-size cutouts were made of them, and they were lined up on the taffrail for Scillato and his comrades to shoot at. At the end of an exercise, they were practically shot to pieces, and they had to make new ones for the next shoot. Captain Lucas had them practising every day. His plan, Mr Banjo reported, was to sweep the enemy upper deck with musket fire and grenadoes and then board. That was what his crew was trained to do.

Nathan was unimpressed. It was big guns that won battles at sea, not small arms, he remarked to Mr Banjo. Mr Banjo agreed, but he said the French had a problem with their powder. He had heard this from the armourer. Gunpowder was three-quarters saltpetre, which was usually made from the excrement of bats. The British got theirs from bat caves in India—a piece of knowledge of which Nathan, despite his long experience of guns, had until then been ignorant. The French usually got theirs from bat caves in South America, but the British blockade had led to a serious shortage in supply, so they had resorted to scraping human urine from the walls of *urinoirs* and cellars because that, too, was strongly laced with saltpetre. But not as much as bats' urine. And according to the armourer, who was from Normandy, the French had very weak piss due to their practice of diluting their wine with water. Thus, it made for very poor gunpowder.

Nathan listened to this explanation with wonder, but was not entirely convinced.

The days grew into weeks, the weeks to months. His parole, he discovered, did not extend to leaving the ship. This was for his own safety, the master-at-arms explained, Cádiz being a dangerous place for foreigners. The injunction did not extend to Mr Banjo, however, and at the first opportunity he went ashore in one of the tenders with a party of French sailors, looking to patronise the bars and brothels of the port. He was gone for several hours and returned with a thoughtful expression on his face, which was the nearest he ever came to looking shaken.

Cádiz was the poorest place he had ever visited, he said, and near to being the most violent. All through the summer there had been an epidemic of yellow fever which had decimated the local population and caused a severe shortage of food and naval supplies. There was famine in Andalusia and in the port itself, hordes of beggars on every street and gangs of ragged urchins as scrawny and diseased and fierce as packs of feral dogs. So many Frenchmen had been murdered, they had been ordered to go ashore armed and in groups of ten or more, and to be back on board before dusk.

As if this was not bad enough, there had been serious clashes between mobs of French and Spanish seamen over what had happened at Finisterre. The Spanish apparently blamed the French for the loss of their two ships, claiming they had been abandoned to their fate. The French infuriated their allies by sneering that the two ships had been part of a Spanish flotilla of five that had surrounded a single English man of war, which had not only managed to fight them off but had taken two of them as prizes. The Spanish ships were seriously undermanned, George reported, and the press gangs were on the rampage, raiding taverns and brothels and even homes, seizing every able-bodied man and boy they could find to serve in the fleet, even if they had never been to sea. Fewer than ten per cent of the Spanish crews were experienced seamen, he had been told.

Meanwhile, the ships remained at their moorings. This was partly due to the wind, which remained stubbornly in the west, blowing directly into the harbour. In the first week of October, it was reported that Admiral Nelson had arrived to take over the British fleet, bringing four ships with him from England as reinforcement. Another rumour had it that there was 'a grand incendiary project' to attack Cádiz with fireships and other devices, as had happened at Boulogne. Nathan wondered if this involved Sir Sidney Smith and his friend Mr Fulton, with their infernal machines, but though these were anticipated with dread, and squads of armed mariners rowed about the anchorage every night in search of them, they never materialised.

Then came the most spectacular news of all: Bonaparte had abandoned his plans for the invasion of Britain.

This had been reported widely in the Portuguese newspapers, Mr Banjo said, and had made its way by one means or another to Cádiz. The French army of England had been withdrawn from its bases on the Channel ports and was marching eastward. No-one knew exactly where or why—except possibly Napoleon himself and a few favoured members of his staff. It was said that he blamed the French navy for the failure to carry out his Grand Plan—specifically Villeneuve. He had publicly declared that the admiral was a cowardly poltroon who did not have the strength of character to command a frigate.

'He said those exact words, did he?' demanded Nathan sardonically.

'Those exact words,' said Mr Banjo, with a straight face, who had it direct from the armourer, he said, who had it from the captain's steward, who had it from the lips of the captain himself, whom he had overheard discussing the matter with the first lieutenant in the privacy of his cabin. Nathan, despite his reliance upon this intelligence, and his own experience of Mr Kidd, was shocked that these private exchanges among senior officers could be so swiftly disseminated among the rest of the crew. But he hungrily awaited further intelligence.

A few days later Mr Banjo reported that Villeneuve's replacement was on his way from Paris. Then, that he had arrived in Madrid, where his carriage had broken down. Villeneuve had been informed by letter, not from the French Minister of Marine, but a 'well-wisher' in the Spanish government. He was to be sent back to Paris for trial, and very likely, execution.

Nathan could believe what he would. It was probably as reliable as the newspapers.

In the second week of October, the wind swung to the east and there was a council of war aboard the French flagship, *Bucentaure*, which was attended by many of the captains, including Lucas. The following day it was reported to Mr Banjo by his usual impeccable sources that the admiral had stated his intention of putting to sea in accordance with the emperor's orders and been bitterly opposed by the Spanish officers present. The Spanish admiral Gravina had shouted in his face: 'Only a madman could think of sailing at this time. Do you not see that the barometer is falling?' This was taken by the Spanish to mean that the October gales would soon be upon them. This would scatter the English fleet, and when the wind dropped the French and Spanish ships could sail out of harbour unopposed.

Upon which, Villeneuve had replied: 'It is not the glass that is falling, but the courage of certain people before me', at which point the Spanish officers had reached for their swords. When order was eventually restored, they had left the meeting bowing ironically to the admiral, 'like gladiators in the Roman arena', George's informants had told him, with the words, *Ave Caesar, morituri te salutant*—'Hail Caesar, those who are about to die salute you.'

This had been enacted with all the dramatic talent of which Mr Banjo was capable, with actions suited to words and splendid characterisations of both French and Spanish antagonists, but though Nathan was vastly entertained, he was sceptical of its authenticity.

However, the Spanish officers turned out to be right about the weather. The day following the council of war it came on a full gale, which lasted a week and a day. Whether this had scattered the British fleet was unknown, even to Mr Banjo.

Then, two months after their arrival in Cádiz, Nathan was summoned once more to the captain's cabin. Lucas was seated at his table, as before, but this time he was alone. He invited Nathan to sit and poured him a glass of wine. But before Nathan could permit himself to relax a little, Lucas revealed that word had finally arrived from Paris concerning his case. An official of the Department of Justice, one Colonel Laurent, had been despatched to Cádiz to conduct an investigation into his true identity and the allegations made against him. He was already in Cádiz, and his arrival was expected in the next two or three days. In the meantime, Lucas had been instructed to hold the prisoner under close arrest.

If this was not the worst news he might have heard, it was quite close to it. Laurent had been the official who had charged him with arson and espionage when he was being held as a prisoner at the Temple. He would know him at once as Captain Nathaniel Peake.

'And so I regret I must release you from your parole and hand you over to the master-at-arms,' Lucas informed him. 'It will only be for a few days, and then hopefully this matter will be resolved.'

'But this is outrageous,' Nathan protested. 'I have already been held here for two months on false charges. Now I am to submit to another investigation. I have certain rights, sir, as an American citizen.'

'This is true,' agreed Lucas, 'if you are indeed an American citizen. But if you are a British naval officer and this gentleman from Paris is able to establish that, you could be charged with being a spy, for which the penalty is death.'

'It is nonsense,' said Nathan, shaking his head.

Lucas sighed. 'Listen, my friend. There are only the two of us. Tell me, in confidence, who you really are. If you are a British naval officer, I will have you transferred at once to the custody of the Spanish authorities ashore, who will treat you as a prisoner of war. This gentleman from Paris will then have to negotiate with the Spanish government for your release into his charge.'

From somewhere within the harbour, they heard the distant sound of a gun, a signal gun most likely. Lucas raised his eyes briefly to the stern windows but then continued: 'Spanish bureaucracy takes a great deal of time to come to a decision, as I am sure you must know, and in this case, they will not wish to make a decision that might compromise the situation of any Spanish officers being held as prisoners of war by the British. Do you understand my meaning?'

Nathan did, and was tempted. But he suspected a trick. And there was Mr Banjo to be considered. He was better off where he was now than in a Spanish prison, which was undoubtedly where he would be held. He might also be implicated in the charge of spying.

'You know who I am, sir. You took me from my ship. Illegally, I must say. Do you think the crew would have subjected themselves to the command of a British naval officer? If you do, you do not know Americans, sir.'

'Unfortunately, the crew were not questioned at the time,' Lucas pointed out, 'and they are no longer available to be questioned now. So, I regret I must hand you over to the master-at-arms until the arrival of Colonel Laurent.' He stood up and raised his voice. 'Guard!'

But with the guard came the ensign who had escorted Nathan from the *Grampus*. He seemed more than usually excited, and with only a brief glance at Nathan he announced: 'Compliments of Lieutenant Vallière, sir, and there is a signal from the flagship.'

He had the message written down. Lucas stared at it for a moment and then looked, not at the ensign, but at Nathan. His expression was one almost of complicity.

'You have been sent a reprieve, sir, if that is the right word. The fleet has been ordered to prepare for sea. Whatever happens now, we are in it together.'

Chapter 22

Trafalgar

It took three days for the Combined Fleet to put to sea. Cádiz was a notoriously difficult harbour to get out of, with a nightmare of crosscurrents and reefs, but above all it needed the right wind. On Friday, October 18, the wind was exactly right, but there was very little of it, and by mid-afternoon it had dropped away altogether. At four o'clock the flagship ran up a new signal. Fleet to weigh anchor and prepare to leave the following morning.

Saturday morning dawned bright and clear, but the wind was still very light. Nonetheless, the admiral signalled, Make sail and proceed. One by one the ships of the Combined Fleet began to move laboriously towards the open sea. By midday nine of them had made it, but then they lost the wind again and attempts were made to warp the ships out. This continued throughout the night, and on Sunday morning they were helped with a light breeze off the land. The walls of Cádiz were packed with thousands of citizens cheering them on, the churches with thousands more praying for their safe return. By midday the entire fleet was at sea. Thirty-three ships of the line, five frigates, and two brigs, a total of thirty-five thousand men.

Nathan and George watched the final act in this slow-moving drama from their usual perch in the maintop of the *Redoutable*, where they were such a regular installation they were no more regarded than a pair of quarter blocks. Far out to sea they could see the sails of the watching English frigates, but no sign of the heavier ships. That they were out there some-where was not in doubt. The only question in Nathan's mind was how many they were and when and how they would attack.

Mr Banjo, of course, had information on this, though not from Brit-ish sources. Naturally, it came from Villeneuve, via Banjo's usual chain of communication. The admiral had held two more meetings with his captains to discuss the likely British approach, and he had expressed the view that if, as suspected, the attack was led by Nelson, he would not proceed in the conventional manner, in a line parallel with their own, but come straight at them, as he had at Aboukir, and seek to break through their line at the centre, envelop the rear, and overpower as many ships as he could isolate or cut off. If this was true, it struck Nathan as extremely perceptive, for Nelson had expounded this same tactic to him at dinner in Merton Place, using spoons instead of ships. It certainly seemed to work with spoons, though a lot depended on the weather, and at Merton Place it had been unusually calm. To counter this tactic, the French admiral proposed to divide his fleet into two divisions, Mr Banjo reported: the main battle fleet, which would await the attack and fight a number of individual ship-to-ship conflicts; and an observation squadron of twelve ships under Admiral Gravina that would stand off to windward, out of the smoke and confusion of the battle, but ready to reinforce the main fleet wherever they were most needed.

There was no evidence of this approach as the fleet assembled outside Cádiz, however. Instead, the ships formed up in three columns and tacked to the south. This was curious. The wind had veered to the south-west and the weather was coming in thick and squally. Heading south meant sailing as close to the wind as possible, and uncomfortably close to the shore, and it soon became clear that it was no temporary measure. They continued in the same direction, following the line of the coast towards Gibraltar. Now that the plan to invade England had apparently been abandoned, or at least postponed, there was no particular need to head north, of course, to reinforce the fleet at Brest. But where else was Villeneuve heading?

For once Mr Banjo had no information on the subject.

His most likely route, they agreed, was via the Strait of Gibraltar into the Med. But then what? This was anyone's guess. Probably Villeneuve himself did not know. His home port of Toulon, Naples, Sicily, the

Levant or wherever Bonaparte was planning to send the former Army of England?

But there were other possibilities. He could be heading for the Canaries, and then the Caribbean. Or down Africa to the Cape and thence into the Indian Ocean. Or he might simply be running away from the gentlemen from Paris and the warrant for his arrest. The important thing for Nathan was that they were leaving Cádiz, for he had his own gentleman from Paris to worry about.

All things considered, he would rather they were heading into the Mediterranean, for although his conversation with Lucas had been ambiguous, it could be interpreted as meaning he was no longer on parole, and at its narrowest point the Strait of Gibraltar was barely eight miles wide. Both he and Mr Banjo were capable swimmers. If they came close enough to the Rock, or even Africa, it was quite possible for them to reach the shore or to be picked up by a fishing boat, or even one of the British sloops that patrolled the Strait. Certainly, it was worth a try.

A little after four in the afternoon, the wind veered to the north-west and the weather cleared. The *Redoutable* was at the head of one of the three columns, with the entire fleet stretched out behind her, covering several miles of ocean. Most of the ships were painted black, Nathan noted, but some had red or yellow bands chequered by black gunports, and the giant *Santísima Trinidad* had white stripes between each of her four decks of guns. Each of the French ships had a shield at the stern, he observed, with the blue, white, and red bands of the national flag, and the Spanish ships each carried a giant wooden cross, also at the stern. Presumably this was to distinguish them from the enemy in a battle. But of the enemy, there was still no sign—at least, not of the main battle fleet, only of the shadowing frigates.

Darkness fell. The two men descended from their perch and joined some of Mr Banjo's friends on the gundeck. They had no more information to impart. The general opinion, as expressed in colloquial French, was *Personne sait que dalle*—which loosely translated into lower-deck English as 'No-one knows fuck-all'—and their admiral, in their view, knew even less. Captain Lucas had cleared the ship for action as soon as they had left Cádiz, but they had not yet beat to quarters. Nor did they expect to, not at least until morning, and even then they did not know if there would be a battle or not. There was considerable speculation as to where they were headed. The smart money, apparently, was on Naples.

At eight o'clock in the evening there was a great exchange of signals, using lanterns now, and in due course the gunners reported that the flagship had signalled 'Enemy in sight'. A little later the news reached them that a fleet of eighteen ships of the line had been sighted to the south-south-west. Nathan and George climbed into the maintop again, but it was so dark now, all they could see were the lights of their own fleet, which was to say, the French and Spanish. 'Like a well-lit street, six miles long,' as Mr Banjo remarked. But then, as the evening advanced, they saw more lights out to the south-west—blue lights, casting a bright and sudden glare in the midst of darkness—and they heard the distant reports of cannon. Nathan assumed they were signal guns. Shortly after, there were a great many different coloured lights, which he could not explain unless it was to sow confusion. It certainly worked with him.

At nine o'clock there was a great deal of activity aloft and alow and they descended to the deck to find that the flagship had signalled the fleet to form line of battle. This had caused a great deal of agitation on the quarterdeck for the fleet was widely scattered and very little could be seen in the darkness except lights. At eleven o'clock the captain issued an order for the men to lie down at their posts and try to get some sleep so that they might be as fresh as possible for the approaching fight.

Nathan decided to go below. His berth, he found, had been turned into an extension of the sick bay, but he made himself as comfortable as possible on a pile of sacks and managed to snatch a few hours' sleep. Mr Banjo stayed on deck 'with his friends', as he put it, to see what he could discover.

At seven o'clock the next morning Nathan emerged on deck in the hope of finding some breakfast. It was still dark but there was some light in the sky to the east. The men were standing by the guns and Mr Banjo, who had been up all night, joined him to report that the enemy had been sighted to the south-west and numbered twenty-seven ships of the line.

Nathan crossed to the starboard rail but it was still too dark to see anything. There was no sign of any breakfast either. The galley fires had been put out, apparently, but Mr Banjo brought him some hard tack which he sucked upon miserably, so it did not break his teeth. It might be the last food he ever ate, he thought. He had barely digested the first morsel when the drums began to beat *Branle-bas de combat!*

The soldiers began to drill on the gundeck, and Lucas and his first lieutenant came down from the quarterdeck and moved from gun to gun, preceded by fife and drums, giving encouragement to the men. They responded with cries of *Vive l'Empereur!* and *Vive l'armée!* Many urged the captain to remember his promise to board at the first opportunity. Nathan kept well out of the way.

At eight o'clock there was another signal from the flagship. From the shouted commands of the officers and all the activity on deck and aloft, it became apparent to Nathan that the admiral had signalled for the fleet to go about, but 'wearing in station'. This meant every ship had to turn individually, so that the rear of the fleet became the van, and they were on the larboard tack, heading back towards Cádiz. Whatever was in Villeneuve's mind, it caused total chaos among the ships of his fleet.

It was daybreak now, the weather clear, but the wind was from the north-west and very light, and it was obvious that some of the ships were finding it very difficult to manoeuvre. This was not the case on the *Redoutable*, but Nathan took advantage of the activity to climb into the maintop again with Mr Banjo, and here for the first time he saw the British battle fleet. It was bearing down from the west in two parallel columns about a mile apart, as near as he could estimate, on a broad reach—and every ship carried a full press of sail, even studding sails, which was unheard of in a battle. The flame from a touchhole could rise for up to fifteen feet or more, and if they did not take in sail, they would not be able to fire the guns on the upper decks, not without a serious risk of fire. More conventionally, Villeneuve had ordered his captains to proceed under topsails and topgallants alone.

Nathan tried to count the advancing ships, but those towards the end of the column were not easily discernible—not less than twenty, he thought, but certainly no more than thirty. Even at a distance of three miles or so he could see that they wore a uniform livery of yellow stripes, presumably to distinguish them from the enemy, chequered with the black of the gunports so that they resembled a swarm of giant hornets. This was the recurring nightmare of Nathan's dreams in the Temple—to be on the wrong side in a battle. He remembered how he used to force himself out of the fog of sleep and emerge with relief in the security of his prison cell. But it would not work here.

His own fleet—the *enemy* fleet—was still trying to form line of battle. There were constant signals from the flagship, presumably trying to enforce some semblance of order, but it would have taken far more expert seamen than they to manoeuvre such large vessels in such a light, contrary wind. Ships were losing way or drifting far to leeward. There were clumps of ships crowded together, two or three deep and more or less in line abreast; at other points there were just one or two ships in a wide expanse of ocean, the whole fleet sagging to leeward in the centre to form a deep curve or crescent. There was no distinction that Nathan could see between the main battle fleet and the observation squadron under Gravina that was supposed to remain to windward. The *Redoutable* was now the third ship in line astern of the flagship, which put her almost at the centre of the fleet and closest to the advancing British.

For two hours or more, the two men had remained undisturbed in the maintop. They were dressed in much the same way as the ordinary French seamen, in blue jackets and trousers, Nathan's only mark of distinction a pair of buckled shoes and the cocked hat he had worn when he first came aboard as Mr Campbell. They had been largely ignored by the topmen passing by on their various duties aloft, but now their luck had run out. Their refuge was invaded by an infantry sergeant and two private soldiers, burdened with bags of grenadoes for throwing down upon the enemy decks, and they were brusquely ordered out of the way.

No sooner had they set foot on the gundeck than they were collared by one of the boatswain's mates who knew them from their months in Cádiz. They were to make themselves useful, he said, and despite Nathan's protests that they were non-combatants and guests of the captain, he ordered them to join one of the work parties formed from among the waisters— those who neither worked the guns nor went aloft, and were generally considered to be neither use nor ornament but only good for hauling upon the mainsheets in the waist, or keeping the decks clean.

And so the two men found themselves taking turns to turn the large grindstones that had been brought up from below to sharpen the cutlasses and tomahawks, pikes, and other edged weapons that were used in boarding, or to repel boarders. The soldiers were still marching up and down the deck to the martial music of fife and drum, presumably in an effort to raise everyone's spirits, though in Nathan's opinion a rum issue would have been more effective, but then, he was English. Then they began to sing 'La Marseillaise' and the whole crew joined in. It was, Nathan supposed, quite rousing, if you were French. Finally, the soldiers were sent to their stations, mostly in the fighting tops, from where they could sweep the enemy decks with musket fire.

The supply of lethal blades requiring attention had eased considerably and Nathan had leisure to study the approaching English ships through his glass—if they *were* approaching, for they did not seem to have moved much since he had last looked. Several of the French and Spanish ships to windward were firing ranging shots which were dropping well awry, for although the wind was still very light and capricious there was a significant swell, which did not make for the most stable of firing platforms. This must inevitably be of advantage to the British, for the Combined Fleet was sailing *across* the swell, which made the problem much worse. In the two months they had been in Cádiz, although the guns were sometimes run out and the gunners went through a pantomime of loading and firing, Nathan had never seen a single gun of heavier calibre than a musket fired, until now.

He felt an urgent tap on his shoulder from Mr Banjo and removed his eye from the glass to see a squad of seamen approaching, led by the same boatswain's mate who had put them on knife-grinding duties. They were pushing and hauling upon a large contrivance which he recognised as a form of fire engine. They had something of the sort on the *Panther*, an adaptation of the normal bilge pump fitted with canvas hoses, mostly used for cleaning the decks, but with an additional lever that forced the seawater through a smaller bore for added pressure. The one on the *Panther* could throw a jet of water a good fifty feet into the air, very useful for wetting the sails in a light wind, though its primary purpose was fighting fires. This was clearly the function of this device, and both he and Mr Banjo were assigned to work the levers that operated the pump, along with four other men who had nothing better to do. All things considered, this was a considerable improvement on the blade grinding, and for the next five minutes they happily practised at pumping water up from the sea and squirting it back under pressure until orders came from the quarterdeck for them to desist on the grounds that they were covering the officers with spray.

It was now noon and the wind had freshened a little and was holding steady in the north-west. Nathan climbed on top of the machine to secure a better view, even at the risk of incurring the wrath of their supervisor. He could see, even without the aid of his glass, that the approaching ships were noticeably closer, less than a mile from the *Redoutable*, Nathan estimated. He also noted that the two ships that had been immediately ahead of them had dropped off to leeward, leaving a wide gap between the *Redoutable* and the flagship—and the British column on the weather side seemed to be heading straight for it.

Lucas had clearly seen this, too, for a stream of orders issued from the quarterdeck to put on sail and close the gap. At least two reefs were taken out of the fore course, and slowly but surely the *Redoutable* began to move up to the stern of the flagship, so much so, in fact, that it appeared to be causing some agitation on the *Bucentaure*'s quarterdeck. A new string of signal flags went up from the mizzen, and lest their meaning was unclear, an officer began to gesture furiously from the taffrail. Lucas remained impervious to this, and within a few minutes his ship had taken up a position just off the flagship's larboard quarter. And at the same time, a new signal was displayed whose meaning swiftly became clear.

'Engage the enemy!'

The first broadside was fired by one of the ships directly astern, though perhaps a quarter of a mile distant. Nathan knew her from their time in Cádiz as the *Fougueux*—a seventy-four of the same class as the *Redoutable*—and she appeared to be firing at a ship that had advanced some distance ahead of the British column on the leeside. Nathan focused his glass on her, and with a shock of recognition saw that she was the *Royal Sovereign*, a three-decker of a hundred guns that he had served on during the Battle of the Glorious First of June, and now the flagship of Admiral Collingwood. She kept on coming, taking fire now from at least three other ships, and finally broke the line astern of Admiral Gravina's flagship, the *Santa Ana*, delivering a thunderous broadside. As far as Nathan could tell, they were the first British shots to be fired. This was one of the problems with the 'go straight at 'em approach' which Nelson advocated, rather than the conventional tactic of drawing parallel with the enemy and exchanging broadsides at a distance. It meant you could only fire with the guns mounted in the bows of the lead ships—your broadsides could be brought to bear only when you had broken through the enemy line, and in the time that took, you were exposed to the raking broadsides of every ship that was within range.

This was what was happening now.

The *Royal Sovereign* was surrounded by enemy ships, all pouring fire into her, with the nearest British ship still at least a quarter of a mile away—and she, too, was coming under heavy fire. She was the exact image of the *Redoutable*, apart from the flags, and Nathan thought she must be the *Belleisle*, a ship of the same class that had been taken prize in the last war. Even as he looked her foremast came down, and by the time she reached the enemy line the mainmast had gone the same way. This was going very badly for the British. Nathan could hear the cheers of the French crews, not only on the *Redoutable*, but on the flagship just ahead of them, with a prolonged cry of *Vive l'Empereur!* But at least no-one was taking any notice of him, and he had a reasonable view from the top of the fire engine, even if it was not as good as the maintop.

He turned his attention to the weather column, now about a half-mile from the *Redoutable*, and apparently heading straight for them—or the flagship. There was no longer much of a gap between the two ships, and at times, their bowsprit seemed almost to be touching the taffrail of the *Bucentaure*, to the considerable alarm of her officers, who appeared to be paying more attention to the *Redoutable* than to the British. The approaching column was now led by not one ship, but two—two almost identical three-deckers, coming straight at them, side by side. Nathan focused his glass on the nearest. She was close enough now for him to see her figurehead—two cupids holding a shield bearing the coat of arms of the House of Hanover. She was the *Victory*, Nelson's ship. Nathan exulted, until he remembered where he was. Nelson's presence considerably increased the chances of British victory, and with it, the certainty of his own death, fighting under a French flag.

Then the *Redoutable* opened fire with her full broadside. Nathan's view was obscured by the smoke of the guns, but when it cleared, he saw that the *Victory* was still coming on, apparently undamaged. But she was under fire from the flagship as well, and from the mighty *Santísima Trinidad* immediately ahead of her, with her four decks of guns. The water was erupting around her as if stirred by the demons of the deep, but most of the shots seemed to be falling well short, even at a range of less than half a mile. This was causing some consternation on the quarterdeck, and the gun captains were sent into the tops to observe why they were firing so badly.

Nathan wondered idly if George Banjo's informant could be right, and that it was down to the weak nature of French piss, the unforeseen consequence of watering down their wine. He looked forward to including this in his report to the First Lord of the Admiralty, if he lived through the next few hours. So far as he could tell, the gun crews seemed to be working the guns as efficiently as any British crew he had served with; he timed how long it took to reload one of the eighteen-pounders, and it came out at just under two minutes—not the fastest in the world, but by no means the slowest, either. And as the column came closer, he could tell from the cheering that they were recording a few more hits, though it was difficult to see anything now, for the smoke from the guns, which was blown back along the upper deck.

When he did, he saw that the lower sails of the *Victory* were as shot through with holes as if a horde of giant moths had been at them, but she was still coming on, and quite suddenly, it seemed, after such a long and slow approach, her bows came bursting through the smoke at the very point at which the bowsprit of the *Redoutable* was tilting at the taffrail of the flagship. Nathan barely had time to register the sight of the shield with the two cupids when she unleashed a rolling, raking broadside into the stern of the *Bucentaure*. This was exactly what Nelson had expounded to him at Merton Place. Break the enemy line in the centre and then come up on their lee, disabling the ships in the rear before the van had time to turn and come back to help them.

But they were not fighting with spoons at the dinner table, and the gap between the two French ships was too narrow. The top deck of the *Victory* now loomed above them, and either Lucas had swung his helm or the ship was being dragged round to starboard. Either way, they were now side by side, the guns of the *Redoutable* firing at point-blank range and men up in the yards throwing grappling irons to lash the two ships together. Nathan just had time to slide down from his perch on top of the fire engine and dive under it. Mr Banjo was already there. Then the *Victory* unleashed her own broadside.

Nathan remained under the fire engine for the next few minutes. It might have been longer, or shorter; he was not timing it. He was making himself as small as possible and holding his arms over his head, pressing the heels of his palms into his ears. He had endured broadsides before when he could not do this, when he had been obliged to stand upright on his own quarterdeck without even flinching while everything disintegrated around him. He marvelled now that he had been able to do this. Perhaps it was lack of imagination, though he had never, in his long career, endured the broadside of a one-hundred-gun three-decker. The overall impression in his present circumstance was, of course, the noise. The thunder of two ships of the line firing heavy artillery into each other at the range of a pistol shot. A number of objects hit the pump above his head with such force, he wondered how it remained intact, but it did.

Then there appeared to be a slackening in the rate of fire, and after a moment or two, he crawled out. Through the smoke he saw Mr Banjo, on the other side of the machine, still in one piece. Then he looked about the gundeck. At first he was too dazed, too deafened, too blinded by smoke to take it in. Then the smoke blew away, like a fog suddenly lifted, and he viewed a scene from hell, but without sound. He could see people making sounds, for their mouths were gaping holes distorted into the shape of a scream, but he could not hear them. Bodies lay everywhere, some headless, others mutilated beyond recognition. The wounded, too, sprawling across the decks, across the guns, torn apart by grape or flying splinters, lying in their own blood and that of the dead, guns themselves dismounted, a thirty-six-pounder carronade burst open with her crew lying about the wreck as if arranged by some demonic hand . . . And then, dimly at first, as through heavy padding, he heard the screaming.

He looked up. To God? Rather to the devils perched gleeful on the mastheads, like gargoyles on a church roof. Then he stepped out of the nightmare into the world of reality, and though it was not so very different, it was, at least, familiar. He had been in battles before. But always as a participant, never a witness. He needed something useful to do.

He picked up a leather bucket of sand and threw it on the blood that covered the deck. Then, as if remembering something from the dream, he looked up again and this time he saw that they were not devils or gargoyles but soldiers. Hundreds of them, it seemed, or at least scores, thickly clustered in the fighting tops and more sparsely in the rigging, firing down into the upper deck of the *Victory*. The yards, he saw, were now lashed fast to those of the British flagship, so she could not move without taking the *Redoutable* with her, and directly above his head, in the futtock shrouds below the mizzentop, he could see a man he knew. Sergeant Scillato, with one arm hooked through the shrouds, peering down as if looking for a target. And then he brought his musket to his shoulder and took aim. In his mind's eye Nathan saw those cutout figures of the British officers against the taffrail and the holes in them afterwards . . . And then he fired.

A great roaring in his ears, not screams now, but roars of exultation: *Vive la France, Vive l'Empereur, Vive la gloire!*

And there came a hellish horde pouring up from below, armed with the swords and pikes and tomahawks he had spent the past few hours honing to a lethal edge. His mind was still too dazed to take it in. He looked up again into the tops. They had stopped shooting and were hurling grenadoes, and through the pall of smoke that enveloped both ships Nathan could see the explosions all along the *Victory's* upper deck, and—significantly—she had stopped firing. Why? The French could not possibly have silenced three decks of guns.

But then it came to him that Nelson or Hardy or whoever was still alive over there would have pulled the men off the guns on the lower decks to repel boarders. Even so, it was working out exactly as Lucas had planned.

But not quite. For he had not planned on boarding a three-decker.

Instead of swarming over the side and onto the *Victory's* upper deck, the boarders were milling around on their own gundeck, staring up at the massive wall of oak that rose at least ten feet above their heads. He saw the young ensign who had taken him from the *Grampus* outside Ferrol—what was his name? Yon—Ensign Yon—with a cutlass in his hand and four men at his heels, climbing the best bower that rose up above the *Redoutable's* forecastle and preparing to leap down upon the enemy deck. Others, their attention drawn to this by their officers, were preparing to follow . . .

And then, on other side of the deck, at the stern of the French ship, like a monstrous vision out of Nathan's nightmare, a great yellow beak appeared out the smoke and the flame of battle. The *other* three-decker, the one he had seen earlier at the head of the British column, side by side with the *Victory*. And he even knew who she was, not from her figurehead, but from the lack of one. The *Temeraire*. 'Reckless' it meant, in the French. Perhaps there was no figurehead that could capture the spirit of reckless.

And then she fired.

The hail of grape sweeping the deck, packed now with men, the bodies thrown this way and that like so many rag dolls, a hailstorm of iron shot, and at the same time, more mysteriously, the decks exploded upwards, punched through with great holes, the splinters flying as high as the lower yards, and men, too, whole bodies and parts of them hurled into the rigging where they hung like the dead crows that farmers hang in the branches of trees as a lesson. And Nathan standing there, by the wreck of the fire engine, too stunned to take cover, a bucket of sand still in his hand, a great wind passing by his head, and a part of his brain that was still incredibly functioning telling him that, of course, they were firing not only from above but from below, from the lower gundecks, with the heavy thirty-two-pounders at maximum elevation, the round shot ripping through the gunports and upwards, smashing through the more fragile timbers of the decking, dismounting guns, unmanning men . . .

And then it stopped. Or something stopped. Possibly it was his brain.

He was aware that he was still alive, somehow, moving among the dead and the damned like the hags he had seen in paintings of Culloden and other battles, robbing the bodies of the dead, save that he was picking them up with Mr Banjo and throwing them on a heap in the middle of the deck, for that was what the French did. The British, more practical, more ruthless, threw them in the sea. It was probably better. It was not good for morale to see what a few pounds of iron shot could do to the human body. But they did what they were told to do—they picked the corpses up and threw them on the growing heap. And if they found one still living, they carried him below, to the hell below, for the lower decks had been smashed to pieces and the dead lay there, too, among the wrecks of their guns, with the gunports smashed into gaping holes in the side of the ship, and the water bubbling up from the deck below, red with blood, and no-one alive to work the pumps. And they laid them down wherever they could find that was dry, and left them, to live or die, whatever their fate determined.

This was the part of the nightmare that happened after he had woken up, that he had never seen until now.

They were back on deck, still heaving bodies, when the boatswain's mate came up to them again. He looked like a corpse. He was certainly as pale as one, and he had a wound in his head, bound with a bloodied scarf. It took a moment for Nathan to make sense of what he was saying. The captain has ordered all hands below, to fire at the British with whatever guns that were not disabled.

But no. That made no sense at all. So, when the man had moved on, to pass on his senseless order to whoever was still alive, Nathan looked about the terrible deck and he saw the anchor that Ensign Yon had tried to climb, and he looked at Mr Banjo and he jerked his head, and they dropped the body they were carrying, and they walked away, stumbling through the smoke and the horror, and they climbed up the anchor and they jumped down onto the deck of the Victory.

It seemed quite ordered here, by comparison, or at least a more familiar chaos. There were men at the guns in striped jerseys or stripped to the waist with their Barcelona scarves tied around their ears, powder monkeys running about with cartridges, officers in blue uniforms and cocked hats, marines in red coats. Nathan stumbled over a water bucket and stared at it, as if surprised it was not a head, staring back at him, but instead there was the insignia of King George, stamped into the leather. Then one of the men in a blue jacket and a cocked hat was coming at him with a sword. Not a man, a boy—he could not have been more than twelve or thirteen—shouting at him in an unfamiliar tongue. But, of course, it was English, his ears just too deafened to hear it. And behind him were two marines with musket and bayonet.

Nathan had been smiling, or making the ghastly pretence of a smile, with intent to reassure, but the snot-nosed brat was waving a sword in his face and swearing at him in a manner he was wont to find offensive.

'Down, sir,' Nathan instructed him sharply, as if he were an importu- nate puppy, which he was, and then more reasonably: 'Your zeal is com- mendable, but I am Captain Peake of His Britannic Majesty's Navy, and I would be obliged if you would remove that sword from my face and take me to Admiral Lord Nelson.'

Chapter 23

Victory—and Death

They had carried him down to the cockpit on the orlop deck and he was lying in a nest of bedding they had made for him against the side of the ship, attended by a number of officers and others, one of whom, Nathan gathered, was the surgeon, another, his chaplain. It was clear, even from where he stood at the fringe of this gathering, that it was the chaplain the admiral had the greater need of. And from what he could hear, Nelson knew it too.

'I felt it break my spine.' The weak whisper of a voice, a ghost of the familiar Norfolk accent. And then: 'I feel a gush of blood inside my chest.' He had been stripped of his upper clothing but partly covered with a sheet, and Nathan could not see the wound. Hardy, who had greeted him on the quarterdeck, had said it was musket fire, from one of the fighting tops on the *Redoutable*.

'I was standing right next to him, as close as I am to you now,' he had told Nathan. 'He had just turned towards the stern and the blow threw him facedown on the deck. Two of the marines raised him up and he told me they had done for him at last.'

The bullet had struck the epaulette on his left shoulder, Hardy said, and it must have travelled down diagonally through his chest. The doctors thought it had punctured his left lung and lodged in his spine. They held out no hope for him. An hour or so, they said. He was only hanging on for news of the battle.

Nathan had served under Nelson twice—once in the Med in '97, when Bonaparte was storming through Italy, and again at the Nile, when he had been with him on the flagship. The last time they had met was at Merton Place, that last dinner together when he had demonstrated his tactics with silver spoons. But the memory sharpest in his mind now was in London during the Peace, when Nelson had taken him to inspect his coffin at the undertakers. It was made from a section of the mainmast from *L'Orient*, the French flagship at the Nile, and he was having it lined in silk. He wanted Nathan to help choose the colour.

'*But I trust it will be a long time before you need it, my lord,*' he heard himself saying.

'*Yes, yes, they all say that, but what do you think—red, white, or blue?*'

'Drink, drink,' he was saying now, and they gave him water to drink.

'Fan, fan,' and they fanned his face with a paper.

'Rub, rub,' and they rubbed his chest, so he could breathe.

Once he heard cheering and asked what it was, and one of the other men who had been wounded, a lieutenant, lying a short distance away, raised himself up and told him another French ship had struck, and someone else said: 'That makes seventeen, your lordship—and more to come.'

And someone else murmured: 'A great victory. The greatest in our history, my lord.'

He died at four o'clock in the afternoon, and Nathan never spoke to him.

Chapter 24

Epilogue

He stood at the top of the Rock looking down into the Bay of Gibraltar with a monkey at his side. Or more properly, an ape. It was eating a nut he had given it.

He had been here before. So had the ape, he thought. He remembered it from the last time he had been here. It had the face of Old Jarvey. Perhaps they all did.

'Been up to much lately?' he asked the ape.

'Not a lot,' said the ape. 'How about you?'

'Not a lot,' said Nathan.

In the bay lay the victorious British fleet. The *Victory* prominent among them, her yards a'cock bill as a sign of mourning, and the admiral's body in a cask of brandy to preserve it until they could get it back to England. There was going to be a state funeral, Nathan had been told. It was what Nelson would have wanted, but Nathan had rather he had been buried at sea by the men who had fought at his side.

The *Panther* was down there, too, with her prize—*his* prize—the *Perle*, flying the white ensign at her stern. And there were four more prizes from the recent battle—three Spanish and one French. There should have been twenty-two, but the rest had been wrecked in the great storm that followed the battle, or set on fire to prevent their recapture.

The news of the victory would not have reached England yet, but the *Gibraltar Chronicle* had hailed it as 'the most brilliant and decisive in the renowned history of the British navy'. Twenty-two enemy ships taken, four thousand dead, seven thousand prisoners—for the loss of just four hundred British seamen, and not a single ship. They were calling it the Battle of Trafalgar, this being the name of the nearest cape on the Spanish mainland. It had saved Britain from invasion, they said, and changed the course of the war.

Nathan knew he should have felt good about that, exultant even, but with the death of Nelson, and so many others, all he could feel was a deep sense of loss, so deep he could not reach it, and something approaching despair. He did not know how he had survived the nightmare on the *Redoutable*—or why. Sometimes he felt as Scillato must have felt, *Lo Spettro*, the revenant. One of the walking dead.

The *Chronicle* had carried a letter from an English merchant in Cádiz. For ten days after the battle, he wrote, the wounded were brought ashore and carried through the streets, many screaming in agony. They filled the hospitals, and several churches and convents had to be appropriated. Women were to be seen everywhere in tears or sitting upon heaps of baggage and broken furniture from the ships, with their heads between their knees. The survivors of the ships that had made it back to Cádiz walked the streets with blank eyes, as if stunned. The churches were filled with the relatives of men whose fate was unknown and Masses for the dead were being chanted every day for those who were known to have been killed. As far as the eye could see, the sandy side of the isthmus bordering the Atlantic was covered with masts and yards, the wrecks of ships and the bodies of the dead.

From other sources, Nathan had heard that on the ten-mile sweep of open beach between Trafalgar and Cape Roque the dead lay thick, drifting up on every tide, intermingled with broken fragments of ships and gear. The coast for miles around was patrolled by men on horseback who notified burial parties to come and dig holes in the sand into which they dragged the dead.

The Neapolitan Antonio Scillato was not among them. Nathan had not seen him among the dead and wounded on the *Redoutable*, and he had not been identified among those brought into Cádiz in the days following the battle—but then the dead often remained unidentified and unclaimed, buried in unmarked graves. Many were mangled beyond recognition. It happened in battles. He remained *Lo Spettro*. The ghost from Naples.

In a later edition of the *Chronicle*, they had reported news of another battle, though by no means so prominently. Bonaparte had marched the former Army of England halfway across Europe, from the Channel ports to the Bavarian border, where he had defeated an entire Austrian army of seventy-two thousand men, with minimal losses. He was now about to fight the Russians. Nathan did not give much for their chances. But then he was a pessimist.

He gave the ape another nut.

'Are we ever going to get any better?' he mused. 'As a species?'

But the ape expressed no opinion on the matter.

There was another ship coming into the bay. It was the Falmouth packet, the *Antelope*. He knew it well, for he had sailed in her from Gibraltar to England on his journey back from India towards the end of the last war. She would be bringing the latest news from England, and the mail. He had not had any news from home for almost four months, not since he had left Portsmouth in the *Panther*. He did not expect any now, for his family did not know where he was.

But he was wrong.

There was a letter from his mother, addressed to Captain Nathaniel Peake of the frigate *Panther*, and the navy, with surprising awareness, had sent it to Gibraltar. It was written with the usual haphazard distribution of capitals and exclamation marks and with a gushing affection that he could never quite associate with his mother, and tended to categorize as parody.

My Darling Boy, it began—(as her letters invariably did, since the first he had ever received from her in his first week at Charterhouse, aged ten. The fear that this would be seen by one of his new associates and that he would ever be referred to by the entire school as My Darling Boy had followed him into the navy as a midshipman, and had never entirely gone away. She did it now, he was convinced, more out of a sense of mischief than affection, but it was probably a bit of both)—

I have no Idea whether you will receive this, but when has this not been the case? A poor Mother must live in hope! I trust you are well and in good Spirits! I trust you think often of your dear Mama who loves you and remembers you always in her prayers.

His mother was, in fact, an atheist, but he knew she loved him.

We are all well here in London, or as well as can be expected in our Want and with this dreadful War taking our Loved Ones away and leading to a

Great Dearth of French Wine and Brandy, which are the only means of consoling us.

I have some News to impart, which has caused me to pick up my Pen and write this Missive to you in the faint hope that you will receive it and act upon it in whichever way you see fit, or at least inform me of your Sentiments in the Matter, and what Action, if any, you would wish me to take. A Draft upon your Bank would also be welcome.

On arriving Home in early August after a visit to the Countryside (how anyone can abide to live in the English Countryside I do not know, for all they do is Drink Beer and Brandy, of the kind one's servants use to clean Windows, and consume vast quantities of what passes in the Countryside for Food and ride to Hounds and go to Church and the fields are full of Cows and, worse, Sheep, and it is always raining, even in Summer . . .

He skipped the next few lines, which were familiar to him from previous correspondence, detailing his mother's visits to the English countryside.

And on my return to Civilisation (in as much as Soho in its present state can be described as such), I discovered I had received a Visit in my Absence from a Lady who had left a Card bearing the name Mademoiselle Louise de Kirouac, with an address in fashionable Saint James where I, of course, used to live before my Great Misfortune.

I did not recognise the name. I wonder if you do.

Well, I was sufficiently intrigued by the short note which accompanied this to send a Reply informing her that I was now back in Residence and inviting her to partake of Tea whenever it might please her to do so, to which she responded with startling Promptitude and arrived the following day, upon which I found her to be a Lady of great Beauty and of an Intelligence that belied her comparative Youth.

Over the course of our Conversation, she revealed some of her recent history in Jersey and in France, and though discreet—as your friends invariably are— her connection to my Darling Boy.

She also informed me—and you might brace yourself, my Dear, and perhaps pause to have one of your Nautical Lackeys pour you a glass of Grogg, or whatever it is you call it—that she is With Child! And though she did not reveal any other details of this Mishap, for she is Unmarried, and did not name the Father, she led me to expect that you would find it of interest.

She was distressed to find that I had no idea of your current whereabouts, though I was subsequently enlightened by a very charming Officer at the British Admiralty, hence this Missive.

She seems a very Nice Person!

The child is expected early in the New Year.

If this is of interest to you, do please respond with more than your usual alacrity, to your dear

Mama.

THE END

Fact and Fiction

I usually feel that if you write a work of fiction based on something that really happened, you should let the reader know the difference between true and false—assuming the distinction is clear.

The main premise—or premises—of this novel are that the British secret service, as we would call it now, was behind the plot to kidnap or assassinate Napoleon Bonaparte, and that this was a primary cause of the Napoleonic Wars. Additionally, that Trafalgar, though one of the most spectacular battles in history, was not the battle that saved Britain from invasion. That battle was the one that preceded it by a few weeks, fought by the same ships in a fog off Cape Finisterre, and largely ignored by history.

We may never know the exact truth, but many of the known historical facts support both of these contentions.

It's true that the British landed agents on the French coast and that some of those agents were involved in a plot to kidnap Napoleon. The conspiracy was orchestrated from Walmer Castle in Deal, on the south coast of England, and Castle Gorey, in Jersey. The principal operatives were Georges Cadoudal, the Breton royalist, and Jean-Charles Pichegru, the former revolutionary general, while the British provided logistical and financial support under the supervision of William Pitt at Walmer Castle, and Philippe d'Auvergne in Jersey.

It's also true that Bonaparte was so infuriated by the plot that in retaliation he ordered his gendarmes to kidnap the Bourbon royal prince, the Duc d'Enghien, from his German exile in Baden. He was then put through a mockery of a trial and shot by firing squad in the dried-out moat of the Vincennes fortress, on the edge of Paris. A willow tree marks the spot. His kidnap and murder, as they saw it, so outraged the rulers of Prussia, Austria, and Russia that it enabled Pitt to form a new coalition against France, and precipitated the Napoleonic Wars.

I've kept to the main facts of this conspiracy, but I've given Sir Sidney Smith more of a role than he probably deserves—and of course, I've brought Nathan Peake into it, and he is entirely fictitious. However, the role I've given him is based on the true story of Captain John Wesley Wright, who landed many of the royalist agents in France in the British brig, *Vincejo*. During one of these clandestine operations, he was captured by the French and imprisoned in the Temple, where he was said to have committed suicide—though many at the time and since have suspected murder.

While this was going on, Pitt, Smith, and others were planning other unconventional means of warfare against the French involving the use of the 'infernal machines' and submersibles invented by the American, Robert Fulton. The raid on Boulogne which I've described is based on the known facts, but again, I've thrown Nathan into the mix.

His rescue from the Temple and transport to Malmaison is fiction, but the story of Josephine and Malmaison is true, as is the remarkable story of her plants being supplied by the nursery in Hammersmith and the British navy allowing the plants to be delivered by cartel throughout the war. I think many of them, or their descendants, are still there.

The story of Napoleon's grand design for destroying the British fleet is true, of course, and well known. I've kept to the known facts of how it progressed—but again, I've inserted Nathan into the plot. His historical role model in this case is Captain Thomas Baker of the frigate *Phoenix*, and the fight between Nathan's ship the *Panther* and the French *Perle* is based on the single-ship conflict between the *Phoenix* and the *Didon*, as described by Baker in his account of the battle.

The Battle of Finisterre is also based on the known facts. It is thought by many historians to be the real battle that saved Britain from invasion, as it stopped Villeneuve from proceeding to Brest and attempting to unite with the French Atlantic fleet. However, some historians pinpoint a later encounter as the crucial factor. After the battle, while Villeneuve and his fleet were in Ferrol, he apparently became convinced that Nelson had joined Calder with an additional eleven ships of the line, and this formidable fleet was waiting for him in the Bay of Biscay—with Nelson in overall command.

Villeneuve had what we would now call a paranoid fear of Nelson—but maybe it wasn't paranoid. He had seen what Nelson could do at the Battle of the Nile. Even so, he brought the fleet out of harbour and appears to have headed north—towards Brest. At this point, however, he encountered three ships—the seventy-four-gun *Dragon*, the frigate *Phoenix*, and her prize, the crippled *Didon*, which she had taken in tow. Convinced that they were scouts for Nelson's fleet and that he stood no chance of taking him on, he turned the fleet about and headed south for Cádiz.

It was this that convinced Napoleon to call off the invasion of Britain. Instead, he marched his army halfway across Europe to fight the Austrians. This is well attested by records of his explosive exchanges with the French Minister of Marine, Denis Decrès, an old shipmate of Villeneuve's, castigating the French admiral for his 'cowardice' and the French navy generally for being completely hopeless.

As for Trafalgar itself, I've based this version of the battle on the accounts of several French captains, especially Lucas of the *Redoutable*, and Villeneuve himself. A lot of what they say is suspect, almost certainly designed in Lucas's case to make a good impression on the emperor, and in Villeneuve's, to save his skin. I've left out the more obvious inaccuracies. However, I was particularly intrigued by the verbatim reports of the council of war and other meetings Villeneuve held with his French and Spanish colleagues—captains, commodores, and admirals—while the combined fleet was moored in Cádiz.

Judging from these, Villeneuve accurately predicted Nelson's tactics and had a plan to counter them, specifically with an 'observation squadron' of twelve French and Spanish ships led by Admiral Gravina, which was supposed to stay to windward of the main fleet and reinforce it wherever it was most needed during the battle. The key thing about the plan was that the squadron would be able to see the battle clearly and not be lost in the middle of it, as Villeneuve was, in the 'fog of war'. In the event, Gravina for some unknown reason disregarded his orders and joined the rear of the main battle fleet, with the consequences that followed.

In researching this I could not help but feel some sympathy for Villeneuve. Well, not sympathy as such, but a feeling that he has never been given a fair trial—either by his contemporaries or by historians. He thought Napoleon's grand plan was absurd, but he allowed himself to be talked into it, even though he did not think it could possibly work. Fleets cannot be moved like armies—something that Napoleon never seemed to grasp. After the battle Villeneuve was taken prisoner by the English, and attended Nelson's funeral, but he was later released on parole and sent back to France. In April 1806 he was found dead at the Hotel de la Patrie in Rennes, with six stab wounds to the chest, five in the lungs, and one in the heart. A verdict of suicide was recorded. Thus demonstrating the difficulty of sorting fact from fiction, even for a proper historian, or a detective. Which rather leaves the field open for the novelist.

Which brings me to the story of Nelson's death—and his killer. No-one knows who killed Nelson. Claims have been made, books written—one by the man who claimed to have shot him, although this was later discredited. All that is known for sure is that the shot was fired from above, probably from the mizzentop of the *Redoutable*. In this book I have suggested that the killer may have been a Neapolitan in the service of the French. I have no evidence for this.

The reason I wrote it is complicated and possibly contentious. Nelson is the sublime British hero, possibly the greatest of all time—a symbol in many ways of the British national character, or of how we would like that character to be perceived. He was a brilliant naval commander and an inspirational leader of men with a weakness for women, or one woman in particular. I admire him for his many qualities, and in previous books in this series I think I have shown him at his best. However, he was not without flaws. I am not talking about his affair with Lady Hamilton, but the other events that occurred in Naples at that time, when hundreds—possibly thousands—of civilians were massacred by royalists, with Nelson's support. He was not responsible for those massacres, but he aided and abetted them, despite the British envoy having made an agreement to give the rebels safe conduct in return for their surrender.

Moreover, Nelson was more directly involved in the execution of the Neapolitan admiral Francesco Caracciolo, Duke of Brienza, who was hanged from the yardarm of his own flagship as a traitor. Caracciolo was a Neapolitan patriot and had served with distinction in the British navy. After the king and queen had fled in Nelson's ships to Sicily, he accepted the command of the Neapolitan navy from the new republican government. This was why he was hanged. Obviously, there are differing views on the rights and wrongs of this, but Nelson was rebuked for it by his contemporaries, and it has cast a lingering shadow on his reputation ever since.

In this book I have made only a fleeting reference to Nelson's involvement in all of this, but I have made it the motivation for Nelson's killer. Why? I thought it made for a more interesting story. Whatever patriots want from their heroes, writers want them to have flaws, or feet of clay. It makes them more interesting as people, less godlike. And I suppose I do think our heroes should not be worshipped as gods but recognised as fallible human beings, with all their faults. Scillato—like Mordred in the Arthurian legend—is Nelson's nemesis—the dark, avenging angel. But he has no basis in reality. He is *Lo Spettro*. The ghost of Naples.

—Seth Hunter, April 2022

Acknowledgments

The Nathan Peake series has been a great adventure for me, and I hope not too boring for everyone else involved, but I'd like to take this opportunity to thank them anyway. I'm particularly grateful to George Jepson, the editorial director of McBooks Press, and his team, especially Brittany Stoner and Melissa Hayes, for their support and encouragement. To Martin Fletcher, who launched the series for Headline in the UK, and Alex Skutt, who bought the US rights and whose passion for nautical fiction almost convinced me I was capable of writing it. To my agent Bill Hamilton at A. M. Heath. To my family for accepting that most of the time I'm in another world and best left there, so long as I don't attempt to explain the intricacies of warping a ship out of harbour or the difference between a cannon and a carronade in the belief that it's something they really need to know. And finally, to Bill Cran, who I had the privilege of working with on the film *Nelson's Trafalgar* for Channel Four. He was the first person to tell me about the battle in the fog off Finisterre and how it was this engagement that changed the course of history, rather than the far more famous battle that followed. This led me to the discovery of the plot to kidnap Napoleon, to the wonderful gardens of Malmaison, the grim fortress of Castle Gorey on the island of Jersey, the white cliffs of Biville-sur-Mer in Normandy—and ultimately, against the odds at times, to this book.